T0366171

OKSANA

OKSANA

A NOVEL

ANIL DHAR

PARTRIDGE

ISBN:	Hardcover	978-1-4828-6796-1
	Softcover	978-1-4828-6795-4
	eBook	978-1-4828-6794-7

Print information available on the last page.

To order additional copies of this book, contact
Partridge India
000 800 10062 62
orders.india@partridgepublishing.com

www.partridgepublishing.com/india

DEDICATION

To the beautiful women of Ukraine and the world
Family, relatives, and friends
To all those who believe in peace, tolerance, and democracy

ACKNOWLEDGEMENTS

I want to sincerely thank my family, relatives, and friends for their love, support, and encouragement. My gratitude to Tricia Dearborn, for her honest critical assessment. I am deeply indebted to Priya Pandya and Kajal Desai of Doonya.com, for allowing me to use one of their clips to describe the dance sequence in the novel.

CONTENTS

CHAPTER 1

My name is Jai Grover, 22, born on 14 November 1992 in a Punjabi Hindu family in New Delhi, India. Today, I am going to talk about the Grovers, i.e. my family. I've always avoided talking about my personal achievements, my family, or the family wealth; but the story I am going to share with you compels me to break the family rule book for the first time. We have a family rule book that was created by my grandfather in the 1970s, which I'll share with you a little later. My grandfather has been deceased for ten years, but the family rule book is still followed by the family.

I completed my engineering degree in computer science from the Indian Institute of Technology (IIT), New Delhi, in 2014. I am currently working as a management trainee with the family-owned business house in New Delhi. The brand Grover's is a household name, and the annual turnover of the Grover Garments runs in millions of dollars. We have a huge market in India. We also export to North America, Europe, Russia, and the Middle East.

My parents think I am a handsome young man. All parents in this world think that their children are beautiful.

All children are beautiful because they are innocent, who have unpolluted minds and are ignorant of many bad things that exist in this world. There might be another reason. My papa is a handsome Punjabi man and my mum a beautiful Punjabi woman. I am not lying because I've seen them.

My hobbies include playing music, singing, dancing, swimming, going to the gym, and reading. I like to look after my health. I don't smoke, drink, or take drugs. I go to the gym three times a week. I also have a little home gym, which I use whenever I feel lazy to go out.

I love and respect my parents. My life has always revolved around my parents, studies, work, and hobbies, which I've already shared with you. My friends think I am a highly matured, patient, level-headed, knowledgeable, well-read, well-spoken, and soft-spoken person. I don't know about that, but I don't engage in unnecessary debates or discussions, but I can debate on anything.

When I was 18 years old in the first year of my engineering, I decided to appear for the Indian civil services exam once I had completed my engineering degree. I started to read books on history, culture, geography, conflicts, and key world events. I extensively read about Indian history, Russian history, and Persian history. I liked the Czar Russian history the most. I was impressed with them the way they expanded from a small Muscovy region to the big Russia we all know of today. Russian expansion still continues: Abkhazia, North Ossetia, and Crimea. I don't like this Russian expansion.

My all-time favourite book is *Two Lives* by Vikram Seth. It is not about history, culture, geography, conflicts, or key world events. It is about a real love story between an Indian doctor and a German Jewish woman set in the backdrop of the Second World War and the Holocaust.

Three years later, when I was in the last year of my engineering, I became wiser. I thought I didn't have to necessarily do engineering to appear for the civil services exam. A BA or a B.Com or a B.Sc. would have made me eligible. But it was too late and unwise to drop out of the engineering course, so I dropped the idea of appearing for the civil services exam. However, the knowledge I gained in those three years will always stay with me forever. Not only did I gain knowledge, but I also learnt to question things and would often relapse into deep thoughts over the issues I believe are interesting, controversial, or disturbing.

I like democracy, personal freedom, freedom of thought, secularism, and pluralism. I believe a free mind is a creative mind. I hate communism, communalism, racism, caste system, discrimination, regionalism, wars, and conflicts. I don't like when countries go on wars over religion, sectarianism, territory, natural resources, or influence. I think war is the worst type of act humans bring upon themselves. It brings suffering to people, especially women and children. I think it is high time that the world needs to do some serious thinking.

I want to now talk about my family in detail starting with my grandfather.

My grandfather was born in 1927 in Lahore, British India. His father was a very wealthy and successful cloth merchant in Lahore. My grandfather was not very educated but very wise. After completing his matriculation, he joined his father's business at the age of 17. He quickly learnt the tricks of the trade and dreamt of expanding his father's business. However, tragedy was soon to strike his family. In 1947, India was partitioned into two countries. It was the worst kind of partition. Many people were killed. Neighbours living together for centuries killed one another.

My grandfather's entire family was slaughtered; and he was forced to flee to Delhi, India, where he became a refugee.

In Delhi, he didn't have any home, job, savings, relatives, or friends. He was only 20 years old then. He stayed in a refugee camp for five years. He started doing odd jobs and after ten years of hard work managed to open a small cloth shop in old Delhi in 1957. He had known the trade from his Lahore days, so he quickly became a successful and wealthy cloth merchant. He married late in 1962 to a refugee woman who herself had migrated from Lahore. My father, his only child, was born in 1964 in Delhi. Finally, he succeeded in establishing a garments factory in 1974. He was a wise man—less educated, though—so he rebuilt his life and died a successful and wealthy businessman in 2004.

My grandfather had seen it all: wealth, poverty, killings, hatred, loneliness, struggle, humiliation, and much more. He made sure that the lessons he had learnt be passed on to his future generations. So he created a list of dos and don'ts, which became our family rule book. The dos contained all good things like education, love, respect, family values, simplicity, relationship, kindness, compassion, value for money and social work, etc; and don'ts contained all the bad things like boasting, show-off, ego, arrogance, jealousy, cruelty, hatred, discrimination etc. The rule book was passed on to my father who, in turn, passed it on to me. The family is supposed to follow all the good things and avoid all the bad things literally.

My father, Vijay Grover, is around 51 years old. He is the CEO of the Grover Garments, the company that was started by his father in 1974. He joined the company after finishing his MBA from the United States some 26 years back. Since taking over as the CEO of the company, he successfully restructured the company. As a result, the turnover has doubled in the last ten years. He is extremely kind to his employees, loyal to his friends, and faithful to his wife.

My mother, Simrin Grover, is 47 years old. She was the only daughter of highly successful doctor couple from Chandigarh, Punjab. Both are now deceased. She met my father in the United States while he was pursuing his MBA and she was visiting her uncle. At that time, she was in her final year of engineering pursuing from a college in South India.

My parents met at a party in the USA. My mum instantly fell in love with Father because she found him very handsome. After my father's return, she got married to him and then moved to New Delhi. After four years of marriage, she gave birth to her first and only child, Jai Grover, i.e. me. She chose to sacrifice her career to look after home and family and carry out social work.

In Delhi, we live in a sprawling bungalow in the upmarket South Ex area. The house is tightly secured by high walls and a large iron gate, which is manned by a security guard. Anyone entering our house from the street is greeted with a beautiful, neatly manicured garden. The interior of our home is nicely decorated with high-quality furniture, Persian rugs, chandeliers, wall paintings, and wall units. However, the entire family's favourite part of the home is the TV room. We relax in the TV room after our evening meals before retiring to bed at around 10.30 in the night. A hallway leads to the four large bedrooms. The other end of the hallway has a door that opens to the backyard.

The backyard is fully covered with pavers. A number of large clay pots are placed along the back wall and the right side wall. The pots contain beautiful plants. They need daily watering in hot Delhi summer months. They never dry or die because my mother looks after them like her own children. On the left-hand side is a swimming pool, which is used by the family in hot months. My father never learnt swimming, hence, can't understand the usefulness of a swimming pool. My mother is a good swimmer, and so am I. She learnt swimming at an early age after an incident. When 8, she nearly drowned in a river but was saved by people around. Her parents understood the importance of swimming that day and took her to swimming lessons the next day. I wish humans were natural swimmers like animals. Why has God been so kind to animals? Probably animals are better than humans.

I know I am lucky because I've very caring and loving parents, and I am from a rich family. But I do feel for the poor, and there are a lot of poor people in India. My mother says there is a god in every poor so we should treat them well. I think apart from treating them well, we should get them out of poverty. My father says this will happen because centuries back, we were the richest country in the world but everything was drained out. It will take some time before we regain our glorious past. I hope it does.

Apart from our Delhi house, we have one more property in Mumbai. A three-bedroom apartment now unoccupied. The apartment brings back many sweet and bad memories of my six-month stay over there last year. These days I don't think much about bad memories. The past is dead and has no future.

My life changed forever between July and December 2014 when I decided to move to Mumbai for one year. Prior to that, I used to think that I was an educated, mature, intelligent, and well-read person. I was wrong. There are more mature, intelligent, and strong people in the world though they may not be very educated or well read. These are ordinary people like you and me.

I learnt a lot from beautiful, smart, intelligent, and talkative Dolce Desai. I am still in touch with her because she is my lifelong best friend. From tall, funny, and business-minded Amardeep Singh Gill. From quiet and intelligent Sachin Joshi. He is Dolce's boyfriend, and they plan to marry after completing their degrees. From the quietest personalities like Ajay Pant and Neel Sharma. They are all in the USA, currently pursuing their undergraduate courses from various universities. From occasionally-normal-otherwise-permanently-abnormal Vishal Singh. From Roshan Ali, whom I saw once or twice at the Starbucks but never found time to speak to him. From Monik de Mellow, whom I spoke once but never met. From evil people like Shabnam Seth, Sharif Ahmad, and Naresh Galhot and many more whose names I don't know.

I met them all in Mumbai. I learnt about the real world that exists out there away from protected home environment. The real-life experience teaches more than one could learn in schools, colleges, or homes.

Above all, the most I learnt from one Oksana Bzovsky. A sharp, strong, proud, intelligent, beautiful, and skilled dancer from Ukraine.

This book is my story, which I want to share with you all.

CHAPTER 2

Friday, 4 July 2014, was a special day at home. It was my graduation ceremony. Earlier in the morning, Mum had prepared *halwa* for *prasad* and offered special prayers. My parents were very happy and extremely proud of my achievement. They felt that I had lived to all their expectations. We left home at 7.30 in the morning for my institute but not before my mum had taken my *aarti* in a traditional Hindu way. We reached the institute at 8.30, parked the car, and then walked towards the registration hall. I stood in a queue for the preceremony registration. The registration staff was working very efficiently. After waiting for little under ten minutes, I was called by one of the female staffs.

"What is your name and branch?" Female staff asked.

"Jai Grover. Computer science," I replied.

"Do you have a formal invitation to the ceremony? Have you paid for the ceremony? Show me your receipt," she asked in one breath while glancing over the growing queue.

"Here is everything," I replied while handing over her the paperwork, which she started to check.

"Who else is attending with you? How many passes do you need?"

"My parents. Two."

"Here are the two passes for your parents," she explained while shuffling my paperwork and then handing them back. "They will have to enter from the left side. You will have to get a gown first and then take the right side. The gown hiring will cost Rs1,000."

She pointed me to the room where I could hire a gown. I walked with my parents who then proceeded to the main hall from the left side. I went to the room, paid up money, chose a graduation gown and a cap, and then proceeded to the hall from the right side. The graduating students occupied the front rows so that they could easily walk to the stage to receive the degrees. There was a gap of four empty rows between the students and the invitees. I took the seat as directed by a staff. The hall was full of parents, relatives, friends, staff, and students. There was a lot of noise and excitement. The stage had a mic placed on the left-hand side for the master of ceremony, and right in the centre were two rows of chairs. The education minister of Delhi was going to be the chief guest of the event, which was about to start in the next ten minutes. I turned around to find my parents. Mum waved at me after I spotted them sitting in one of the back rows.

An announcement was made to observe complete silence as the ceremony was about to start. The central door of the hall opened. The vice-chancellor (VC) of the Delhi University, deans, departmental heads, and the registrar entered the hall and then started to proceed to the stage. Once they took their seats, the registrar read out the programme and then requested the VC to welcome the education minister. The ceremony went through the usual course, e.g. giving speeches by key speakers, calling out names, receiving degrees from the VC, and taking a picture with him while receiving the degree. When my name was called out, I felt a sense of achievement because this was the first real milestone of my life. While on the stage, I looked at my parents and felt that they were very proud of me. I received my degree from the VC and then took a picture with him.

After the formal ceremony ended, I ordered replication of my degree in a plaque form and also took a photograph with my parents. The plaque and photograph were going to be ready in two weeks' time, I was told. We left the institute at 3 in the afternoon. Papa first dropped me near a metro station as I wanted to visit one of my friends' place, Mum at home, and then he had to go to his office to attend a meeting at 4.30. Mum was going to cook something special for the evening, so she instructed both of us to be back home by 6.30.

After spending a couple of hours with my friend, I returned home at 6 soaked in sweat after braving Delhi's blistering July heat. I straight went to my room, took a nice cold shower, got ready for the rest of the evening, and waited for Papa's return. Meanwhile, it looked like Mum had finished her cooking, and she started to place the food on the table. While we were waiting for Papa, we heard the noise of a car entering the house. It was Papa right on time at 6.30.

"Ki haal hain ji [What is up, dear]?" I heard Papa asking Mum in Punjabi as he entered the home.

"Vadiya ji vadiaya. Tussi aa gayey? [All well. Are you home?]" Mum also replied in Punjabi.

"Na ji na. Mera bhoot bol raha hai. [No, dear. It is my ghost who is talking.]"

"We received many calls." Mum chirruped like a happy bird. "Everybody was asking for a party. I told them we will have one at a later date. Tussi tyaar hoge [Would you freshen up]?"

"Give me ten minutes," Papa replied.

I left my room to greet Papa, who had recently arrived, still talking to Mum. I was wearing a spotless white *kurta* and *pyjama*. They both looked at me in admiration, which I felt very flattering.

"My son is the most handsome boy in the world, isn't it, Vijay?" Mum said, proudly looking at me affectionately.

Mum was like that—always said that. I felt embarrassed because it was too much of adulation.

"Sada Punjabi Munda [Our Punjabi boy]," Papa replied in Punjabi.

"You said that in the morning also," I said, irritated. "You both have to stop now. I am feeling hungry."

"Because you are. Why should we lie?" Mum said. "Vijay, quick."

"I'll be back in ten minutes," he replied while disappearing into his room.

Ten minutes later, we all were at the dining table. Papa took the smaller side. Mum and I sat together on his right side.

"Smells good. What is in the food?" Papa said, inviting me for a small drink before dinner. "Jai, should we have a single shot of whisky? After all, it is a happy occasion."

"No drinks today. It is an auspicious day. Jai anyway doesn't drink much. Whisky toh naa baba [For him, it is no to whisky]," Mum objected.

I thought in India every day was an auspicious day. I never liked to drink much, but today was a good reason for a small one. However, Mum's ruling had the final say, so we had to drop the idea.

"As you say," Papa said, dejected.

"Look what I've cooked for dinner," Mum said happily with a hint of pride about her choice. "Chhole bhature, basmati rice, Punjabi dhal, and matar paneer in the main course. We also have halwa and rasgulla as the dessert."

"Everything smells so good," Papa remarked, possibly trying to flatter Mum. He told Mum, "After dinner, I need to discuss something important with Jai in your presence."

We had our dinner rather quietly, occasionally requesting one another to pass this or that. After meals, we proceeded to the TV room. Mum requested the domestic help to clear the table. Mum never ordered but always requested because she had always been kind to the domestic help. We were feeling energetic after the meals as we settled in the TV room. I started flicking through various channels but couldn't find anything interesting. I wondered how people remained glued to the TV sets. How did they remember what was on which channel? There were around 600 channels in India, which was crazy. I turned the TV off and noticed that my father was looking at him.

"Do you want to watch something?" Papa asked and added quickly. "Go ahead."

"Naah [No]. There isn't anything interesting," I replied.

"Suno ji [Listen, dear]", Mum said impatiently as if Papa was going to forget, "you had to discuss something important. Do you recall?"

"Ji, Ji [Yes, yes]. I wanted to discuss Jai's future plan," Papa replied and, turning to me, asked seriously, "Jai, what do you want to do now?"

"I'm not sure," I replied. "I hardly got the time to think about. I had been busy with my final exams. The last three months had been very tough for me."

"Let him relax for a day or two," Mum said while adjusting her sari. "Meanwhile, he can think of his future plans."

"I agree with you," Papa said. "However, I've got a couple of suggestions."

"I don't see any harm," Mum said. "Jai, what do you think?"

"I am always with my parents," I replied politely.

"Jai, you have two options. First, you join the company now. However, you will have to start from the bottom. For the first two years, you will have to move around all the divisions so that you understand all the areas of the business. After two years, we will see which position to offer you. Are you listening?"

"Yes, Papa."

"Second, you can pursue further studies. Go and acquire an MBA degree from the US. Come back and join the company. However, the rules of joining the company remain the same."

"I think you should do an MBA first," Mum suggested. "By the time you return, you would be around 23 or 24, mature enough to take responsibility."

However, they noticed that I was thinking about something. In fact, I had heard everything that Papa had said, but I had my own plans.

"Did you hear what we had been saying?" Papa asked in a raised voice.

"I want to ask you both one thing," I asked nervously. "Have I lived up to your expectations so far?"

"Way, way more than our expectations," Mum replied, concerned. "You have been a good boy. Our dream child. Why? What is the issue?"

"I was thinking. Umm . . . can I get a year off? I want to create something on my own. I want to test my ability. Either I fail or pass, I am eventually going to do what you both want. It is just a year of my own," I concluded with a hopeful face.

"What is the problem?" Papa asked, slightly worried. "What do you want to create?"

"You both know that besides my studies, I've always been interested in singing and music. I've taken a formal training in both."

"And bodybuilding and Bollywood songs," Mum interrupted, excited. "Don't forget that."

"I just want to create a dance group and an events management company."

"What is the future in a dance group and event management company? We have an established business. Why not something similar?" Papa argued.

"Exactly. That is the idea. Do something different. Moreover, I am a trained singer and musician, so it is like similar to my skills," I counterargued.

"Is that what you want to do first?" Papa asked, somewhat uncertain, and then turned to Mum. "What is your opinion, Simrin?"

"If you both are happy, then I am also happy," Mum replied.

"Just one year, Jai," Papa said, forcefully looking straight into my eyes.

"I'll have to move to Mumbai, the entertainment capital of India," I disclosed.

"Will you leave this home for one year?" Mum asked anxiously.

"Mum, for the MBA degree, I'll have to leave the country for two years. I am just moving to a different city within India."

"In any case, I am sad. But call me every day," Mum said, pretending to be sad. "I am not going to call you. I want to see how much my son loves me."

This was my mum—always expecting more from me. I didn't tell them how much I loved them both, hence, would miss them too.

"When are you planning to move?" Papa asked.

"On the 20th of this month," I replied.

Mum looked at me slightly distressed because I had less than three weeks left. We had been talking for a long time without realising that it was close to midnight. So we decided to call it a day. I fell asleep thinking about the work ahead leading to my departure to Mumbai.

CHAPTER 3

Today was my last day in Delhi. I was flying down to Mumbai tomorrow at 7 in the morning. The last three weeks had passed quickly as I had been busy with many things. I had made the booking for Mumbai. I had packed my musical equipment and gym equipment, which took me almost three days because I had been working very slowly. Next was the packing of my warm clothes in a large suitcase. Mumbai doesn't get that cold compared to Delhi in winters, but Mum insisted that I should keep warm clothes. Once the big items were packed away, I then booked a transport company to ship them to Mumbai. The cargo was expected to arrive around the time I would arrive in Mumbai.

Meanwhile, Papa had opened a bank account for me and also stood as a guarantor for my credit card. He had deposited Rs750,000 into my bank account to make my new life a little easy. Also, a party was thrown at our place last weekend as promised by Mum.

I was very satisfied with the preparations so far and was looking forward to my new life in Mumbai. Another good news was that I didn't have to pay any rent. We owned a three-bedroom apartment in a modern high-rise building in Mumbai. My parents had bought the apartment last year for our private use if we ever visited Mumbai. However, we had never been able to use it because Papa always remained busy with his work and I remained busy with my studies. Poor Mum didn't have any choice but to stay busy with us. I had never visited Mumbai in my life, so I didn't know much about the apartment. The apartment was partly furnished.

Being the last day in Delhi, I called all my close friends from my engineering days to bid my last goodbye. Many were surprised at my choice to move to Mumbai for a year because all of them were about to start their careers with big IT companies like IBM, Google, Microsoft, or large Indian BPO companies like TCS, Infosys, or Wipro—all multibillion-dollar companies. I passed the day by making sure everything was in order—suitcase, hand luggage, driving licence, and wallet—and moved heavy items to the TV room. I watched TV for some time and waited for my papa's return from his office, eager to have our last postdinner meeting.

Papa came back from his office at his usual time at 7.30 in the evening. We quickly had our dinner and then settled in the TV room for the postdinner discussion, which, unfortunately, was going to be my last one for quite some time.

"Everything in order?" Papa asked, looking around as if searching for a missing item. "Are you ready for tomorrow's journey?"

"Yes. Everything is packed," I replied while pointing to the items.

"Jai, make sure you call me daily. I want to know how your day went," Mum reminded yet again and then ordered, "Take care of your health and always be good to all."

"I will."

"Now, listen carefully," Papa said, moving close to me. "I am going to give you a long lecture. So be patient and attentive."

"I have always been patient and attentive," I replied, slightly irritated.

"I've deposited Rs750,000 in your bank account. You also have a place to live in," Papa gave a fatherly talk. "It is a big amount. Only lucky ones can get such a big help from their parents. This amount will help in getting few things you will need, such as a car, TV, music system etc. Are you listening?"

I was feeling overwhelmed by the kindness of my parents, so I exclaimed, "Vijay the great!"

"Of course, your papa is great," Mum replied, delighted, and looked at Papa, smiling.

Papa shook his head and then resumed his fatherly talk, "I want you to value money. Spend carefully. You have to plan your year in such way that you don't run out of money. You should plan monthly expenses in such a way that you spend less than the planned expenditure."

"How do I do that?" I asked, puzzled.

"You will know," he assured. "Responsibility will teach you."

"Oh, how do you know?"

"How do I know?" he replied, laughing, and continued, "I've studied in the USA and travelled overseas a lot for business. I've seen in the Western society boys and girls leave their parents' home at 17 or 18."

"What have I to do with that?"

"There is a lesson for you," he explained. "They leave not because they don't like their parents or their parents ask them to leave."

"Why then?"

"Because they want to grow in the real world, experience early-age responsibility, contribute to the society, and then become good citizens."

I knew about that, but when it was happening to me, I couldn't make much about it. What one had heard is different from what one faced in reality.

"How do they start?" I asked, confused.

"Like you are starting," he replied, disappointed. "Their parents also help them initially like giving them, say, $5,000, depending on the capacity."

"That is why you are giving me money."

"He likes everything about America," Mum joked.

"There are good things and there are bad things in every society," he said in a serious tone and then finished with a good reasoning, "You take good things and ignore bad things."

"What bad things?" Mum asked with raised eyebrows.

"What bad things?" Papa mimicked, laughing gently.

"You know what I mean," Mum said, slightly jealous.

"You had a girlfriend in America?" I asked casually. "What is wrong in having a girlfriend?"

"Yes. I had a girlfriend there." He laughed. "Jai, I agree with you."

"See, Jai, I told you, but he never told me anything about her," Mum started a mini family war.

"What was her name?" I asked.

"You really want to know?" Papa asked.

"We both want to know," Mum said, even more jealous this time.

"Simrin Kaur. Your mother," Papa killed the mystery.

"So you never had any girlfriend?" I asked.

"Where was the time? She came to the US, and we liked each other."

"Indian love story made in America," Mum said, loudly throwing her arms up.

"One last thing, Jai," Papa warned. "This money is a gift from us to you. Don't expect further help from us. You don't have to buy an expensive car. Settle with little ones like Alto etc. Even better if you buy a second-hand. Do you agree?"

"Yes," I said, almost repeating everything. "I won't ask for any further financial help even if I am in deep financial trouble. That is a promise to you both. Also, I'll value money and spend carefully."

"Changa munda [Good boy]," Papa remarked, smiling.

Now it was Mum's turn to lecture me, and it was not going to be an easy one. I thought Indian parents think that their children never grow. But my parents were a bit different, so I never minded their lectures.

"Be good to all," she started, reminding me of our family rule book. "Respect others' opinion. Don't hurt anyone. Do not boast of your parents' wealth. I particularly want you to be good towards women. Respect is all that you need to show towards women."

I nodded.

"I don't mind you find a girlfriend but always be good to her. Promise you won't deceive her or take undue advantage of her or ditch her without any valid reason," she lectured as if she was an advocate of women's cause.

Since she was a social worker, besides being a housewife, her feminine logic was strong and unshakable.

"Mum, I never had any girlfriend," I protested.

"I always wanted you to find a beautiful Punjabi girlfriend," she said, disappointed. "That is the only thing you have disappointed me so far."

"Where was the time?"

"Now you are talking like Papa." She chuckled, looking at Papa, and they both smiled.

"You both know how tough my engineering course was," I argued. "And those three years I thought I would prepare for the civil services exam."

"Now do something," she kind of ordered.

"Jai, we both have a deep faith in you," Papa interrupted. "Don't let us down."

"Yes. Yes. Yes," I replied, irritated.

"Chal bache der ho gayi [Come on, son, it is getting late now]," he reminded me of my early morning flight. "We have to leave at 5."

"Jai, make sure you exercise daily," Mum made a last-minute comment. "Maintain your chiselled body."

I laughed at her chiselled-body comment.

"Vijay, samjao ise [Vijay, explain to him]," she complained innocently, which made me laugh even louder.

"Jai, she is right. Do what she says," Papa said seriously.

When it came to choosing between Mum and me, he was always by Mum's side.

"I'll try. The gym equipment is already on its way to Mumbai. Anything else?"

"Let us all go to sleep now," Mum said with a touch of good sense of humour.

Next morning we all were woken up by the buzz of alarm at 4. It took us 45 minutes to get ready, leaving 15 minutes to spare, so I started to put my luggage in the boot. I made sure my air ticket, mobile, wallet, access card, and keys were with me secured. We left for the airport exactly at 5, reaching the airport in 45 minutes.

I quickly checked in, secured the boarding pass, and then prepared to head towards the terminal. I hugged my parents, kissed Mum, and then proceeded towards the terminal. I turned back last time and waved at them. I saw fake smiles on their faces, implying that they were feeling sad. I was sure once I was out of her sight, Mum would surely break down. I somehow controlled my emotions and headed towards the terminal without looking back.

I boarded the plane, and soon we took off exactly at 7. Once airborne, I could see Delhi, the city I had lived all my 21 years, underneath me. The plane went past the famous Lotus temple belonging to the Baha'i faith. It was standing majestically, basking in the Delhi sun. Suddenly, I felt depressed, tired, and sleepy. I didn't tell my parents that I had not been able to sleep whole last night thinking about them. I always disliked air travel, finding it very boring, uncomfortable, and uneasy. I knew that I wouldn't be able to sleep until I reached my Mumbai apartment.

Finally, the plane made the touchdown at 9, two hours after it had taken off from Delhi. The weather in Mumbai was cooler than Delhi but very sticky. The other passengers and I started boarding off the plane and then headed towards the luggage claim area. The conveyor belt kept going in rounds without any items for a long time. After waiting for ten minutes, suitcases, bags, and boxes of all sizes and colours started appearing on the belt. I didn't have to wait for long to claim my luggage. I headed out and hired a taxi, taking me about an hour to cover the distance through the busy Mumbai traffic. I paid the fare, offloaded my luggage, and then entered the building.

It was a modern skyscraper with the glassed exterior. I thought Papa would have paid millions for the apartment. The building was manned by a security man who was sitting behind the reception-type setting inside the building lobby. I started walking towards the lift when he stopped me. He asked me to produce an ID because it was a key requirement to enter the building. He said the security had been tightened in Mumbai since the 2008 terrorist attacks. I showed him my driving licence. He registered me as a permanent resident and then activated my lift access card. Before I left, he told me that the lifts were programmed in such a way that only authorised persons could use the lifts. My access was restricted to only level 5. That is where my apartment was situated. I didn't ask him how guests gained access, though.

I took a lift to level 5, unlocked the door, and checked water, electricity, and gas connections. It looked like Papa had been paying the bills on time because everything was working. I made a quick inspection of the apartment. I couldn't make much out of the inspection because I was very tired. I had already informed my parents about my arrival from the airport. The time was 12.30 in the afternoon. I set the alarm for 5 and then dozed off in one of the rooms.

I woke up at 5 and got up lazily with a heavy head and feeling very hungry. I had missed a call from Mum; so I called her back, explained everything, and promised her to keep calling every day at 7 in the evening. She told me that because it was my first day, she had called me; otherwise, it was my duty to call her daily, to which I agreed.

I made another inspection of the apartment. This time, it started to make sense to me. The door opened to an L-shaped hall. The longer side had a formal area with a couch, a coffee table, and two side tables. There were two paintings resting against a wall. Probably, no time was found to hang them. The shorter side had a small round dining table with six chairs exactly in front of the open-plan kitchen, which wasn't very big. The narrow hallway led to a toilet-cum-bath and a large room on the right side. On the left side of the hallway were two more rooms, one small and a large room with an attached toilet-cum-bathroom and a tiny balcony. There were also a small laundry and a pantry to store cleaning material and items. The apartment was self-contained. It wasn't bad at all for me. I decided to sleep in the large room without an attached toilet-cum-bathroom in order to keep the other large room vacant for an unexpected guest.

I took a quick shower and then headed down to buy something for dinner. As soon as I got out of the lift, I noticed a man talking to the security man. I wanted to let the security know that I was heading out for a while, so I went to him. The man stopped talking to allow me to talk to the security man. When I finished talking, I noticed that the man was staring at me. He was of medium height and built. He had a funny look. He was wearing loose jeans and a white shirt tucked inside. Every now and then, he would pull his jeans up with his hands. I looked at him and then smiled.

"Are you new in the building?" he asked authoritatively.

"Yes, I arrived this morning from Delhi," I replied softly.

"I don't like North Indians."

"Why is that?"

"Because they think they are smart and handsome," he said in absolute terms. "Also, very showy?"

"I don't think they are."

"What? You don't think you are handsome?" he asked, surprised. "Have you ever had a close look in a mirror? I think you are handsome."

He paused and then with a shake of his head said, "Smart, I am not sure."

"I've to go now." I found him a bit unstable person, so I thought of getting away from him.

"Wait. My name is Vishal Singh," he said stylishly. "Call me VS."

"Vishal Singh?" I asked, surprised. "Aren't you yourself a North Indian?"

"I was born in Mumbai, but my parents are originally from Meerut."

"But, Vishal, Meerut is very close to Delhi. That makes you a North Indian."

"I said call me VS," he said, annoyed.

"What is wrong with Vishal?"

"It sounds old-fashioned. VS is modern," he replied, leaving me a bit confused with his logic.

"How?" I laughed.

"Haven't you heard of PZ or PC?"

"Who are PZ and PC?" I asked, confused.

He started to giggle and then looked at the security man.

"Suresh, Suna tu ne isko [Suresh, did you hear him]?" he asked the security man, waving his hand and giggling as if I had asked something very funny. He turned to me. "Gaon se aye ho kya [Are you from a village]?"

I started to get some idea about him. Though born in Mumbai, he had all the symptoms of an idiot from North India.

"No, Delhi," I protested.

"Which world do you live in?" he said, coming close to me, and then muttered as if saving me from a big embarrassment. "PZ means Preity Zinta and PC means Priyanka Chopra."

He was talking about popular Bollywood female actors. It probably was the press that had started addressing them in their name acronyms. I pitied his level of maturity, but I didn't say anything.

"What are you thinking?" He woke me up.

"I think both are actually from North India," I replied coolly.

"I know," he said. "But they are my favourite actors, so it doesn't matter."

I was getting frustrated with him, but he wouldn't leave me.

"I am feeling a bit hungry, so I've to go now," I said flatly.

What he said next totally shocked me. "Mar nahi javo gay. Ruko [You won't die. Wait for some more time.]"

"What do you want?" I asked, irritated.

"Give me your mobile number."

"Why?"

"You don't want to become my friend?"

I laughed and cursed myself for the timing I had chosen to go out. I didn't have any choice but to exchange mobile numbers.

"I live in the same building, level 11."

"What do you do, Vishal—sorry, VS?"

"What do I do?" he mocked and then said very proudly, "Ask what I don't do."

"What don't you do?" I mocked back.

"I am a very busy man," he boasted. "I've contacts with all the production houses in Mumbai. They always need my help."

"Why do they need your help?"

"Don't you know my father is the regional officer of Mumbai with CBFC?"

Oh my god. How was I supposed to know that? I thought, if the son was like him, how would the father be like?

"What is CBFC?"

"Look at him now," he told the security man, laughing. "He doesn't know what the CBFC is."

"Seriously, I don't."

"It's the Central Board of Film Certification." His boasting continued, "No movie can publicly be exhibited without its approval."

"I've to go now," I made a last-ditch effort to get away from him.

"I know you are handsome but not smart," he reminded me of my deficiency once again. "You should have known what the CBFC was."

"I now know. I've to go now," I replied, hastily preparing myself to leave.

I left the place, fearing he would start a new topic. *Why didn't I leave earlier?* I thought. Probably, I myself was enjoying his stupid talk. I ran to a nearby shopping centre where I bought enough ready-to-cook food for the next couple of days.

CHAPTER 4

My last four days in Mumbai had passed off busy partly in setting the apartment up. I chose to place the musical instruments and gym equipment in the small room. However, most of my things were still scattered around. I was not used to this lifestyle. I thought of rearranging the apartment in the coming weekend. Earlier in the week, I bought a used Alto, a new 36-inch LED TV, and a good music system needed for my singing practice. I had spent around Rs130,000, leaving my bank balance at Rs620,000. With no major expenses expected now, I had to plan my monthly expenditure. Things were taking some time to settle, but I was sure that with the passage of time, everything was going to be okay.

It was my first Friday in Mumbai. In the afternoon, not sure of what to do, I decided to take a nap. I lay upon the bed and closed my eyes, trying to sleep. I was in semi-sleep when my mobile rang.

"Jai, hi. VS speaking," a male voice said.

"Who?" I asked, confused.

"VS. Remember, we met another day in the lobby."

"Vishal . . . sorry, VS. How are you?"

"What are you doing in the evening? Around 8."

"Why? Nothing."

"Good. Come with me. I'll take you to a nice place."

"What place?" I asked suspiciously.

"You ask many questions," he replied, incensed, and then threatened, which made me laugh, "Do you want to come? Otherwise, I'll look for another person."

I thought for a while and then realised that I didn't have much to do in the evening.

"I'll join you."

"Meet me at 8 in the lobby," he said and cautioned, "Don't get late. IST doesn't work in Mumbai."

"What is IST?"

"Indian Standard Time," he replied, sounding irritated with my questions.

IST is a term that is often used in India for the latecomers.

"No, I won't be late. I'll see you at 8," I assured and then disconnected the call.

I thought Vishal was not a bad company to kill time. But I still wasn't convinced whether to join him because he hadn't disclosed anything. Laughing at Vishal, I realised that I still had three hours until 7, so I decided to doze off.

As usual, the buzz of the alarm woke me up. I stayed in the sleep position for a while and then made a call to my mum. I then took a nice cold shower that refreshed me from the lethargy I had felt whole day. I wasn't sure what to wear. I had always liked to dress appropriately for an occasion, but Vishal hadn't told me exactly where we were supposed to be going. I thought of calling Vishal before I got dressed. I dropped the idea of calling him because I wasn't sure what unexpected might come from him.

I decided to wear a suit without a tie. It was too warm and humid for a tie. I got ready, combed my hair, applied aftershave, and sprayed a mild scent. I felt satisfied the way I looked after having a last look in the mirror. There were seven minutes left to 8; so I picked my wallet, mobile, and keys and then left the apartment. I locked the door, rechecked the lock and within minutes raced down to the lobby. It was empty with only the security man sitting in his usual place. Not wanting to disturb the security man, I waited for Vishal at the entrance of the lobby. Five more minutes passed, and there was no trace of Vishal, so I continued to wait for him. After a couple of more minutes, I called Vishal, but he didn't answer. I had no choice but to wait for Vishal, so I decided to talk to the security man until he showed up. It was a different person today. He was tall, well-built, and had a big moustache.

"Where is the guy who normally sits here?" I asked.

"He is on leave for a month. He went to his village," the man replied politely.

"Do you know him?"

"Yes, we are from the same village."

"Which village?"

"In Rajasthan near Kota."

"What is your name?"

"Jai Singh Rathore."

That brought a big smile on my face.

"My name is also Jai," I told him, beaming. "Jai Grover. Are you a Rajput?"

"Yes, but Suresh isn't."

I tried to recall the name I had heard somewhere earlier. I couldn't recall, so I asked, "Who is Suresh?"

"The guy who went on leave."

That reminded me of my first meeting with Vishal. I had completely forgotten about Vishal when I suddenly heard the noise of a lift door opening. Vishal appeared from that lift, walking straight towards me. He was wearing once again the same loose jeans and a striped matching full-sleeved shirt.

"This is the first time I am late," he tried to justify his late arrival. "I wasn't able to find a matching shirt."

"I tried to call you," I said, laughing.

"I didn't hear anything."

"Check your missed calls."

"See? There are no missed calls," he said while showing me the screen of his mobile.

"Let me show you my screen." I decided not to let him go so easily. "The last call I made was to your number, which means you have seen my missed call."

"Let me check again." He pretended not to have seen my call and then quickly changed his tone. "Oh! Yes, I saw this one. I can't answer all missed calls. I was going to see you anyway."

He checked the time—it was 8.25—and blamed me, "You wasted ten minutes in an unnecessary argument. The programme starts at 9."

"How are we going?" I asked, realising futility in arguing with me.

"In my car," he replied and then asked, "How do you commute?"

"I use public transport as much as possible, walk short distances, and use the car only when no other option is left."

"So you have a car?" he asked and complained as if I was duty bound to inform him. "You didn't tell me."

"I bought it three days ago," I replied calmly. "Where was the time to tell you?"

"Still, you should have phoned me." He was not convinced with my explanation. "Anyway, I am not taking my car now. I want to test drive your car."

"I've already bought it," I told him. "You test drive before buying a car."

He probably didn't understand me. He hastily suggested that we leave now because the time was 8.35. I agreed, so we took the lift down to the parking area. When he saw my car, he jumped as if stung by a bee.

"What? It is an old car," he said, shocked and surprised.

"Yes, but it is in good condition. It is only 5 years old. It has clocked only 80,000 kilometres, and I got it serviced, so it is almost a new car."

"You should have told me," he complained yet again. "How much did you pay?"

"One hundred thousand."

"Really? That is not bad for this car," he praised, sounding normal for the first time.

I started moving to the driver's side when suddenly he pulled me back.

"Do you know the way?" He became abnormal again. "I'll drive."

"Vishal, let us leave this place," I pleaded while agreeing, having no option left because we were getting late.

We took our respective seats. He turned the ignition, and then the car started to move. At last, we had hit the road. He told me that we would miss the start by ten minutes.

"Where are we going?" I asked eagerly. "What is happening there?"

"We are going to a five-star hotel," he replied and then said in a very low tone as if it was a crime to watch an exotic dance. "Every Friday night, they've exotic dancers performing in the bar."

I didn't know what to tell him because I had never been to such events before.

"Will it cost?" I asked innocently.

"Nothing is free these days," he castigated me and lectured as if I were a schoolboy. "The entrance to the bar costs Rs2,500 per head. Then you order drinks and food, which is always at an inflated price. Separate cost for a personal audience."

"What is the personal audience?" I asked curiously.

"Oh, you don't know personal audience?" he ridiculed. "You can make a request for a dancer of your liking to sit with you, flirt with her, eat and drink with her."

"Well, this is not my type of stuff." I thought of warning him beforehand, expecting anything unexpected from him. "Anyway, I'll pay for the entrance and anything I order. I am not sure whether I would enjoy the dancing. The personal audience is out of the question for me."

"You will like the dance," he said confidently.

"How do you know?" I asked with raised eyebrows.

"Arerry yaar [O friend], you don't have to pay for anything."

"Why? How?" I was comprehensively bowled by his googly.

"I've got entrance passes and coupons for drinks and food."

"Which passes and coupons?"

"I told you I've contacts," he said while flashing a smile. "One of the production houses gave me."

"Really."

"But you don't drink too much." Suddenly, he became my guardian in Mumbai and then delivered the final blow. "I am driving now, but when we go back, it is your turn to drive."

He was right. I wasn't a smart person. I realised that the actual reason wasn't that I didn't know the way but he wanted to drink and needed me to drive him back.

"I don't drink anyway," I said, laughing.

We stopped talking because the traffic was too heavy, so I let him drive in peace. We reached the hotel and soon found a vacant parking spot. I observed that Vishal was a good driver, skilfully negotiating the traffic, changing the lanes swiftly, driving at legal speed limits, and not breaking any traffic rules. We walked towards the main entrance, which was manned by a burly Sikh.

The lobby was large and nicely done up with couches in different parts mostly occupied by the waiting guests. There was a large reception area on the right side where the staff was very busy in the check-in/check-out process. The left side of the lobby had a small arcade consisting of small cabins for a travel agency, a flower shop, and a book and souvenir shop. The lifts were located on the left side after the arcade. Farther down the lobby, directly facing the main entrance, was the restaurant, a café on the left and the bar on the right side.

As we approached the bar, we heard loud music coming from the bar. Vishal produced the passes, and the doorman issued us the formal tickets. We entered the dimly lit bar but soon noticed that in the opposite end was a brightly lit small stage where some dancers were performing. People were enjoying the dance quietly; occasionally, the silence was broken with the rattling of glasses and cutlery. The orders were being placed in hushed tones, and waiters were moving efficiently to fulfil the orders. We finally located a table, which was few metres away from the stage. A waiter came to take our order.

"Good evening, VS saab," he said while greeting Vishal. "How are you? What would like to order?"

"Double-shot whisky on the rocks and sheesh kebab," Vishal placed his order like a VIP guest. "What do you want, Jai?"

I was fairly impressed the way waiter had greeted Vishal.

"I'll have a Coke—" I couldn't complete my order when he cut me off.

"And biscuits, isn't it, Jai?"

He made fun of me with a loud laugh as if I were a kid. Next he himself decided for me. It was a full-on entertainment for me.

"Get salted peanuts for him," Vishal told waiter in a very impressive way. "Get this first. We will order the main course later. I've got the coupons. How much did we miss?"

"It started half an hour ago at 9," the waiter replied. "The main attraction, Natasha and her group, will perform at 10."

"Is she from Russia?" he asked, lewdly winking his left eye.

"Yes, sir. Should I get your order?" the waiter said hastily, probably trying to get away from Vishal.

"Yes. Listen, where is Vinay? I need to talk to him," Vishal asked.

I smiled, knowing he wasn't going to let the waiter go so easily.

"He is in his room. You can see him there."

"I'll. You can go now," Vishal dismissed him like a king.

"Jai, do you know who Vinay is?"

"How would I know him?" I said, laughing. By now, I was used to his illogical questions. "I am new in Mumbai."

"He is the manager of the bar," he informed and then advised, "One should know people like him."

I smiled and thought that Vinay should have been the first person I should have met. Vishal made it sound as if he were talking about the prime minister. The order arrived in ten minutes. The dancers had finished their performance, and there was a break for ten minutes for the next performance by Natasha. Vishal was enjoying his drinks but struggling with knife and fork. Every time he wanted to cut a piece of kebab, it was moving up. He tried many times but soon got frustrated with his failed attempts. Finally, he gave up, looked left and then right over his shoulders, and then used his hands to make small pieces. I smiled with squeezed lips but didn't say anything.

At 10 all the lights of the stage were turned off. Nothing was visible. Suddenly, taps of feet could be heard on the stage. It seemed that the dancers were moving to their predetermined positions. An announcement was made that Natasha's performance was about to start. Slowly, the lights turned on. It was a group of one lead dancer and eight supporting dancers. Their backs were facing the people. The lead dancer was right in the middle; supporting dancers formed a group of four to her left and remaining four to her right. The supporting dancers were standing two arms' length ahead of the lead dancer. This whole order would be reversed when they would eventually turn their faces towards the people. Lead dancer in the front and supporting dancers behind her.

The lead dancer was wearing light-red shoulder-less cropped top, strong-red skin-tight trousers slightly loose in the bottom, shiny golden-coloured small hat normally worn in parties, and black high-heeled shoes. The supporting dancers were wearing the same attire but grey tops, black trousers, silver hats, and white shoes.

They were standing in a starting position with their hands curled up in a lotus shape and right legs behind their left legs. They all looked very attractive although their faces were still hidden from the crowd. The guests were impatiently waiting for their performance.

"They are looking very sexy," Vishal spoke in a hushed tone. "I think the lead dancer is a bomb. What do you say, Jai?"

"Did you notice all the dancers have the same height, beautiful bodies, and all are thin?" I said, ignoring his last statement. "There isn't any excessive fat around their waists. This is very rare. I think the choreographer has a good sense of symmetry."

"What are you looking at?"

"I've to remember these things when I form my own dance group."

"This not a college. Just enjoy the dance," he chided me.

"Every place is a learning centre," I replied casually. "It all depends on you."

Suddenly, music started. With the beat of the drum, they turned and then started to dance. I noticed that their trousers were ripped at three places from knees upwards, and the bottoms of their trousers were slightly loose like a bell shape. The supporting dancers were all good-looking.

However, the lead dancer was out of this world. She had a smooth flawless skin, perfect body, beautiful long face, curved nose of excellent proportion, big blue expressive eyes, big lips, and a very enchanting smile. She was a rare beauty who could easily turn heads, and it would be hard for anyone to take his eyes off her face. The exposed midriff and shoulders were adding to her beauty. She was extremely appealing and sexy.

She was lip-syncing to an erotic Bollywood number. She was an extremely good dancer and her style very exotic. Her performance was creating allure, excitement, and arousing feelings in male guests, who were panting, huffing, and puffing. Every eye was glued on her. I hated those types of male guests. I thought they should have appreciated the dance and her dancing skills. My eyes were also fixated at her in admiration. I soon got lost in the dreams of my future plans. I needed to form a group of musicians, dancers, and singers. I dreamt of my group with beautiful and skilled dancers. I really appreciated the dancing skills of the lead dancer and wished her to be the lead dancer of my group.

Suddenly, the dance was over, and I was woken from my dreams. I got the feeling that I was alone. I looked around and found Vishal was missing from the table. He had not handed over the coupons for food and drinks. I called him on his mobile, but he didn't answer my call. I looked around, searching for the waiter who had served us earlier. I located him standing in a corner, taking orders. I walked to him.

"Do know where Vishal is?" I asked, immediately correcting myself. "I mean VS Saab."

"No," the waiter replied.

"Did he pay for the food and drinks?" I asked, worried.

"No."

"I can't trace him. It is already 10.30." I was getting very annoyed at Vishal. I requested, "Can you talk to the bar manager? What was his name? Vinay."

"Please wait here," he said politely.

The waiter went away and returned in ten minutes. He told me not to worry because Vinay would fix the matter with Vishal. I sincerely thanked the waiter and thought of leaving for home. I got out of the bar. I started to walk towards the lobby door when I thought, *Who is going to drop Vishal back?* I knew he had had a couple of double shots of whisky, so I decided to wait for some more time before making another attempt to call him. I decided to kill my time in the café. I went there and found it nearly empty. I looked around and then chose a quiet corner, which had a small round table with two chairs. I took one of the chairs with my back to the wall. I noticed that right in front of my table, a large sitting arrangement was created by joining four square-shaped tables. I went there and counted 12 chairs.

"This one is reserved," I heard someone saying. "Do you have an order?"

I turned back and saw a man, who was a waiter. *Who could reserve such a large table in a café at this time?* I asked myself, perplexed.

"Sorry, I am there." I pointed to my table. "Yes. Just one cappuccino. How long will it take?"

"Sure. In ten minutes."

I went back to my table when my mobile rang. It was from that abnormal Vishal.

"Jai, I had an important appointment with someone at 10.15," Vishal said, very relaxed and casual as if nothing had happened.

"Where was your appointment?" I asked coldly.

"In the restaurant."

"Which restaurant?"

"Same hotel."

"Are you still there?"

"Yes. Have you left?"

"Yes," I lied because I didn't want to give him the impression that I was actually waiting for him. "Why didn't you inform me?"

"I didn't want to disturb you," he replied as if having done me a big favour. "You were enjoying the dance. Did you like the dance?"

"I don't know," I replied, annoyed.

"I'll see you later," he said and then disconnected.

I still hadn't fully understood him. I took a deep breath and thought all sorts of people make this world, and Vishal was one of them. I had been waiting for my coffee for over ten minutes when I noticed the same waiter marching towards my table.

"Sorry, sir. We had a number of orders from many rooms prior to your order. Would you mind waiting for another ten minutes? This time, ten minutes mean ten minutes. I apologise for the inconvenience," he said apologetically in crisp English.

"I will wait." I accepted his apology.

"Thank you, sir," he said, slightly bowing down. "Sorry once again."

I checked the time. It was five minutes to 11. Suddenly, I heard a little commotion in the café. I looked up towards the entrance, and I noticed a group of women entering the café. They were giggling, talking, and laughing. They were all walking towards my table. An average-height, fair-skinned, good-looking, but very fat woman was leading the group. She might have been in her late 30s. She wore jet-black hair in straight style. The rest of the women were young and looked almost the same in every sense except for the one who looked like a foreigner. She and the fat woman looked serious, with upsetting looks on their faces.

They slowly made their way into the reserved area opposite my table and soon settled down. The foreigner sat on the chair directly opposite facing me. The fat woman sat in front of her, blocking her view completely from me.

I moved my chair for a better view of the foreigner. All the girls including the foreigner were in casuals. The foreigner was looking very beautiful and smart in her casuals. The fat woman was in a traditional Indian lady's low-cut *kurta*, exposing her cleavage, and *chudidar pyjama*. She had a mobile in her left hand, which she was constantly thumbing with. I had been looking at them with a lot of attention, especially the foreigner.

My attention was diverted when I saw the waiter placing the coffee on my table. He then went to them to take their order. They placed the order and then started talking, which I could hear loud and clear.

"Tonight's dance performance was good", Girl 1 said, "isn't it, madam?"

"It has to be good," the fat woman replied arrogantly. She boasted, "After all, you girls work for my company. You know, I make a lot of effort to get you all good shows. It is not easy these days with so much competition around."

"But we are all talented dancers and give our best," Girl 2 tried to answer back.

"No one cares about talent," she said in a raised voice, and then her boasting continued, "It is all about connections and good contacts. I've worked in many movies before I started my company."

"I don't think it is hard to start a company," Girl 3 commented in a typical innocent girlie way. "All that is needed is money."

"Really," the fat woman shot back. She had a heavy voice often found in people who drink and smoke a lot. "Money, beauty, and talent mean nothing. It is all about contacts. I've always been liked by all. That is how I established contacts. I still get calls from producers for various roles."

"Why don't you accept?" Girl 1 asked, probably teasing her.

"Because I've to manage girls like you," the fat woman replied sarcastically, pointing to the foreigner. "Tolerate your tantrums. Still, I am good to you all, and I pay you all good money. Don't forget that."

And then she stopped talking. There was complete silence. The foreigner looked at the fat lady briefly, placed her elbows on the table, and rested the chin on her palms. She didn't respond to the fat woman's taunts and then looked away. I felt a lot of pain in her eyes, which she was trying to suppress.

"Some girls are never happy," the fat woman started again, taunting. "What do you have to say, East European beauty?"

So the foreigner was an East European. By then, I had figured out that they were the same dancers whose performance I had watched few hours ago. They were all looking different with their makeup removed and now in casuals. But I couldn't recall the name of the lead dancer. The waiter brought their order. When he placed a cup in front of the fat woman, she looked at him with raised eyebrows.

"Pagal hai ka tu [Are you mad]?" she shouted. "I ordered whisky, and you got me this lousy coffee. Who drinks coffee at this time? Get me a double-shot whisky with ice and soda."

The waiter apologised and quickly ran back to get her order. I finished my coffee without feeling the taste because I was enjoying their conversation more than my coffee. I didn't like the way the fat woman was treating the East European woman. I felt for her. She was the only person who had not participated in their discussion. She then looked at the fat woman without any expression or emotion. I thought for a moment and then decided to order one more coffee.

"I've come a long way," the fat woman's lecture continued. "I've always been a real professional. Whatever was told by my directors, I would always obey. As an actor, you have to behave professionally. You can't show attitude."

"It's getting late now," Girl 3 said and then looked at other girls. "Quick. We should leave now."

It seemed the girls were getting bored at her constant lectures, so they decided to leave. Soon they finished their coffee and started to get up.

"You all can leave except Oksana," the fat woman ordered. "I need to talk to her in private. The hotel's courtesy van will drop you all off."

"Bye, madam," the girls said while preparing to leave.

"See you tomorrow," the fat woman said. "We have another show tomorrow."

"Bye. See you. Tata," the girls bid goodbyes in their own way.

The supporting dancers then left the café. Oksana? That was her actual name, but they had announced something else. I thought they probably wanted to conceal her identity.

"The clients are not happy with you," the fat woman complained without looking at Oksana, instead checking something on her mobile. "I get a lot of complaints about you."

"Are you sure, Shabnam?" Oksana asked softly.

The fat woman's name was Shabnam. What a beautiful deep husky voice the European woman had. It felt music to my ears.

"Do you think I am lying?" Shabnam asked curtly.

"Why are your clients complaining?" Oksana replied in the most graceful manner. "I am a good dancer, and I work very hard. I am a lead dancer now."

"I made you lead dancer so that you could entertain guests," she said arrogantly. She did want to give her any credit for her dancing skills and kept harping. "Still, I receive complaints from clients."

"I know what your clients want from me," Oksana replied firmly. "I can't sleep with them."

"Oh! Ho! Look at her. Starry tantrums," she ridiculed. "You think you are a Bollywood superstar?"

"No," Oksana replied and then shot back, "I am not a Bollywood superstar, but I am not a prostitute either."

I liked her style. She was not aggressive but very assertive in full control of the situation.

"Prostitute?" she asked, surprised. "All you need to do is to escort lonely rich gentlemen."

I took a deep sigh and thought what a lowly woman Shabnam was. What a wrong name for this woman. Shabnam is of Arabic or Persian origin, which means *of the morning's dew*. The fat woman had nothing close to her name. She was rude, brash, a big bully, and a lowly woman.

"Escort service is another form of prostitution," Oksana explained in a cool manner. "It is like sleeping with strangers without working in a brothel."

"Is that your final decision?" she asked, seriously looking straight into Oksana's eyes with wide open eyes.

"I want to work as a dancer," Oksana pleaded.

"Listen, you blue eyes," she said in a raised voice. "I got you from Ukraine, paid airfare, arranged a work permit, gave you the job, a place to live, and promoted you to the lead dancer."

Shabnam was talking as if she had done a big favour to her. If she was paying, so was Oksana getting her business; otherwise, why would Shabnam have promoted her to the lead dancer?

Meanwhile, the waiter got Shabnam the double-shot whisky. She took a large sip, held it in her mouth while puffing up cheeks, and then gulped it down with a little head shake. She quickly gulped down the remaining drinks as if she was too stressed.

"Now you want to make me a prostitute," Oksana said sadly after waiting for Shabnam to finish her drinks.

Her beautiful face had dropped, and she looked very distressed.

"Come to the office on Monday," she said, sternly giving her a final warning. "We will finalise everything."

"Please don't do this," Oksana pleaded.

I thought if Shabnam had continued with her rant, Oksana would break down anytime soon because she was mentally torturing her.

"I've to go now," she said, coldly ignoring Oksana's plea. "Come with me if you want to be dropped back."

"You go ahead," Oksana replied. "I'll manage."

I really liked her reply. She was showing her stronger side. There was no point in accepting Shabnam's offer because she was a ruthless woman who only wanted one thing from Oksana. Shabnam started to walk out of the café. The waiter waved at her. She didn't pay, which I couldn't understand. Oksana folded her arms and then buried her head. *What did Shabnam expect from the Indian dancers?* I questioned myself. They didn't seem to be taking her bait. I felt very sorry for Oksana. I never imagined that the world could be such a bad place. I had a protected environment in Delhi. I wondered how a woman could force another woman into prostitution. Should I help her? I thought she was a helpless woman in a strange country needing help. That country happened to be my own. So I decided to help. My parents would have expected the same from me. I asked the waiter to bring two Cokes. The waiter got the Coke swiftly. I took the two glasses from him and went to her.

"Drink this," I said very politely, not wanting to sound like another bad Indian. "You don't look well."

"Who are you?" she asked while lifting her head. She looked at me, amazed, and, pointing to the table where I was sitting, asked, "Were you sitting there?"

"My name is Jai Grover," I replied in a soft voice. "Yes, I was sitting there."

"What do you want?"

"I want to help you. What is your name?"

"Oksana Bzovsky. What help?"

I had never heard anything like Bzovsky in my life. Even Oksana was relatively new to me, but I liked the name.

"I heard your conversation with the fat woman."

"Fat woman. Her name is Shabnam Seth," she said in a very musical way, smiling. She then taught me ethics. "Why were you listening to our conversation? It is bad to listen to someone's private chat."

"I was sitting just there," I explained, a bit ashamed and partially agreeing with her. "You guys were talking very loudly. It is very quiet here. It was hard for me not to hear you both."

"Sorry, we shouldn't have spoken loudly," she said innocently.

"Can I sit here for some time?"

She nodded, so I took a chair beside her.

"Thanks for the Coke. My throat is dry," she said in a heavy voice.

"Why are you sad? Can I help?"

"You want to help me?" she asked with a surprising smile. That was the first time I had seen her smiling so close. Her smile was so enchanting, which really moved me. She continued, "You look very young. How old are you?"

"Twenty-one."

"Only 21?" she said, surprised, and taunted, "Shouldn't you be with your parents like other Indians?"

"Twenty-one is not a kid," I argued, not minding her taunt. "I've finished my engineering. I used to live with my parents until few weeks back. What has age to do with helping someone?"

"Can you really help?"

"Try."

"I may lose my job on Monday. I'll have to vacate my apartment," she said, distressed.

"Why in a week?"

"My two-year contract is expiring next week," she said slowly while opening up. "Shabnam will not renew it unless I—"

"You do what she wants you to do?" I completed her sentence. She nodded. I said sympathetically, "It is a shame a woman can ask another woman for such a thing."

"She wants me to do bad things," she said innocently, which melted my heart.

"No, you shouldn't do anything you don't like," I lectured. "Do you have savings?"

"Yes, I've enough for now."

"Why don't you go back?" I asked, eagerly not able to comprehend why a European would be so helpless in India.

"To do what?" she asked and then started to state the facts, "There is an ongoing war. The economy has collapsed. There are no jobs there."

"Oh! But you can take a break and then come back."

"I've a single-entry visa," she said and then complained, "Your country has stopped issuing a visa to the Ukrainian woman between 18 and 40."

"Do you know why?"

"Because some girls do bad things in India."

"Which girls?"

"From other countries."

She didn't give me the names of the countries. I didn't insist either. I wanted to help her rather than worry about which girls did what in India.

"You said bad things," I asked in an investigative-journalist style. "Did you mean the thing Shabnam wanted you to do, isn't it?"

She nodded slowly.

"Anyway, do you have a valid visa in India?"

"I've a valid work permit for another 12 months."

"Look for another job. Why do you worry then?"

"I don't know how long it would take to find a new job. I really don't want to blow up my savings. I've to pay debts," she said and disclosed her main worry. "I will lose my apartment."

"You can find another apartment."

"Indian people are strange," she said and stopped, probably realising her mistake that she was talking to an Indian. I smiled and nodded, so she resumed, lamenting, "They avoid renting apartments to single European women."

I had to agree with her. I recalled how even Indian Muslims had found it hard to find a place in Mumbai, which was widely reported in various news channels. I thought that India needed strong tenancy laws.

"Where will I live if I don't find a place on time? I can't afford to live in a hotel. My savings will dry up in weeks," she said hopelessly.

It was not hard to realise that she was in deep water. However, there was an immediate solution to her problem. I could easily help her, but I wasn't sure whether she would accept my offer. Since we had been talking to each other for about ten minutes and she had not shown any hesitation or displeasure, I decided to make the offer.

"There is an immediate solution."

"How could there be an immediate solution to such a complex problem?" she asked, amused.

"You can move into my apartment," I said honestly and added, throwing a freebie, "Moreover, you don't have to pay any rent because I am not paying any."

"You said you were living with your parents," she asked, probably not having heard me.

"I said when I was in Delhi," I replied softly. "I am from Delhi."

"Why don't you pay rent?" she probed.

"My parents own it," I replied and added further, like a salesman makes a sales pitch, "It is a three-bedroom self-contained apartment. There is a large room with attached toilet and bath. You can take that."

"First, you got me Coke," she asked suspiciously while narrowing her eyes. "Then you wanted to help me, and now you want me to move into your apartment. What's next?"

"You decide and then move," I replied, casually ignoring her question, which I understood very well.

"What do you want next from me?" she repeated, stressing every word.

I had to come clean now.

"See, I want to start my own dance group and then set up an events management company. I am a good singer and know most of the musical instruments. I want you to be the lead dancer and choreographer for my group," I explained while looking at her to gauge her reaction.

She thought for a while. Next, she turned the tables on me and started interviewing me.

"How much money?" she asked seriously.

"Nothing at the moment," I replied cautiously. "I've to set up the group first. Slowly, we will find some work."

She rested her left cheek on her palm and went into deep thinking like a Greek philosopher. I waited for her reaction. She remained unmoved, so I decided to wake her up. "The good thing is that you don't have to pay any rent. You have a long-term visa. You worry about your expenses, and I'll worry about mine. But—"

"Common expenses would be shared by both," she completed my sentence.

"Yes."

"But you still haven't answered my question." She went back into her probing mode. "If I decide to move into your apartment, what will you want next from me?"

"While we are looking for work, we will create some compositions that you will have to choreograph," I replied, ignoring her question again.

"Gosh! You don't understand," she said, shaking her head in disbelief.

At that point, I almost lost my patience. I burned inside because I was trying to help, but she was suspecting me. For once, I thought of leaving the place but decided to confront her.

"I don't want anything that you have been thinking about," I said politely, which mellowed her down.

"Do you need permission from your parents?" she asked.

"No," I assured. "However, I don't hide anything from them. I'll let them know the day you decide to move."

Suddenly, I realised that we had been talking for a long time, so I decided to end the conversation. I offered to drop her off, which she accepted. Once inside the car, she leant back and closed her eyes. We didn't talk to each other until we reached her apartment. I stopped the car outside her building. She got off, thanked, and started to walk inside the building. I slowly started to move my car when she suddenly turned back.

"Give me your mobile number," she asked.

"So you are moving?" I asked.

"I'll call you."

I nodded and asked casually, "Which level do you live in?"

"Tird," she replied, pronouncing *third* as *tird.*

I gave her my mobile number and then sped off. It took me around 90 minutes to get back to my apartment.

Back at home, I started to think about Oksana appreciating the fact that she had a good command over English. But she pronounced all the words that began with *th* as *t,* hard *t* as soft *t,* hard *d* as soft *d*, and *w* as *v* like she had pronounced *third* as *tird.* I really liked her accent because it was so different from the British or the American we had become used to or our own English accent, which was so flawed.

I felt very satisfied the way I had held my discussion skilfully. I thought these negotiating skills would come in handy in the future when I joined my family business. I wasn't fully convinced, though, that Oksana would move. However, I decided to wait for few more days; otherwise, I would start searching for another dancer.

CHAPTER 5

It had been almost a week since I had met Oksana, but she hadn't called me back. The hopes of Oksana moving into my apartment were sinking. I thought I might not have been able to fully convince my prospective dancer-cum-choreographer. I was wrong about my negotiating skills. There was no way I could contact her because she hadn't given me her mobile number.

I had to search for a new person. How would I proceed? Internet search was the best way to proceed. But I didn't have a proper internet connection, which I needed so badly now. I called a number of ISPs to shop around for a good deal. I felt satisfied with the deal offered by Airtel. I ran to the nearest Airtel shop, picked a tower-shaped Wi-Fi modem, and quickly returned home. It took me around 30 minutes to configure the connection. I successfully tested a couple of websites, so I was now well and truly connected to the Internet world.

I then searched the keyword *dancers and choreographers wanted in Mumbai* in Google, which returned me over two hundred and fifty thousand results. Happy with the result, I decided to work in the night to shortlist ten to fifteen people in order to start calling them one by one in the coming days.

I took a bath, had lunch, and then decided to doze off, which I needed to enable me to work in the night for my search work. The time now was 2.30 in the afternoon, so I set a wake-up alarm for 6.30 to leave me half an hour for myself to call Mum for the daily update. I went to the bedroom and after some twisting and tossing soon fell asleep.

I dreamt of being in Delhi with my parents, having our daily evening discussion in the TV room. We all looked happy, laughed, teased one another, and joked around. Mum said soon I would be going to the United States for my MBA degree. I could hear that the domestic help was working in the kitchen, loading the dishwasher. Suddenly, she dropped something from her hands, which made a loud sound of a crockery breaking, which woke me up.

I looked around, trying to figure out what exactly had happened but soon realised that it was a dream. I tried to reach for my mobile, which I normally left on the bedside rack. It wasn't there. I looked around on both sides of the bed, but it wasn't on the either side. I went to the hall and found it on the couch as I had forgotten to pick it from the hall after setting up my internet connection. I checked the time. It was 6.25. I went to the bathroom to wash my face and then to the kitchen to make a cup of coffee. Suddenly, the alarm on my mobile started to buzz. I ran to the hall to turn the alarm off when I noticed two missed calls and an SMS.

3.15pm – It was a missed call from a private number.

4.32pm – Message "Call me on 9822xxxxxx. Need to talk urgently. Oksana"

5.10pm – Voicemail "Jey, I am Oksana calling. I am waiting for your call until 5.30. It is urgent."

She had pronounced my name as *Jey* instead of *Jai*. I was late by over an hour but still called her. It went into her voicemail. I left a message to call me back as soon as possible as I had to call my mum, hence, didn't want to miss her call again. I waited for her call, holding my head with both my hands. After seven long minutes of agonising wait, my mobile rang. I lunged on my mobile like a hungry lion that hadn't eaten for days.

"Hello, Oksana," I spoke with a sense of urgency.

"Jey, how are you?" she spoke softly. "It is Oksana."

"It is Jai, not Jey," I told, slightly annoyed.

She apologised and then started practising the correct pronunciation of my name. Soon she got the pronunciation right, which pleased me a lot.

"Sorry, I missed your call," I apologised. "I was sleeping."

"I lost my job," she said, distressed. "Tomorrow morning, I've to vacate my apartment before 10."

"So what are you planning?"

"Can I move into your apartment? But I am not sure," she requested, confused.

"Your statement is very contradictory," I replied calmly. "For me, you are welcome to move."

"Are you sure?"

"I was sure on the first day I met you."

"I'll start packing now," she said, giggling, and then went a step further, which pleased me a lot. "Can you pick me up from my place tomorrow?"

"SMS me your address."

"I'll," she said. "I've to start packing now."

"Wait," I stopped her. "Why did you say that you were waiting for my call until 5.30?"

"When did I say?" she protested.

"In your voicemail, which you left for me."

"Oh, that. Don't worry. We are now talking, so it doesn't mean much."

"You are right. I'll see you tomorrow," I disconnected, puzzled.

I called my mum whom I spoke for about 15 minutes. I told Mum about Oksana. She warned me to be careful with strangers. Only if she knew Oksana herself was stranded in a strange country. I was relieved because I didn't have to search for a dancer now. I stopped for a while and started to think, *Would it work with Oksana?* Unsure, I decided to carry out the search work anyway. If it worked out well with Oksana, then I wouldn't call anyone; otherwise, the caller list was ready. I sat on the couch and started to search for people, taking me about three hours. Satisfied with my search, I turned the notebook off and then went to sleep.

Next morning I left the apartment excited to pick Oksana. It took me 40 minutes to reach her apartment. After finding a place to park, I ran towards the lift and soon escalated up to level 3. I pressed the bell and waited for her to answer. A woman, who didn't look like an Indian or East European, opened the door.

"Yes?" she asked, smiling.

"I want to see Oksana." I smiled back.

"She left," she replied in broken English.

"Where?" I asked, surprised.

"Down," she replied in a cryptic manner, also pointing down with her index finger. "Two minutes."

I guessed she probably was saying that Oksana went downstairs two minutes back. Relieved that Oksana was still around, I started to head back to the lift, but then I stopped.

"Can I ask a question?"

I really wanted to know her nationality because she was not only attractive, but her smile was like one of those you really liked.

"You want to ask me a personal question?" she asked shyly, probably trying to gauge my age.

"No. No. It is not like that," I clarified. "I just wanted to know your country of origin."

"I am from Russia," she replied hastily and then slammed the door.

I got the feeling that she had lied to me. I called Oksana who was waiting for me downstairs. It was a coincidence that while I was going up, Oksana was coming down. I raced down to find her waiting with two very large suitcases, a large bag, a carry bag, and a laptop hanging by her left shoulder. She was looking stunning in her casual attire and a pair of big oval-shaped sunglasses. Her hair was loose, which was coming on to her face because of the wind. She was occasionally moving it back with her hands.

"Are you ready?" I asked.

"Where is your car?" she asked.

"It is there." I pointed towards the car, which was parked some 20 metres down. "Can we walk there?"

"Can you bring it here? I am tired," she requested.

I went to the car, reversed it, and then slowly drove towards her. I unlocked the trunk and then got out. She opened the back door; shoved her big bag, carry bag, and laptop in; and then she tried to lift her suitcase. It was too heavy for her. I asked her to wait. I then put her large suitcases in the trunk with great difficulty. They were too large and heavy but somehow fitted in my small car's trunk. I sat back in the car and then waited for her to get in when she asked, "Where should I sit?"

"Wherever you feel comfortable," I replied casually.

"I'll sit with you." She giggled, which pleased me because we were now becoming friends, not just acquaintances.

She sat inside, and I moved the car. For some time, we didn't talk to each other. She was looking straight down the road. She looked confident, relaxed, and beautiful. I thought she would have used a high-quality body lotion as fragrance started to fill inside air. I decided to break the silence, which sounded eerie to me.

"How did you spend the last few days?" I asked casually.

"Busy," Oksana replied and then complained, "Shabnam is a bad woman."

I nodded and then asked, "How did your meeting go with her?"

"Not well. I will tell you everything in detail in a couple of days."

"Why in a couple of days?"

"It is very distressing. I want to relax for few days."

I didn't press her further, so I chose to drive quietly. We approached a traffic signal that had turned red. I looked out of the window and found not much traffic around. Suddenly, a motorbike pulled up on my side, and the man on the bike started to stare at Oksana who was looking straight down the road. Oksana, intuitively sensing being watched, looked into the eyes of that man who then quickly turned his gaze away from her. She looked at me red-faced. I felt very embarrassed at the bad habit of some Indian men to stare at foreigners or beautiful Indian women. The signal turned red, and I started to drive again. I decided to resume my conversation to divert her attention from that ugly incident.

"Who was the woman who answered the door?" I asked.

"I don't know. There are two left now," she replied without looking at me.

"She told me she was a Russian, but she didn't look like a Russian."

"Was she blonde?"

"No."

"Oh! She is from Uzbekistan," she told. "She is known by her Russian name Natasha."

"Why Russian name?"

"I don't know, but every woman from ex-Soviet republic is called Russian here."

"What does she do?"

"Dance like me."

"And more than that?"

"I don't know," she replied curtly. "Don't remind me of that."

"Sorry."

I preferred not to disturb her further, so I drove quietly. We reached the apartment in 50 minutes. With a lot of struggle, I managed to bring her luggage up inside the apartment. Once inside, we sat on the couch, trying to get our breath back to normal. She was sitting cross-legged in a very comfortable manner, which made me happy because I wanted her to feel comfortable. I got two Coke cans from the kitchen fridge and then gave one to her. She started to sip the Coke, looking directly into the floor, and then she started inspecting the hall by rolling her big blue eyes all around. She put the empty can on the table, got up, pulled her T-shirt down, and then asked for her room. I gave her a guided tour of the apartment. She inspected her room and bathroom and had a look at the balcony from inside. She asked me not to open the balcony door because she had a height phobia. I told her that the balcony was being used to dry the wet clothes. She told me that she would take care of that because once in a while going out on the balcony was not an issue with her. I noticed that she didn't take much interest in other parts of the apartment except for her room.

"There is no dressing table here," she said, somewhat surprised.

"There was no woman here until you arrived," I replied.

"I mean I'll have to buy one," she clarified and then pointed to the right side of the wall directly opposite to the bedhead. "I'll keep the table there. When can we go?"

"Is it very urgent?"

"Yes, but we can wait until next weekend."

"Do you want a new or a used one?"

"Used one."

"I'll call someone to find out the best and cheapest seconds shop."

She then asked me to leave the room. She said she would be busy for a long time, wasn't feeling hungry, so I didn't have to worry about her lunch. She then looked at me, expecting me to leave. I started to leave the room when she suddenly asked me, "Do you have a hammer?"

"Do you want to keep it with you as a personal weapon?" I asked, smiling.

"I need to hang pictures." She burst into laughter. "I don't like bare walls."

"How will you hang the pictures?"

"I've the picture nails."

"I don't have a hammer. But I'll get one later."

"I should have known that."

"How?"

"I saw a couple of paintings resting against the wall outside," she said casually, which impressed me for her attention to the minutest detail.

"I was thinking of hanging them but couldn't find the time," I said, embarrassed.

"Don't worry about the hammer today," she said, unimpressed. "I can wait. I'll start unpacking now."

I left the room and then heard the sound of the door being closed. Realising that she would be busy in unpacking for hours, I decided to go to the shopping centre to kill my next three to four hours. At the shopping centre, I went around from one shop to another without any intention of buying anything. I still had plenty of time left, so I decided to watch a movie in the multiplex theatre, which I left halfway as I found it very boring. I sat on a bench in an open area inside the centre and then started to think about Oksana. I had to talk to her about her role as a lead dancer-cum-choreographer in the group, which I needed to form quickly. I already had a cursory discussion with her about it. Moreover, it was the main condition of her sharing my apartment. But I still needed a firm commitment from her, so I decided to discuss in detail in the evening.

I headed back to the apartment; and when I opened the door, I found her sitting on the couch, staring into the vacuum. She turned her head, looked at me, and then went back to her original position. She had changed, and her big luscious lips were a standout, which she had painted with cherry-red lipstick. There was a special aura on her face. I felt inferior in front of her, so I went to the bathroom to take a self-appraisal. I didn't look that bad, so I came back and sat with her. She kept staring into the vacuum. My presence meant nothing to her.

"Are you going somewhere?" I broke the silence.

"No. Why?" she replied with an expression as if I had asked an unusual question.

"Why are you dressed up like this then?"

"I like doing up," she replied with a lot of pride. "I like to look good all the time."

"You don't like the casual look?"

"Sometimes. Mostly at night when I don't have to go out."

"How long does it take you to get ready?" I asked. "I mean right from bath to makeup?"

"It depends on the type of makeup and hairstyle I choose."

"Say, around 90 minutes?" I guessed.

"Yes," she replied, somewhat appreciating my guess.

"How long do you want to remain dressed up like this?" I asked, changing the topic.

"Am I distracting you?" she shot back.

"Not at all. I thought we will discuss business."

"Do I've to change for that?" she continued with her rant.

"No," I replied softly, not wanting to upset her further. "We can discuss at dinnertime."

"I take my dinner at 7. What time do you take?"

"I call my mother at that time." I was not expecting any relief from her. "It takes me 10 to 15 minutes to finish with her."

"We can have dinner after you have finished the call," she said magnanimously.

"You are very kind," I said with a hint of sarcasm.

"I am going to my room." She started to walk back to her room. "I still haven't finished unpacking. I'll see you at quarter past."

"What do you want for dinner?"

"Anything."

"Do you like Indian?" I asked fearfully.

"Yes."

Soon she disappeared into her room. I sighed a big relief because I didn't have to worry about her food. I went to the kitchen to cook food. I had plenty of ready-to-cook stuff. I decided to cook rice, tadka dhal, butter chicken, and Indian-style salad. It took me half an hour to finish my cooking, placed food on the table, and then headed to my room to make a call to Delhi. I spoke with Mum for ten minutes. When I returned to the dining area, she was already at the table.

"Did you call your mother?" she asked.

"Yes," I replied.

"Do you call her daily?"

"That is what she wants me to do."

"Otherwise, you wouldn't call her."

"I love my parents. I would have called them otherwise also," I told proudly and then asked, "What about your parents?"

"I don't discuss my family," she replied coldly.

I decided not to get involved with her personal life, so I started filling the plates. She liked the aroma of rice and spicy accompaniments. She picked tomatoes and carrots from the salad, discarding onions.

"You don't like onions?"

"They leave a bad smell in the mouth," she replied with a "yuck" face. "Only cooked ones."

That was the signal that raw onions were out of salad as long as she stayed in the apartment.

"Should we discuss the future plan?"

"What is your future plan?"

"I told you that I have to form a dance group and establish an events management company. I need people for both."

"What is my role?"

"I need a lead dancer and a choreographer," I said. "Can you choreograph?"

"Of course, I am a dancer."

"We also need a songwriter, a guitarist, a drummer, a flautist, a tabla player, and a harmonium player."

"What will you do?"

"I'll sing. I also know how to play few instruments."

"How long will it take to form the team?"

"July is ending soon. I suppose by August end. Once we have a team, we can then write new songs and choreograph dances," I replied, hoping that the things would start happening soon.

She didn't say anything, so I continued, "We will perform in various events and also create an album of our creations."

"So there won't be any income for quite some time."

"Yes. Do you have a better idea?"

She shook her head and said, "We will go your way."

"There is one thing I didn't tell you."

"What?" she asked suspiciously.

"You are going to be the USP of the group."

"What is USP?"

"Unique selling point," I replied, unsure of her response. "In every advertisement, we will highlight you. You know, glamour sells."

"Actually, it is sex sells," she refuted me.

"Is there any problem?" I asked fearfully.

"Jai, you are not that innocent," she told sharply. "Your brain works like a shrewd businessman."

She wasn't wrong. I thought whenever I joined my father's business, I would be the third generation in my family business. Although I had never been involved in my family business, it came naturally to the Punjabis, the

Gujaratis, the Marwadis, and the Sindhis. I recalled my father telling me once that these communities owned and controlled more than 90 per cent of India's private wealth. I was convinced that she had a sharp brain.

"Are you lost somewhere?" She woke me up.

"Sorry, I should have told you," I replied.

"That is okay."

"So you are okay?" I asked like a happy child.

"Yes, but on one condition."

"What condition?" My face dropped.

"You will pay me extra for modelling work," she said very calmly and confidently.

She was one step ahead of me. I had offered her free accommodation, but I didn't know why I felt powerless in front of Oksana. I decided to remind her about the free accommodation.

"Since you don't have to pay rent", I said slowly and carefully, "could that be considered as the payment for your modelling job?"

"You offered me free accommodation I didn't ask for. You approached me, didn't you? Had you told me beforehand, I wouldn't ask for any extra payment."

She was right, so I lost my case.

"How much do you want?"

"Five per cent of revenue that is generated through me," she replied like a shrewd negotiator.

"Can I ask you a question?"

"What question?"

"Are all Ukrainians bloodsuckers?" I asked, smiling.

"Don't talk bad about Ukrainians," she admonished.

"Sorry, I was just joking."

"Was it a joke? I know similar jokes about Indians."

"I said sorry." I regretted my foolishness about the bloodsucker remark.

"You think I'll forget." She was not going to give up. "I'll tell you a joke about Indians at an appropriate time."

I did not say anything but reminded myself to remain careful towards cultural sensitivities. I now had to wait for the time when she was going to fire a joke away about Indians.

CHAPTER 6

It had been a couple of days now since Oksana had moved into my apartment. She was slowly settling down and looking relaxed. On that day after dinner, I reminded her about her meeting with Shabnam. For some strange reasons, I was very eager to know about her meeting. She asked me to wait and then went to her room. She came back soon with three to four sheets of paper in her hands. We both settled down on the couch, and then she read something from the sheets.

She started off by telling me that on Monday, 28 July, she left her apartment to meet Shabnam in her office. She hated to get up early, but she had no choice because her appointment was at 9. She was kind of "late-bed, late-rise" type of person—never out of her bed before 10.30. She very much enjoyed morning sleep. That was the first time she was visiting Shabnam's office. She had always been contacted on her mobile by someone from Shabnam's office. She decided to catch the metro but wasn't sure how far Shabnam's office was from the station. She boarded the metro and reached the station in about 40 minutes. She enjoyed the ride.

She added that the commuting had become safe and comfortable since the metro became operational in Mumbai. In the past, she had preferred to commute through the BEST buses over overcrowded local trains. She had a terrible experience in the past when she boarded a crowded local train. It was like a thousand people being stuffed into a box that had a capacity of accommodating only a hundred people. Moreover, prying eyes had made her very insecure. She virtually felt being stripped and raped by those prying eyes. She had to get off at the next station, which was five stations before her destination.

At that point, she stopped and again looked at me. I again felt embarrassed having myself witnessed such an incident a couple of days back. I apologised on behalf of some Indian men and then affectionately patted her hand to give her some comfort. She smiled, read something again, and then resumed.

She got off the train and went to the enquiry counter. The lady at the counter was very friendly. She gave her directions to Shabnam's office. Pointing to the exit, she told her to first cross the road, turn right, walk 50 metres, turn left, and walk another 20 metres, turn left into a small lane, and the building was second on the right. The lady, seeing her confused face, wrote up the directions on a piece of paper. Oksana thanked her and started walking towards Shabnam's office. After walking a labyrinth of streets for ten minutes, she finally reached the building.

It was a four-storeyed dilapidated building. She took 20 flights to reach the second floor. The office had a very ordinary setting. There were four people in the office, busy working on their old-style desks and chairs. Shabnam had a larger desk and was sitting close to the window. As Oksana entered the office, Shabnam lifted her head and with her right-hand index finger gestured her to come through. She sat on one of the two chairs directly facing Shabnam.

"What have you decided?" Shabnam asked in a very authoritative tone, which she didn't like.

"Hello, Shabnam, how was your weekend?" she asked politely.

"I asked you a question," Shabnam said curtly, looking at her abhorrently.

"My reply is the same as it was on last Friday," she replied calmly.

Shabnam didn't say anything but kept staring at her somewhat in awe. Realising that Oksana was firm in her decision, she bent down to open the drawer and then pulled something out.

"This is your final payment," she said, annoyed, and issued an ultimatum. "Vacate the apartment on Friday morning by 10. Someone will come to collect the keys from you."

"Can't you reconsider your decision?" she made the last plea.

"There are thousands of Russian girls in India," she shouted loudly. "I don't have time for your nonsense. Now leave me alone. I've got lots of work to do."

Oksana felt humiliated. She got up, red-faced, without saying anything and started to walk out of the office. As she was about to cross the door, evil Shabnam growled, "Blue eyes, I'll make sure you pay for your refusal."

"I don't care," Oksana shouted back angrily and then screamed, "Do whatever you like."

She kicked the door in anger, scaled down, and then left the building. She boarded the metro back to her apartment. Upon reaching her apartment, she locked herself in her room and started to think about her options. She had four more days to ponder.

She stopped again. I noticed some hesitation in her.

"What happened afterwards?" I asked.

"Umm . . . I am not sure whether I should tell you this."

"What *this*?" I asked, confused.

"It is about India and you," she replied, confused.

"I have no problem as long as it is true," I assured.

She thought for a while, probably still not sure; but finally, she agreed. Glancing over papers, she told me that she hated being in India and thought Shabnam was one of the rudest persons in the world. She thought how stupid we Indians were. We think every woman from East Europe and Central Asia is a Russian. She hated to be called a Russian. She also told me that she thought about our meeting in the café. She thought I was either very clever or a naïve. She recollected that during the entire conversation, I hadn't laughed or smiled even a single time. I looked serious while talking to her. She regretted not using my offer as a bargaining chip when she had gone to see Shabnam that morning.

She continued by telling me that for the next two days she had called all her contacts for a job. Everybody promised to talk to their managers, but they all came back with the same answer, i.e. a big NO. She came to know through her close circles that Shabnam had spread a word against her. She had branded her everything other than a dancer: a thief or a drug addict or a prostitute. It didn't surprise her because she knew that Shabnam could stoop low.

She further added that the word *prostitute* hurt her the most. The reason she left Shabnam was becoming one of the reasons for her disqualification to find a job. She was aware that a couple of years back the Indian government had reportedly asked the country's diplomatic missions in Ukraine, Russia, Kazakhstan, and Kyrgyzstan to tighten the overview of visa applications by women aged 18–40 in an attempt to stop the inflow of sex workers to India. The topless FEMEN activists in Kiev had protested outside Indian embassy in the subzero temperature, demanding an apology from the Indian government. She hated women from her country to be dubbed as prostitutes. Her country was trying to get out of that image.

She concluded that not being able to find a job and the fear of being on the road left her with no choice but to contact me.

She stopped, tossed the sheets on the table, took a deep breath, and then looked away. There was complete silence for a while. I didn't know how to react, so I decided to leave her alone for some time. I went to my room and spent the next ten minutes thinking about Oksana. When I returned, she wasn't there. I noticed that she had left behind a sheet on the table. I picked the sheet and started to read:

> My parents once told me that life was so good during the Soviet period. Everybody had jobs, food, and there was peace everywhere. Students from a number of countries used to get scholarships to study in ex-Soviet republics like Russia, Ukraine, Uzbekistan etc. Indian students used to be everywhere including Ukraine. Ukrainians were never rude to them despite paying for their fees and accommodation. Times have changed because now we have to seek opportunities in India. The only difference is that Indians are rude. We weren't. After all, we believe in EUROPEAN ETIQUETTE AND CHRISTIAN VALUES. I'll visit Goa for a few days. A large number of

> Russians live there. No, I don't like Russians. Instead, I'll use the next four days to find a job or an apartment. If push comes to shove, I'll pack up and then go back to Ukraine. Kiss my ass, India. I am not going to sleep with any Indian.

I kept the sheet back exactly the way she had left. I looked at the wall clock. The time was 11.30. I switched the light off and then went to my room. As I was preparing to sleep, I heard the sound of a door being opened. After waiting for few moments, I got out of my room and noticed that the light in the hall was on. I guessed that Oksana must have gone to the hall to pick the sheet. Not wanting to disturb her, I slipped back into the bed and soon fell asleep.

CHAPTER 7

It took Oksana about a week to settle down in the new environment. She had made sure that her room looked exactly the way she wanted it to be. She told me that I was not supposed to enter her room in her absence or without seeking her prior approval. She always kept her room door closed. I didn't have any problem because I very well understood the privacy of a woman. She used to spend most of her time locked in her room. She had left the apartment only twice since her move. She never discussed her plans or how she spent her time while away. She had a habit of sleeping late and never getting up before 10.30 in the morning.

Meanwhile, I had been carrying out online searches to find appropriate people for the group. I spoke to around 30 to 40 different people, shortlisting three groups whom I decided to meet in person. Each group consisted of a songwriter, a guitarist, a drummer, a flautist, a tabla player, and a harmonium player. Most of them were either new or struggling or out-of-work type of people. I lined up a meeting with two groups for tomorrow at 11 in the morning and 2 in the afternoon respectively in the food court of a shopping centre.

While having dinner, I decided to discuss my tomorrow's meeting with Oksana.

"Tomorrow, I would be out most of the day," I said.

She shrugged her shoulders without saying anything.

"I've to find people for the group," I explained politely. "We need to form the group by the end of this month. Do you want to join me?"

"I don't think I can contribute much," she backed out. "How did you find?"

"Online search."

"Oh!"

"When do you want to buy your dressing table?" I asked, preferring to change the topic.

"Saturday," she replied. "Did you find the shop?"

"I'll find out before Saturday," I replied.

"What time do you have to leave tomorrow?"

"Ten in the morning."

"I am going now."

She got up and soon disappeared in her room. I called Vishal about the used furniture who gave the name and address of the shop at Chembur. I cleared the table and then headed to my room. I started to think about Oksana. I wasn't sure whether she was the right type of person for the group. There was no camaraderie between us. She hadn't, so far, shown any interest in sharing the workload. I decided not to worry too much about the workload. It was a small thing. I felt exploited, though.

Next morning I got up at 6.30 with the intention of leaving home at 10 to meet the two groups. I removed my mobile from the charger, put my notebook in the bag, made a cup of coffee, and then went to the small room for a workout. I finished everything by 8 and decided to start getting ready at 9.15. It was a sticky day; so I chose to wear a white cotton shirt, jeans, and sneakers as I had to walk a lot. I had some time left, so I sat on the couch and then started to think about Oksana. She must be still sleeping. Last night, when I went to the bathroom before going to bed, I saw the light in her room still on. I also heard music being played at a very low volume. The time was 11.30. I hadn't been able to make out what time actually she used to go to sleep, but something was strange in her personality. Something like enigmatic and reticent. Whatever her personality, she was a good dancer. That was what mattered most to me.

I realised that it was time to start getting ready; so I quickly took a shower, got ready, and then sat back on the couch, waiting for the wall clock to strike 10, which was still ten minutes away. Suddenly, my concentration was broken with an alarm going off. Then I heard the sound of a door being opened. I looked over my shoulders towards the rooms. It was Oksana in red shorts, matching tank top, and thick black thongs. Her hair loose, which she was constantly adjusting. For the first time, I saw her without makeup. She looked more beautiful without makeup because she was naturally beautiful. She came to the hall, stopped, adjusted her hair to the right with her left hand, and then tilted her neck to the left. She kept using her left hand to hold her hair like a hairclip. She had a piece of paper on her right hand.

"This is the list of items I want you to buy," she said in semi-sleepy eyes.

"When?" I asked.

"I need in about an hour."

"I've to meet someone at 11," I said, astonished. "I have to leave in five minutes."

"They will deliver," she said casually. "You just hand over the list."

"Give me the list," I said, annoyed. "I've to rush now."

I quickly ran to the shopping centre. At the store, I gave them the list and the delivery address, rushed to the railway station, and soon boarded the train. I didn't have time to look at the list.

I reached the food court of the shopping centre ten minutes early. I picked a spot near McDonald's, big enough to accommodate six to seven people. I sat down and called one of the persons from the first group to give them my exact location. I waited for them, looked around, and realised that it was a huge shopping centre. Mum once told that before I was born, shopping centres were almost nonexistent in India; but in the last 20 years, they had mushroomed everywhere. Some of the shopping centres in big cities like Mumbai, Bangalore, Chennai, Delhi, Gurgaon, and Noida were so huge, probably among the biggest in the world.

I didn't have to wait long because my candidates arrived on time. They were a group of seven people, two girls and five boys. Why seven? I needed only six. Soon I found that one of the extra persons was the brother of one of the girls. They were in casual attire, and all looked like college students. They wanted to order food first, so they went around different stalls. Around 20 minutes were wasted, but they refused my offer to pay for their food, which impressed me because they didn't look like to be taking advantage of my situation. I started off with my plan and then asked each one to talk about his or her specialty. They seemed to know enough about their instruments, which they had played many times in their school events. They all were university students pursuing undergraduate degrees in various disciplines. I started to like them and thought that I might have hit the bull's-eye.

As things seemed to be going well, I disclosed that there was no immediate money until I found some work. Their faces dropped, and then they started to look at one another as if they had smelt a rat. I immediately knew that I had hit the wall. After a while, the leader of pack agreed, but they wanted some retention type of fees, mainly to cover their day-to-day expenses. They gave a figure, which was not hard to meet. I told them that I needed some time to get back to them. I thanked them for their time and then shook hands one by one. How could have I agreed without meeting the remaining two groups?

I had one hour left for the next meeting, which was due at 2. I decided to stroll around the mall and within half an hour trudged back to the food court. I bought the food and started enjoying my food. I finished my food and then called one of the members at around five minutes to 2. It was a girl who answered my call. She told me that they had already arrived but were struggling to find a parking spot. She then hung up, saying that they might be late by five to ten minutes.

I waited for further 15 minutes when I saw a group of four young men and one young woman heading towards me. The girl stood out because she was very attractive. She was wearing a printed singlet, tight jeans, high-heeled sandals, and an expensive wristwatch. She was tall and had a round face and straight black hair. The young men were also smartly dressed in designer clothes. They all looked teenagers from very rich families. I wondered if they would join my group. They introduced themselves as Dolce Desai, Ajay Pant, Neel Sharma, Sachin Joshi, and Amardeep Singh Gill.

"Did you finally get the parking?" I asked.

"After a bit of struggle," Dolce replied in a typical girlie manner. "Thank god, we finally found it."

"Parking is always a problem," I said and tried to be a good host. "Do you want anything?"

"No thanks. We are fine."

"Should we start then?"

"Sure," Amardeep said.

He was a tall Sikh.

"Tell me about yourselves."

"I am the drummer, Ajay plays the flute very well, Amar guitar, Sachin tabla, and Neel harmonium. Neel is good at saxophone also," Dolce spoke for all.

"I sing and also know how to play a few instruments," I said and then disclosed, "Oksana would be our lead dancer and choreographer."

"Is she an Indian?" Dolce enquired suspiciously.

"No."

"I bet she is a Russian," Amardeep said in a funny style, thumping the table with his right hand.

"Ukraine."

"No problem," Neel said quietly and then justified himself with a good logic. "It would add value if we have a foreigner in our group."

"Are we all happy to include her in our group?" I asked, trying to seek a consensus.

"We have no problem," Dolce replied, again on everybody's behalf.

"But there is a small issue. There is no money until we find some work."

"No problem," Dolce spoke once again very casually.

"Are you sure?" I asked, shocked and surprised.

"Yes. Didn't I say that?" Dolce chided me.

I really liked the way she chided me because it spoke of her nature, someone who could make friends in minutes and I needed friends in Mumbai.

"Money is no worry," Sachin spoke for the first time in a very cool manner. "Just form the group first."

"Why isn't money any worry for you guys?" I probed.

They looked at one another for a long time. It seemed they didn't want to disclose the reason. I started to grow suspicious.

"Jai, don't worry about money. We are friends now," Dolce replied seriously.

"There has to be a reason," I said, not fully convinced with Dolce's logic. "How could you trust someone you didn't know until now?"

"Jai, we are not boasting. We all are from very rich families. We all went to the same school, Dhirubhai Ambani International in Bandra East. Have you heard?"

"No, I am from Delhi," I replied.

"We are all 18. We recently finished our HSC. Next year we are all heading to the US for our undergrad courses."

"Next year?" I asked. "When?"

"July 2015," Amardeep replied.

"We have little time in India," Sachin said, adding more. "US is going to be a hard time because you have to do everything on your own."

"Little time. It's almost a year away. Why are you wasting a year?" I asked, acting like their guardian.

The explanation they gave me really amazed me. But they had a valid reason because they were all from Mumbai where winter temperature averages early thirties.

"We can start in January," Dolce replied. "But it would be very cold there—"

"If we start in July, that will give us some time to acclimatise," Sachin completed her sentence.

"So we want to enjoy our remaining time." Amardeep giggled.

"Do you know which universities are you going?" I asked, showing interest in their future plans.

Having recently left my institute hadn't killed my excitement about the campus life. Moreover, I thought, I myself might be heading to the United States in a year's time.

"We are going to different universities." Dolce again. "But Sachin and I are going to the same university in New Jersey."

"You both opted for the same degree?"

"No, he is my boyfriend," she said matter-of-factly. "That is why."

"Oh!"

"So when do we start?" Ajay asked, drawing my attention back to the main point.

"We need a songwriter first."

"That is my department," he said, surprising me even more because everything seemed to be falling in place as per my plan. "I am basically from Uttarakhand. My grandfather was a renowned Hindi poet."

"What has your grandfather to do with us?"

"I also write in Hindi. I learnt from him."

"I can't imagine how happy I am," I said, feeling over the moon. "I will pay you for songs as well as for playing the flute if required."

"When do we start?" Dolce asked impatiently.

"Soon. But I want a firm commitment from you all," I said forcefully.

"Don't worry. We won't let you down," Dolce replied.

"And a promise."

"What promise?" Neel asked this time.

"When we start making money, you all will have to accept."

"Of course," Dolce said loudly. "There are no free lunches in this world."

"Where do you live?" Neel asked. "Where will we practise?"

"I live in a three-bedroom apartment. We can practise at my place in the hall. I'll SMS you my address," I replied, not willing to disclose my address until I had met the third group.

"You don't have any furniture in the hall?"

"Yes, but I can move that to make a room."

"Don't worry," Amardeep said. "I know a place behind the Churchgate station that we can use for our practice."

I felt that I was very lucky to have met them all because they were resolving all my issues.

"What is it?" I enquired.

"It's an apartment that is unoccupied at the moment."

"Whose apartment is that?"

"One of my close relatives," he explained. "They are an old couple. Currently in Toronto until next year."

"Don't you have to take their permission first?"

"I've a duty of looking after it in their absence," he said plainly. "So I've a permission."

"We will have to move the instruments there."

"We have to move the stuff from the hall first. I'll let you know."

"Can we start by next week?" I asked and then to Ajay. "Can you write a couple of songs?"

"Next week? Yes," Amardeep replied.

"What type of songs?" Ajay asked.

"Modern type. Fusion between Hindi and English."

"Duet or solo?"

"One apiece."

"I can do one by next week. Which one do you want first?"

"Make the duet first," I replied and then turned to all. "Come to my place on Sunday. We will work out our schedule for the coming weeks."

They all accepted my invitation.

"I have to go now. Is there anything else we need to discuss?"

"How old is this Oksana?" Dolce asked.

"I don't know. Maybe in her late 20s or early 30s."

"Good," Dolce commented, very pleased.

"Why?"

"Nothing. Don't bother."

"Are you worried about Sachin?" I asked, smiling.

"Nothing like that." She blushed.

"There is one small problem," I said, worried. "I don't know how to compose music."

"Amar, how many times have I created compositions for our school functions?" Dolce asked proudly.

"Don't you know? Why are you asking me?" Amardeep replied, irritated.

"Music was one of her subjects," Sachin said calmly.

"So you can do it?" I asked, still not fully convinced.

She looked at me and took a deep sigh as if asking me, "Why don't you trust me?" Next she started off with an impressive speech on the composition.

"Composition is a process of creating a new piece of music. It consists of two things. The first is the ordering and disposing of several sounds in such a manner that their succession pleases the ear, which is called melody. The second is the rendering of two or more simultaneous audible sounds in such a manner that their combination is pleasant, which is called harmony."

"How do you approach?" I asked, curiously fairly stunned by her knowledge.

"Horizontally, that is, write a melody first or vertically, that is, write harmony first," she replied confidently.

"You know too much about composition," I praised, trying to stop her. "Is that all?"

"Please, let me complete. If you want to compose fast, one should practise composing non-ambiguous music—that is, compose both melody and harmony at the same time, which is what we will do. You can use the notation software like Sibelius 7, but I prefer writing it out by hand. We will finalise the notion during our practice, which we will use in creating a track," she concluded and looked at me, smiling mysteriously as if asking, "Happy now?"

I kept looking at her totally mesmerised because she had bulldozed me with the long explanation.

"I am sorry. I am now convinced," I said and then enquired, "How long will it take to compose?"

"It may take a week to a year depends on what you want and how complex a composition is," she replied confidently.

"A year?" I asked nervously.

"What did I say, a week or a year? We will do in a week," she comforted and continued proudly. "You don't know how many competitions I won for my house, Tiger."

"Zero," Amardeep snapped her.

"Zero," she mimicked him. "Every year."

"Before we leave, I've a question for you, Dolce," I said.

"What?"

"What degree are you going to do?"

"Journalism. I want to become a TV reporter."

"I think that suits your personality," I said admiringly.

She was smart, presentable, and very talkative. We finished our meeting. We walked together for a while and then parted our ways. I soon boarded the train for my back journey. The train was half empty, so I chose a seat by the window for the next 45 minutes of my journey. I started to think about the two meetings I had today. I decided not to contact the third batch. I was happy with the outcome so far. But which one to pick? The first batch also looked good. I could afford the retention money they needed to cover their day-to-day expenses. It was a fair demand. But what about the second batch? They were rich so didn't need any money immediately. They just wanted to enjoy their lives for the next few months. I realised that I had already, indirectly, finalised the second batch. They were visiting my place on Sunday. I had no choice but to go with the second batch. These were the bunch of rich teenagers who wanted to enjoy their lives, living in secure and cosy homes and unmindful of contradictions in India.

I thought India was full of contradictions. There are extremely poor who live, eat, and breathe on roads under open-sky-like grubs. Then there are daily wagers who earn money on a daily basis, not sure about tomorrow; salaried class who earn on a monthly basis but are always short of money much before their next salary; and millionaires and multimillionaires and billionaires and multimillionaires. There are other contradictions apart from economic one. Corrupt, honest, patriots, nationalists, caring, callous, religious, atheists, secular, communal, dark, and fair—the list goes on and on. Then there are fault lines like frequent communal clashes, dissatisfaction, industrial strikes, underworld, intimidation, inefficient bureaucracy, and poverty.

I wondered what was keeping this country united with some many different states, cultures, languages, religions, shades, and colours. Probably, secular constitution, democracy, tolerance, vibrant civil society, and freedom to ask uneasy questions. There is no country in the world that is as diverse as India. If at all there was one, they would be at one another's throat, and rivers of blood would be flowing everywhere.

My concentration was broken by a train coming from the opposite side that just passed by. I again went into my thoughts. This time, I started to think about Oksana. Why was she like that? She could have given me the list a day earlier. Had I questioned her logic, she surely would have come up with a reply that would have left me speechless. The train started to slow down and eventually rumbled to a halt at a station. That one was mine. I got off the train and started to walk to my apartment.

I opened the door. The apartment looked completely different because it was spotlessly clean and looked very bright. Oksana, as usual, was sitting on the couch, staring into the vacuum. She looked over her shoulders. Our eyes met. With no expressions on her face, she quickly returned to her previous position and then continued with her favourite pastime of staring into the vacuum. She was in her full regalia as if she were soon going to attend a dinner party at the White House.

I went to the bathroom. It was sparkling clean. I checked other rooms. Everything had changed. The rooms looked like five-star hotel rooms waiting to be occupied by guests. So she had cleaned the whole apartment. I thought it would have taken her the whole day to clean the apartment. I went to my room to change, and when I came back, she wasn't there. I knocked at her room door. She said she would meet me at the dinner table. I enquired about dinner to which she replied that she had already prepared dinner. I returned to my room, inspected the rearranged settings, and then made sure nothing was misplaced.

I thought she not only was beautiful but also had a great sense of dressing, knew how to decorate and keep a home neat and tidy. My negativities about her disappeared. Did she ever have her own family or a home, or was it all passed on to her by her mother? There was no way of knowing this because I was sure that she would never disclose and I was never going to ask.

I called Mum, briefed her about my meetings, and assured her that the group was about to be formed. I went back to the dining area for dinner. She had placed the dinner on the table, waiting for me. I sat on the chair directly opposite her. There were two soup plates, a bowl, and garlic bread. I lifted the lid of the bowl but couldn't make much out of it. It was something soaked in red liquid. I pulled my hand back and then looked at her.

"What is this?" I enquired.

"Borshch," she replied and explained, "It's a Ukrainian soup made of beets, cabbage, potatoes, carrots, onions, garlic, and dill."

"So it's all vegetarian?" I asked, still not convinced whether it's suitable for me. "No beef or pork?"

"This one is made of only vegetables, but one could include meat or fish also," she assured.

We poured the soup into our plates and started to eat. It tasted sweet and sour. With garlic bread, it tasted perfectly fine and very filling. She didn't bother to ask me whether I liked it or not. Probably her philosophy was "This is what is available. Take it or leave it."

"Where did you get the stuff from?" I asked.

"I gave you the list in the morning," she replied.

"That is what was on the list?"

"Lots more."

"What is that lots more?" I asked curiously.

"Detergent, floor mop, floor cleaner, disinfectant, dishwashing liquid, and few more items," she replied while counting the items on her fingertips.

"Those items were already here," I asked quizzically.

"I threw the old ones," she replied impassively.

"Why?" I asked after giving her a quick glare. "I got them recently."

She didn't answer. She placed her elbows on the table, rested the chin on the locked hands, and then looked at me, smiling. That was her second favourite pose. I immediately knew the reason.

"You didn't want to use the used ones."

"I don't know," she replied, looking away.

"What are you made of?"

"Flesh and bones like you."

She got up and ordered me to clear the table. Before disappearing, she told me that she needed to wash the dishes once I had cleared the table. She also told me to clean the kitchen after she had washed the dishes. She wanted to discuss something serious once I had cleaned the kitchen. I nearly fell off my chair. That was her new avatar.

Later that night, we sat together to discuss her "something serious". She said that she wanted to share domestic workload with me. She explained to me my duty: dust the furniture, clean rooms and toilets, clear the dining table, clean the kitchen, and shop for grocery after dark if required. For herself, she decided to take the responsibility of cooking, cleaning dishes, doing the laundry, and ironing.

That was not all. She came up with a schedule. The rooms and toilets needed to be cleaned once a week on Saturday mornings. The kitchen had to be cleaned daily after dinner to make sure it was ready for use the following day. The weekly grocery shopping on Sunday mornings together. She insisted that things have to be returned to their proper place after use. She emphasised that she liked discipline, order, and cleanliness, enforcing them on me without worrying about my consent. I looked at her in total disbelief. She got up, smiled, and disappeared into her room. She was now in total control of my apartment and life, and I couldn't do anything. Basically, she had announced my status that of a servant-cum-landlord.

CHAPTER 8

We got ready to leave for Chembur to buy the dressing table for Oksana. Thankfully, she didn't take much time in dressing up, choosing to wear smart casuals. I looked at her in admiration because whatever she wore looked fabulous on her. At 11.30 in the morning, we left the parking area, turned right then left, and I saw him standing near the building entrance. He was in long shorts, tight V-necked T-shirt, and sunglasses, looking like an absolute joker. As I approached the entrance, he indicated me to stop. I stopped the car and then rolled down the window. Oksana looked at him and turned her face in the opposite direction, pretending to be looking out. She took him as my acquaintance or a friend. I noted that he didn't recognise Oksana, not knowing it was because of him I had come to know her.

"Where are you going?" Vishal asked but kept his gaze at Oksana.

"Chembur to buy a second-hand dressing table," I replied, sensing some new nonsense in the offing.

"Do you know the way?" he asked seriously.

"I'll manage."

"Get off the car," he ordered to my utter dismay.

"Why?" I protested in pain.

"I'll drive you to the place," he volunteered himself without any such request from me. "I know the quickest way."

"Why can't you sit and guide me to the shop?" I asked, agonised.

"If you want the quickest way, then I'll drive," he replied, forcing his opinion upon me, and then said something that made laugh, "I am not good at giving instructions."

I gave up like I had many times in the past. I got off and took the backseat. Oksana started to get off probably to sit with me, but Vishal had already started to move the car.

"Hi, my name is Vishal but call me VS," he said, introducing himself to Oksana in English, chuckling. "I am Jai's best friend in Mumbai, isn't it, Jai?"

I nodded reluctantly, sulking over his best-friend remark.

"Did you want me to sit with Jai?" Oksana asked in the sweetest way possible that would have melted many.

He shook his head, assumed everything for Oksana as well as for myself, and concluded with a pronouncement, "You are not disturbing me. Jai can sit alone. He is not a kid."

She laughed without saying anything.

"Jai, tumari girlfriend toh ek item hai. Kya maal hai [Jai, your girlfriend is an item. What a beauty]," he said, laughing loudly, which sounded very cheap to me.

I looked at Oksana, embarrassed, but couldn't do anything to Vishal because he was on the driver's seat.

"Oksana is not my girlfriend," I said calmly, trying to appear normal. "Moreover, she can speak and understand Hindi."

He didn't apologise to Oksana, probably not understanding the severity of his comment, and then he became quite open to her but didn't stop his nonsense.

"Oksana, what kind of name is this?" he asked, giggling. "But you foreigners are very intelligent. You so quickly pick foreign languages. I don't know a single foreign language."

"Oksana is a Ukrainian name," she explained in a very graceful manner. "You introduced yourself in English. Why did you say you didn't know any foreign language?"

"I didn't know English was a foreign language," he remarked like an ignorant person only expected from an idiot like him. "There are so many languages in India. You never know which one is Indian and which one is a foreign language. For me, all South Indian languages are foreign."

Oksana smiled at him, encouraging him to dish out more nonsense. Soon, I realised that she herself was enjoying free-of-cost entertainment, and he didn't disappoint her.

"I know what Russian girls do in Mumbai," Vishal said, giggling.

I decided to withdraw myself from their cosy conversation.

"I am not a Russian," she reacted sharply.

"You look like a Russian."

"How?"

"Other day I saw the picture of a girl in a fashion magazine." Vishal's stupidity continued, but Oksana no less than enjoyed every moment. "She looked like you. She was a Russian."

"You said you knew what Russian girls do in Mumbai," she asked, smiling, actually pulling his leg. "What do they do?"

"Should I tell her?" he asked me, giggling while looking through the overhead mirror.

"Why are you asking me?" I replied, uninterested.

"No." He suddenly turned serious and then remembered his family values. "I am from a good family. I can't use that word."

For some strange reason, he stopped talking and continued driving in complete silence. Oksana, sensing that Vishal's entertainment was over, pushed her seat back for more legroom and lowered it to rest her head for extra comfort. She closed her eyes, probably pretending to be sleeping. There was calm inside except for the noise of the moving car. I started to look out to watch the moving traffic aimlessly when, all of a sudden, I heard a screech. The car came to a sudden halt, throwing everybody forwards. I noticed that Vishal had applied full brakes, pulled to the side, and then started to unbuckle himself.

"I've some work nearby," he said seriously while preparing himself to get off the car. "You will have to go to the shop yourself."

"Did you remember now, or you knew beforehand?" I asked, completely astonished.

"This place was on your way, so I thought why not take a lift?" He giggled shamelessly.

"Why didn't you tell me?"

"What if you had refused?"

His question shocked me. I thought he was an idiot of the highest order. Actually, a thick-headed ass. The other day also, he had ditched me, disappearing in the middle without letting me know. I had forgiven him for that because I would have otherwise never been able to meet Oksana.

"Why would I refuse if it was on the way?" I asked, puzzled.

"I can't trust people," he replied seriously. "That is why I insisted on driving myself."

"I don't understand," Oksana asked, amused.

"I'll tell you. If you guys had agreed to give me a lift but Jai wouldn't stop the car, what would have I done? I can't jump out of a running car," he explained, totally ignoring me and assuming everything wrong about me.

"Please get off now," I told sourly. "How do I go from here?"

"Use the GPS. Do I've to spoon-feed you?" he barked while getting off.

I slipped into the driver's seat and started to move the car when he stopped me.

"What now?" I asked, frustrated.

"What is your problem?" he complained. He was my self-proclaimed friend, but I had become the source of his every problem. "I've to say goodbye to Oksana. Let me go to her side."

"Bye, Vishal," she said while rolling down the window.

He walked to her side, rested his hands on the window, and poked his face inside close to that of Oksana.

"Call me VS," he corrected politely. She moved her face a bit away from him, looking amused and moving her eyes left and right. He then proposed, "Have you seen Mumbai? I can take you around."

"I've seen Mumbai," she replied, smiling.

He quickly changed his proposal. "Have you been to Lonavla?"

"No."

"I am going there soon. I can take you." He wouldn't leave her easily. "You will enjoy."

"Umm . . ."

She looked at me, which Vishal didn't like.

"Why are you looking at him?" he chided and then complained, "He is not your boyfriend."

"She doesn't need my permission. Do whatever you both want to do," I told them.

"Jai, if you wish, we take you also." He became generous to me. "Do you mind, Oksana?"

"I am not interested," I told him flatly.

"Do you drink beer?" he asked her, ignoring me.

"I don't drink at all," she lied.

"I'll then get scotch for you," he said innocently that made Oksana laugh so loudly, but he still didn't realise his stupidity.

"I don't drink anything," she told him again.

Suddenly, he looked at his watch and realised that he was getting late.

"I'll give you a call, Oksana." He expressed his love for Oksana in no uncertain terms.

"Bye, Vishal."

He acknowledged her bye with a hand wave, stared at me for a while in a meaningful way, came around, and then whispered in my ear in Hindi, "Mujhe patta hai ki tum smart nahi ho. Ab bacche nahi ho badey ho jayo. [I know you are not smart. But you are not a kid either, so try to grow up now.]"

I looked straight down through the windscreen, shocked, and decided to give him at least a glare. By the time I turned, he had already crossed the road and soon disappeared into a building. We looked at each other, and then she burst into laughter, but I didn't. They had been enjoying each other's company like lovebirds, deliberately denying my presence. To them, I was the idiot odd man out. Next I burst into loud laughter, thinking about what Vishal had whispered in my ear. Actually, he meant that I should have left the two lovebirds alone. Oksana looked at me in total amazement, thinking that I was mad, but didn't say anything. So I chose to drive silently. She went back to what she did best: sleep. We reached the shop where she took a long time to finalise her dressing table because she didn't like anything. Finally, she picked one rather reluctantly and paid for the table and the delivery charges. Her table was expected to be delivered tomorrow afternoon around 4. We headed back home.

Next day I received a call from Amardeep at 9.30 in the morning. He informed me that they were all heading to my place and expected to arrive at 10.

Although I had invited them, we hadn't discussed the time. I had no option but to receive them at 10. There was no chance Oksana was going to be up by that time. I thought of letting her know. I went to her room and knocked at her door. There was no response. I waited for few seconds and then knocked again. I could hear the noises of her twisting, turning, and then nothing. Silence again. I opened the door slowly. She was awake; her head rested on the bedhead, rest of her body still inside the quilt, staring straight at the door. She looked at me with her big blue eyes as if a cat had spotted a rat. Her face had a stern, scary look. Next, her right hand went under the pillow, and she pulled something black out. It was a sleeping mask, which she put around her eyes, and went to sleep again. I retracted, closing the door behind. By nature, I've always been very cool, calm, and patient, never losing my temper ever in my life until that moment. I decided to keep calm because the team was expected to arrive soon. I didn't want to give them any wrong impression on the very first day.

Few moments later, the doorbell rang. I went to answer the door. It was Dolce, Ajay, Neel, Sachin, and Amardeep. I let them in, and we sat anywhere one felt comfortable.

"This is where I live," I told.

"This is a very good place," Dolce, as usual, spoke first. "How much rent do you pay?"

"Nothing. This belongs to my parents."

"How old are you, Jai? What have you done?" Amardeep asked.

"Twenty-one. I completed my engineering last month."

"Really, just 21?" Dolce asked, surprised. "You talk and behave like a very mature man."

"You are embarrassing me," I replied honestly. "You all are too good."

"Should we come to the point?" Sachin cut us out.

"Do you guys want anything?" I asked like a good host.

"Nothing, Jai," Dolce said. "We know you are a bachelor, so Amardeep and I got food with us."

"Did you buy?"

"No. I got dokla. What have you got, Amar? Where is the food?" she spoke authoritatively.

"I forgot in my Scorpio. I'll get it."

Amardeep went down to get the stuff up. I felt blessed to have such friends who not only had agreed to work for free but were also very kind, considerate, and generous. It was like winning a jackpot. Amardeep came back up with a rectangle-shaped cane basket, which he was carrying with both his hands.

"Where should I keep it?" he asked.

"What is in it? Is it for lunch?" I asked.

"Chhole bhature from my home."

"I'll keep it in the fridge. We can heat it up later."

"Where is your partner? What was her name?" Ajay opened his mouth for the first time.

"Oksana. Why do you forget names?" Neel chided him.

"She should be with us in about an hour," I replied with some uncertainty.

"Has she gone out?" Ajay asked.

"No. She sleeps late, so she wakes up late."

"These Europeans have got strange habits," Amardeep commented.

"What are you talking?" Dolce snapped and then gave him some intelligent lesson. "She must be like that. Do you think Europe would have made such a progress with the people like her?"

"I think you are right."

"We can discuss few things," I said, intending to divert their attention from Oksana.

They all nodded.

"Amar, when can we move the stuff to Churchgate?" I asked, concerned.

"We still have to clear the hall. We'll have to move the stuff to other rooms. I am hoping by 23 August, and then we can start our rehearsals from 25 August."

"What about the timings?" Dolce asked.

"Eleven to 4," Neel proposed.

"I am not sure about Oksana. Why don't we do in the evenings? Four to 9, Monday to Friday?" I said.

"No. I've to be back home by 8," Dolce said.

"What about 2–6?" I proposed.

We all agreed. I noticed that most of the talking was done either by Dolce or Amardeep. Sachin, Neel, and Ajay, by nature, were very quiet. But they all bonded well like a good bunch of friends who had no friction. Dolce was smart, talkative, and intelligent whereas Amardeep was jovial, carefree, and their most trusted friend.

At 11.30 we saw Oksana making her way into the hall, smiling in a very cheerful mood, all dressed up. Her hair was pulled up into a knot at the top of the head. Two long pointed hairclips were sticking out through the knot. Just to top it up, she had applied glossy red lipstick. She waved, greeted everyone with a broad smile, and then sat on the couch cross-legged like a queen makes an appearance to her subjects.

"Wow, you are very beautiful," Dolce complimented her.

"Thank you," she replied, delighted.

"Rabba [God]! Russians are very beautiful," Amardeep exclaimed.

"Actually, she is from Ukraine," I corrected.

"That is okay," Oksana said.

"Are you going somewhere?" Amardeep asked her.

"No."

"We should come here daily then," he flirted.

"Actually, I am not feeling well today," she complained. "I got woken up in the middle of my sleep."

Middle of her sleep. I had woken her up at 9.30. I stared at her. She stared back with a little forward head jerk, trying to scare me off. Amused, I shook my head when Amardeep broke the silence.

"If sick Oksana looks like this, how would then healthy Oksana look like?" Amardeep's flirting continued.

"You have a good sense of humour," she praised him and then returned Dolce's compliment, "Dolce, you are a pretty-looking girl. How old are you?"

"Thank you, Oksana. We are all 18," Dolce replied gracefully.

"I am very happy that we have two girls in the group," she said, seriously giving the impression as if she had been feeling unsafe up until now.

"No problem, Oksana," Dolce said cheerfully. "You and I are friends now."

I could hardly suppress my laugh at her two-girls remark. Oksana and Dolce went to the kitchen to heat up the food with Amardeep who helped them in moving things around. Oksana liked chhole bhature so much that she licked her fingers to polish the last bit off. Amardeep seemed to have struck a nice chord with her. In fact, I noticed that Oksana was very happy to meet everyone. She talked, giggled, and joked with everyone. Even yesterday, she was quite normal with Vishal also.

So why me? She didn't talk to me at all. She was still upset with me about the morning episode. I consoled myself. At least, she had liked the group. That was more important than worrying about her mood and attitude towards me. Her dressing table arrived at 5 that cheered her up. She asked Amardeep to help the man take the table to her room. The group left at 6 but not before helping us in cleaning the kitchen.

We both returned for dinner at 7.15. There were enough leftovers from the morning. Oksana preferred to have a couple of doklas with green chutney. We didn't talk to one another or even looked at one another, so our dinner was over in ten minutes. She went to her room while I started to clear the table. She came back fuming.

"Why did you wake me up in the morning?" she complained angrily.

"The group was coming," I replied calmly.

"So?"

"So what? Aren't you part of the group?"

"I can't sacrifice my sleep. I need to sleep well."

"Why don't you sleep early?"

"What will happen with that?"

"You can get up early."

"I've to do many things before I go to sleep."

"Why can't you do things during the daytime?"

"I want complete silence."

"What do you do before going to sleep?" I asked sarcastically. "Meditation?"

"I can't tell you."

"Why can't you tell me?"

"I really liked Dolce and Amar," she said, cleverly changing the topic. "What was on Amar's head?"

I looked into her eyes, but she turned her gaze away. I chose to move away when she repeated her question.

"It is called *patka*," I replied while shaking my head.

"Why don't you wear a patka?"

"Because I am not a Sikh."

"What is a Sikh?

"It's a different religion," I explained in brief. "You can distinguish them from their appearance. They keep a beard and wear patka or turban."

"Do you know about their religion?"

"Yes, my mother is a Sikh. I am half Sikh."

"And half?"

"Hindu."

"How are Sikhs by nature?"

"They are brave, enterprising, hardworking, honest, and very jovial," I replied, giving an honest description of Sikhs. I asked jokingly, "Why? Do you want to marry a Sikh?"

She didn't like my comment. Suddenly, she got up, pulled a receipt from her pocket, and said, "This is the receipt of the items we purchased on Friday. You have to pay half."

I nodded. She went to her room. I cleared the table and waited for her to wash the dishes because I still had to finish my last duty of the day, i.e. to clean the kitchen. While waiting for her, I started to think, *How many shades are there in her personality?*

CHAPTER 9

We still had five days to move the equipment to Amardeep's Churchgate apartment. Our rehearsals were due to start following Monday. Meanwhile, I decided to form a company in partnership with Oksana. However, I wasn't sure whether a foreigner holding a type E visa could become a partner of a company that was incorporated in India. I went to the Ministry of Corporate Affairs (MCA) website, which I found very detailed and user friendly. First, I made a quick check on the availability of the name I had chosen for my company. Luckily, the name was still available, so I needed to register my company soon before the name was taken by someone else. I soon found that any foreign national bringing foreign direct investment into India was allowed to become partners. But Oksana's case was totally different, so I decided to seek an expert opinion.

I continued to sift through the website. I found the easiest way to incorporate a new company was as a one-person company (OPC). The process to complete the registration under the OPC was rather simple, so I downloaded all the necessary forms for online submissions at a later date.

The cost to register a company under the OPC was only Rs2,000. I wondered how technology had made life easy. I was able to complete my work in three hours from home, which otherwise would have taken weeks. No visits to offices, no long queues, and no need to grease one's palms.

I had been working on the computer for almost three hours, not realising it was close to midday. Oksana hadn't woken up yet. I wasn't sure what was wrong with her, so I decided to check myself. I knocked at her door. As usual, there was no response from her. I decided not to put with her nonsense, so I gently opened the door to find her sleeping. Not sure of her reaction had she found me inside her room, I retracted and closed the door. I waited for few more seconds and then knocked at the door again. This time slightly with a little more force. Again, there was no response from her. I opened the door again to find her still in bed, but this time, her head rose, and her eyes were fixed at the door. I looked at her, waiting for her to say something. I should have known that I was expecting a miracle. She was not going to do that, and she didn't.

"Why aren't you up?" I asked anxiously.

She stayed in the same position but didn't answer me. I was losing my patience with that woman. The team had just been formed, but I was not sure about the lead dancer. Would she come for the rehearsals?

"You don't look good," I said.

She nodded.

"What is it?" I asked.

"I don't know," she replied and said, "You go. I want to sleep."

"Do you want to see a doctor or need medicine?"

"No. I'll be fine by tomorrow."

"How do you know?"

"I am just feeling weak."

"Do you need anything?"

"I don't need anything," she replied, irritated.

"Do you want someone else for help?"

"Who?"

"Someone you like?"

"Who do I like?" she asked, annoyed.

"Amardeep," I joked. "You told me yesterday that you liked him."

She looked at me with angry eyes, rested her head on the pillow, and then closed her eyes, pretending to be sleeping. I thought she didn't like my joke, which was a poor joke anyway. I decided to leave her alone until tomorrow. I spent the whole day alone, praying for her quick recovery.

Next day I started to fill out the forms for my company's registration. The forms needed a lot of information. It took me close to two hours to complete the forms. I decided to wait to submit them until I had spoken to Oksana. I turned my notebook off and got up to walk to my room when I saw Oksana coming out of her room. She looked fresh and happy. Health-wise, she looked hale and hearty. I laughed, thinking, true to her words, she had miraculously recovered from her yesterday's weakness. I needed to talk to her.

"Are you going out?" I asked.

"Yes," she replied.

"I need to talk to you."

"About?" she asked me as if I had dropped a bomb.

"I am applying to form a company."

"How long will it take?"

"It is important, so it will take minimum 30 minutes."

"We will then have to do it in the evening," she said and started to walk. "I won't be back until 5."

"At least give me your passport."

"Why?" she asked with raised eyebrows.

"I'll explain to you in the evening," I replied. "For now, I just need to scan the first page and the visa page."

She looked at me suspiciously for a moment but then went to her room and came back with her passport. Her passport was a blue book with something written on the top, which I couldn't understand: an emblem in the middle, "UKRAINE PASSPORT" written below the emblem, and a chip symbol printed in the bottom. I took the pictures of the first page and the visa page. I gave her passport back, which she kept in her bag, and then started moving towards the door. I was pleased with her changed attitude, so I raced past her and opened the door for her. She widened her eyes in surprise as if not expecting that type of gesture from me. I stood at the door, watching her, waiting for the lift. The lift arrived. As she was about to step in, suddenly, she turned and waved at me, smiling. This was for the first time I had seen her in that mood. I waved back, and next moment, she went inside the lift. I squeezed my lips, shook my head in disbelief, and thanked my stars for that moment.

I came back to resume my work. I printed the forms, signed, and then scanned them, ready for online submission. However, I still needed to find out whether I could have Oksana as one of the directors. I called up the Mumbai office of the regional directorate of the MCA. I was put on hold for a long time before someone attended my call to give me the bad news that Oksana wasn't eligible. That sucked. Anyway, I uploaded the forms into the MCA website, paid Rs2,000, and then pressed the Submit button. Within moments, I received an acknowledgement email, informing me that the formal documents would be posted in two weeks.

I didn't need Oksana's passport details anymore, so I decided to delete the pages from my notebook. Before deleting, I had a cursory look at each page. The first page contained her personal information and her photo. My eyes fell on her date of birth. It was 27 November 1981, which meant she was 32 and soon to turn 33 in little under four months. I created an entry in my calendar to remind me of her birthday. The second page contained a valid type E visa, expiring in around ten months. I deleted the pages from my mobile. I killed the rest of time doing nothing productive but mucking around, just waiting for Oksana's return.

She returned at 5 in the evening and sat on the couch cross-legged without saying anything. She looked tired, so I enquired whether she needed some coffee. She looked back over her shoulders and nodded. I went to the kitchen, turned the kettle on, picked a large mug, and put two tablespoons of granule coffee and a teaspoon of sugar. I heard the click of kettle going off. The hot water was ready to be poured into the mug. I added milk, and her coffee was ready to be served. I came back with her coffee and handed it over to her, which she started to sip.

"Did you like the coffee?" I asked, initiating the conversation, hoping to find out how her day went.

"Yes. Why?" she replied, surprised as if I had asked her to jump into a river.

"Why?" I said politely. "That is how you ask?"

She didn't say anything but rolled her big eyes all around as if asking, "Really?" I didn't know how to deal with that woman. I felt that I was stuck between a rock and a hard place. I was damned either way. I couldn't let her go because I needed a dancer and wasn't sure how much interested she was. With no immediate solution in my mind, I decided to put up with her for a little longer, so I changed the topic.

"I need to talk you," I said softly.

"At the dinnertime," she snapped at me.

"But give me at least 30 minutes," I pleaded. "I've to discuss many things."

"Fine," she said, accepting my plea like a magistrate accepts the plea of an accused and went to her room after keeping the mug in the kitchen sink.

I laughed and vaguely started to recall her behavioural pattern. She would sit on the couch cross-legged, staring into the vacuum for hours, which was her first favourite pose. Her second favourite pose was to sit with her elbows on the table, chin on hands, and look at me, smiling. Her third quirk, which I had observed, was actually a problem. Whenever I would say something she didn't like, she would stare at me, say nothing, get up, and disappear into her room. The biggest worry for me was her abnormal behaviour towards me. She was normal with everybody else, especially with Dolce and Amardeep, and strangely enough even with that occasionally-normal-otherwise-permanently-abnormal Vishal.

Oksana returned to the dining area, put food on the table, and we started to eat.

"Don't you have to make a call?" she asked.

"Not today," I replied, fairly impressed with her concern.

"What did you want to talk to me about?"

"I am a bit concerned since you moved here," I asked, showing some concern. "Are you happy here?"

"Did I say?" she shot back.

"You don't talk to me properly."

"Don't worry," she replied casually.

"Don't worry?" I said with bitterness.

"Can I ask a question?" I asked, preferring to change the topic.

"What?" she asked with raised eyebrows.

"Will you come to the rehearsals by next week?"

"Yes. Why?" she enquired.

"Just wanted to be sure," I replied, feeling a bit relieved.

"If I've given a word", she said with a lot of pride and stressed, "I'll keep it."

"Can I ask you a personal question?"

"What?"

"Where do you go? Whom do you meet?"

"Why do you want to know?" she reacted sharply.

"For emergency?"

"What emergency?"

"Accident etc."

"I'll call you in that situation," she said calmly and after a brief pause asked, "Why did you need my passport?"

"I have formed a new company. I thought I'll include you as one of the directors, but I couldn't because you are not eligible."

"Why did you want me in your company?"

"To secure a firm commitment from you," I replied, smiling.

"You don't have to worry about my commitment."

"Do you want to know the name of the company?"

"What is it?"

"JO-D Private Limited. JO-D in short."

"What does JO-D mean?"

"*J* for *Jai, O* for *Oksana,* dash *D* for *dancers*," I replied and then revealed, "JO-D, if spoken like *Jodi*, means *a pair* in Hindi. Did you like?"

"I don't know. Why my name?"

"Because we are a pair of dancers?"

"Can you dance?" she asked, surprised.

"I know the basics. But I can learn quickly."

"How will you learn?"

"You will teach me," I replied.

"You still are trying to secure a commitment from me," she said sharply and left for her room.

There was no way I could beat the intelligence of that woman. She was very sharp. Why didn't she use her brains somewhere else like science, technology etc? Surely, she might have been a really good student in her school. Impressed with her, I went to my room to sleep, hoping to overcome challenges that lay ahead of me.

Next morning Amardeep called at 9.15 to inform that he was arriving at 10 to move the musical instruments. In the next 15 minutes, I moved the stuff from the small room to the hall near the apartment entrance. I took a quick shower, got ready, and waited for Amardeep's arrival. Amardeep arrived on time. He inspected the instruments and declared that they would fit in his Scorpio. I suggested that we have a cup of coffee before leaving. He liked the idea. While having coffee, we started to talk.

"Where are the other members?" I enquired.

"They will meet us at the apartment at 11," Amardeep replied.

"So we have to be there by 11."

"Yes, otherwise, they will have to wait because I've the keys."

"How long would it take us?"

"Forty to 45 minutes," he replied. He looked around as if searching for someone. "Is Oksana still sleeping?"

"What do you think?"

"Should we?" he said while getting up, ignoring my question. As we were walking to leave, he stopped. He said hastily, "Jai, take your clothes with you."

"Which clothes?" I asked, surprised.

"Extra set," he replied. "It would get messy. You can take a shower there."

"Why do I need the extra set?" I asked, confused.

"Later, we are going to Gaylord's," he said hastily. "Quick. We will talk in Scorpio."

He didn't give me a chance to ask about Gaylord's. I rushed to my room to pick an extra set of clothes, a towel, and a soap and put them all in a backpack. We quickly moved the instruments downstairs, which luckily fitted well in his Scorpio. Amardeep got into the driver's seat, and I took the front passenger's seat. As we were about to move, I realised that I had left my keys and mobile on the dining table while we were moving the instruments downstairs. Who would open the door for me now? I had no choice but to try my luck, so I dashed up my apartment. I pressed the bell once, twice, and thrice; but there was no response. She was not going to open the door for me. I thought of leaving without my keys and mobile, so I headed back to the lifts when I heard the click of the door opening. She stuck her head out and saw me. She looked annoyed. I entered the apartment, pointed towards the table, picked my stuff, and quickly turned back towards the door. I stood at the door for a while, looked at her, smiled, waved, and then closed the door behind. There was no response from her. I knew that she would still be staring at the door.

I came back to the waiting Amardeep, apologised, took my seat, and he moved his Scorpio. After negotiating our way out of narrow lanes, we soon hit the main road.

"It is already 10.30," I said, concerned. "Can we make it by 11?"

"Don't worry," he assured. "I already phoned Dolce. They will wait."

"What is Gaylord's?" I asked.

"Restaurant."

"Where?"

"Just near the apartment."

"Oh! In Nariman Point," I said, trying to act smart as if I knew enough about Mumbai.

"No, in the Churchgate area," he corrected. "Nariman Point is the next suburb."

"These are expensive suburbs of Mumbai, aren't they?"

"Whole of South Mumbai is expensive."

"Like South Delhi," I boasted.

"I don't know much about Delhi."

"What key suburbs fall in South Mumbai?

"Marine Drive, Churchgate, Nariman Point, Colaba, etcetera, etcetera."

"I've heard about them all."

"Where?"

"In the movies."

"This is the first time in Mumbai?" he asked while looking through his overhead mirror.

"Yes?" I replied.

Amardeep was driving in the middle lane when suddenly a car from the left lane changed to the middle lane very close to our vehicle. He had to apply full brakes to avoid the collision, causing us to be thrown forwards. He recovered and then swore in Punjabi, "Teri Ma Di Fudi Marun [F—— your mother]" and then looked at me red-faced, a bit embarrassed. I thought the Punjabis traditionally swear after every second sentence but not in our family because it was against our family rule book. Papa had once called me *Ullu Ka Patta* (son of an owl) jokingly, which infuriated Mum so much that she didn't talk to him for one full week.

Amardeep quickly regained his composure and then continued with his driving.

"What were we talking about?" he asked, trying to recall the conversation where we had left. With a little nod, he resumed, "Mumbai is the only place you have been other than Delhi?"

"No. Chandigarh, Shimla, and Bangalore," I replied.

"You keeping going there?"

"Chandigarh is my mother's hometown, so we keep going there. Shimla we go every summer to beat the Delhi heat. I just went once to Bangalore for my industrial training."

"What is industrial training?"

"I had to do one-month industrial training in the fourth year of my engineering."

"Why did you choose Bangalore?"

"Because it's the IT hub of India."

"Did they pay you?"

"No. It is a part of the course."

"Which company did you work for?"

"Infosys."

"Fifteen more minutes, and we will be there," Amardeep informed.

He stopped talking, choosing to concentrate on his driving. I had been very eager to know more about his Churchgate apartment. I looked down the road and around. There wasn't much traffic, so it was safe to resume our conversation.

"Whose apartment is this?" I asked, still looking down the road.

"The old man is my grandfather's brother," he replied.

"So he is like your grandfather."

"That is what I call him."

"How old is he?"

"I don't know their exact age, but the couple must in the late 60s or early 70s."

"Have they always lived in this apartment?"

He shook his head and revealed, "This is not his apartment. It was bought by my grandfather in the sixties."

"Why is he living there?"

"My grandfather is two years younger than him," he replied and revealed the most common tradition in the Indian families. "It is like younger brother looking after his older brother. You know what I mean?"

"Typical Indian."

"Exactly," he agreed and continued with more revelations. "He retired as a lieutenant general. He has a son and a daughter. Son is a successful businessman in Toronto. You know, Toronto is full of Punjabis."

"There are more Punjabis in Toronto that Canadians," I said, stating a fact he found so funny that he started to laugh loudly.

"What about his daughter?" I asked.

"She is an IFS officer currently posted in Kenya," he replied.

"With her family?"

"She is a divorcee," he replied. He took a deep breath. He disclosed the most common reason of a divorce. "Her husband left her for another woman."

"No kids?"

He shook his head.

"So the old man is financially sound."

He nodded and revealed more than I had expected, "He has got everything. Land in Punjab, one flat in Chandigarh, and another in Gurgaon. But they are old, nobody to look after them in North. So my father asked them to move to Mumbai."

"Who looks after their land and the flats?"

"No one looks after land. It is close to the city. They are waiting for the municipal corporation to bring it within the city limits so that they could sell it to builders at a good price. One flat is always locked, and another has been rented out."

"Why don't they migrate to Toronto?"

"They are very particular about their independence."

"Who looks after them here?"

"Me."

"So you live with them?"

"No. I visit them twice a week," he informed. "We are almost there."

He made a left turn and then parked his Scorpio outside a block, which was third on the right side. Dolce, Ajay, Neel, and Sachin were waiting there. These were the old three-storeyed blocks built in the 40s or 50s close to the Arabian Sea, Churchgate station, and Brabroune stadium. Amardeep suggested that we leave the stuff in his Scorpio until we cleared the hall. There was no lift, and his flat was on the second floor. We started to walk up via the staircase.

"Where were you, guys?" Dolce complained. "We have been waiting for half an hour."

"It's just half an hour," Amardeep said while trying to calm her down. "You, anyway, don't have to do anything."

"I am not going to move the stuff," she said while shaking her head. "I'll just give directions."

"Dolce, we anyway wouldn't have let you do the physical work even if you had offered to help," Amardeep said affectionately.

We reached the second floor. Amardeep unlocked the door and let us in first. We went around the apartment. It was a decent-sized two-bedroom self-contained apartment, which was nicely decorated. We started to move the stuff when Dolce suddenly interrupted.

"Wait, Amar," she said, shrieking.

"Ki Hoya [What happened]?" he asked, confused.

"Amar, first take pictures of the hall from different angles."

"Why?"

"So that you know where to keep what when you move the stuff back."

"Changi Kudi [Good girl]," Amardeep praised, fairly impressed with her suggestion, and then complimented, "Sachin, your girlfriend is very intelligent."

"Sachin ko patta hai [Sachin knows that]," she replied shyly in Mumbai-style Hindi.

"Sometimes you should let him talk," Amardeep said, laughing. "Tu bol Sachin [Sachin, you talk]."

"Don't waste time," Sachin said, coming straight to the point, ignoring both.

"Jaldi Karo [Move your hands quickly]," Neel and Ajay said in tandem.

We first started to wrap the decorative items in newspapers, putting them in buckets carefully. They all fitted in two buckets. Amardeep moved them away into one of the bathrooms along with side lamps. Next we moved the coffee table and two side tables, placing them on one of the beds. We had now been working for 40 minutes, so Amardeep called for a short coffee break when he noticed Dolce sitting on one of the couches, busy on her mobile.

"Who are you sending messages?" he teased. "Sachin, she is up to something."

"Can't I've more than one boyfriend?" she shot back.

"Sachin, tu to gaya [Sachin, you are gone]," he said, giggling.

"Go and make coffee now," Sachin responded maturely, ignoring them again. "Don't waste time."

"I am tired," Neel commented.

"Really, what did you do?" Dolce pulled his leg.

"And what did you do?" he shot back.

"I am supposed to give only directions," she replied crisply.

"Dolce, can you please make coffee?" Sachin requested.

"Amar, show me the way to the kitchen."

Amardeep showed her the way to the kitchen.

He came back and commented, "She only listens to Sachin. Had I asked, she would have never agreed."

"Uski girlfriend hai, yaar [Friend, she is his girlfriend]," Ajay said.

"We have to get the stuff up from Scorpio," Sachin responded in his usual style to divert their attention from Dolce.

Dolce came back with coffee and went around us to pick one. We finished having coffee in ten minutes. Dolce refused to keep the used mugs back in the kitchen, which I had to do. We now had to move heavy items like the couches, dining table, and a small wall unit.

"We should be finished in 30 minutes," Amardeep said. "The wall unit is a bit of problem."

"Where will you keep the dining table?" Dolce enquired.

"What is your problem?" he replied, irritated.

"Problem? I am supposed to give you directions," she said forcefully. "That is the problem."

"On the other bed," he replied, irritated. He turned to us and ordered after giving Dolce a quick glare. "Sachin, Neel, and Ajay, you guys start moving the chairs."

"What are you saying, Amar?" Dolce asked, disappointed.

"Why? What happened to you now?" he asked, seething and red-faced.

"Amar, move the table first," she suggested, softly looking into his eyes to bring his temperature down. "Place it upside down. That will give you space for the chairs."

"Man na padega [I'll have to accept]," Amardeep remarked, conceding to Dolce's suggestion.

"You now understand the value of bringing Dolce," Sachin remarked.

"Yes. Happy," he replied grudgingly.

We started moving the remaining stuff but decided to leave the wall unit in its place because it was too heavy to move. I cleaned the floor, which was now ready for our rehearsals. We had a quick bath and then headed to Gaylord's at around 2.

It was a very elegant restaurant on Veer Nariman Road. We picked a spot and sat down for a well-earned lunch.

"I'll pay for lunch," I said.

"Don't talk rubbish. You're in my area, so I'll pay," Amardeep blasted me.

"What type of logic is this?" I argued. "You don't own the area except for an apartment here."

"Sardar se panga na ley [Don't mess with a Sikh]," he roared.

"I am not paying anyway," Dolce disassociated herself from the unnecessary argument. "What is the point in going out with boys if I've to pay?"

"We won't let you pay anyway, so don't worry," Amardeep shut her up.

"Accha [Really]," she said, blinking.

"Everybody pays for his food. Sachin will pay for Dolce," Neel tried to resolve the issue in vain.

"Bakas mat kar. Maine kaha na mai pay karoonga. [Shut up. I said I'll pay.]," Amardeep shouted at him.

I laughed at Amardeep the way he was trying to convince us. It reminded me of my mum. Every time we had relatives or friends visiting Delhi, she would take them out to restaurants, shops, and places. At the time of payment, she would say, "Na. Maine nahi man na. Paise toh mai hi doongi. [No. I won't agree. It is me who is going to pay.]" Probably because she was also a Sikh like Amardeep. But she was 47 and wife of a rich businessman, so she could afford. Amardeep was only 18 and working for my group for free, so it was not appropriate for him to pay the bill.

"We will do one thing," I said, trying to resolve the issue with a threat. "Amardeep and I'll split the bill. Otherwise, I am leaving."

"Baith Na. Kidar jar raha hai? [Sit down. Where are you going?]" Amardeep cajoled me.

"I can't let you guys pay," I told them honestly. "You all are only 18, not working and not charging anything."

"It is okay if you want to pay. But there is only three-year difference between us and you," Amardeep finally relented.

"But he is very mature," Dolce needled him. "He is not an idiot like you."

"Sachin, manine ise maar dalana [Sachin, I'll kill her]," Amardeep said, annoyed.

"I am hungry. Order now." Sachin tried to control the situation.

"Dolce will order," I suggested.

"You guys take a lot of time. Order two pizzas, one veg and one chicken, and Coke," Dolce said without going through the menu and wasting further time.

We all agreed and placed the order. We were told to wait for ten minutes.

"I can't believe you are just 21," Dolce praised me. "You are so mature, Jai."

"Don't embarrass me," I said humbly. "There are millions like me and much better."

"Like?"

"Take Malala Yousafzai who at so young age became a household name for her activism in female education."

"Give us Indian examples."

"There are many, but I'll give you a couple of examples—" I paused to remember appropriate examples. "Take S Ramanujan who mastered advanced trigonometry at 13, and by the time he died aged 32, he had resolved some many complex problems."

"I was always weak in mathematics." Amardeep sighed in grief.

"And Sachin Tendulkar. He started playing international cricket at 16, and by 19, he had scored three centuries not in India but away in England and Australia."

"The Australian cricket team is awesome," Sachin commented. "They play hard but fair."

I regretted quoting Tendulkar as an example because I knew that the discussion now would only focus around cricket.

"They sledge a lot," Amardeep complained.

"What is wrong with that?" I argued. "It is a part of the game."

"I know a good sledge," Ajay said, not wanting to be left behind.

"Batta. Batta. [Tell us.]," Amardeep asked, very excited, moving close to him.

"Ready?" Ajay asked in a funny way, shaking his head as if we were participating in some kind of sprint.

"Ab Bol bee. Kya Tha us mey? [Now tell us. What was it about?]" Amardeep said restlessly.

"Pay attention," he said seriously. "Australians were fielding. They got someone out. Ian Botham came out to bat. When Botham started to take his guard, Rodney Marsh asked apparently to unsettle him, 'How are Mrs. and my kids?' Botham turned to him and replied, smiling, 'Mrs. is fine, but kids are retarded.'"

We all laughed because it was a very witty reply.

"Jai, who is your favourite cricketer?" Sachin asked.

"I don't follow cricket much," I replied.

"What sort of Indian are you?" Neel asked in utter disbelief.

"A sensible sort," I replied calmly. "Who is yours, Sachin?"

"I like Mitchell Johnson."

"Why?"

"He is a cool bowler," Sachin replied, and then he started to give a running commentary on Johnson. "I like the way he walks to the mark, turns, starts running slowly, body slightly bent, picks up the pace, and then bang. It is all so rhythmic. Moreover, he used to play for Mumbai Indians. My IPL team."

"Now he plays for Kings XI Punjab. My Preity Zinta's team. Ting." Amardeep said, excited ending with a *ting*, a word often used by Preity Zinta when she points to her dimples.

We had now moved from cricket to Bollywood.

"You like Preity?" I asked him.

"Of course, she is so cute and bubbly," Amardeep said with a broad smile. "Moreover, she is a Punjabi."

"She is not Punjabi," I corrected. "She is a Rajput from Himachal."

"Really?" he said, disappointed.

"You are like my mother."

"Why?"

"She is so biased," I said. "She only likes Punjabi actors. That is the only blemish in her."

The waiter brought the food, and everyone jumped to grab a slice. There was a momentary silence. While having pizza, I started to think the only sports Indians love is cricket. The cricketers are treated like gods in India. The people in India discuss cricket for hours and hours. The sports channels show the repeats of a game for weeks. No one minds because there is always an audience. If you didn't like or knew about cricket, you were an abnormal person. Besides, cricket people love discussing Bollywood and politics.

"Enough of Punjabis," Dolce said. She had been very patiently listening about the Punjabi actors, but she wasn't the one who would sit back. "They are so loud and showy. There is a new Gujarati actor who is going to blow away all Punjabis."

"You are talking about Tiger Shroff, aren't you?" Amardeep said.

"Hey, his real name is Jai Hemant Shroff," Dolce said in a bit of style.

"Gujaratis are ruling India these days," Neel commented.

"Hey! Go, Modi. Modi. Modi. Modi," Dolce said, very excited. "You know, he is the second prime minister from Gujarat."

I tried to test her general knowledge.

"Who was the first?"

"Her uncle," Amardeep said, laughing loudly. "Morarji Desai."

Everybody except Dolce started laughing, which she didn't like.

"Shut up," she said, annoyed. "My dad was just 9 years old when he became the prime minister."

"But you are also Desai," Amardeep continued with his senseless argument.

"I can expect this from you," she chided. "All the Desais are not related to one another, idiot."

"Sachin, Dekh, dusri baar. Mey iska galla gont dunga. [Sachin, a second time. I'll strangle her.]," Amardeep said, annoyed.

"We call it a day," Sachin said in a bid to end the little war between Dolce and Amardeep before it escalated to a serious one. "It has been a good day. We will meet again on Monday at 2."

I paid the bill, and we started to head back to our homes. On the way, I started to think about Sachin. He always very intelligently changed the topic when he found Dolce in an awkward situation. He was right. It had been a good day. The most satisfying thing to have happened was, finally, the Churchgate apartment was ready for rehearsals.

CHAPTER 10

When I reached home, Oksana wasn't there. I made a cup of coffee and sat on the couch, relaxed. I was very satisfied with the progress so far. The company has been registered, the team formed, equipment moved, and our rehearsals about to start from Monday. Ajay had promised to write a duet song, a new piece of music had to be created for the song, and finally we needed to choreograph with Oksana's help. That was going to be our signature song and dance. Something new created by us from the scratch. We also decided to practise dances on various popular Bollywood songs. However, I needed to learn to dance properly. I was confident that it wouldn't be that hard because I knew the basics. It was now up to Oksana to transform me from a mediocre to a dancer of some quality.

I heard the sound of the door being unlocked from the outside. Oksana came in, and I looked at her and then burst into laughter. She was looking like a college-going teenager. She was wearing a tight round neck white T-shirt tucked inside a very short black leather skirt and tall boots. A bag was hanging by her left shoulder. Her hair parted down the middle and tied into two ponytails on both sides and those big lips neatly painted in glossy pink lipstick. She was amused by my laughter.

"What?" she asked innocently. "What are you laughing at?"

"You look like a fashion-conscious college-going student," I replied.

"This is my favourite dress."

"I never saw you in this."

"I haven't been here for that long," she said and added unconvincingly, "I wear this on special occasions."

"What special occasion was today?"

"You don't need to know," she said, smiling. "I am going to change now."

"You look like in a good mood today," I tried to flatter her but in vain.

"I've to cook. I better go and change now," she said, smiling, ignoring my flattery; and off she went to her room.

I started to think about the day. Overall, it had been a good day. I really enjoyed their company because everybody was so friendly. We discussed many things: Amardeep's grandparents, cricket, Bollywood, South Mumbai, and also something funny Dolce had mentioned. I tried to recall and then laughed what she had said. It was her Modi, Modi, Modi chant.

That was the usual chant during the last general elections. In the May 2014 general elections, Narendra Modi managed to do something unthinkable. In the last three decades, not a single political party had managed to get an absolute majority. He was dynamic, energetic, a good orator, and, above all, made an effective use of social media to connect with the youth. He promised development, jobs, and corruption-free India, which he said plagued the current government. He was drawing large crowds to his rallies. Unable to counter him, his opponents branded him a communal, an ultra-nationalist Hindu, a danger to unity, and a destructive politician. Modi's opponents had to eat a humble pie. On the election day, people gave Modi a thumping majority. His government had been performing well so far, but some of his colleagues were dishing out communal statements against certain communities. He needed to control them. Not everyone liked him. He has his own detractors. Modi is the second prime minister from the state of Gujarat, Dolce's Gujarat.

Meanwhile, Oksana had changed and went straight to the kitchen. I followed her, thinking that she was in a mood today.

"What are you cooking for tonight?" I asked softly.

"Nothing special. Italian pasta," she replied casually without looking at me.

"Is it hard to make?"

"No. Just boil in water for some time and then mix sauce."

She cooked the whole dish in just one sentence. I kept bugging her, knowing that the worst could come anytime soon.

"Do you need any help?"

"Yes."

"Tell me," I asked enthusiastically.

"Just leave me alone. I'll call you when the food is ready."

I felt humiliated, and I didn't know how to react back. I looked left and right, expecting her to take pity on me; but she kept cooking, unmoved. She wasn't going to change, so I left her alone. No sure of what next to do, I turned the TV on. It was an ad about the expert panel discussion on the forthcoming Cricket World Cup. The tournament was scheduled to start in February 2015 in Australia and New Zealand. At 8.30 they were going to discuss the prospects of India retaining the title. There was nothing interesting, so I turned the TV off and decided to make a call to Delhi. I dialled the number, which nobody answered. I disconnected and then called Mum on her mobile. After few rings, she answered my call.

"Hello," Mum answered.

"Mum, Jai."

"Oh! Jai," she said. "I heard the ring, but I was out in the garden. By the time I reached to pick the phone, it went off. I knew it was you."

"Why didn't call me back then?"

"Remember, I told that you have to call me."

"How is Papa?"

"He is fine but still in the office. You know winter is approaching. They are introducing a new fashion wear. These days, he is busy with that."

I didn't say anything but kept listening.

"What did you do today?"

"We fixed the apartment for our rehearsals."

"Good. How is your apartment mate?"

"She's fine."

"Be careful," Mum warned once again.

"There is no problem."

"If you are happy, then we are happy."

"I've to go now."

I went to the bathroom to wash my face and then returned to the dining area. Oksana had neatly set the food on the table, waiting for me, which I greatly appreciated. We started to eat.

"You know what is tomorrow?" I asked deliberately to test her memory.

"You have to clean the apartment," she replied so quickly that my jaw dropped in awe.

"How did you know?" I asked, surprised.

"I've set the schedule," she replied forcefully.

"Do I need to clean your room and bathroom also?"

"When I cook, do I only have it?"

"So the answer is yes."

"I'll make sure to remove my stuff," she said, looking away from me in a very heavy voice.

"What stuff?" I asked eagerly to know what treasure she wanted to hide from me.

"Stuff you are not supposed to see," she replied, incensed.

"Like?" I asked again, laughing unnecessarily.

She gave me a nasty glare and said angrily while getting up, having finished her dinner, "I was in a good mood, but you ruined my mood."

"What did I say?" I asked, shocked.

"What did you say?" she yelled, enraged, and ordered, "Clear the table. I'll be back at 9."

"Why 9? You normally do at 8."

She walked off without answering but not before giving one more little glare. I had one additional hour to clear the table. I thought I didn't have to necessarily follow her instructions. I killed my time shuttling between my room and back in the hall, browsing the net, and also making a call to Amardeep, which lasted for about 25 minutes. I checked the time. It was 8.25, so I decided to watch the expert panel discussion. I turned the TV on and waited for five long minutes for never-ending commercials to finish. Finally, the discussion started with the introduction of the two experts by a good-looking host. She had a very nice and clear voice required for TV anywhere in the world. The host opened the discussion with a remark that, although

India was the current world champion, it would be very hard for them to retain the cup under the tough Australian conditions. She then invited the experts for their opening comments.

"We have a very good chance to retain the cup," Expert 1 commented. "Our team is young. But we have a good mix of batsmen, seamers, spinners, and all-rounders. It won't be hard to adjust in Australia because we are playing a test series and one-day series before the World Cup. If we could make it to the semis, then our chances would increase."

"I don't agree with him," Expert 2 disagreed with Expert 1 on everything. "We cannot win this. Last time, we won under home conditions. I don't see any all-rounders in the team he was talking about."

"Dhoni, Jadeja, and Ashwin?" Expert 1 started to justify his opening comments. "We have a very good opening pair in Rohit Sharma and Shikhar Dhawan. Rohit holds the world record of 264 runs in ODI. Moreover, we won our first World Cup in 1983 in England, not under the home conditions."

"Dhoni is a wicket keeper batsman. Jadeja and Ashwin are more of bowlers than batsmen," Expert 2 again disagreed with him. "Dhawan hasn't played in Australia. He remains untested under Australian conditions. If we can make it to the quarter finals, it would be a good outcome. But retaining the title is out of the question."

They both kept on disagreeing with each other. The host was having a field day to get a consensus. I thought, how could she get a consensus from two opposing persons? There should have been at least three people on the panel. It was getting pretty boring, so I decided to turn the TV off. Suddenly, the TV went blank. Someone had turned the TV off. I looked up and found Oksana standing in a tank top and shorts, enraged but looking beautiful. Her face was red, eyebrows raised, and nostrils blown up. What happened to her now? She pointed towards the dining table. I checked the time. It was five minutes over 9.

"I'll clear the table," I said casually.

"I've been watching you for five minutes now," she screamed, breathing heavily, her body trembling in anger.

"Why didn't you tell me?" I asked, holding my breath.

I had never faced a situation like that in my life. Only seen in movies. Her behaviour unsettled me. I thought, what if she knew martial arts, trained by deadly Russian commandos? She would bleed me to death.

"Don't do anything crazy," I warned to pre-empt any such possibility.

"When did I tell you to clear the table?" she snarled like a wild cat, which scared me.

"How does it matter? I'll clear it now," I replied after mustering some courage.

"How does it matter?" she fumed. "I've to wait now."

"Two minutes," I pleaded, which enraged her more.

"It is about discipline," she said sternly and then pointed her index finger at me. "This is your responsibility."

"You imposed on me," I protested meekly.

"Uuf!" She shook her head and said, "I imposed. I am not doing anything now."

She stomped the floor, left the hall in a hurry, banged the door of her room, and then turned the music on loudly. That was the first time I had seen her in that hysterical mood. I stood motionless. I was very annoyed with myself because it was basically my fault. I should have cleared the table soon after dinner. I decided to do the cleaning. In the next 20 minutes, I cleared the table, collected the waste, washed the dishes, and finally cleaned the kitchen.

It was humid August. I was sweating, so I decided to take a shower. I went to my room, grabbed my washed track pants, and went to take a shower. I turned the shower tap on. Cold water gushed out and slowly started wetting my entire body. I felt very nice as the sweat from my body started to wash away.

I started to think about Oksana's weird behaviour. I thought, what was the big deal? In a matter of few minutes, I could have cleared the table. Should I ask her to move out? I shook my head. No, I couldn't ask her to move out. Where would I get a new dancer so quickly? The rehearsals were due to start on Monday.

Thinking about Oksana, I started to apply soap on my face when it slipped away from my hands. The soap went inside my eyes, and I felt a deep burning sensation. With my eyes tightly squeezed, I bent down to retrieve the soap with both hands. After a bit of struggle, I managed to find it, finished my shower, wiped my body, tossed the towel on the floor, and put my track pants on.

It was still humid inside, so I opened the bathroom door partly. I stood in front of the mirror and started to comb my hair. While in the middle, I got the feeling that somebody had just passed by the hallway. I stood motionless for a while, shrugged my shoulders, and then continued combing my hair. After a little while, I again got the feeling that someone was standing outside. I wasn't wrong because someone opened the door from outside.

It was Oksana standing outside the bathroom. Our eyes met. I looked at her embarrassed because I was shirtless. I didn't know what to do. My used towel was lying on the floor. I could still pick it, but I couldn't move. I could quickly go past her and then run towards my room. But she was standing at the door, not moving. She was looking at me with her big, blue, bright, and sparkling eyes. She wore a different look I hadn't seen before. I moved close to her and innocently told her that I had cleared the table, washed the dishes, and cleaned the kitchen.

She was still standing on my way but started to melt, and her eyes became moist. Then she lifted her right hand, put it on my chest, and started to stroke my chest. I felt the softness of her hand. It was a nice feeling. After few moments, she held my head with her hands, pulled me down, and kissed me. It was a long and passionate kiss. I liked her big lips. I felt my body had started to stiffen, heartbeat was racing up and down, and I was breathing through my blown-up nostrils. After a while, she released my head and asked, "Did you like it?" I nodded without saying anything. She held my hand in her hand and said, "Come with me." She started taking me to her room. She didn't have to make much effort because I followed her without much resistance.

CHAPTER 11

Next morning I woke up lying on one side of Oksana's bed. I got up not knowing the time. I put my clothes on and started to move towards the door. I looked back before exiting the room. She was lying on the left side, her back towards me slightly exposed. Her beautiful skin was glowing radiant. I thought of reaching to her to touch her back but dropped the idea because I didn't want to wake her up.

I brushed my teeth and looked into the mirror. I kept staring and touching my face, not knowing how it had happened last night. Why did she do it? Our relationship until last night was far from normal—at least, from her side. I had always seen a dancer in her—nothing more—never interfered in personal life or questioned her freedom. I never had any relationship in my life, so I was unaware of such things. She had never given me any hint that could prove her liking for me. Did she always like me? Was her love for me accumulating, which burst last night like a volcano? She only knew the answer. I made coffee, came back to the hall, and sat on the couch. I put the mug on the side table after taking a sip or two. I saw the steam emitting from the mug and then started to recall everything about last night.

Once inside, she closed the door behind. This was the first time I had gone inside her room since she had moved in. Everything looked neat, clean, and orderly. She had a lot of makeup stuff on her dressing table. Her suitcases were safely kept away in one of the corners. The whole room smelt her perfume and the body lotion she always used. We stood near the bed, staring at each other. She kissed me again, this time rubbing her lips in a circular motion, which lingered for a while. My body stiffened again with some strange desire I had never felt before. She pushed me gently and then went to the side of her bed. She looked at me mischievously. Next she started to remove her clothes, first her tank top and then her shorts. She was now in a black laced bra and black boy shorts. My gaze fixated at her bra and shorts instead of her exposed body because I felt they were revealing more than what they could hide. The black colour of her bra and shorts complemented her body. She then went inside the quilt, which hid her body, leaving only her head exposed. The body I had been enjoying was now hidden inside, which excited me more.

She was staring at me with a mischievous smile, slowly shaking her head. We didn't talk to each other. Didn't people talk to each other in that situation? How would I know? That was the first time I was in that situation. My body was still stiff; breathing heavily, I felt a desire to see her body once more. She took her arms out and extended towards me as if she was saying, "Come close to me." I tried to remember those extended arms. Where had I seen like that before? Oh! When I was small, Mum used to ask me to move to a corner. She would then extend her arms and say, "Jai, c'mon, hug me." I shook my head. What was I thinking? That was motherly affection. This was something else, which I still didn't understand.

Oksana was still smiling with her arms extended towards me. I rushed and stood by the bedside. She asked me to remove everything, which I did without any hesitation or thought. I was now fully naked. I looked down to find myself fully erect. It looked very odd and ugly. She moved the side of her quilt to let me in. I placed my legs between her legs and then slowly dropped my body weight onto her body. I felt the warmth of her soft velvety body. It was a nice feeling I had never experienced before. I stayed like that with my head by her right shoulder. I then held her head with both my hands and for the first time kissed her myself. We both were rubbing each other's lips in a circular motion. Next, I lifted my upper body with the support of my left hand and pushed my right hand under her bra. I really enjoyed that experience and wanted to hold both the breasts. She understood what I wanted. She lifted her upper body, removed her bra, and tossed it on the floor. Her beautiful breasts were now at my service. I held them with my hands and then started to gently squeeze them. I touched her nipples, which I felt were hard and fully erect. I enjoyed the experience of playing with her breasts.

I didn't know what to do next. I looked at her, confused. She asked me to get off her body. She then removed her shorts and tossed that also in the same direction where her bra lay. She again lay upon her back, stretched her legs up, spread them apart for me to come on to her, and then said, "Now do it." I placed myself between her legs with the support of my hands, which I placed above her shoulders. Once properly positioned, I struggled to find the target. Every time I made a forward move, it was either going up or touching her sides. It did give me some pleasure but not the one I was looking for. The tension in my body was constantly building. I looked at her. She had her right-hand index finger placed on her lips, wondering what exactly I was doing. I was feeling embarrassed at my inexperience. I made few more futile attempts. Fed up with me, she told me to use my hand. I asked her which one. She giggled and told me that it didn't matter and said, "Use any." I balanced my body with my left hand, held it on my right hand, and then made a forward move. Soon I found the target. It slowly started to go in. I made a forward thrust with a loud groan. I felt hot and sticky inside. Pleased with my success, I started stroking her gently and enjoying every bit. After few strokes, I felt a lot of tension. I started to breathe very fast and heavy, trying my best to control my breath. Suddenly, my strokes became fast and furious. That continued for a while, and then with my final thrust, I released something inside her. I collapsed by her left shoulder, still breathing heavily and trying to control it. It took me a while to bring my breath back to normal.

I just lay there motionless. All the tension and strange feelings experienced earlier had disappeared. What was that? I couldn't understand. After a while, with a deep sigh, I lifted my head and looked at her. She was normal. I rolled over to the other side of the bed, looking straight at the ceiling without any purpose. There was a complete silence for a while. I then rolled to my left side in a curled-up position and put my left hand under my head. She also rolled to my side, and we looked at each other, smiling.

"Did you enjoy?" Oksana asked.

I squeezed my lips and nodded without saying anything.

"First time?" she teased.

I rolled over to my back, covered my eyes with my left hand, and laughed.

"Yesssss . . ." I replied. "What about you?"

"I lost my virginity at 16 while I was in school," she replied, smiling, and disclosed, "But first time here."

"How many years back?"

"You want to know my age, don't you?"

"No," I lied, taking my eyes off her momentarily to hide my lie. I returned my gaze at her and complimented, "It didn't matter whether you were 20 or 40. You are still green, and green is always fresh."

"How do you know when this was your first time?" sharp Oksana probed.

"I felt it," I replied honestly.

She seemed to have liked my comment because she put her left hand on my cheek and started to scratch.

"Really?" she asked, smiling.

"I was very excited, but I didn't find the same feeling in you."

"We women know how to control our emotions and sexual desires. That is why most rapists in this world are men."

"You are right," I said, agreeing with her. Seizing the moment, I thought of extracting some information that had been bugging me from her. I asked cautiously, "Can I ask you few questions?"

"I won't answer if I didn't like," she replied.

Nodding, I asked, "Where do you go?"

"To meet my friends. We practise dance and meet at different places. Leopold's is our favourite meeting point," she replied, revealing much more that I had expected, which surprised me.

"Where is it?"

"You don't know about Leopold's? It was one of the sites attacked during the 2008 Mumbai attacks. It is in Colaba."

"Now I remember. By the way, do you have a boyfriend?"

"What do you have to do with that?"

"Don't worry."

"Why should you worry? You got what you wanted."

I was completely thrown off balance with her weird allegation.

"I wanted?" I asked in utter disbelief. "When did I want?"

"Then why did you do?" she said in a complaining tone.

"How many Oksanas are there in one Oksana?"

"What do you mean?"

"You really want to know?"

"Yes."

"Sad and helpless Oksana I met for the first time. Confused and indecisive Oksana when she didn't know whether to move here or not. Beautiful Oksana who has a great fashion sense. Strict Oksana who wants order and discipline. Enigmatic Oksana who wouldn't reveal her past and discuss her family and—"

"Anything else?" she cut me off in the middle.

"Hysterical Oksana, emotional Oksana, soft Oksana, and this Oksana whom I liked the most."

"No more Oksanas. I am going to sleep now."

"Are there more Oksanas?" I asked, laughing.

"You will know soon. I want to sleep now," she replied lazily.

I rolled over to my back. She put her hand on my chest, started stroking gently, and then it stopped. I looked at her and found her sleeping. I carefully removed her hand from my chest and then rolled my index finger over her big lips. Next, I stared at the ceiling and recalled what she had said about men: "That is why most rapists in this world are men."

She was right. I recalled that in the recent years, there had been many rape cases reported in India. One of the most prominent cases was that of the *nirbhaya* (fearless) rape case or the 2012 Delhi gang rape case involving a 23-year-old female physiotherapy intern who was beaten and gang raped in a private bus. She eventually died of her injuries. The incident generated widespread national and international coverage and was widely condemned both in India and abroad. Her life and death came to symbolise women's struggle to end rape.

My concentration was broken by the noise coming from the neighbouring apartment. I had been thinking about last night for so long that my coffee had turned cold. How long had I been thinking? The time now was 9.30. I decided to make a new cup of coffee, so I went to the kitchen.

The coffee re-energised me. I now had to follow her weekend schedule. I guessed that it would take me an hour to clean the apartment. I first dusted the coffee table, side tables, TV, two wall pictures, and the dining table. I cleaned the bathroom followed by vacuuming the floor one room after another. It took me longer than expected because the time now was 11. I took a breather. I felt like not having seen Oksana for a long time. I was now ready to clean the most important room of the apartment.

I slowly opened her room door and looked around. She wasn't in the room. I entered the room to find her bathroom door closed. I heard the noise of running water. I thought that she must be taking a shower. I looked around and saw a thick black-covered notebook on her bed. I picked it up. I unfolded and turned to first few pages. It had handwritten notes with dates on top. I couldn't read anything because everything was written in a language I didn't understand. I rapidly flicked through all the pages. I noticed that after every three to four pages, new entry started from the fresh page with a new date. It must have been her personal diary she maintained and the reason of her sleeping late. I quickly flicked to the last entry. There wasn't any entry for yesterday. I laughed how there could be one for last night. Last night she was maintaining a different type of diary. I folded the diary back and put that away on the dressing table.

Suddenly, I recalled having read the sheet about her meeting with Shabnam. That was a couple of days after she had moved into my apartment. Why did she use the sheets instead of her diary to record that event? Why did she use English then? Did she deliberately leave the sheet for me to read? She sounded so complex to me. I didn't know what more to expect from her.

I looked at the bed and then sat on the side where she was sleeping last night. I ran my hand over the bed as if I were running my hand over her body. After a while, I took a deep sigh, got up, and started to fix her bed. I then ramrodded vacuuming the floor, taking me hardly five minutes. I waited for her to come out. Now the noise of running water had stopped. I thought she might now be wiping her body. I excitedly desired to see her taking a shower and wiping her body.

Suddenly, the bathroom door opened. She had a long white thin towel wrapped around her body, which she held with her left hand from the middle. She stood there motionless as if not expecting me to be in her room. I smiled at her, but she showed no reaction. She bore a very stern look and kept staring at me with her big blue eyes. She gave me the impression that she was not happy. She then walked past me towards her dressing table. She stood in front of the mirror. I could see water droplets dripping from her hair onto her bare back. I found her back very exciting. I felt so much love for her. My emotions for her started to overwhelm me. She bent down to open the top drawer. I quickly moved and hugged her from behind. She straightened her body, shook it violently to release from my grip, and then hit my stomach with her left elbow. I felt deep pain, released her, and sat on the bed, holding my stomach with my hands. I looked at her, nonplussed and shocked. She still had the same stern expressions on her face. She didn't say anything or talk. Why? Oh! It could be because I was sweaty, which she didn't like having just taken a bath.

I decided to leave her alone, got up, and started to limp towards her bathroom. I closed the door behind, thinking where to start first. I looked around and spotted her black bra hanging on the shower screen. I grabbed it, joined the two cups, and started to smell it. It was the same intoxicating smell I had enjoyed last night. While I was enjoying the smell, someone knocked at the door. I partly opened the door and stuck my head out. Her facial expressions hadn't changed. She told me that she needed to grab something from inside she had forgotten earlier. I knew what she had forgotten and thought of cheering her with a practical joke. I held her bra on my right hand from the straps and started to dangle it in front of her face. She kept looking at the dangling bra with angry eyes for a while and then pounced on it with both her hands snatching it away. She pushed me inside the bathroom and closed the door behind. I could do nothing but to finish up cleaning the bathroom.

I finished cleaning her bathroom in 20 minutes, totally exhausted. I hadn't done this type of work before but thanked her for teaching me something new. I went back to the hall to keep the stuff back when I saw her sitting in her first favourite pose. She looked over her shoulders and rolled her big eyes all over me. I ignored her because I was feeling exhausted and hungry. But first, I needed to take a nice cold shower.

I came out fresh from the shower and decided to prepare breakfast for myself. Although cooking was her responsibility, she looked in no mood to do anything. *Small things,* I thought. I decided to make an Indian-style omelette, which was easy to make because I had done that many times in the past in Delhi. I grabbed four eggs and broke them all in a large mug. I needed to add finely chopped onion and tomato. I decided to involve her in order to test her mental state, which didn't look good to me since the morning. I went to her and asked if she could help me. She didn't say anything to me but headed to the kitchen. I followed her like I had been following her every time.

"How will I chop?" she asked angrily.

I grabbed the knife and the chopping board for her without reacting back.

"How do I chop?" she asked coldly.

"A quarter onion and a half tomato finely chopped," I replied very politely, and then I asked, "I am making an omelette. Is that okay with you?"

She didn't reply, which I took as a yes. I finished preparing breakfast and then placed everything on the table. I asked her to join me, which she did without any fuss. By the time we started our breakfast, it was already midday. We started to have our breakfast quietly but not for a long.

"What happened last night was a freak accident," she said coldly.

"Freak accident? After all that? Your behaviour towards me had been so indifferent that I could never imagine in my dreams that something like last night could ever happen," I said, surprised.

"I felt very bad at my behaviour. I know I was rude, so I decided to apologise. I searched for you everywhere but couldn't find you."

"I must have been taking a shower."

"I now know," she said in a heavy voice. "When you told me that you had cleaned everything, I felt even worse and . . . umm . . ."

"You decided to pay me back," I reacted sarcastically, feeling bad at the reason behind our sexual encounter.

She rested her cheek on her left fist and stared at me in a meaningful way while bringing a mysterious smile on her face. I couldn't make out what her eyes and mysterious smile were conveying. I felt restless to know the reason, so I stared back, expecting her to reveal the truth.

"You are a handsome young man," she said, shyly looking away. "You also have a nice body."

I ignored her compliment, knowing that she had so many contradictions in her personality; and talking about her mood swings, I could count them on my fingertips. I wasn't wrong because soon she dropped an unexpected bomb.

"I don't feel safe here anymore."

"Why?" I asked, shocked.

"You know what to do now."

"I didn't know, but you taught me," I protested.

"I shouldn't have done it," she regretted.

"Do you want to undo it?"

"How?"

"Last night, I came on top of you," I said, smiling, and then I burst into laughter. "Tonight, I'll lie down and you come on top of me."

She brought a broad smile on her face and started to laugh uncontrollably. *Was that so funny?* I thought. I never imagined that I had that great sense of humour. Perhaps I myself was changing with her.

"It is the same thing," she said, blushing.

"Really? I didn't know that," I scoffed.

"But you didn't know yesterday this time," she teased.

"I am getting smarter every day in your company."

"Don't pull my leg."

"If you don't want to do, then don't do it," I lectured.

"Do you want to do it?" she teased, smiling.

I looked directly into her eyes in utter disbelief.

"We will do when I tell you to do," she said, winking.

"What is new in it? I have been doing everything that you have been telling me," I said bitterly.

"Never touch me without my permission," she said seriously.

"Why?" I asked, surprised.

"I don't like people touching me unnecessarily."

"How will I do without touching?" I asked, laughing.

"Shut up," she said, laughing.

I realised that since I saw her this morning, her mood swung so many times, leaving me totally confused beyond my imagination. I started to recall last night's conversation when I had asked, "Are there more Oksanas?" Her reply was "You will know soon."

"I am seeing a new type of Oksana this morning," I said, resuming the conversation.

"What new type of Oksana?" she asked, confused.

"A weird type of Oksana," I replied. She looked at me, slightly unhappy. We had been talking for over an hour, basically wasting our time in an unproductive discussion. I changed the topic. "We start rehearsals from Monday. Are you ready?"

"How many times?" she scolded. "We need to start making money. I don't want to blow up my savings."

"How much have you spent so far?"

"Ten thousand."

"You have got plenty left," I comforted. "We should be able to make money very soon."

"I hope so," she said while getting up. "I've to go now."

"Where?"

"To my room."

"What is in there?"

"I've to finish something," she put in. "I couldn't do anything last night."

"You didn't do anything last night," I teased, smiling.

"Don't be funny," she said, squeezing her lips to the left.

"Honestly, I liked every moment last night. I never had enjoyed so much in my life," I said, filled in joyous emotions.

She didn't say anything. She smiled, gave a little left-handed wave, and vanished into her room. I again started to think about last night. She had a beautiful body, and that fragrance emitting from her body drove me mad. I couldn't have ever imagined losing my virginity to someone so beautiful. She had a strange attraction. I started to like her despite strange behaviour and drastic mood swings. I myself had changed. I was maturing, flirting, and developing a good sense of humour, possibly going through the best phase of my life.

I couldn't think of my future without her. I couldn't lose her and needed to win her heart. I didn't know how. She also looked so happy last night and eventually today. Why shouldn't she? She was living on her own terms, having total control over me. Her gamble to move had finally paid off.

CHAPTER 12

The first day of our rehearsals had finally arrived. In two hours from now, we both would be heading to the Churchgate apartment. I really liked the 2pm start as it enabled us to leave soon after lunch. Everything was going well as per plan. I was still waiting for the documents of my company. It had been ten days since I had submitted my application online. Being a Monday, there was a good chance of receiving them today. So I went downstairs to check the mail. I saw a large envelope sticking out of my letterbox. I pulled it out and then looked inside the box. I took everything out that I could see inside. Except for the large envelope, everything else was junk mail, which I quickly trashed away. I checked the sender's address on the envelope, and it was the thing I had been waiting for.

I decided to open the envelope upstairs, so I quickly dashed up via the lift. Once inside, I sat on the couch and then carefully tore it from the top. I had the formal documents of my company containing vital information like corporate identification number, company name, registration number and address etc. I read the documents once, twice, and then many more times. I felt a special sense of achievement that I was the sole director of my own company. I started to dream about money flowing in, expansion from one person to a hundred to a thousand persons, meetings, large clients, and big events. I took a deep breath and then laughed at my daydreaming. Nothing is easy in the world because there are no shortcuts to success. It takes a lot of hard work, time, and luck to become a successful businessman. But I could dream. If one didn't dream, how would he then realise his dreams?

My daydream was broken by the taps of Oksana's feet. She was ready in the same college-going teenager dress she had worn last time when she had gone out. She sat down, assuming her second favourite pose. She looked her best. Exceptionally attractive.

"What time are we leaving?" she asked.

"After lunch at 1," I replied and reminded, "You have to cook first."

"We will have Chinese noodles, so it won't take long."

"As you say," I said while getting up. "I'll go and get ready."

"What is in that envelope?"

"Our company registration papers."

"Our papers?"

"Mine," I continued. "But I'll project you as one of the partners. Don't tell anyone."

"Why this lie?"

"For your benefit. People will listen to you when you tell them that you are one of the directors."

"Do I've to sign anything?" she asked while growing suspicious. "I mean any payment cheques?"

"No. Say Jai has that authority."

"I don't want to get into any trouble later."

"What trouble?"

"Disputes and all, you know."

"I won't let that happen. You can count on me," I assured.

"You surely will get me into some trouble one day," she scolded.

"Never," I said, irritated. "You got to learn to trust people. Now let me get ready."

By the time I got ready and finished our lunch, it was already 1 in the afternoon, so we decided to leave for Churchgate. She sat with me on the front seat, frequently adjusting her short skirt, looking straight down the road through her large oval-shaped sunglasses. I wanted to keep looking at her but couldn't take my eyes off the road. We didn't talk at all for about ten minutes until we hit the freeway when she served me her first ace of the day.

"What time will we have a coffee break?" she asked casually.

"Coffee?" I reacted, amazed. "We haven't started yet. How could you think of coffee break?"

"We can decide now," she chirruped.

"We will decide together," I said forcefully.

"So many people."

"What is the problem in multiple opinions?"

"It takes too long to decide. That is the problem."

"What time do you want?"

"At 4."

"We can discuss with others. If they agree, then it is 4."

"They've to agree."

"Why?" I asked, surprised while looking at her.

"Because I am one of the directors of the company."

"They are not your employees," I scoffed. "They are doing it for free."

"Is there any Starbucks around there?" she asked, cleverly changing the subject.

"I don't know. There should be one around," I replied, irritated.

She was driving me mad with her tantrums. Today she was not only looking beautiful but also showing her clever side.

"You have to pay for my coffee." She chuckled.

"I can pay today."

"Always."

"Why?"

"Because I am also doing it for free."

"Few moments back, you said you were one the directors of the company."

"That is the lie you told me to tell others," she continued. "Otherwise, I don't like to lie."

"I'll pay." I gave up and requested, "If some ask, just say we settle our expenses in the evenings at home."

"I don't lie."

"Don't say anything," I yelled while gesturing to keep her mouth shut by joining all my fingers, moving them across my mouth. "Just zip. I'll tell them."

"Not my business," she replied calmly much to my chagrin.

"Can I drive now?" I asked seriously.

"What have you been doing then?" she replied calmly, once again driving me almost crazy.

I took my eyes off the road and stared at her, but it turned out to be a futile exercise because she was calmly looking down the road. For the first time, I had felt so much anger that I wanted to throw her out of the car. Suddenly, I heard the noise of the tyres hitting the surface markers. I was going off the lane, so I quickly moved the car back on the right lane. I once again looked at her with an angry face, but she had closed her eyes and taken a nap as if nothing had happened. I shook my head in disbelief and continued to drive quietly.

We reached the apartment in the next ten minutes. I parked the car and looked at her. She adjusted her skirt and then got off without looking at me. We entered the building complex and started to walk towards the staircase.

"There is no lift," she complained.

"The apartment is on the second floor," I said with great difficulty while trying to control my anger. "Moreover, these are old apartments built in the 50s."

"That is why it looks so old."

"You know how much each apartment would cost?"

"How do I know?"

"At least ten crores, that is, around $2 million."

"If they install the lift, how much will it go up by?"

"I don't know, but it would certainly increase the maintenance cost," I replied sarcastically.

We walked up the stairs and pressed the bell. Amardeep opened the door with a smile on his face. His face beamed like a glistening pearl when he saw Oksana in a short skirt. He made an okay sign, admiring how beautiful she was looking. She returned his compliment with a beaming smile, which simply burned me up inside. But I had another worry. There was no one there other than Amardeep. I looked at him with enquiring eyes.

"They should be here anytime," Amardeep said. "They've been arguing about who picks whom. They should be here in about 20 minutes. Oksana, kya lag rahi hai tu [Oksana, you are looking smashing today]."

"Really?" she asked while trying her best to suppress her delight.

"I really like Russian girls. They are cool."

"I told you she is not a Russian. So be careful in future," I warned.

"Sorry," he apologised and asked as if he intuitively knew how to please her. "Oksana, you know the problem when you have so many people in a group?"

"No, I don't," she replied, pretending ignorance, and then went on and on, "How do I know? This the first time I am joining a group in India. I don't have a very large friend circle in Mumbai. In Ukraine, I was never a part of any group but . . . but Jai knows," she completed her sentence after a brief pause, looking at me, and then started to blink.

I looked away, choosing to ignore her second ace of the day. I was getting worried about the missing members of the group.

"Too many cooks spoil the broth," Amardeep replied, unmindful of the pain his intellectual talk was inflicting on me.

She looked at me, smiling, like a winner as if saying, "See, I told you." I again chose to ignore her.

"Should I make coffee?" Amardeep asked, thankfully changing the topic.

"We will go for a coffee break at 4," she almost ordered.

"Where?"

"Starbucks."

"Cool," Amardeep said. "There is one very close in the Elphinstone building in Fort. Hardly ten minutes' walk from here."

"Amar, what can be done while we wait for them?" I asked, disrupting their cosy chat.

"You decide."

"We really can't do anything. I thought we will discuss our schedule for the next two to three weeks. But I need everybody present. We will wait."

"We can do something without them," Oksana intervened.

"What?"

"Go there," she ordered, pointing to the open space. "I want to see how much dancing you know."

"Which song do you want me to dance on?"

"Wait. I'll tell you in a moment. I don't remember the song."

She got busy with her mobile. After few taps here and there, she showed me a YouTube clip. It was "Dil Na Diya" from Krrish.

"What? I can't do," I said, shocked. "They've used a harness in this song."

"Show me the first two minutes. They have used harness after that."

"But it is Hrithik Roshan. He is a good dancer," I protested.

"I know. But this song has got every motion. I mean hips, hands, shoulders, waist, legs, head, and neck," she explained impressively.

I watched the clip, convincing me that she was a keen observer. Otherwise, how could have she remembered one such song among millions of songs?

"How do I remember the steps and sequence?" I asked nervously.

"I've never danced on this song, but I can show you," she said confidently and then threw a challenge. "Do you want me to show you?"

"If you could."

"Amar, I need a big screen. Do you have a notebook?"

"No. There is a desktop. Should I get that?" Amardeep replied.

"Don't worry," she said, carefree.

I regretted my decision of leaving the notebook in the apartment.

"Amar, hold my mobile straight in front of me a little away," she ordered.

I once again checked the time. It was 2.30, and the missing group had still not shown up. Meanwhile, Amardeep stood some distance away from Oksana, holding the mobile straight on his right hand. She looked at the screen for a while. She then started to imitate the moves, occasionally looking at the screen. Her moves were very close to the original, surprising me a lot. Her concentration was so intense that she forgot that Amardeep and I were around her. She finished her trial in about three minutes and sat quietly on the chair, trying to catch her breath back. *What a dancer,* I thought. How did she remember the moves when her eyes were away from the screen? I thanked my stars for meeting her. She was the most valuable asset of my nascent group. My bitterness about her once again turned into an admiration. I sat there looking at her like a fan who was looking at his idol for the first time. She was busy on her mobile, so she didn't notice my admiration for me. She didn't need that from me anyway.

"Should I start?" I asked, bringing her attention back to me.

"Watch the clip a few more times and then try to memorise the moves," she ordered like a schoolteacher.

I nodded and then turned to Amardeep. "Amar, please call them again."

"Don't worry, you concentrate on the clip," Amardeep replied.

While I was watching the clip, they started to talk to each other.

"Amar, what instrument do you play?" Oksana asked, smiling.

"Guitar."

"I like guitar."

"You know how to play?"

"Little bit not much."

"I can teach you," Amardeep said, offering his good services gleefully, probably sensing an opportunity to come close to Oksana. "When do you want to start?"

"I'll let you know," she replied, smiling.

"Oksana, I am ready," I said like an obedient student.

"Good," she said. "I will hold the screen for you."

"I have a question. How did you remember the steps when you took your eyes off the screen?"

"It is called instinct. A way of behaving, thinking, or feeling that is not learnt. I am a dancer, so I can overcome interferences. But you have to train hard and practise, practise, and practise," she replied, brimming in confidence.

"I haven't seen you practising since you moved."

"Start now," she said curtly.

I took my position, requested her to wait, closed my eyes to remember the moves, and then let my body move. According to me, everything was going right when she suddenly moved the mobile away from my sight, and I stopped.

"Why?" I asked, dejected.

"Don't worry," she consoled. "We will start again. But don't stop this time."

I started once again. This time, the moves were much clear to me. Suddenly, she took the mobile away, but I continued to dance the way I thought was the best. After a while, she asked me to stop. I sat on the chair, huffing and puffing. I looked at her, but she was thinking about something. My eyes fell on her thighs, which were a bit overexposed because her skirt had moved up. I felt a burning urge to stroke her thighs with my hands. Knowing that was not a possibility, I kept staring at her thighs. Suddenly she turned to me to say something when she noticed me staring at her thighs. She first adjusted her skirt and then gave me a glare, her cheeks flushing. I knew I was in trouble because she had yet to deliver her verdict.

"Better pay attention to your dancing," she rebuked.

"Was there any problem?" I asked, pretending not to have understood her. "I told you I am not a trained dancer."

"You should be in two weeks provided you work and practise hard."

"Really? How?" I asked, overjoyed.

"You have a natural body for dance, but you first need to know the elements of dancing."

"What elements?"

"I'll explain to you tonight."

"What time?"

"After dinner."

I felt very happy and relieved at her observation. I became relaxed after having secured her commitment to teach me dancing. There was nothing else to do until the missing members showed up. I decided to have a bit of fun with her.

"Where? In your room," I flirted.

"Outside," she replied sternly. She advised, "Bring some more energy in your dance."

"How do you bring energy?" I flirted again.

"Like you brought on last Friday night," she replied aloud and moved away.

She knocked me out with her reply. I thought she was always one step ahead. Then I realised that the missing members were still missing. This is typical of Indians. Never be on time, never keep the promise, or never call to report late. I laughed while recalling what Vishal had told: IST doesn't work in Mumbai. But what could I do? They were all working for me for free as amateurs. I recalled having asked Amardeep to contact them about an hour ago.

"Amar, where are they?" I asked, frustrated.

"They were stuck in traffic somewhere. I'll call again," he replied.

"Don't call them, Amar. It was their responsibility to call back," Oksana said sternly.

"You are right. I am not calling anyone," Amardeep replied, agreeing with her, leaving me in the minority.

"Forget about responsibility. Give me the number, Amar," I pleaded.

"Don't give him anything. They are late anyway," she said forcefully.

I looked at her, trying to understand her logic.

"Why?" I said, looking at her helplessly.

"It won't make any difference. They have to understand their responsibility," she lectured.

"Why are you doing this?" I begged.

"Di . . . rec . . . tor," she replied in a slow motion with a knowing wink.

"Oh! Now you are a director. You are—"

I couldn't complete the word *mad* when someone knocked at the door. Finally, the missing members showed up at ten to 4, only an hour and 50 minutes later. They all looked tired, so I requested Amardeep for water who went inside to get water for them.

"Hi, Oksi, how are you?" Dolce asked sweetly.

"Good. How are you?" Oksana reciprocated sweetly.

"Sorry, we are very late," Dolce apologised to Oksana only.

"Take it easy," she said coolly and then served her third and the deadliest ace of the day. "I told Jai to call you to tell you not to worry."

I looked at her like a wounded tiger but was beaten back by her mischievous smile. She raised her eyebrows and started to shake her head slowly, smiling as if asking me, "Now reply, Dolce." Amardeep came back with water, which diverted my attention from her.

"Jai, why didn't you call us?" Dolce groused.

"I don't always have to listen to her," I replied coldly.

"Jai, it is very bad. See how much concern she was showing for us?" she commented, which Oksana enjoyed but miffed me.

"Oksana, let us have a coffee break?" Amardeep suggested, ending the showdown that was silently building between Oksana and me.

"Yes, I need coffee," Oksana agreed gleefully.

"Even I need a break. I am so tired," Dolce said, yawning, and then stretched her arms.

If Oksana was a drama queen, Dolce was no less. We got down and started to walk to the Starbucks. Ajay and Neel were muttering with each other. Dolce started talking to Sachin. Oksana and Amardeep were chatting in a flirtatious manner. I was the only person walking alone, feeling jealous of Amardeep. We reached the shop and grabbed a round table. Dolce insisted on sitting with Oksana, and the other person who sat with Oksana was Amardeep, which made me more jealous. We ordered coffee. I thought the best way to overcome my feelings was to talk about work.

"We have to finalise the schedule for the next two to three weeks," I said.

"Good idea," Sachin said. "What do we do?"

"Composition, choreography, and marketing."

"How will you market?" Dolce asked.

"Digital. We need a website, social media, and emailer system," I replied.

"What is an emailer system?" Amardeep asked.

"It will enable us to send bulk emails."

"I remember. We used to send one email to all parents for notices, functions etc," Dolce said.

"Exactly."

"Do you know how to do?" Neel asked.

"No, we need to engage a company that does all. It may cost Rs50,000 to 60,000."

"Who will pay?" Dolce asked.

"Oksana and me," I continued. "We will have to finalise a company to carry out this work. Oksana will help me."

"How can I help?" she asked, concerned.

"We need to take your pictures."

"Do you want to hear the song now?" Ajay asked.

"Not now. You can start your practice to create new music in our absence."

"We can do it after the break," Amardeep suggested.

"No. We are leaving from here."

"Why early?" Dolce questioned, shrugging her shoulders, but quickly realised her mistake. "Because we came late."

"Exactly," I replied and came up with a strange logic. "You came late so you leave early."

"This won't happen again," Dolce regretted and blamed someone. "They've to do something at the cross-section. We were stuck there for half an hour."

"So you left late?" I asked, little annoyed.

I saw a Starbucks staff heading towards us with a tray in his hands. He came around the table and stood by my right side directly opposite where Dolce was sitting. I looked up at him and noticed a pin on his right pocket, which had his name "ROSHAN ALI" engraved. I really liked what he did next; he bent forwards and placed the coffee cup first in front of Oksana, then Dolce, and finally the men. He seemed to be aware of the etiquette to serve ladies first. Maybe it was the Starbucks training or his own personality or better upbringing. Whatever it was, I really liked him for that. We started to have coffee when I looked at Oksana. She took the first sip, which left a layer of cream on her upper lip, which she quickly licked with her tongue. Our eyes met, and I got the feeling that she was fairly impressed with me the way I had handled the proceedings so far. I then turned to Dolce when she dropped the bombshell. She said that she would be away between 26 September and 30 September because she was going to track Modi's first US visit.

"I am giving an advance notice," she told, which I highly appreciated.

"How would you track his visit?" Amardeep enquired.

"How? TV and social media."

"You can track him from anywhere," I said.

"No. I'll be in Baroda with my cousins."

"Why do you need to track his visit?"

"Our family is a long-time follower of BJP," she revealed. I noticed that she hadn't touched her coffee so far. She started to scratch her forehead, trying to recall something. "In fact, in the May elections, I worked as a volunteer for him in Baroda."

"He quit that seat for Banaras," Amardeep commented.

"How does it matter? He won from both the places. So he had to quit one."

"Are you originally from Baroda?" I asked.

"We have a business interest there, but basically, I am a Mumbai girl."

"You can go. But I still don't understand why you need to track his visit. It is a waste of time."

"Jai, she's nothing else to do," Amardeep teased her.

"Tu bakwas bandh kar [You shut up]," she shouted.

"Did US give him the visa?" Amardeep taunted her.

"Please, Amar," I pleaded, requesting him not to raise the issue.

"When did they deny him?" Dolce scolded.

"In 2005," Amardeep replied coolly.

"That was the Bush administration, which had no moral authority."

"What do you mean?"

"Didn't he kill people in Iraq? He lied to the world that Saddam had WMDs and then attacked Iraq. How many people have been killed in Iraq since then? The country is in ruins. They had Saddam hanged. There are double standards in this world," Dolce spoke like an expert analyst.

Her analysis left all of us speechless. Dolce had a point.

"And—" Dolce tried to start again when I snapped her.

"Stop. Everything was very unfortunate. No innocent should be killed."

"Sorry," Dolce apologised.

"Should we pack up?" I asked and then turned to Amar. "I'll call you if we can't make it tomorrow."

"What will we do in your absence?" Ajay asked me.

"I told you to practise on the new music."

We got up to leave. I picked my empty cup and that of Dolce. Her cup was still full because she hadn't touched it. I started to dangle her cup in front of her face. She told me to throw it away. We shook hands, and soon we were heading back to home. I was in no mood to talk to Oksana, so I decided to drive quietly. Barely had I driven for ten minutes when she opened her mouth, which made me laugh because I had told her my age when we had met the first time.

"How old are you?" she asked.

"How old are you?" I imitated her.

"That is a question, not an answer."

"Why do you want to know my age?"

"You handled them very maturely," she praised.

"They are all younger than me. So it is not hard to handle people younger than your own age."

"Really."

"But I don't know how to handle you."

"Are you implying I am older than you?" she asked with wide eyes.

"Don't put words in my mouth. You said that. I didn't," I replied, annoyed.

"You want to know how old I am?"

"It makes no difference to me."

"It makes no difference to me either," she said while adjusting her skirt. She looked down the road with an upsetting look on her face. Suddenly, I recalled what she had told Dolce earlier today.

"When did you ask me to call Dolce?"

"I was joking," she replied in a flattering tone.

"No, you weren't. You wanted to look good in their eyes," I protested.

"What is wrong with that?" she contested.

"What about me?"

"You are an Indian in India. Nothing will happen to you."

I kept quiet, choosing not to respond to her weird logic.

"What was that about sharing Rs50,000 to Rs60,000? Do I've to share?" She asked.

"Do you think I am an idiot?" I replied unkindly while giving her a quick glare.

"No. Why?" she asked casually, yawning, looking straight down the road as if I was really an idiot.

"When you can't pay for you coffee", I said clearly, "how could I then ask you to share such a big amount? I just had to say that in front of them."

"You are very nice," she said in a flattering tone and closed her eyes.

I concentrated in driving in peace. After a while, I started to think about Dolce's decision of throwing away her coffee without touching it. Why didn't she drink her coffee? Was it because it was served by a Muslim? Hindus have this prejudice against Muslims. They think they are unclean because they are nonvegetarian, especially since they eat beef. Hindus worship cows. I felt Dolce was a bit communal. She was too young to start thinking on communal lines. I personally hated communalism. The people with such views are narrow-minded who can't think out of the box. It is a mindset that needed to be changed. If my reading about Dolce was correct, then I needed to talk to her about it. I was sure I could convince her with my arguments buttressed with good examples in order to remove her prejudices against Muslims. Moreover, Roshan Ali was a good reason to talk to her. I had personally liked him, but I wasn't sure whether such opportunity would ever arrive.

CHAPTER 13

Around 8 that evening, when I finished cleaning, Oksana came around to check my availability for the theoretical lessons on dance. Seeing me ready, she went back to her room to fetch her notebook. I sat on the couch, hoping that she would sit beside me so that I could enjoy her body fragrance. She came back with her notebook and asked me to move to the dining area.

"Can we sit on the couch together?" I requested.

"No. We need to sit facing each other," she replied firmly.

"Why?"

"You need to concentrate on something I am about to show you."

With no option left, I reluctantly went to the dining area and sat on the chair across her. She pushed her notebook towards me and asked me to read from the screen. She also told me that she would explain further once I had gone through the online material. I started to read from the screen, which described the elements of dance in detail.

I went through the screens, casually concentrating only on the significant portions:

> The elements of dance are the foundational concepts and vocabulary for developing movement skills as well as understanding dance as an art form. All these elements are simultaneously present in a dance or even in a short movement phrase. In order to recall the elements of dance, an acronym BASTE (body, action, space, time, and energy) helps educators and students.
>
> **Body** - In dance, the body is the mobile figure or shape, felt by the dancer, seen by others.
>
> **Action** - It is any human movement included in the act of dancing such as dance steps, facial movements, lifts, carries, and catches.
>
> **Space** - Dancers interact with space in myriad ways. They may stay in one place and move parts of their body or their whole body, or they may travel from one place to another.
>
> **Time** - The keyword for the element of time is *when*. Human movement is naturally rhythmic in the broad sense that we alternate activity and rest.
>
> **Energy** - Energy is about how. It refers to the force of an action and can mean both the physical and psychic energy that drives and characterises movements.

It took me about 30 minutes to go through the elements. It wasn't hard to understand, but I didn't know how to apply them. I looked at Oksana who was directly looking at me. She had been monitoring me. In my whole student life, I never had anyone monitoring me. I was naturally brilliant at studies. I had never needed any monitoring or private coaching. After all, I was the product of elite IIT, which had a worldwide reputation. Only if she knew that IITians are admitted straight into elite Ivy League universities in the United States. But who could explain to her? On second thought, I realised that she was right. It is not only those who have degrees who are intelligent because intelligence has many dimensions. I indicated to her that I was done with the reading.

"Fold the notebook down," she ordered, like a schoolteacher. I followed the instruction under her watchful eyes. She resumed, "Now, answer my questions."

"What?" I asked, puzzled. "Is it a kind of viva voce?"

"Do what I am saying," she asked sternly.

"Give me a second," I asked, agreeing reluctantly.

She nodded. I closed my eyes and tried to recall. What are elements of dance? What is BASTE? What is the each element about?

I looked at her, unhappy, and indicated that I was now ready for her Q&A session.

"What is BASTE?" she asked, looking straight into my eyes.

"Body, action . . . umm . . . space . . . time, and energy," I replied slowly.

"What is time?"

"When to move."

"What is energy?"

"Like I brought last Friday night," I replied, winking.

"What is energy?" she repeated sternly.

"How much force you apply in an action," I replied, quickly falling in line.

"Good. That is enough on elements."

"How do you apply them?" I asked curiously.

"If I ask you to take a circular action, what elements are we applying?"

"Time, energy, and actually . . . all," I replied slowly while trying to match her question with the definition of BASTE.

"Yes," she said without appreciating and asked quickly, "Now if you are close to a wall and I ask you to take a big jump towards the wall, what would you tell me?"

"There is no space," I replied quickly.

She nodded. She didn't give away much. I was still not sure whether I could deliver. I needed to ask more questions.

"Do I've to remember everything about the BASTE during my lessons?' I asked.

"No," she replied while shaking her head. "Just remember the basics. When you dance, leave your body free, dance for yourself, enjoy it, overcome interferences like the audience, obstacles, stage fright etc. Always remember it is the first few moments you have to manage well. Good beginnings and endings leave lasting impression."

"Are you a trained dancer?" I asked in admiration, impressed with her knowledge about the subject.

"Self-taught," she replied crisply.

She got up, grabbed her notebook, and then, as usual, disappeared into her room, leaving me alone to scratch my head. She was not only a skilled dancer but also a good teacher. I went to my room confident and happy that there wouldn't be any issue with choreography. I was in the company of a brilliant dancer. Thinking about tomorrow, which was going to be another busy day, I went to my room a satisfied person.

Next day I did an online search for a web development company. I spoke to four different companies, explaining the requirements in detail. Finally, I selected one at Fort and secured an appointment with them at 3 in the afternoon for tomorrow. We also needed to buy Indian dancing costume and fake jewellery for Oksana for her pictures.

I went to my room to get ready for Churchgate for our rehearsals. When I came back, I found Oksana waiting for me, busy on her notebook, browsing something. I really admired her memory to remember to keep the notebook with her, which we had failed to do yesterday. We left the apartment after having a quick lunch and reached the apartment in under an hour to find, to our pleasure, everybody present there. After exchanges of greetings and few handshakes, we settled down for real work.

"Should we go through the song?" Ajay asked.

"Yes," Dolce replied.

Ajay started to read the poem, which was a duet. He read the lines for male, female, male, female, both, female, male, and so on. The poem basically was on the pattern of usual Bollywood-style songs in Hindi and occasional use of English words to ensure proper rhyming. I thought the use of English words or sentences mixed with the Hindi language had become kind of trend or norm for the past few years. The poem sounded fine to me. I was confident that we could approve the poem after a few rounds of practice, improving it in the process.

"What do you think?" I asked.

"Fine by me," Sachin replied.

"Should we approve then?"

"Wait. Ajay, one more time," Dolce suggested.

"No. That round is over," I said, rejecting her suggestion, which she didn't like. Ignoring her, I started to think about the next move. Something from my engineering course gave me an idea. I needed to cheer up Dolce now. "Dolce, what do you think about peer review?"

"What is peer review?" she replied, confused.

"Each of us, except for Oksana, will pick a quiet place in one of the rooms, recite the poem loudly in a lyrical manner, feel it, and then come back with the feedback."

"I can't sing well," Dolce regretted, cutting a sorry face.

"How can we do without you, Dolce?" I cajoled.

Her face blossomed. She asked, surprised, "Really? I will try then."

"Don't do it, Dolce, if you can't sing," Oksana gave a free advice while nudging her to throw the spanner in the works, inviting my glare.

"You don't have to recite in front of us," I explained. "It won't take long. The poem, if recited at normal speed, won't take more than three minutes. Amar, you go first."

Amardeep went away, disappearing into one of the rooms. He came back in a couple of minutes, as expected, totally confused. Dolce, Sachin, Ajay, and I went in one by one. Everything was over in 30 minutes. It was feedback time. Everybody liked the lyrics except for Amardeep who said he couldn't make out anything, so he was unable to give any feedback. I then suggested doing the last test, which was that of group singing. We all recited the lines together, which we did once and then the second time. There was complete silence for a while, and then we all burst into laughter, clapping our hands. The poem was approved 5–0 in favour with Amardeep choosing to abstain. Oksana's vote didn't count, anyway.

"Jai, that is how you do it?" Amardeep asked.

"I don't know," I said, laughing loudly. "I applied the software testing technique. Unit test, peer review, and concurrent testing. If it worked, so be it."

"I don't understand. Oksana, let us go for a coffee break," Amardeep said as expected.

"Where are we going today?" Dolce asked, looking worried.

"Same place."

"I'll stay back."

"Why?" I asked.

"Can we go to a different place?"

"We are going to the same place," I insisted forcefully.

"Why can't we go somewhere else?" she pleaded like a child.

"We have to be back quick."

"I'll go, but I won't have anything."

"Fine."

We reached Starbucks and ordered coffee for all minus Dolce. The same guy, Roshan Ali, served us. I made sure that he didn't, by mistake, serve coffee to Dolce because I didn't want him to serve a communal customer. We finished our coffee quickly. I chose to stay back while others left for the apartment.

I started to look around for Roshan Ali but couldn't locate him. I waited for five minutes, but he was nowhere to be seen. I then went to the counter and enquired about him. A young girl busy on the grinder told him that he would be back in 15 minutes after his break. I decided to meet him some other day, so I left. I started to walk back thinking how to resolve Dolce's issue. How could I? I couldn't because she hadn't made anything explicit. I decided to forget the whole issue until I got an opportunity to talk to Dolce. Soon, I joined others in the apartment.

"Oksana, when can we start choreography?" I asked.

"Not until the song is fully composed," she replied.

"Why?"

"You said the poem was three minutes long. After recording the voice over the music, it could grow to four to five minutes."

I thought for a while. She was right, realising that she couldn't design the moves properly until the song was fully composed. I looked at her and nodded.

"What element?" Oksana asked.

"All but action," I replied swiftly.

"Why?"

"Because you have to design the moves."

"What are you guys talking about?" Dolce asked, puzzled.

"She is testing my knowledge on the elements of dance," I clarified.

"Oh!"

"You need a proper place for your dance lessons," Oksana said.

"Dolce, can we find a proper place?"

"Consider it done," Dolce replied in style.

"Will it cost?"

"Not sure, but I've to check with someone. It is a school auditorium."

"Where?"

"I have to check first. I'll send you an email tonight or by tomorrow."

I had full faith in Dolce, so I stopped worrying. But I had another worry. I needed a female singer who would sing the duet with me.

"We need to create a track and record the song over it," I said and threw a couple of questions. "Where can we record? How much would it cost?"

"Mumbai is full of recording studios. The charges are generally per hour," Neel responded.

"Who will do the female voice?"

"Will find someone," Neel assured. "There are so many out there who are struggling. They will do cheap."

"Get the cost."

"Tomorrow."

"We need to finish recording in two weeks. After that, Oksana can start working on her choreography."

"I don't have much work for the next two weeks," Oksana said, pleased, while clapping her hands.

"You have to do dance tutoring," I told, which took a bit of shine off her face. I turned to Amardeep. "How many instruments will we use?"

"Guitar, drum, tabla, and harmonium," he replied.

"We need a lot of practice before we do the final recording."

"We need to create a new music first."

"Initial music should start with a melodious tune and end with a high beat of the drum. Like bang," Oksana suggested, swinging her right hand like a drummer.

"Good one, Oksana," I said, fairly impressed. "Let us call it a day. We won't be coming tomorrow."

"Why?" Dolce asked.

"We have an appointment with a web development company."

"Oh! I'll miss you, Oksi," she said dramatically.

"I'll miss you too," Oksana responded, equally matching her drama, and then made a comment and pointed at me, "It is going to be boring tomorrow."

"You guys work on the music in our absence. Neel, I want cost from you when we meet on Thursday. Dolce, email me about the auditorium. Also, I need passport-sized pictures of all of you. Just the faces," I said, ignoring Oksana's comment.

"What for?" Dolce asked.

"For our profiles on the website. You take responsibility of getting me all the pictures. I want them by tonight with your email."

"Will do."

We all left. While driving back, I started feeling a lot of work pressure and strain of responsibility. The next two weeks were going to very busy in music creation, singing, and recording, and dance practice. The bigger expenses were about to come. How would I manage with the money that was left in my account? I needed to check my balance, which I hadn't done for a long time. To compound my problems, Oksana had been nagging me like an Indian mynah. She complained about her less involvement. She said she wanted to meet her friends tomorrow, but I had kept an appointment without her knowledge. We hadn't started making money. Her savings were depleting fast, never caring about my own depleting savings. It didn't occur to her that most of the time she and Dolce just talked. On top, she had been taunting me whenever she saw an opportunity. She was proving to be more of a burden than a help. I thought apart from beauty and dancing capability, there was nothing appreciable about her. She was not adding any value to the group. I remembered my mother warning me to be careful about her. For the first time in the last six weeks, I felt like running away from Mumbai back to Delhi. I was really angry with her and needed to do something.

CHAPTER 14

I got up late at 9.30 in the morning with a heavy head. There were only two more days left in August. I had been thinking about everything until late last night. The more I thought, the angrier I became. I needed to control my emotions and start thinking with a clear head. I decided to make use of the three *R*s technique, which I knew is used for anger management. The three *R*s, i.e. retract, relax, and react. I decided to retract by keeping a distance from her, wouldn't flirt with her anymore or respond to her flirty talks and keep the relationship purely professional. Relax by controlling my emotions using my head and acting normal. React by taking saner decisions, wouldn't run away from responsibilities, and keep her in my group because it was too late to part ways with her. I felt much better at my thought process.

I checked my bank balance, which stood at healthy Rs596,218.55. I checked my emails and found an email from Dolce. She had sent everything that was needed, about a school auditorium and passport-sized pictures of all. The school auditorium was close to my apartment, which lit my face up. It would cost Rs500 per hour, which was lower than the normal rate. She had managed to extract concession for us using the influence of her uncle who happened to be one of the trustees of the school. Happy with her details, I emailed her back, requesting her to book the auditorium for one hour in the evenings starting at 9 between 15 September and 10 October.

Oksana suddenly appeared all dressed up, ready to go. There was still one hour left to turn midday, so I decided to seize the opportunity to have a quick chat with her.

"We have to do shopping at noon," I said.

"What shopping? Where?" she enquired.

"I'll tell you at the shopping centre. The one we normally go to. You are free after that."

"Yesterday you told me that I had to go somewhere. I don't remember some company."

"Web company. You don't need to go. It is too technical for you."

"Why didn't you tell me yesterday? I could have planned my day accordingly," she moaned.

"Sometimes things are planned on the fly."

"You always have your way."

"It was your way up until yesterday," I said forcefully while turning the notebook off, finishing with a warning. "Now onwards, it's going to be my way or the highway."

"You want me to leave?" she asked furiously.

"No."

"What does highway then mean?"

"No highway if you go my way."

"On one condition."

"What condition?" I asked, worried.

"For dance and choreography, you will follow my instructions."

"Agreed," I said, relieved. I realised that her hairstyle didn't look right for the Indian costume. "Your hairstyle is not good for the pictures you are going to take."

"What do you want me to do?"

"Simple. Parted from the centre and twisted waves on the sides. Can you do that?"

"I can do anything with my hair," she replied, delighted, and asked, "It will take me 15 minutes. Can you wait?"

I nodded, and she went away for her new hairdo. I went to my room to get ready and within ten minutes was back on the couch. I picked a magazine to kill my time while waiting for her. There was nothing interesting, so I tossed it back on the table. I stretched my arms and then closed my eyes for a brief nap. I couldn't sleep. I checked the time and realised that 15 minutes had passed, but there was no trace of her. I thought she must be checking and rechecking her new hairdo until she was fully satisfied. I remembered how Mum would adjust and then readjust her sari or bindi many times whenever she had to go out. Finally, Oksana appeared after 25 minutes, but her new hairdo was exactly the way I wanted.

"Jai, how do I look?" she asked, expecting a praise.

"Did you look into the mirror?" I asked seriously.

"Yes. Why?"

"That's how you look," I replied, which didn't please her much.

I had already moved to the door ready to go, leaving her with no choice but to follow me. We reached the centre in ten minutes. The Indian costume shop had a lot of varieties. Oksana had never visited any Indian costume shop, so I decided to pick one for her. After sifting through various designs and colours, my eyes got fixated on one particular costume. It was a red-coloured combination of blouse and *ghagra* with a border made of golden tape. I chose the costume deliberately because it would expose her midriff to increase the attention of the viewers visiting our website. I asked her to try the costume. She went to the fitting room, came out soon, and the costume looked fabulous on her. I paid for the costume and then went to a shop selling fake jewellery. We both selected silver-coloured necklace, earrings, a nose stud, two bangles and a hair ornament that had a pin, and a maple-shaped thing that would sit right in the middle of her forehead. We finished our shopping, costing me Rs4,000.

Next, we headed to a studio to take her pictures by a professional photographer. Upon reaching the studio, Oksana changed into the costume and wore fake jewellery. When she came back, I asked her to stand in the centre with her left foot bent behind her right foot, hands curled up in a lotus shape, and to bring a broad smile on her face. I advised her to hold the same pose for four different pictures. I then directed the photographer to take the first picture covering her full body, i.e. head to toe, the second one a bit closer from her lower ab to head, third one closer from her breast to head, and finally close up of her neck and head.

Once the pictures were taken, we both felt pleased with the outcome. She looked stunning in her pictures, and her smile was worth a million dollars. The photographer also had done a good job showing full professionalism visible from Oksana's pictures. I paid the photographer Rs2,000 and then left the centre. I headed towards the metro station whereas Oksana chose to head back home.

It took me about an hour to reach and locate the office of the web development company. The office of the company was in an old colonial building. I walked up via old-style wooden stairs, which still looked solid despite, probably, being more than a hundred years old. I entered through a large door into a small-sized office with five to six staff who were all busy with their heads down. I went to a table where a woman was working and told her about my appointment with Jignesh Patel. She didn't say anything but pointed me to a corner table where a man was sitting with his face down, reading something. I walked to the person who looked up and then smiled. His face was big, a small chin and bald in the middle, which he had covered with hair bringing from one side over his head to the other side. I found his hairstyle very amusing. I suppressed my laugh at the thought that on a windy day he might be having a field day trying to maintain his hairstyle. He must have been in his 50s. He greeted me with a soft voice and told me that he had been waiting for me.

After some personal talk, I started to explain my website requirements. Patel asked me whether I had the domain name registered. I shook my head. He suggested registering the domain name first. He informed that the domain registration would cost Rs999 per year. I agreed and gave him my company's domain name. He did a quick search and after few moments nodded, indicating that the name was available. I nodded back, and he started to register the domain name. About ten minutes later, the domain name was registered. He gave me all the necessary access details.

I then started to explain my requirements. I told him that I needed a very simple website consisting of only five to six pages, a slideshow in the middle, company name in the bottom, and finally a link to the social media applications appearing top right on the homepage. We needed a logo, so we decided to design a black silhouette image of a man and a woman in a dancing pose. I also told him that the website should work across all types of browsers and be accessible from any device. He informed me that all websites these days are developed based on responsive web design, enabling users to access from any device. I told him that I also needed hosting service for my website on his company's server. That was the end of my requirements.

Patel suggested me to opt for the search engine optimisation (SEO), a process that would affect the visibility of my website in a search engine's unpaid results. I knew what he was talking about. Basically, it would have ranked my website higher on the search engine's result page. But the yearly cost associated with the optimisation didn't convince me, so I declined, saying that I would rather rely on organic growth. Still he kept on insisting on the benefits of SEO like a good salesman would often do but failed to convince me.

He excused himself for ten minutes to work out the total cost involved and then got busy jotting something down. While he was busy, I started to look around his office. There were only six people including him. *Where was his development team?* I thought. I needed to ask him.

He got back to me with his cost. He told me that the total cost would come around Rs42,999, which included the website, the back-end panel, the domain registration, and the hosting service fee. I was happy with the cost, so I paid him in full. We then discussed the process involved from page design to go live. I enquired about his development team. He replied that he had a virtual team working for him in various cities across India. Fully satisfied with my discussion, I left his office.

I scaled down the wooden stairs, came out of the building and then stood at the edge of the pavement, thinking. I thought, how many websites had I developed during my engineering days? It is so easy these days. Just download the templates, and within hours, the website would be up and running. But the professionals do a better job; moreover, I didn't have time for that. My core objective was to functionalise my dance group. My engineering degree was useless for that. I checked the time and realised that I had been sitting in Patel's office for more than two hours. I looked around. There were colonial structures all around. There was the BMC building, Flora Fountain now called Hutatma Chowk, and down that way was the famous Victoria Terminus station now renamed as Chhatrapati Shivaji Terminus. Change is the only constant, I sighed. I decided to board the train for my back journey to home.

By the time I reached home, it was already 7. I quickly changed and then made a call to Delhi. After dinner, I sat down to calculate the money I had spent today: Rs4,000 for costume and fake jewellery, Rs 2,000 for pictures, and Rs 43,000 for the website so all up Rs49,000. I still needed to pay for song recording, auditorium, and female singer. My wallet was becoming lighter every day.

It was the time to talk to Oksana. She came out, took a chair across me, and then raised her eyebrows as if asking, "What do you want from me?" She was looking very attractive in that pose, but I was in no mood to fall into her trap.

"I am going to be busy for a couple of weeks," I said. "You know, there is this composition, recording, and website etc."

She didn't say anything but shrugged her shoulders as if saying, "Nothing to do with me."

"You can take some time off until—"

"You're throwing me out, aren't you?" she interrupted.

"No. Meet your friends."

"Can't I do something else?"

"Then go and have a look at the school auditorium."

"Which auditorium?"

"I've booked a school auditorium for our dance practice."

"Where is it?"

"Very close. I've booked between 9 and 10 in the evening."

"What dates?"

"15 September to 10 October," I told. "Go and have a look."

"I can't do that," she said while scratching the surface of the table. "I don't know how to talk to Indians."

I looked at her surprised because I didn't like what she said. I thought she was trying to avoid going to the school because she didn't like Indians. But I was an Indian; and she had no problem with Dolce, Amardeep, and others.

"Who are you talking to now?" I asked with a raised voice.

"Who else should I talk when I am living here?" she replied plainly. "I also like talking to Dolce and others because you all have treated me well."

I mellowed down and became a bit emotional. I thought she might have come across bad Indians who would have looked down upon her because she was a dancer, a foreigner, and a beautiful woman who could easily be trapped. She had a point. I felt ashamed.

"I understand. We both will go together with Dolce," I said softly and stressed, "But we need you in our group."

"I've done the grocery shopping," she said innocently like a kid.

"When did you go?"

"This morning."

"But we came out together."

"Is it hard to go back?" she shot back.

"No. How much did you spend?"

"You don't have to pay for the home expenses anymore."

"Why?"

"It is my choice," she replied in the most affectionate manner as if we were in some kind of relationship.

I refused by saying that I had enough money to look after myself. She relented after a lot of persuasion. We remained silent for a while, looking at each other in admiration. My respect for her grew for showing the caring side of her personality.

"Why did you take my pictures like that?" she asked.

"Oh yes!" I explained. "They were deliberately taken that way. On the slideshow, we will organise the pictures in a particular order."

"Which order?"

"First full body, then second, third, and finally the close-up."

"What will happen with that?"

"Viewers can feel that you are coming closer and closer to them every time a picture changes on the slideshow to create some kind of illusion."

"You are using me," she said, pretending to complain.

"Who wanted 5 per cent?"

"You are bad."

"There are no free lunches. Wait."

I recalled having promised Jignesh Patel to send him the pictures. I went to my room to get my notebook. I came back, cropped Oksana's last picture into passport size, and then saved it as a separate file. I zipped all her pictures and other passport-sized pictures into one file and then emailed to Jignesh.

"Sorry," I apologised for keeping her waiting. "I was emailing your pictures."

"Who did you email to?"

"Hrithik Roshan."

"Really? Why?" she asked, surprised, taking me seriously.

"He is single now. He may like your picture and then decide to marry you."

"Very funny. I am going now," she said while getting up.

I followed her soon to my room for a goodnight's sleep, satisfied with my today's efforts.

CHAPTER 15

After reaching the Churchgate apartment, I found Dolce on the drum, Sachin on the tabla, Amardeep on the guitar, and Neel on the Harmonium. There was no flute involved, so Ajay was just hanging around. I noticed that they had progressed a lot with their practice to create a new track. Dolce wasn't wrong when she told me that she had won many music competitions for her house in her school days. They assured me that within next four to five days, new music should be ready for recording. But first, we needed to practise the song. Where was the female singer? After few minutes of wait, they stopped for a break.

"How did you like?" Dolce asked.

"Great," I replied. "What is involved in the process?"

"The studio will do everything."

"But we should have some idea."

"I had got a rough idea," she spoke at length. "First, we need to create a track, record the song or voice over the selected audio track, edit, mix, and finally master."

I was fairly impressed with her explanation, proving her know-how about the subject.

"How long is your composition?" I enquired.

"Four minutes and 28 seconds," Amardeep replied.

"Jai, you need to practise a lot before recording," Dolce advised.

"Neel, where are the costs and the female singer?" I asked, concerned.

"Recoding would cost Rs2,700 per hour in Mumbai," Neel replied. "But if you go to Pune, it is just Rs1,200."

"Forget it. We can't go to Pune for just one song. It makes no sense. Where is the singer?"

"I can call her here if you like."

"How much would she charge?"

"I don't know. Do you want me to call her?"

"Call her now. Can she come today?" I said with a sense of urgency.

"I've to call her to find out."

"Do that."

Neel called the singer. He spoke to her for about ten minutes and then announced that Mini was coming at 4. The coffee break was not possible today. I turned to Amardeep.

"No coffee break today. At least, Neel and I can't go."

"We can," Amardeep said, shrugging his shoulders.

Dolce wasn't in the hall while I was talking to Amardeep, probably gone for a bathroom break. She came back rubbing her hands with her kerchief. Seeing her back, I thought, *Would she go for a coffee break today?* That was the least of my concern as I needed to talk to her about something more important.

"Did you book the auditorium?" I asked.

"Yes," she replied. "You have to pay in advance on a weekly basis."

"I'll pay full. Will I get a refund if we don't use it?"

"I'll have to check. Why do you want to pay everything in advance?"

"I don't have time to remember things. I want to start every new day with new things."

"That is strange," she said. "You can set reminders in your mobile."

"I'll do next time. How do I pay?"

"I'll email you the details. Put my name somewhere in the description."

"Thank you, Dolce," I said, pleased.

It had turned 4, so Amardeep and others left for the coffee break. Dolce, as expected, chose to stay back for the reason I knew very well. In a way, it was good that she had stayed back because it would be easier for me to talk to a girl in the presence of another girl.

It was 30 minutes over, but there was no news of Mini. I looked at Neel who tried to reach for his mobile when someone opened the door from the outside. Amardeep, Sachin, Ajay, and a girl entered the hall. There was Mini. She waved to Neel and introduced herself to Dolce and me. She was short around five feet, slim, dark skinned, and had curly hair. She must have been in her early 20s and wore jeans, loose shirt, and flat shoes. She spoke very fast but in a clear voice, never fumbling or missing a word.

She told us that few years back, she had participated in one of the singing reality shows but got eliminated in the fifth round. She grumbled that she was unfairly eliminated because judges were biased. She was struggling to get a foothold because every year new people were entering the industry. Moreover, she didn't have any good contacts, which was making it all too difficult for her.

I thought, with around over six hundred channels in India, every channel competed for space, creating own reality shows. The big channels acquire international formats and telecast them as Indian versions. Even the winners of these shows get two-minute fame and then quickly fade away from the scene. Every day thousands of artists of all forms land in Mumbai, hoping to make it big. Very few succeed. It was a sad reality.

After listening to her story, I thought of coming to the point.

"We just have a song for you, which you have to sing with me. It is a duet."

"How much will you pay me?" she asked, coming directly to the point.

"I want to explain to you what is involved," I said. "You have to be here for two weeks for the practice. Then for the recording at a studio."

"Two weeks . . . umm . . . every day . . ." she mumbled, hesitating and pausing in between.

"I'll charge separate for practice and recording," she said, thoughtfully completing her sentence.

"Why separate?"

"In case you don't record, then I should get paid for practice. Will I get credit for the song?"

"Yes," I said. "But we own the song."

"Will I get a copy?"

"Yes. But you can't upload into any social medium."

"What is a social medium?"

"Gosh," Dolce intercepted, surprised at Mini's lack of knowledge about social media, and explained, "Jai is talking about YouTube, Facebook etc."

"Oh! How much will you pay me?" Mini asked.

"How much do you want?" I asked.

"Ten thousand for practice and Rs3,000 for recording."

"First, prove your skills. You have to sing something."

"Can I sing a song of my choice?"

"But you have to sing another song of our choice."

She nodded and asked, "Should I start?"

I nodded. She chose a popular Bollywood solo sung by a female singer and started to prepare herself for singing. She requested for a glass of water, which she drank slowly in two to three gulps; closed her eyes; cleared her throat; and then started to sing. She started with a low pitch, then went to high pitch, bringing variations in between wherever and whenever required. There were times when the song needed her to complete two to three lines in one breath. She had an exemplary voice. I wondered why she didn't get noticed. Some people have bad luck. Her day would come. I hoped and prayed for her success.

She finished her song in style and waited for our response. I then asked her to sing the song that was written by Ajay. She sang the female portion of the song very well. Being a new song, she needed a bit of practice, but that was true for me also. I couldn't find any fault in her singing, but I decided to continue interviewing her.

"You have to be here every weekday between 2 and 6," I said and cautioned, "Two means 2, not like today."

"Should I start on Monday?"

"Neel will let you know in the evening."

"Do you have more people to interview?" she asked anxiously. "I can charge Rs8,000 for practice and Rs2,000 for recording."

"That is fine, but Neel will let you in the evening."

"Can I leave now?"

"Yes."

She left, and then I turned to the team. We all agreed that she had a beautiful voice so should be taken.

"Neel, call her tonight," I said. "We will pay her Rs10,000 for practice and Rs5,000 for recording."

"Are you mad?" Dolce yelled. "She asked for Rs8,000 and Rs2,000. Just pay her that."

"There are many reasons."

"What reasons?"

"One, never exploit anyone. Two, respect talent and pay accordingly. Three, if we pay her more than her expectations, she'll give her best, and last, I have already budgeted this amount so I am not losing anything."

"Where did you learn these things from?" Dolce asked, amazed.

"My father."

"I wish I could ever get more than my talent."

"You are also very talented," I commented.

Amardeep laughed at my comment. They had a very strange love-hate type of relationship. Could that have been the Gujarati and the Punjabi factor? The rivalry between these two communities is well known. Both the communities are very enterprising, prosperous, hardworking, and resilient. They can start anything with a cent and turn it into a million dollars within no time. Failure doesn't deter them. They fall, get up, walk, and then start running again. No wonder why both the states have a higher income than the national average.

Their rivalry was not going to end soon as Amardeep made the first move.

"You know, Jai, Gujjus pronounce *hall* as *hole* and *Coke* as *cock*," Amardeep joked, giggling.

"It was from some movie. I don't remember which one," Dolce wasn't going to allow Amardeep dominate her, so she retorted back, "My aunt lives in South Hall, London. She once told me that Punjjus pronounce it as *Suthal*."

"Suthal . . . what Suthal? There is no punch in it," Amardeep made fun of her.

Dolce wasn't the type to give up easily. She was a little dynamite. With her hands, she gestured him to calm down and told him that the worst was yet to come.

"What worst is coming?" Amar made fun yet again.

"I've not finished yet."

"Bakko [Spit it out]."

"A Punjabi in *Suthal* went to attend a wedding in a *hole* with a large *cock* in his hand," Dolce said, laughing loudly and ending with a final blow. "Did you feel the punch now?"

This was enough to break the ice. Everybody started to laugh. Dolce, mindful of the meaning of *cock* when used as a slang, blushed but kept laughing, covering her face with hands. The rivalry was over. I, myself a Punjabi, thought that she had mixed the three mispronounced words so intelligently to create a funny joke. After a while, when everyone had recovered from the joke, she resumed where I had left earlier.

"You were talking about my talent. What talent do I've?" Dolce asked, curious.

"You showed your talent in the form of that joke. Actually, I wanted to say that you're a good company."

"That is all you want to give me?"

"Dolce, I promise you to give something bigger. It may not be money, but it will make you a better person."

"What is that?"

"Wait for the right time. Should we wrap up?"

All agreed.

"Neel, contact Mini. Dolce, send me the email," I said, issuing last-minute instructions before leaving.

Later that night, I received a call from Neel who told me that everything was sorted out with Mini. She was very happy with the payment. Dolce also emailed about the payment details. I transferred Rs10,000 for 20 days into the school account.

Before going to bed, I once again assured Oksana that she didn't have to worry about bearing the home expenses alone. She appreciated my gesture. As a gratitude, she said that she wanted to return an immediate favour by reminding me of something. I asked her what that something was. She reminded me that it was Friday today. Did I remember what happened last Friday? I sat motionless, staring at her, nostrils slightly blown up and breathing slowly. She started to walk towards her room, giggling. I followed her. She stopped at her room door and then stuck her tongue out at me. I gave her a nasty glare and then went into my room, slamming the door behind. I just wanted to strangle her because I knew that it would be hard to sleep now.

Two days later, on 1 September, I sat down to prepare a to-do list for the next two weeks. My hands were full. I had to create social media accounts, test the website, create content for the website, practise the song with Mini, and record the song. I dropped the idea of an emailer system as it was time-consuming to prepare a large email list.

I thought, with Oksana out of sight for a while, I could concentrate on achieving my target without much hassle. Oksana—what did she say last Friday? She wanted to return my favour by reminding me about the Friday night a week before. I started to think about last Friday night. I couldn't sleep up until early morning. I kept on thinking about her body, breasts, lips, and that intoxicating fragrance. I desired her to be with me so that I could touch her, feel her, and make love to her.

I had to get up twice. First time at midnight. I could hear music and saw the light in her room on. I stood outside her room, hoping that she would open the door to let me in by her side. It didn't happen. I couldn't muster enough courage to open the door. Had I opened the door, I would have breached the trust. The trust that brought her here, the trust that was keeping her here, and the trust that made her feel secure.

Instead, I went to the hall and then sat on the couch for some time. I thought of calling Mum because I was feeling lonely. But I didn't because I thought Mum would be frightened to receive a call at that time. I thought about Dolce, Amardeep, and others. They thought I was a mature person and had started to look up to me. I wasn't sure, though.

The second time, I got up at around 2.15 in the morning. There was no music and no light in her room that time. She had gone to sleep, unmindful of my condition and dilemma I was facing. I immediately went back to my room. I thought that there was one definite way to release the tension. I knew that. I had tried that in the past. Everybody does. But I didn't want to try that method on that night. I decided to test my tolerance to control the urge. If I succeeded, I would be fine in the future. But how could I control? I recalled two incidents where people had tried.

Few months back, I had watched a portion of a Japanese movie. A man entered a room in the Japanese attire and then sat on the floor like Japanese do, on his knees. He waited for few moments. Then an extremely beautiful young girl, around 18, entered the room. She was naked—absolutely naked. She sat exactly opposite the man few metres away, exposing her very thing. The man kept on looking at the girl, trying to hold his sexual urges. The girl remained calm, showed no emotions, and kept looking at the man. After some time, he squeezed his lips, and his body started to shake. Few moments later, he exploded within and died.

Gandhi is also believed to have experimented to test his sexual desire. He had asked a young girl to lie down by his bedside naked. After looking at her for some time, he had turned to the other side; and then whole night, he remained like that, never looking back at her. Gandhi had succeeded and didn't die.

But what the Japanese man was doing was acting, not a real thing. Gandhi was Gandhi. The world called him Mahatma. I was neither Gandhi nor an actor. But I had one advantage over them. They both were in the company of a naked girl, but I was alone, so I could succeed. I had to divert my attention and keep my brain busy. I started reverse countdown by 3 starting at 100: 100, 97, 94, 91, 88. Soon I fell asleep.

Last Friday was another first for him like the Friday one before. Every day I was learning something new. I was happy that I had handled situations well. I was also happy that Oksana had changed. She was talking, joking, and behaving normally like two friends sharing the apartment, occasionally driving me mad like the last Friday night.

CHAPTER 16

Thursday, 4 September 2014. Oksana, Dolce, and I were visiting the school to inspect its auditorium for my dance lessons. Dolce was expected to arrive soon.

Earlier on Monday, I started practising the song with Mini. After a number of practice sessions and improvements, we finally got the song right in just three days. Mini turned out to a good singing partner. She not only sang her portion well but also gave me a number of suggestions that improved the overall quality of the song. During the practice, we also finalised the key recording issues, such as initial music, time to sing, time to pause, time to sing together, and the end music. The group had done an excellent job practising hard to create a nice new piece of music. We were almost ready to take the composition to the studio for recording. We were extremely happy and satisfied with our efforts, so we decided to book a studio. Neel spoke to a studio who assured that five hours were sufficient enough to record one song. I paid the studio Rs13,500 and booked the date for 10 September.

Meanwhile, Jignesh Patel had sent me the design pages of the website. After a quick look, I had advised few changes to the logo and the homepage; otherwise, everything looked fine. So I approved the design. He assured me that the development work would start soon to enable me to test the website from mid next week. I had also created social media accounts for the company. I made Dolce responsible for spreading the word in social media in order to increase the followership and the subscription base. Soon the numbers started to increase but only in hundreds, which was actually low. I hoped that within weeks, hundreds would become thousands and eventually millions etc. Anything above 100,000 was a good number, though.

The bell rang. I answered the door. Like a breath of fresh air, Dolce came in smiling. She straight went to Oksana's room. I wondered what they did, but they came out soon; so we left the apartment, taking us little over ten minutes to reach the school. Dolce took us to the room of the principal, whom she knew very well. We were greeted with a cup of tea. The principal then tried to reach to his buzzer apparently to call an assistant to take us to the auditorium. But Dolce stopped him, telling him that she knew the way and the people who could show us the place. We thanked the principal and walked to the school office.

A man greeted Dolce, picked a key from the holder, and then escorted us to the auditorium. It was a five minutes' walk. He opened the central door of the auditorium and let us in. I had a cursory look around and guessed that it had a seating capacity of 500 people. The stage was medium size but big enough for our practice. The man and I took seats while Dolce and Oksana went up the stage, talking and giggling, normally expected from girls. They went around from one end to another, one corner to another, tapping the floor, and then asked the man to turn the stage lights on, which he did.

A large light placed on the left side had gone off. They came down the stage and asked the man whether the light could be fixed. I argued that we could do without the light, but Oksana wouldn't agree. She counterargued that she wasn't worried about herself but was thinking of me. She wanted me to have a real stage feel. I wanted to thank her for thinking about me but kept quiet, thinking about her favour, which she had returned to me on last Friday. She had actually ruined my Friday night's sleep. Eventually, the man promised them to have the light fixed before our first lesson started.

We left the school and then headed to the shopping centre for a nice cup of coffee. Oksana and Dolce were talking to each other like college friends, overlooking the age gap that existed between the two. After finishing our coffee, Dolce suggested having a day off tomorrow from work. She said we could instead have a group lunch paid by me to which I agreed. Oksana said that she's unable to join us because I didn't want her until the start of rehearsals. Dolce looked at me angrily, but I told her that was a lie, and she could join us anytime she wanted. Dolce convinced her, and she agreed, looking at me with those big, blue, and bright eyes as if seeking my permission. By then, I was fully convinced that she was a drama queen of high calibre. I asked Dolce to get in touch with others and also inform Mini not to show up tomorrow. We soon left the centre. On the way back, I enquired about Oksana's drama. She said, giggling, that she was just following my instructions, inviting another glare from me. Our rest of the day passed without talking to each other. I hadn't completely forgiven her for her last Friday's return favour and now the lie she had told Dolce earlier that day.

Next morning we left for the Gaylord's at 11. Oksana, as usual, was looking fabulous. For a change, she wore flat shoes. That was the first time I had seen her going out without high heels. The journey to Gaylord's was smooth. We reached there ten minutes early. Gaylord's was Amardeep's favourite. He had insisted he would join us only if we agreed to go to Gaylord's. We were the first to arrive, so we waited outside. Soon we spotted Dolce who was looking very beautiful in her Indian kurta and pyjama and high-heeled black sandals. Both women kissed and hugged, admiring each other's dresses. We went inside, settled on a table, and waited for others to arrive. By 1 our group was full. Sachin, Neel, and Ajay, as usual, didn't matter much. They never talked much most of time, looking at one another's faces, occasionally expressing their opinion. But Amardeep and Dolce were different breeds.

"Oksana is looking beautiful today, isn't she, Amar?" Dolce commented.

"I like her dress sense," he complimented. "She always picks the best for the occasion."

Oksana smiled and acknowledged the compliment with a bow, her left hand on her chest. I knew how happy she must have been feeling inside. All women like to be admired. I decided to change the topic.

"Next week this time we should have finished recording," I said.

"Jai, no. I told you we have a day off today," Dolce chastised.

"What do you want to discuss then?"

"Anything but work."

I nodded and decided to change the topic once again.

"Why are you all going to the US? Why not somewhere else?"

"Like?"

"Like England, Canada, Australia, or New Zealand."

"We can go anywhere."

"Then why not to Germany or France?"

"Language problem. We like English-speaking countries."

"Because Indians can understand them." Amardeep came up with a strange logic.

"Amar, you always talk nonsense," Dolce ridiculed him. "It is not Indians only. They also have to understand us."

"What is the reason then?" he retorted.

"We are all colonial cousins."

"Matlab [Meaning]?" he asked, puzzled.

"Leave it. It is not your cup of tea," she dismissed him. Turning to me, she commented, which actually was directed at Amardeep, "You know, Jai, my mother says you should have four almonds with a glass of milk every night to sharpen your brain."

I laughed gently, but Amardeep didn't get the joke; otherwise, a mini war between him and Dolce wasn't far off. Fearing that Amardeep might get the joke, I decided to change the topic a third time in the space of ten minutes.

"Should we order? Dolce and Oksana will decide."

I turned to Oksana when I noticed that she was not paying any attention to our conversation. She had a glass in her left hand, which she was gazing into, and was busy chewing something like a cow. It was her new pose, which I hadn't seen before. I laughed, finding her new pose amusing. *What should I call her?* I thought. Probably holy-cow Oksana. In a way, it was good she wasn't participating in the discussion; otherwise, she would have been chewing my brain.

"Oksana, what should we order?" Dolce asked, breaking her concentration as well as that of mine.

"What do you all want?" she asked.

"You both decide," Sachin suggested, stepping in for the first and right time.

They both started to browse through the menu with their heads close to each other. They moved their fingers from top to bottom, turned the pages—this, not this, that, not that—and finally were happy with their selection.

"We are having Indian today," Oksana said.

"Kebab and samosa to start with. Butter chicken, aloo matar, dhal, naan, rice in the main course, and ice cream in the end," Dolce read the order, occasionally glancing through the menu.

"Mere ko meetha chahiye. Main ice cream nahi loonga. [I want something sweet. I won't have ice cream.]," Amardeep said, outrightly rejecting Dolce's choice of dessert.

"Tabi to main sonchu to ita meetha kiyun bolta hai [That is the reason I think you talk so sweetly]," Dolce commented, pulling his leg.

"Sachin, Dekh subah se bol rahi. Main kucch nahi keh raha hoon [Sachin, see, she's been rubbishing since morning. I am not saying anything.]," Amardeep complained.

"What do you want?" Sachin asked calmly.

"Rasgulla, and I want four of them."

"Dolce, note that. Otherwise, we are fine. Order now," Sachin said firmly.

I laughed at the war of words that had taken place between Dolce and Amardeep. Dolce placed the order, instructing to get the entrée first. It would take ten minutes, she was told.

"Oksana, tell us something about Ukraine," Amardeep resumed the discussion with a new topic.

I really liked the topic Amardeep had picked. It would give Oksana a chance to involve herself in the discussion.

"It is a very beautiful, green, and fertile country," she spoke. "It's the second largest country in Europe. Kiev is the largest city and the capital of Ukraine."

"Are you from Kiev?" Dolce interrupted.

"No," Oksana replied while taking a deep breath. "I am from Donetsk in Eastern Ukraine. Donetsk is one of the major sites where fighting has escalated since April 2014."

She paused; took a deep breath again, which touched our hearts; and resumed, "The whole of Ukraine was self-sufficient in agriculture. We had a large industrial base during the Soviet time. Life was good then."

"What happened then?" Dolce asked in a pensive mood.

"There is a war with Russia. They took Crimea from us."

"Why?"

"Because Crimea has large Russian population, so they think they should have it. But Crimea is ours."

"What have your governments been doing since the fall of Soviet Union?"

"They are all corrupt. They rig elections. Some are pro-America, some pro-Russia."

"So there is some kind of proxy war going between Russia and America," I commented.

"Yes. But the people suffer. I don't know for how long."

"Simple. As long as these two countries agree. You need a government that is acceptable to both. Is that hard?"

"I don't know," she replied. "We used to produce a lot of wheat and export to many countries. My parents told me that the Soviet days were happy days. These days, women have to look for work outside. Old Americans come to take young women as their brides."

She took a deep sigh. I noticed her eyes had misted over with grief. She grabbed a tissue, blew her nose, and then stopped. Everybody was silent, didn't know what to say; and then Dolce, as usual, said something lovely, "O, Oksi, you can stay in India as long as you like. We will never ditch you," Dolce concluded while hugging her. "What do you all say?"

We all nodded.

"Do you get Bollywood movies in Ukraine?" Dolce asked.

"Not sure. I didn't know much about Bollywood until I arrived in India," Oksana replied. "But they show dubbed movies and songs on TV."

"Do you know any movies or song?"

"Not movie but one song is very popular everywhere in Russia, Ukraine, and other ex-Soviet countries."

"Which one?"

"'Jimmy Jimmy Aaja Aaja.'"

"Which one?" Dolce asked, surprised as if she never heard of it.

"You guys don't know this song. It's old from the 80s."

"Really? Let me check."

Nobody had heard of that song. Dolce quickly checked on her mobile and informed that it was from some old movie called *Disco Dancer* released in 1982. We were all 90s kids who had seen different India, different movies, different stars, and heard different songs. The year 1982 was very ancient to all of us. Meanwhile, the main course arrived, so we started filling our plates.

"Today is 5 September. Few more weeks to go," Dolce said out of the blue.

"In what?" Neel asked.

"Modi's US visit," she replied calmly.

"Oh no!" Amardeep jumped. "Why are you getting so mad about it?"

"Mad? What do you mean?" she yelled.

"Is he going to get a gift for you?"

"I can expect this nonsense from you."

"Nonsense? I don't care where he goes."

"Why? Isn't he your prime minister?"

"Yes, but he has to first fulfil the demand of Sikhs."

"What demand?"

"Punishing the culprits of 1984 anti-Sikh riots."

"That was Congress Party."

"That is why. There is no hope from that party. They themselves were involved," Amardeep thundered in anger, red-faced.

I thought what topic had Amardeep raised. We were too young to discuss such a painful subject. We should move on and contribute something positive in the emerging India. I didn't want any discord in the group. I had always avoided the topic because it was so painful for me. After all, Mum was a Sikh. She herself had lost a number of her relatives. I was never told anything about it, but later I read myself. The whole tragedy again flashed in front of my eyes: Indira Gandhi, terrorism in the Punjab, Bhindranwale, Operation Blue Star, assassination of Indira Gandhi, Sikh guards, and the Sikh massacre. I needed a break; so I got up, walked to the restaurant toilet, locked myself in, stood in front of the mirror, and then went into a deep thought.

During the height of terrorism in the Punjab, Indira Gandhi launched an army action dubbed as the Operation Blue Star. The idea was to flush out the terrorists from the Golden Temple who were holed inside led by dreaded Jarnail Singh Bhindranwale. The holiest Sikh shrine came under attack for days, causing considerable damage to the structure. Sikhs all over the world protested. The building was eventually cleared of terrorists, but Sikhs never forgave her.

She was eventually assassinated by her Sikh guards in 1984. Her assassination triggered a backlash against the Sikhs. Hindus in Northern India went berserk and started killing Sikhs in the most brutal manner. The police looked the other way because some leaders from her own political party, Congress, were involved in the massacre. When the dust settled, some 4,000 Sikhs had lost their lives. A number of enquiries were conducted; many people were arrested and eventually sentenced. But few local leaders from the Congress Party directly involved were found not to be guilty. Sikhs have since demanded justice and arrest of those culprits, but nothing has happened so far.

For me, it had always been a dilemma. Being half Hindu and half Sikh, I didn't know how to look at it. I was a product of the perpetrator and the victim. But my parents loved each other. Papa was a gem who had never given a chance to Mum to complain about anything. Mum never accepted Bhindranwale as Sikh. She always thought that he was a terrorist. Papa was always supportive of Sikh demand, but Mum had moved on. So had I.

I had been thinking for long, so I decided to go back. When I returned, everything seemed to be normal. The dessert had been served. Dolce and Amardeep were doing what they did the best, i.e. pulling each other's leg. Oksana was on her mobile, tapping and poking. The other three were looking at one another without any real purpose. I thought those three could survive anywhere even in an isolated island. Dolce spotted me and started first as usual.

"Jai, where were you? I thought you had left."

"Where?" I asked, confused.

"Left for home. Who would have paid the bill?"

"You think I can do that?"

"I was just joking. Now have the ice cream. Otherwise, Amar will lunge on it."

"Why? He said he wanted something sweet."

"He had them all. All four. Didn't share with anyone."

"Did you share your ice cream with him?"

"He doesn't like ice cream."

"How do you?"

"We all ordered ice cream," Dolce quipped. "He was the only one who didn't."

I looked at Amardeep who put his index finger on his temple and then started to move it in a semi-circular motion, a gesture to denote "Don't worry about her. She is mad." Their rivalry relieved me a bit. I didn't ask them about the conversation we were having before I left. There was no reason to ask, so I started to enjoy my ice cream. It was a good suggestion by Dolce to take a day off for the team bonding.

Back at home, I started to think about Amardeep's controversial topic, which he had raised earlier in the day. I became very disturbed at the thought, *Was India really bad for minorities?* No. Not really. After all, Dr Manmohan Singh was the prime minister for ten years. Singh, himself a Sikh, was the first prime minister from a minority community. He became PM in 2004 much before Barack Obama became the first black president of the USA. Besides Singh, there have been several presidents, vice presidents, army chiefs, chief justices, chief election commissioners, and key ministers from the Muslim, the Christian, the Parsi, and the Sikh communities.

With the satisfaction that India was not dead but well and alive, always providing equal opportunity to all its citizens, I retired to bed for a goodnight's sleep.

CHAPTER 17

Finally, the day of recording had arrived. We had booked our recording hours between 11 and 5. The group had to record the audio tracking first. I decided to join them at 12.30 to record the song over the selected audio tracks. Oksana had decided to take that whole week off. Before leaving for the studio, I called Jignesh Patel who assured me that the development work would be completed by afternoon. He promised to email me the test server details. I decided to test the website in the night-time, hoping that the website might be up and running by Friday.

I left for the studio at 11.30 while Oksana was still in her room. I boarded the train that took me 40 minutes to reach. I got off the train and walked out of the station to be greeted by a crowded street where traffic was chaotic. I didn't know the exact location of the studio, so I requested a passer-by to tell me the way to the studio. He said he didn't know. I crossed the road and enquired at a shop selling sweets. He didn't know either. Frustrated, I called Dolce who told me that they had finished creating the track and were waiting for me. She gave me instructions and told me that it would take me further ten minutes from the point I currently was, not far from the station. I literally lumbered through noisy traffic and small lanes for the next 12 minutes, finally reaching the studio. The entrance to the studio was shocking. It was a very small door, which led to an office. The office was very dusty and disorderly. I was led to another door, which opened to the main studio. It looked anything but a studio. It actually was a big room—nothing more. They were all standing around a person who was sitting on his workstation. Sachin saw me first and waved to join them. I went to them and saw the man was checking something on the screen. I noticed that a pattern of bars was displayed on the screen.

"Tony is checking the tracking we recorded earlier," Sachin said.

Tony didn't look at me but kept his eyes fixed on the screen while stroking his lips with his left hand as if thinking of something important.

"How are things looking?" I asked Sachin.

"Don't know yet. He is checking."

"Where is Mini?"

"There in that room," Sachin replied, pointing to a room.

I went to the room. It was a small recording room that could barely fit two people. It had two mics. Mini greeted me with a smile. We talked for a while when I saw Sachin waving to draw my attention. They were calling me out to join them, which I did.

"This is good. I've checked individual instruments and melody etc," Tony said, feeling satisfied.

Sachin introduced me to Tony. We shook hands. I asked him about the pattern on the screen.

"Oh! This is your music. See these bars? They are individual instruments." Tony scrolled down and showed me the harmony.

"Why isn't there any sound?" I asked, concerned.

"Sorry, I've to detach the headphone from the computer," he replied while removing headphone.

He detached the cable, and the sound of the music filled the whole room with a blasting noise.

"When can we start recording?"

"Soon. I'll be back in five minutes," Tony replied.

He left the room, and we started to chat with one another. Tony came back and asked me to proceed to the recording room. Mini and I put the headphones on and waited for Tony's instructions. He waved, and I started first. We waited for some time, and then Mini sang her lines. There were retakes on some lines. It took us over an hour to finish the first round. We both came out and listened to our recording. There were problems at some places, which we had to re-record. Finally, the recording was over in about two hours. Tony said it would take him further two hours to finish the editing, mixing, mastering etc. We decided to come back after two hours. We all thanked Mini for her efforts, and she left.

We killed our next two hours sitting in an Irani café ordering *khari chai* (very strong tea), *bun maska* (bun and butter), *nankhatai* (sweet, crisp flaky Irani biscuits) and Dolce's favourite: heart-shaped large sweet biscuits. We chatted about cricket, Bollywood, politics, and Dolce's favourite topic Modi.

Two hours later, we picked our song in a CD. It had taken only four hours to complete the recording, but we didn't get any refund from Tony. Before leaving, I requested Dolce to come to my place tomorrow at 2 in the afternoon. She agreed. The Churchgate apartment was no longer required. I had to move the equipment back to my place and also help Amardeep to move the furniture back into the hall. Amardeep said we had until next year, so there was no immediate need to move anything now.

I reached home at five minutes to 7 totally flat out. At least, we had achieved our first milestone—that of song recording. After dinner, as I was about to clear the table, my mobile rang.

"Hello, Jai."

"Yes, Dolce?"

"I won't be able to come to your place tomorrow."

"Why?"

"I am going out with Sachin."

"But you have been meeting him daily."

"With the group."

"Oh! Like that."

"Yes. Like that."

"Can I ask you a question?"

"Which one?"

"You and Sachin are two different personalities. He talks less. You never stop."

"That how it should be. Men should talk less and always listen to women," she replied, giggling.

"You guys planning to marry?"

"Why are you asking?"

"Because I consider you as my best friend. I really like you and appreciate your help so far."

"Emotional blackmail," she said jokingly.

"Leave it. But I meant what I said," I replied, pretending to be upset.

"Don't be so serious, Jai. Yes, we will marry once we come back from the States."

"So your families approve?"

"Of course, Sachin is very good, but I am the best."

"I am sure you are."

"Jai, do you have a girlfriend?"

"I never had and don't have any," I replied, gently laughing.

"What about Oksana?"

"Who?" I asked, jumping as if I had touched a live wire. She had asked me an unexpected question, which I didn't know how to answer.

"Oksana."

Suddenly, I felt someone was standing behind me. I turned and saw an angry, flush-faced Oksana. I thought how timely her sudden appearance was. "Speaking of the devil, the devil is here." She pointed to the table, which was yet to be cleared. I gestured her to wait and then put Dolce on hold.

"I am talking to Dolce," I said, irritated.

"Why didn't you clear the table?" she fumed.

I got a strange thrill at the imagination of fumes emitting from her ears and nostrils.

"I was about to when she called," I replied, laughing, which irritated her.

"You could have asked her to call you back."

"No," I asserted. "That is not appropriate. I'll do it when I finish with her."

She looked at me for a while and then returned to her room without saying anything.

"Yes, Dolce, sorry. Where were we?"

"Jai, I forgot to tell you one thing."

"What?"

"The guys were asking what is there for them now," Dolce asked, which relieved me because she had forgotten about Oksana.

"Nothing for the time being. We need them when we get some work," I told. "Can you come to my place on Friday at 11?"

"Why so early?"

"We don't have time. I want you to explain the song to Oksana so that she could choreograph it properly."

"Explain? Properly?" she asked, confused.

"She needs to understand each word. It is mainly in Hindi."

"I now understand."

"Also, I'll show the website"

"Cool. I got to go now. Bye."

"See you on Friday."

I really liked Dolce. She was smart, intelligent, friendly, and ever ready to help. I took a deep breath, cleared the table, and then went to my room to fetch my notebook. On my way back, I knocked at Oksana's door. I sat down to check my emails. There was one from Jignesh Patel, which didn't please me. He had put the development work on hold because one of his production servers was down, which was severely impacting his customers. I needed to wait until Friday to start my website testing. Meanwhile, Oksana had washed the dishes. I saw her going back to her room when she suddenly turned.

"Do you like Dolce?" she fumed.

"Yes. As a friend," I replied casually.

"Just as a friend?"

"What do you mean?"

"If she was you best friend, then you could have requested her to call you back."

I chose to ignore her dumb statement, so I kept quiet. Realising that she wouldn't get anything back, she left the scene without saying anything further. At least, she didn't get hysterical this time. I thought that generally she was sharp and intelligent, but sometimes she wouldn't mind using the dead cells of her brain.

CHAPTER 18

Yesterday, I had managed to draw a marketing plan to contact TV stations, events management companies, hotels, and the government departments like Mumbai police that regularly hold their annual events. I decided to contact them once the website had gone public. I was hesitant to perform in private functions like birthdays, weddings, and anniversaries etc; so I decided to perform only in public functions. India is a country of festivals—every month there are two to three festivals—so it wouldn't be hard to find some work.

Someone rang the doorbell. It was Dolce arriving on the dot at 11. Oksana still hadn't shown up, so we sat on the couch and started to chat.

"How is Amar?" I asked casually.

"Must be fine. I don't know," she replied while shrugging her shoulders.

"You didn't meet him?"

"No, since the day we had lunch together."

"Do you think he is funny?"

"Funny? He is mad. You know what he said once?" she replied, laughing. She kept on laughing while holding her stomach with her hands.

"What?" I asked, bemused.

"Because South Indians are very intelligent, that is why all the IT companies are in the South Indian cities like Bangalore, Chennai, and Hyderabad."

"There is no doubt that India's real brain is in South India and West Bengal, but that is no reason to have companies there," I said, laughing.

"That is correct, but who can argue with him?"

"You can. I think he must have been joking."

"I know. He acts dumb, but he is very sharp. I've been knowing him since the first standard."

"So you like him?"

"Yes, he is my best friend and very helpful. I can call him anytime for help, and he'll never refuse."

"That is the way it should be between friends."

"You know, he is only 18, but he feels that he can take over his father's business and run it better," she said, laughing.

"What business?"

"They've a big construction company. They build, you know, these high-rise residential buildings."

"How is it so easy for him?" I asked, surprised.

"He has proven it."

"How? Where?"

"It is an interesting story," she said. "Last year in our school, we had this, you know, speech competition on a given topic. The topic was on modern living. It was kind of open speech where parents were also present."

"Yes?"

"The school principal picked the best five speakers. Amar wasn't among them. He went to the principal and argued that he also should be in the list. Anyway, the principal included him but on one condition that he would be the last speaker. He agreed."

"Why last?"

"The principal would have thought if people got bored with his speech, they could leave. At least, they would have heard the first five."

"Uh-huh."

"Each speaker was given ten minutes maximum," she continued. "On the day, everybody reported at 9, but Amar didn't turn up until 9.20. He looked relaxed whereas others looked very nervous. He told everybody that he hadn't done any preparations, which made others more nervous."

"Really?"

"Yes," she carried on. "The speech finally started at 9.30. Speaker after speaker started to speak about modern living like, you know, green, environment friendly, rainwater storage, less energy consumption etc."

She paused to catch a breath but resumed quickly, "Finally, his turn came. He had a notebook in his hands, which he connected to the projector first. He told the audience that now they knew what modern living was about, he would demonstrate."

"Wasn't he supposed to speak?"

"He did but in a different way. He brought up a PowerPoint slideshow. They were the slides of his father's company about the project they had recently completed but still selling. He told them the building was 'modern living' compliant. Twenty-four hours uninterrupted gas, electricity, rainwater harvesting, energy-saving globes, better waste management etc."

"Very interesting," I commented.

"Then he gave the tour of the apartments in . . . in . . . reality—what is that called?"

Dolce struggled to find the right term.

"Kind of virtual reality," I replied.

"That is the one. He asked people interested in buying the apartments to contact him after his presentation."

"Presentation. He was supposed to deliver a speech," I said, laughing.

"I know. He then folded his notebook. Everybody clapped except for the principal who was fuming."

"Did people see him after his presentation?"

"Not one," she said. "Many. He gave them information packs, his contact details etc."

"Did he win the competition?" I enquired.

"No. On the contrary, the principal rusticated him for one week. He told the principal that he didn't care."

"This is called horses for courses," I said instinctively.

"What?"

"Don't worry."

"I have to," Dolce said. "You meant something good about Amar, didn't you?"

"Yes," I replied and explained, "It means pick the right people for the right job. There was nothing funny about Amardeep. In fact, he showed his genius. His platform might not have been the right one, but he showed application whereas others just spoke. If one has natural ability to apply, why does one need to know theory? Do you agree with me?"

She nodded while taking a deep breath. I took her deep breath as her indigestion at the fact that Amardeep was being praised. I smiled but didn't say anything.

Oksana appeared from nowhere and started talking to Dolce, totally ignoring me. She then decided to take Dolce to her room to better understand the meaning of the song. I wasn't allowed to enter her room except on Saturdays to clean. The apartment belonged to my parents, but she had reduced me to next to nothing.

Both came out in about two hours happy, giggling, and laughing. Oksana assured that she had fully understood the song because Dolce had explained her well. She was very confident that she could work out something in the next two days. Dolce said she would be leaving in the next ten minutes.

"Jai, show me the website," Dolce asked eagerly.

"It is not ready. Jignesh will send something by evening," I replied.

"Blast him."

"For what?"

"He should keep his word."

"There is a small delay. You don't blast people for small things."

"What is his name?"

"Jignesh Patel."

"Oh! He is a Gujju." She was adamant. "Give me his number. I'll blast him in Gujarati."

"I said no blast. It's a small thing," I said forcefully.

"As you wish. I am leaving now. Should I come here on Monday?"

"You are always welcome."

Dolce left. Late that evening, I decided to confront Oksana about the tantrum she had thrown few days ago while I was talking to Dolce on the phone.

"Why didn't you scream the other night like you did the first time?" I asked seriously.

"I don't understand," she replied, confused.

"Other night when I was talking to Dolce on the phone."

"You really want to know?"

I didn't say anything but kept looking at her.

"Did you want me to scream?" she asked angrily.

"Answer the question," I asked, frustrated.

"I know why you wanted me to scream at you," she said, still furious. "So that you could clean everything and—"

"And what?"

"Get an opportunity."

"What opportunity?" I asked, bewildered.

"Like that Friday. Today is Friday. You like Fridays, don't you?" she fumed.

I kept looking at her, totally lost.

"Do you believe in God?" I asked.

"Yes," she replied.

"Do you think there is God?"

"Yes. Why?"

"Because there is a difference between believing in God and existence of God."

"What difference?"

"If someone told me that he believed in God, I would trust him because it is a personal belief. But if someone said there was God, I would ask him to prove first."

"So you think there is no God?"

"Yes."

"Why?"

"Why? Because if there was any God, he wouldn't have made specimens like you."

I had other things to do, so I got up and started walking towards my room not before giving her a nasty glare. I checked my emails. There was another upsetting email from Jignesh. He was unable to deliver tonight but promised to deliver tomorrow morning. Dolce was right. I should have let her blast Jignesh Patel. I decided to sleep but feared that there was a long Friday night ahead.

I woke up fresh after a goodnight's sleep. Last night, I had fallen asleep rather quickly. I stepped out of my room and started walking towards the bathroom. On the way, I heard the loud noise of someone yawning. It was Oksana who was yawning. I drew a lot of pleasure at the thought that she might not have slept the whole night thinking about my specimen remark. So what? I also couldn't sleep few Fridays back. It was one all between us. I then started my most important work of Saturday mornings—that is, to clean the apartment.

After the shower, I checked my emails. Jignesh had kept his promise, so I decided to test the website. I tested homepage, menus, and links to social media. I received an email from the Contact Us menu. I created real content from the back-end application. The website was now ready to be migrated. I called Jignesh Patel who assured me to make the website public by Monday.

Next, I uploaded the recorded song into the social media applications. I checked the numbers. They had hardly moved up. I thought the song and the website might bring the numbers up. I felt happy with the progress. I was hopeful that soon our phones would start ringing and emails would flood my notebook.

As I was about to turn my notebook off, my eyes fell on the slideshow. Oksana's images kept changing from a full length down to her face. It did give the impression that she was coming closer and closer with every changing image. She looked much better than real Oksana.

CHAPTER 19

On Monday, 15 September 2014, morning, I woke up late at 9, excited. I turned and twisted under the soft cushion that covered my bed. For some strange reasons, still half awake, I felt the warmth of the imaginary sleeping figure of Oksana and then acted to snuggle closer so that her buttocks pushed into the base of my stomach. Suddenly, I felt a false pain in my lower abdomen as if she had elbowed me like she had done the day after that Friday night.

My excitement was justifiable as the website had gone live yesterday evening. Also, I had to start my four-week dance lessons from Oksana in the evening. I was elated because dance lessons would naturally bring me closer to her, giving me an opportunity to touch her and enjoy her body fragrance from up close. The thought of that moment excited me so much that, for a moment, I thought I was a kid. But I quickly controlled my excitement and decided to suppress my real feelings, at least, to behave and appear like a mature person in front of Oksana.

However, she had spent last two days sounding upset and looking somewhat off colour probably because of lack of sleep. I wasn't sure how much she had progressed on the design of choreography, but I couldn't care less because she was the in charge of choreography. I hadn't told her anything about the website either.

I was expecting Dolce to arrive any moment, so I was standing in the kitchen with my back resting against the wall. The doorbell rang. As I prepared myself to answer the door, Oksana appeared from nowhere through the hallway like a chirrupy bird and beat me in the race. She opened the door, and there was the smiling Dolce. They hugged and kissed each other. I went to Dolce and gave her a big hug. We sat down, and I fired my notebook up to show them the new website.

"The website is online now," I said while trying my best to suppress my excitement. "You want to have a look, Dolce?"

"Show me," Dolce replied. "Has Oksana seen?"

Oksana shook her head, appearing slightly upset, which I liked because she was looking pretty.

"Jai, why didn't you show her?" Dolce demanded.

"It became online last evening."

"But you told me on Friday that you would receive in the evening."

"Jignesh sent me the test site on Saturday."

"When did you test then?"

Dolce was sharp, so I had to confess, "Saturday."

"Then why didn't you show her?"

"What was the point in showing the test website?" I argued and said, my lips close to her ear, "How could I show her without you? I wanted you two to be the first to see my website."

Dolce looked, eyes filled with emotions, at me. She rested her head on my shoulder. I gently pushed her and gave her the notebook. Sensing the importance of the moment, Oksana looked into my eyes and then drew a deep breath.

"Oksana, your pictures are looking so nice," Dolce praised. "Look at the last one. Isn't she looking beautiful, Jai?"

"Only in pictures," I joked and then burst into laughter.

"These are not my best pictures," Oksana said coldly, completely ignoring my laughter.

"Should we then put Dolce here?" I tormented.

"I don't care."

"Dolce, I am asking her again."

"Dolce, I am telling him again. I don't care."

"Dolce, I want your pictures exactly the way Oksana took her pictures."

"Why? Oksana, what is wrong?" Dolce asked, confused.

"Nothing is wrong. She doesn't want her 5 per cent," I said, laughing gently.

Oksana didn't react but squeezed her lips to suppress her smile.

"I think if someone sees these pictures, he would fall flat," I said diplomatically.

"Really?" Oksana reacted, surprised.

"Of course," Dolce said. "Oksana, why did you say these are not your best pictures?"

"She comes from a cold place. That is why her response is always cold," I intercepted before Oksana could respond.

"But she is very hot," Dolce said admiringly.

"People from the cold are generally hot," I teased again.

"I don't know what he is talking about," Oksana said, pretending ignorance. "Actually, I've not been feeling well for the past two days."

"What happened?" Dolce enquired, concerned.

"Actually I couldn't sleep on Friday night and Saturday night."

"Why? Did you sleep last night?"

"I don't know what happened to me. Last night was okay."

"Are you okay for tonight's practice?" I asked anxiously.

"Yes."

"Were you able to work on the song?" I asked. "Did you design the choreography?"

"Yes," she yelled, irritated.

I felt relieved then enjoyed the moment at the thought that she had not been able to sleep for two nights. The score had moved to 2–1 in my favour.

But at the same, I felt bad that I had failed to notice her sickness. After all, I had some duty of care. I couldn't face Oksana more, so I asked them to carry on and started to walk to my room, pretending some work. In my room, I started to think about my relationship with Oksana. Was there anything more than the fact she was sharing my apartment and that one-night stand? I started to get strange thoughts. An Indian man and a Ukrainian woman living together. This was unheard of. The relationship between Indian and American or Indian and British or Indian and Canadian was quite possible because people from these countries have fallen in love and married. I couldn't find the answer. But I decided to apologise to Oksana once Dolce had gone. I diverted my attention in collecting the names and places I had to contact in the coming weeks.

Later in the evening, we were preparing to leave for the school for my first dance lesson. I chose to wear something comfortable for the practice: track pants, T-shirt, and sneakers. Oksana knew what she had to wear: black tights, red T-shirt, and flat shoes. Her hair was tied back in a ponytail style. She put a satchel bag across her body. I decided to appear a hard student in order to test her patience and style of teaching. We left the apartment at ten minutes to 9. It was a ten-minute walk to the school, which I thought was a good opportunity to talk about her sickness and tender my apology.

"How are you feeling now?" I asked.

"What happened to me?" Oksana replied casually.

"Didn't you tell Dolce that you were not feeling well?"

"Lack of sleep."

"That is all?"

"I don't feel good. It is the sixth sense that is saying something is not good."

"What is not good?"

"I don't know."

"Next time when you can't sleep, let me know."

"How would you put me to sleep?"

"By being with you or by your side," I quipped, which didn't sit well. She gave a strong glare and looked directly at me as if asking, "Again?"

"We are room partners," I said, showing genuine concern. "I've a duty of care, so I need to know these things."

"We are sharing the apartment, not room," she said crisply. "Don't worry about me."

We reached the school gates. Oksana proffered the permission papers to the security guard. He checked the papers, escorted us to the auditorium, opened the door, and then he left. Once inside, we turned the lights on. The light that was not working the other day had been fixed. While walking up the stage, she pulled out a bundle of papers from her bag.

"Tonight we will just go through the schedule, the design, basics, and few steps," she told.

"What is the design?" I asked, excited.

"On these papers. I'll explain."

"When?"

"First, the schedule," she explained. "For the first five days, just learn the steps. There would be a lot of confusion in the first four days. Fifth day, things would start becoming clear to you."

"This is not new," I said, laughing. "There is always confusion between you and me."

"Stop this rubbish," she yelled. "Do you want me to teach you?"

"Are you going to shout at me? What if I commit mistakes? You will kill me?" I asked, shocked.

"I'll not shout if you commit mistakes, but I won't tolerate this rubbish," she said firmly.

"Can I ask you a question?"

"Yes."

"Is it true women look more beautiful when they are angry?"

"Ask your mother," she shouted and started to walk down the stage.

She sat on one of the front-row chairs, staring straight and rubbing her palms. I thought this was not going well because she had taken her most favourite pose, in which she could sit for hours. I had to try something else. I sat down cross-legged directly opposite her. I rested my left elbow on the thigh, placed my cheek on my palm, and then started looking at her stylishly. She quickly turned her gaze away. My trick had failed. I thought it worked only in the movies. Fifteen minutes passed with no change in the situation. I had to break the impasse. I got up, walked down the stage, and sat by her side. I pulled my mobile out of my pocket and then faked to dial a number. I waited for few moments and then pretended to talk.

"Hello, Mum."

She looked at me, surprised, and asked, "Are you talking to your mother?"

"Just a minute, Mum," I said, pretending to put my mum of hold. I covered my mobile with my hand and then turned to her. "Yes."

"Why this time?"

"You told me to ask my mother."

"No. No. No. Don't do that," she pleaded while trying to snatch the mobile from my hand.

She failed to get hold of my mobile. She looked at me defeated, breathing slowly.

"I was just pretending," I said while showing the screen of my mobile.

"You are sounding very difficult today," she complained. "Do you want to practise?"

"I have been waiting for this day for weeks," I replied, looking at her with hopeful eyes.

She held my hand and gently dragged me up the stage.

"Let me repeat," she said seriously. "Tonight we will cover the schedule, basics, design, and few steps if time permits."

She started telling me that in the first week there would be a lot of confusion. By the end of the week, things would start becoming clear. The confusion might return on the first day in the following week because I might start recalling the last week's moves and steps. By the end of the second week, confusion would be completely over, and things would start becoming clear. In the third week, we would perfect the dance; and finally in the fourth week, we would just practice. Next, she lectured on the BASTE—the elements of dance, the basics—and reiterated the importance of the good start and the end.

She took the papers out on which she had scribbled something. It was about the design. The whole song was choreographed into six parts. The first part was about the start position from the centre of the stage; second to break into opposite directions with a lot of dance steps, moves, and shakes; third to come back to the centre; fourth part to repeat the second part; fifth to come back to the centre to prepare for the ending part; and finally the execution of the ending part.

She started to demonstrate the steps. Everything looked so difficult to me. The confusion she had told me had already started to grip in. She demonstrated the steps in the most beautiful and graceful manner. I looked at her, mesmerised, but couldn't remember any of the steps she had demonstrated. I started to get worried whether I could match her skills. There was no time left for me to practise any steps, so we headed home. We didn't talk during our walk back to the apartment. Once we reached the apartment, I decided to discuss the matter with her.

"It looked so difficult," I said, worried. "Do you think I can do it in four weeks?"

"You will," she replied confidently.

"How?" I asked, confused.

"Because it's me, Oksana, who is your teacher," she said proudly, looking straight into my eyes. "You know, who is Oksana?"

"Beautiful Oksana, big-eyed Oksana, blue-eyed Oksana, strange Oksana, weird Oksana, and that Oksana," I replied mischievously.

"Who is that Oksana?" she yelled.

"That Friday Oksana," I replied, bursting into loud laughter, which annoyed her.

"You are mad. You can't learn unless it is my way—"

"Or the highway," I completed her sentence.

She gave me a glare and then disappeared into her room. Our day ended with a little fight.

We continued our dance practice. For the first three days, I found it hard to execute steps, moves—in fact, everything. My head, shoulders, hands, legs, hips, and feet were not moving in harmony. The forward steps, the backward steps, and the sideways steps, along with moving body, were a real challenge. On top of this, I had to match the steps with the music and the song. I found it equally hard to properly coordinate everything with Oksana. However, I was confident. With Oksana by my side, I would be able to improve quickly. She had shown extreme patience, proving that she was not only a good dancer but also a good instructor.

Meanwhile, I had prepared a list of ten TV stations I decided to call one by one starting from the top of the list.

"Hello," a female voice answered my call.

"Hello. My name is Jai Grover," I spoke courteously.

"Jai. Who's Jai?"

"I've a dance company, so I am looking for some work," I said. "Can you put me through to someone?"

"Call tomorrow," she said hastily.

"Why tomorrow?" I protested.

"Wait."

She put me on hold for about two minutes.

"The person is not on his desk. Try again tomorrow."

"Can I leave my details for him?" I said forcefully.

"You are very pushy," she said, annoyed. "Anyway, give me your details."

"Jai Grover and Oksana Bzovsky from JO-D."

"Jai Grover . . . Oksana what?" she asked, confused.

"Bzovsky."

"Is she a Russian?"

I was sick of the Russian tag but decided to accept it as a harsh reality.

"Yes."

"How come she is in your group?" she asked suspiciously.

"We just met and decided to form the group."

"Does she only dance?"

"Yes."

"Nothing else?"

"What is nothing else?"

"You know what I am saying. Anyway, give me your number."

I gave her my number and then asked, "What time should I call you tomorrow?"

"We now have your number so don't call us. We will call if we need you." She hung up.

I immediately knew I would never get a call from them again. I kept calling one station after another without any success. Their responses were weird: "We don't need dancers." "We are a news channel." "Are you from Delhi? Try there." "Stay away from Russian girls because they are bad or drug addicts or prostitutes. So many have been caught, didn't I know?"

One channel put me through to a male, who suggested me to send Oksana alone for an audition.

I got fed up, so I decided to check the website and the social media numbers. No one was looking at our website or social media. The number had barely moved to a few hundred. There weren't any emails either. I thought that the digital marketing was crap because it was not working for us. I couldn't afford newspaper advertisement. TV ad was out of the question.

I got frustrated, so I called Dolce for a mood change. I told her everything. She was outraged at how people had spoken about Oksana. She told me not to worry because she would do something, and then she hung up. She was the only person in Mumbai whom I trusted the most. I thought Sachin was so lucky to have a girlfriend like her. To my surprise and extreme pleasure, Dolce called me back in less than 15 minutes with encouraging news. She gave me a number to call. It was a small TV station recently launched.

I called the number and surprisingly enough was greeted by a very sweet female voice, "Hello, Monik de Mello."

de Mello—I thought she must be a Goan Catholic or a Mangalorean. I felt the politeness in her voice that is found in every Indian Christian. They always talk with utmost manners. The Christian nurses from Kerala work in every corner of India. They work hard and selflessly. They say they are serving God by serving the sick.

"Hello. My name is Jai Grover," I said softly.

"Yes, Jai. What can I do for you?"

"I've a dance company. I'm looking for some work."

"How many people do you have in your company?"

"I am the singer, Oksana is a dancer, and there are five musicians."

"Let me think who to put you through to." She paused.

At that point, I decided to disclose Oksana's nationality before she asked any question about her.

"Oksana is not Indian. She is a Russian," I said cautiously.

"Russians are very good dancers. You know ballet? It is not easy."

"No. I don't know much about ballet."

"I learnt ballet when I was a kid. Just a sec." She paused for a while. She said, which lit my face, "I'll put you through to Vikas Jain. He is the programme director of our morning show. Putting you through now."

Monik transferred me to Vikas Jain. After few questions, he asked us to appear for an audition on Friday, 26 September 2014, at 9 in the morning. I thanked him and then hung up. I regretted not getting a chance to thank Monik. Dolce never disappointed me. The last ten minutes had been very reassuring. But I had less than two weeks to prepare for the audition.

CHAPTER 20

The last ten days had been rather dull. We didn't have much to do except for the dance practice. I was showing a marked improvement at the end of every lesson. Oksana had very skilfully somehow managed to polish me. I wasn't a perfect dancer. Nonetheless, I had managed to develop a good grip over that one particular dance sequence based on our song.

Earlier in the week, I had managed to secure appointments with two events management companies for today. My first appointment at 11 in the morning at Fort and another at 3 in the afternoon at Kalyan, one of the outer suburbs of Mumbai. Luckily, there was a direct rail link between the two suburbs.

Tomorrow we had to meet Vikas Jain for the audition. I had given enough notice to Oksana, so she had agreed to sacrifice her sleep for one day.

I left the apartment at 10, reaching my first port of call just five minutes before my appointment. The office of the first company was in the same old colonial building where I had met Jignesh Patel few weeks back. It was a fairly long two-storeyed building made of limestone. I walked up the stairs where I was told to see a person sitting on one of the workstations. They didn't give me his name, so I walked straight to meet him.

He seemed to be of an average-height person with a thin moustache. He indicated me to sit on the chair in front of his workstation. He didn't introduce himself but asked about my details. I thought of impressing him, so I gave him the address of the website, which he readily brought up on his screen. He enquired about Oksana while looking at her changing images on the slideshow. I informed him that Oksana was my dance partner and she had taught me how to dance. He laughed but kept looking at the changing images. He called a colleague who was passing by and repeated to him what I had told him about Oksana. His colleague smiled and then went away laughing.

I thought that those guys were also interested only in Oksana. But I wasn't very sure what type of person he was. He leant forwards and then told me not to fool him. One could use any image and then claim to be their partners. He further told me that many girls or boys use images of Bollywood stars on their social media profiles. I tried my best to convince him that the images were that of a person I knew. He wouldn't trust me. Frustrated, I left that office to head to the train station for my next appointment.

On my way to my next appointment, I started to get some idea why I wasn't getting many hits. Could it be because nobody believed that Oksana's images were that of a person I knew? Immediately, I realised that I needed to have real dance clips with Oksana for people to believe me.

I hoped that my next appointment turned out to be a good experience. I had already emailed my details including my website to them yesterday. I reached their office at ten minutes to 3, taking me close to two hours. I hadn't had any time to have anything, so I was naturally feeling hungry. I was asked to wait as the owner had gone out for some work. I waited for some 20 minutes before the owner returned. The receptionist pointed at me.

He shook hand with me, introducing himself as Sharif Ahmad. He asked me to follow him to his office. We sat down in the office. Much to my delight, he first ordered tea and biscuits. I thanked him for his courtesy. He reminded me of Roshan Ali of Starbucks. I felt assured that something positive would come out of that meeting. When the tea and biscuits arrived, I pounced on the biscuits like a kid. I had four out of six biscuits. Sharif Ahmad just had one. I was still hungry, so I kept looking at the last biscuit but felt very embarrassed to pick that. Sharif Ahmad moved the plate towards him and asked me to finish the last one off, which I did a bit embarrassed, though.

Sharif Ahmad must have been in his late 50s. He had a wheatish skin, grey hair, and beard, which he used to stroke occasionally. He spoke in an all-too-familiar Bihari accent. Sharif Ahmad asked me about my family and other stuff. He told me that he was originally from Patna, so we, in a way, were both North Indians. He started telling me his story on how he had progressed from his Patna days to his current position. He used to supply tents, chairs, lights, mics etc to religious functions for all faiths in Patna. He was the first choice for all the Hindu festivals like Holi, Diwali, and Ram Leela because his name was Sharif. He then established contacts with influential people in the film industry and moved to Mumbai five years back. He said he was doing very well in Mumbai.

Next he unfolded his notebook, typed in, waited for few moments, and then moved the notebook so that we both could see together.

"So this is your company?" Sharif Ahmad asked, still looking at the website.

"Yes, sir," I replied politely.

"Is she American?"

"No. Russian," I replied, deliberately using Russian for Oksana.

"Too many Russians in Mumbai these days. They are spoiling our youth," he regretted.

"How?"

He didn't answer me but kept looking at the slideshow. Suddenly, his facial expressions changed, and then he leant forwards, stroking his beard. He didn't look like the same Sharif Ahmad.

"Milao Kabhi [Introduce me]," he muttered, never taking his eyes off the slides.

"Who?" I asked, amazed.

"Is Chidyya Se [To this bird]?" He grinned sheepishly.

I started getting some idea why he had ordered tea and biscuits. I thought he might have been looking at the slides since yesterday.

"What for?" I asked, astonished.

He didn't answer but winked as if saying, "You know what I mean."

"Didn't you say that they were spoiling our youth?" I lampooned him.

"Ha-ha-ha. That was for the youth." He laughed shamelessly. He sighed and said, regretting, "I am no longer young."

"So okay with you?" I ridiculed and then expressed inability. "Not in my hands."

"You can also come. We both will have fun."

"Where?"

"We will book a room in any hotel," he said shamelessly without showing any remorse and then winked once again.

I had heard so many bad comments about Oksana in the past, but this was the worst kind of remark. I had no relationship with Oksana but had become close to her that I couldn't possibly tolerate such low comments about her. Sharif Ahmad was worse than Shabnam Seth. Even she had put forwards her indecent proposal in a slightly better way. I decided to leave the place but not before teaching him a lesson. Until then, I had been avoiding to confront people who spoke badly about Oksana. Not anymore.

"I can introduce but on one condition," I said seriously.

His face shone brightly.

"Any," he said.

"Do you have a daughter?"

"Two."

"How old?

"Twenty and 15."

"Bring the 20-year-old with you. I'll enjoy with her, and you enjoy with Oksana."

I stood up to leave. I left the office without looking at his face for any further reaction.

On my way back home, I felt very sick. I had carefully planned the two meetings, but the people I had met had ruined my day. There was no comparison between Roshan Ali and Sharif Ahmad. Roshan means *shining light* in Sanskrit and Sharif means *noble* or *highborn* in Arabic. Light shines on all, but nobles have always been known to live for themselves. Failure to get any work and constant insult of Oksana were adding to my frustration. I laughed at the irony. Oksana wanted to dance, but Shabnam wanted her to be an escort. I wanted some work, but people wanted me to act like a pimp. I felt disgusted at the way I had spoken about Sharif Ahmad's daughter. She might not even know how her father was like. There was nothing I could do other than regret my foolishness to unnecessarily drag her. I hope that one day I could meet her and apologise.

I reached home at 7.30 exhausted, agonised, and disappointed only to find Oksana relishing her dinner. She had a chicken leg in both her hands, which she was biting like a cute little poodle, which frustrated me more. I sat across her silently, admiring her beauty. *Why is she so beautiful?* I thought. I got up and told her that I was not feeling hungry. She looked at me and shrugged her shoulders as if saying, "I don't care." I left for my room. Before entering the room, I looked back and found her busy with the leg piece. I stayed there for a while, kept watching, and then went into my room. I was so depressed that I decided to skip calling Delhi. I switched off; went to bed early, hoping tomorrow's audition would bring some cheer; and unexpectedly soon fell into a dreamless sleep.

Having slept early, I woke up at 5 in the morning an hour earlier than usual. For the first few seconds, I couldn't open my eyes properly. I rubbed my eyes and then massaged them few times. I folded my legs, stretched both my arms, and then rolled my body left and right few times. I slipped out of my bed; went to the toilet, spending my next 20 minutes there; and then went to the kitchen to brew the first coffee of the day. The coffee refreshed me. Suddenly, I heard some noises coming from one of the rooms. I rushed towards my room but soon realised that the noise was coming from Oksana's room. She had gotten up early for the auditions. The time was 6, meaning she had sacrificed her sleep, at least, by four and a half hours. Our plan was to leave at 7.30, so I decided to get ready.

We left our place at 7.30 for our half-an-hour journey to the TV station. On the way, I felt nervous at the thought of my first audition. Oksana assured me since I had to dance with her, I shouldn't worry or think too much. However, she warned me to remember the basics and the steps she had taught me. I felt assured. I told her about my two meetings and how hard it was to find the work, choosing not to disclose how people thought or spoke about her. She consoled me that something would materialise soon because I had been working hard. She preached me not to lose heart because these things happen when someone started a new business. I felt happy to see her fresh, smiling, and as usual beautiful.

Upon reaching the TV station, we were shown into Vikas Jain's office exactly at 9. He was a tall man with a deep thick voice. He had been an Indian classical singer. Vikas led us to a small hall, which had a stage, and then asked us to start our performance. We took our starting positions. With the start of the music, we started to move and shake. I thought I had passed my first test because we both started well. We were very close to completion when things started to go haywire. I couldn't reach the centre in time for the ending part. Oksana was unaware as she had her back towards me. Expecting my stretched hand, she prepared to drop her body backwards. Realising that I was late, I ran towards her and then extended both my hands to prevent her from falling. That was an ugly end to our performance. We quickly recovered and bowed red-faced to indicate the end of our performance. Oksana looked at me very gracefully, which I really appreciated even though I had goofed up the ending.

Vikas Jain praised Oksana's performance but told me that I needed more practice. However, he was happy to give her a chance to appear on his morning show on Tuesday, 30 September 2014, provided she was ready to perform a different song, a female solo. She agreed after hearing the song Vikas Jain played for her. She quickly recognised the song as she had performed on that song many times in the past. She would be paid Rs10,000, they told her. We left the station happy, having managed to secure our first business for the company. But it was due to Oksana, not me. I was sure after Oksana's appearance on the morning show, we would start getting more business. We had our lunch at a Gujarati vegetarian restaurant and returned home at 1 in the afternoon.

I had to find work, so I decided to surf the internet. After a couple of hours, I compiled the contact numbers of a dozen hotels. I started calling the numbers but faced rejection after rejection. No one wanted to meet me, but I kept trying. I finally managed to convince one who told me to see him on Wednesday, 1 October, at 11 in the morning. I dialled the last number, which kept ringing for a while. I decided to hang up when suddenly a male voice answered my call. He spoke in thick Tamil accent and told me that his name was S Ranganathan. He added that he was the general manager of the hotel. He asked me few questions and agreed to meet on 2 October at 11 in the morning. I felt very pleased with my efforts, having secured two appointments in two consecutive days. I thought that things had started to move in the right direction.

CHAPTER 21

I received a pleasant call from Dolce on 29 September. She was in Baroda, tracking Modi's US visit. She was very happy the way his US trip had gone so far.

She enquired about Oksana. I told her that Oksana had gone out to meet her friends. I thanked her for advising me to contact the TV where Oksana had passed her auditions. She became very happy to know that Oksana would be performing on Tuesday.

We also spoke about my two meetings with the events management companies. She became enraged after learning how people were talking about Oksana. She advised me to make sure that Oksana never came to know about those things. She went a step further. She asked to make a pledge that I would always protect her from such idiots.

She then asked the same question again, "Jai, what do you think about Oksana?"

"Why are you asking me?" I replied.

"No. Is there something between you and her?"

"Why do you think that way?"

"Because sometimes I see a tension between you and her."

"We are sharing the apartment, so it's bound to happen."

"It is not that type of tension," she said. "It looks like the tension between the two people who love each other."

"How do you know that?" I challenged.

"This happens between Sachin and me."

"You make his tension. Otherwise, Sachin can't give you any tension."

"Don't divert. Answer my question," she insisted.

"There is nothing."

"I don't agree with you," she said, disappointed.

I heard someone calling Dolce's name. She put me on hold and started to talk in Gujarati, the language I didn't understand.

Meanwhile, I started to think about Oksana. I had always admired her for her dancing skills and beauty. After that Friday, I had definitely drawn close to her. But there wasn't any hint of love from Oksana. We hadn't spoken or talked about it except for occasional flirtatious remarks we passed at each other. I couldn't talk to Dolce about that Friday encounter.

The whole thought confused me so much that, for a moment, I forgot I was talking to Dolce. Dolce came back, so I decided to change the topic without giving her a chance to resume the talk where she had left.

"I've managed to secure two more appointments," I said hastily.

"Where?" Dolce asked.

"With a couple of hotels."

"Who are you meeting?"

"His name is S Ranganathan," I replied, giving her the name of my second appointment because I couldn't remember the name of my first appointment due to confusion.

"South Indian," she nearly screamed, which confused me more.

"Yes."

"That too, a Tamilian."

"What about a Tamilian?"

"He'll rip you apart," she warned. "Do you know his position?"

"Why? He is the general manager."

"I am sure he must an MBA from a top institute like IIM."

"I think you are right. He asked me about my qualifications, institute etc. When I told him that I had done engineering from IIT, he agreed to meet me."

"They don't study for the sake of a degree. They go deeper into knowledge to learn more."

"What is wrong with that?"

"But they expect the same from everyone."

"How do you know?"

"One of the friends of my cousin was interviewed by a South Indian."

"Where?"

"I don't know. Some IT company in Mumbai."

"What happened to her?"

"She is also a South Indian, so he had a lot of expectations from her. He asked her so many hard questions. He ridiculed her when she couldn't answer properly. She broke down in the middle."

"What happened then?" I asked with a lot of interest.

"He called his secretary and told him to throw her out."

"Why?"

"He said if she wants to weep, then she should sit at home."

"Very strict person," I commented.

"They all are," she continued. "They couple their intelligence with hard work. That is why they occupy top positions in government, public sector, and IT."

"I agree."

"Just go there in a simple way," she advised. "Don't wear too flashy."

"Why?"

"They believe in simple living and high thinking."

I didn't say anything because I was really enjoying her analysis on South Indians. I heard her saying something in Gujarati to someone, which I picked like "Vōlyuma vadhārō."

"Modi has reached Madison Park now," she declared, excited.

"What were you saying in Gujarati?" I asked curiously.

"Oh, I was asking my cousin to increase the volume," she replied casually and then hastened to add, "I've to go now. Modi is waving to the crowd."

Next, I heard a kid screaming cutely, "Voovanine."

"Who is this kid saying voovanine?"

"Oh, he is Zev, my cousin's 5-year-old son," she replied. "What did you hear?"

"Something like voovanine."

"Not voovanine," she chided and said, extremely pleased, "He was saying Wolverine for Hugh Jackman. He is also there on the stage."

"When are you back?" I changed the topic.

"In three or four days."

She disconnected the call without saying bye. I laughed for a while, thinking about my conversation with Dolce.

Oksana came in crashing. Without looking at me, she went straight to her room. Her presence reminded me of her performance tomorrow at the TV station. I was very confident that once people saw her live on TV, our company would be inundated with work.

Next day we reached the TV station at 7 in the morning. We first completed the formalities at the reception area. After some wait, we were ushered into the morning show studio. At 9 Oksana went to the stage to deliver her dance performance. It was all over in ten minutes. I requested the channel for the clip of her performance but was flatly refused because of copyright issues. Oksana collected her performance fees, and thereafter, we headed back to home.

During our journey back, we didn't talk at all. I started to get strange jealous feelings about her. I had set up the company, found her, given her shelter, interviewed people, and formed the group; but all that came to a naught. It was Dolce who had been instrumental in introducing me to the TV station. Without Oksana passing her auditions, we would have never made our first earning. People would never know or recognise my efforts. They would always remember Oksana having seen her performance live. She would soon overshadow me, reducing me to almost rubble. I had never been jealous of anyone, but I had never faced such a situation in my life.

Back at home, we sat on the dining chairs facing each other. Oksana ripped the packet, counted the money, and then started making five separate bundles of Rs2,000 each. She folded each bundle separately and then put them together. What she did next was an absolute shock. She was wearing a pocketless shirt, so she put the money inside the left side of the bra. I looked at her smiling. She smiled back, having realised that I had seen her putting money inside her bra. Happy at our minor success we had achieved earlier in the day, I thought of having a bit of fun with her.

"Are you hatching them?" I asked, smiling.

"What hatching?" she replied, smiling.

"Just to double the money."

She didn't say anything, but her smiling face and sparkling eyes said it all. She got up and started to walk back to her room. While still in the middle of the hallway, I called her name. She stopped and turned, still smiling.

"In case you can't get it out, let me know. I'll help," I quipped, winking.

She went away giggling without saying anything. I felt there was a definite change in her. Otherwise, why would she do such a thing in my presence? Was that a hint? I wasn't sure. What mattered most was that she was in a good mood today. She came back with five envelopes in her hand. She sat across and then pushed the envelopes towards me.

"What is this?" I asked, puzzled.

"Give them to Dolce, Amardeep, and others," she replied seriously.

"This is your money."

She shook her head without saying anything.

"I said this is your money."

"Our money," she said, looking straight at me.

There was certain honesty in her eyes, which made me emotional. For the next few moments, we kept looking at each other in admiration in complete silence.

"Who is our?" I asked while drawing a deep sigh.

"You and me."

"I didn't do anything."

"You have done so much," she said. "Just give them to Dolce."

"I can't," I said while shaking my head. "You talk to her when she is back."

"I want to talk to her now," she insisted like a child. "I am missing her."

"Why?"

"Because she's become my best friend. I share many secrets with her."

Secrets. What secrets? I recalled Dolce having asked me about Oksana twice in the past.

"Have you told her anything about me?" I asked, alarmed.

"Why should I tell her anything about you? She is your friend also."

"Never mind," I said, relieved.

I called Dolce. They spoke for about ten minutes. From their conversation, I got an inkling that Dolce had refused to take the money.

"What did she say?" I asked.

"She doesn't want," she replied, disappointed.

"I knew that."

"You take half."

"If I need, I'll ask you. For now, it is yours."

She agreed reluctantly. My jealousy about her turned into calmness. I foolishly had ignored the fact that it was I who wanted her to be the lead dancer of my group, which is what she was doing. I was also very impressed with Oksana's positive thinking. She had tried to offer money to others, knowing that they were doing us a lot of favour. My admiration for her increased in many folds.

CHAPTER 22

I reached the hotel at ten minutes to 11 in the morning for my meeting with S Ranganathan. It was a typical five-star hotel building, not different from any other five-star hotel building. I went to the reception where I was pointed to his office.

I was greeted by his secretary. She asked me to wait and went away to let her boss know. His office was partitioned into his secretary's small chamber and his own chamber. The two chambers were separated by the floor-to-ceiling plywood wall with a door on the left corner.

Ranganathan called me exactly at 11, exemplifying his punctuality. I greeted him, and he told me to take a seat. He looked like a typical Tamilian Brahmin. He wore a simple but neat attire and a long sandalwood called *tilak* on the forehead. Exactly above his head hung a large picture of Lord Balaji. I silently sought blessings and waited for Ranganathan to start the conversation.

"So you have done engineering from IIT Delhi?" Ranganathan fired the opening shot.

"Yes, sir," I replied politely.

"My daughter also did her engineering last year from IIT- Chennai," he said, beaming.

"Where is she working now?"

"Google. You know Google?" he asked as if it was an unknown company.

I pretended not knowing about it and thought of having a bit of fun with him.

"What is Google?" I asked innocently.

"You don't know Google?" he asked, surprised.

"No," I acted dumb.

"I'll tell you. Wait."

He typed something and then turned his notebook towards me. It was actually Yahoo.

"But this is Yahoo," I said, surprised.

"What is Yahoo?"

"It is a search engine."

"If you know Yahoo, then you know what Google is."

He was a smart guy because he had beaten me in my own game.

"Sorry," I apologised.

He asked me for tea. The thought of tea scared me. What if he turned out to be another Sharif Ahmad? So I refused. He spoke to his secretary in Tamil, probably ordering tea for himself.

"Have you heard about Ramanujan?" he asked, expecting me not have heard.

"Yes. The great mathematician?" I replied.

"Do you know what was unique about him?"

"He never earned a degree."

"Why?"

"Because he couldn't pass other subjects except for mathematics. His focus was always on mathematics," I replied confidently.

"What does that teach you?"

"If you are a genius, you don't need any degree."

He looked at me, smiled, and started scratching his left cheek, probably thinking of next set of questions.

"Are you a Punjabi?" he became direct.

"Yes."

"Punjabis. Make money, eat, drink and show off, and—" he paused for some reasons. I somehow controlled my laugh and waited for him to complete his sentence. "They talk so loudly and *bhangra* and *balle balle*."

He threw his arms in the air in the "balle balle" style. I couldn't control my laugh, so I burst into a laughter. I couldn't understand which way our discussion was going. Meanwhile, his tea arrived, which he started to sip. All of a sudden, his face turned serious.

"Why are you doing this?"

He questioned my decision to form a dance group despite having a degree in engineering. I explained to him everything in detail.

"Doesn't make sense to me. You know why I called you?" he asked.

"Possible business opportunity for me in your hotel?" I replied.

"No," he thundered. "To tell you that you are wasting your time."

"Why do you think I am wasting my time?"

"With that Russian."

"Which Russian?"

"I am in the hospitality business. I know all."

"How do you know about her?"

"Didn't you send me the details of your website?"

"Yes. Then what?"

"When I saw her on your website", he said, leaning back, "I immediately recognised her."

"How?"

"Didn't she work for Shabnam? She's performed here many times. That is how."

"What has that to do with Shabnam?" I protested.

"Shabnam told me everything about her. She is not a good woman," he spoke contemptuously about Oksana.

"Shabnam is wrong. She is a liar. Oksana is innocent. I know her very well," I rebuffed him in one breath.

"Shabnam knows better than you," he said, undeterred. "Again, I am telling you that she is not a good woman."

"What does not a good woman mean?"

"I can't use that word. It is below my dignity."

"If she wasn't a good woman, why did you let her dance in your hotel?" I challenged.

"This is a five-star hotel, so we need dancers. Dancers who only dance because—" he paused to clear his throat and then resumed, "Dance is an art. It is a dignified profession, but when a person does something else than—"

"What something else?" I cut him off disdainfully.

"Again. Now listen carefully. I gave you my time because you are an educated person from a very reputable institute."

"If I can't defend an innocent woman, then my education is a total waste," I lectured.

"Are you lecturing me?" he asked, annoyed.

He started to get up, indicating that my time was up.

"You can leave now," he said sternly and warned, "As long as you are with that woman, you will get nothing. Shabnam will not let that happen. She is very influential."

I sighed and started to leave not before reminding him that I wasn't the only person in Mumbai with Oksana, but there were five more. One of them was a teenager called Dolce who herself was a woman.

I left the hotel enraged and disappointed. My meeting yesterday also hadn't gone well. In fact, it never took place. When I reached that hotel, I was asked to wait. They kept me waiting, but no one attended to me. I had to leave without meeting anyone despite my prior appointment.

I laughed at Ranganathan's opinion about Punjabis. I thought Punjabis are different who had a great sense of humour. I didn't end my meeting with Ranganathan the way I had ended with Sharif Ahmad because he had not used any bad word or language for Oksana except for indirect remark. Dolce was right. He ripped me apart. In fact, he ripped all Punjabis apart.

I failed to understand why everybody was after Oksana just because she wanted to stay a dignified dancer. Had she played the game by Shabnam's rule, she would be minting money. Minting money by selling her body, sharing a bed with the people she didn't know, faking a smile, fulfilling every fantasy of men whether she liked or not, and then ending her day drained and without a soul. Ranganathan spoke about dignity. He should have met the people who badmouthed her and gazed at her body in a measured and lustful way. They think she doesn't notice them. She keeps her calm, ignores them, and moves on with utmost dignity. For me, Oksana was the ultimate definition of dignity. Period. But what else could I do for her? There wasn't any business coming soon. I had to make a quick decision about her. I had been thinking about one. I decided to wait until Dolce's return, discuss with her, and then reveal to Oksana. But one thing was sure: I was not going to deceive or ditch her.

CHAPTER 23

It was the last week of my dance lessons. I was extremely satisfied with my progress. Oksana also felt that I was good enough to dance with her as a pair. However, my worry about attracting more business continued despite my best efforts. I still had a healthy bank balance of Rs485,200.65, but my dreams didn't look like to be materialising. At least not in Mumbai.

I called Dolce, explained my future plan, and requested her to break the news to Oksana. She promised to be at my place in about an hour. I felt very depressed and low. I thought of killing my time by having a look at the website and social media numbers. More depression. The followership and the subscription numbers had started going down because I had not been uploading any new content. Apart from Oksana's slideshow, there was nothing that was exciting. There was a great possibility those images would also fade away soon.

I knew it was Dolce when someone pressed the bell. She came in beaming. She was happy that Modi's US tour had been very successful. She told me that Obama had greeted

Modi in Gujarati, "*Kem Cho* [How are you]?" His address in the Madison Square was a big hit. Overjoyed, she told me that the press had dubbed him as the rock-star prime minister. I was least interested in Modi's US trip but had to listen to her because she was my best friend and now a close confidante. She went to Oksana's room and came back with a smiling and happy Oksana. I thought her smile would soon turn into grief. It was now purely up to Dolce how she conveyed the message. We settled on the dinner table for our round-table conference.

"Oksi, I am going to say something you may not like," Dolce spoke slowly and cautiously in a measured tone. "Jai has decided to go back to Delhi soon."

Oksana kept quiet and didn't say anything. There was no expression on her face other than those big blue eyes searching for answers. I didn't say anything. There was a complete silence for few moments, which was broken by Dolce again.

"Not immediately," Dolce comforted. "But in six weeks around November end."

"That is fine. There is no work here anyway," Oksana said, calmly trying to conceal her real emotions.

"Don't worry. You can move to my place after November."

"Don't you live with your parents?" Oksana enquired by rolling her big blue eyes.

"Yes. But I've a big room enough for two of us."

"No. I am not used to living like that."

"What do we do then?" Dolce asked, dejected.

"Go back."

"But you said there was a war going."

"It is not empty. People still live."

"But—"

"She can go now," I interrupted. "She can come back later."

"Really? Do you think I'll get a visa?" she shot back angrily.

"Why not?"

"No. I'll go back," she replied sternly.

"Jai, she is right," Dolce said maturely. "She should be with her people."

"I will book the ticket for her," I said while getting up.

"No. No. No," Oksana reacted, nearly screaming.

"Oksi, let us go to your room," Dolce said.

Dolce took her to the room, not before gesturing me to remain calm. Within the next five minutes, I heard the sound of the door being opened. I got up and saw Dolce first who hurriedly gestured that everything was fine and I should quickly go back to my chair. They started to walk towards the door without looking at me.

"Where are you going, Dolce?" I asked.

"To the shopping centre," Dolce replied. "To buy the ticket from the travel shop."

"Why soon?"

"Jai, Oksana is sorry," Dolce said and then turned to Oksana. "Isn't it, Oksi?"

She nodded.

"On two conditions."

Oksana gave me a quick glare and then looked away, pretending not to listen to me.

"What conditions?" Dolce asked.

"She books the ticket for the last week of November and stays here until that time."

"Of course she'll. Jai, we will be back in half an hour," Dolce said hastily without waiting for Oksana's reaction.

That was the quality Dolce possessed. She was capable of handling situations like that very well. Dolce thought I was a mature person, but I was nothing compared to her. There was a natural bonding between Oksana and Dolce. Probably it's because both were women. My thought then turned to Oksana. Why did she get angry with me? Was she expecting me to break the news to her? I killed the rest of my time restlessly, worried thinking about my future without Oksana.

Dolce and Oksana came back from the centre. Oksana headed straight to her room without looking at or talking to me. Dolce said she was about to leave but wanted to have a brief chat with me.

"Jai, you don't look good," she asked assertively.

"Why? What is wrong with me?" I replied, appearing to be normal.

"If everything was good, then why would you ask me to break the news to Oksana?"

"Because—"

"You don't want her to go?"

"What else could I do?"

"Talk to her."

"She is not interested at the moment."

"I saw that. She became angry with you because she is also in the same position."

"What position?" I asked, pretending to be ignorant.

"Jai, I am your friend so don't hide anything," she continued. "I tried to ask you twice, but you always avoided."

"When did I avoid you?"

"No, not me. But you changed the topic whenever I asked you about Oksana. You both can change this. So talk to each other," she lectured like a grandmother.

"There is an age gap," I said, dropping a hint for the first time about my liking for Oksana.

"Don't be old-fashioned," she chided.

"Ten to 12 years," I said, surprised.

"Even 100 years mean nothing in such cases," her grandmotherly lecture continued.

I suppressed my laugh at her "100 years" remark, but she actually was trying to put some extra weight to her argument.

"I can," I said with some uncertainty. "But she should be ready to talk to me."

"She'll. She'll be here very soon."

"What did you tell her?"

"Nothing other than to talk to you."

"Did she agree?"

"She promised me. I've to go now."

Dolce got up to leave. I opened the door for her when I remembered to ask her, "When is she leaving?"

"Ask her. Make sure you'll be nice to her," Dolce said in a haste and then headed towards the lifts.

I shut the door and sat back on the chair, waiting for Oksana to appear. I covered my eyes and started to think. I decided not to be direct with her. Suddenly, I felt the familiar nice smell of her fragrance. I opened my eyes and found her readying herself to sit on the opposite chair. She looked upset.

"You know, I've learnt a lot from you," I said.

She showed no reaction, probably thinking that I was lying, flattering, or trying to please her. I decided to keep talking.

"I learnt how to clean, keep things in order, discipline, and do things when they are supposed to be done and—"

I stopped for her response, directly looking into her big, blue, bright, and sparkling eyes. All she did was gesture with her right hand as if asking, "What else?" But she didn't talk. I had never won in the past, so how could I win now?

"How to do it?" I completed the sentence nervously.

"I think that is the only thing you learnt," she chided.

"I wasn't very mature, but I am now."

She was not interested in whether I was a mature or immature person. She was acting cold, which I had never felt before.

"Amardeep will miss you," I continued with the silly remark, which I knew she hadn't liked in the past. I had contradicted myself within the space of my last two sentences. I asked, almost pleading, "Will you miss me?"

She shook her head violently, implying a definite no. My hopes were shattered. I had hit the wall. I decided to ask the last question. "When are you flying out?"

"Twenty-seventh of November," she replied casually, got up, and disappeared into her room.

The date of her departure added further pain to my injured heart. I had planned something big for that day. I wanted to buy her a gift. See her happy, smiling, and coming close to me. It was her *birthday*.

I was feeling a bit lethargic, so I decided to take a shower. I took my mobile out, put it on the table, went to the bathroom, and after the shower went straight to my room.

I tried to sleep, but I couldn't because I was feeling very desperate and depressed. I thought I would fly back to Delhi the next day after Oksana had left. However, the memories of the apartment would always stay with me. I would miss the hall, the dining area, the kitchen, my room, small room, and *her room*. I would miss daily mornings when I waited for her to wake up. I would miss her cooking. I would miss her sitting on the couch and staring into the vacuum. I would miss every little thing about her.

It was the worst emotional pain I had been through in my life, by far. It felt like everything was meaningless without her. Although my parents were there for me who would try to make me laugh and be okay again, the only person that could make me feel better was the only person that wouldn't be there for me. Deep down, I knew that the hurt would eventually disappear; but at the moment, I couldn't fathom my life without her. I started to wonder about the three *R*s technique. Retract, relax, and react. The crux of the matter was that the three *R*s technique had failed on me. I had to divert my attention from her and keep my brain busy elsewhere. I started the reverse countdown—100, 97, 94, 91—and fell asleep, heavy heartedly.

Something disturbed my sleep. But I felt like I was awake. I squeezed my eyes and then opened them slowly. I raised my head and started to look left and right. I realised that someone was pressing the doorbell constantly. I checked the time. It was 6.30 in the morning. I yawned, stretched my arms, rubbed my eyes, and quickly slipped out of bed. Who could come so early in the morning? I went to answer the door, and she came in blasting.

"Jai, are you mad?" Dolce yelled. "I called you three times last night."

"You called me? Where?" I asked, confused, trying to understand why Dolce was here so early in the morning.

"Where else? On your mobile." Her yelling wouldn't stop.

"I didn't hear anything," I said. Looking around confused, I muttered, "Where is my mobile?"

"Here it is," she berated after spotting it on the dining table.

I tried to recollect last night's events. I remembered pulling out the mobile from my pocket before I headed to take a shower, leaving it behind. I checked the missed calls. There were three at 10.52, 11.27, and last one at midnight. I tried to recall what exactly I was doing at those times. Was

I thinking or had fallen asleep? I couldn't recall anything. I turned to Dolce.

"Sorry. I forgot to pick it from here," I said apologetically.

"I was so worried about you last night," she said, distraught. "I thought of coming to your place."

"Why didn't you then?"

"I wasn't sure which state I would find you both in," she said, which brought the first smile of the day on my face. She enquired, "Did you talk to her?"

I nodded, and she asked, "What happened then?"

"Nothing happened. We just spoke normally."

"Jai, I now know what is bothering you," Dolce spoke with absolute certainty.

I didn't say anything. I didn't want to think about it.

"Anyway, I've got good news for you both," she said, preferring to change the topic.

We both sat down on the dining chairs facing each other.

"What is it?" I asked curiously.

"Brush your teeth first," she ordered. I followed her order when I heard her yelling, "I want coffee. I will make."

I brushed my teeth, washed my face, and then looked into the mirror. I had looked into the same mirror few weeks ago the day after that Friday. That morning I was searching for answers, but today I didn't have any questions. I came back and found Dolce with two mugs in her hands. She gave me one, and we sat down on the couch.

"You look much better now," she comforted.

I didn't say anything because I wasn't feeling better inside.

"Listen carefully," she said, underlining every word. "There is a chance. Last chance for both of you."

"What chance are you talking about?" I asked, confused.

"Have you heard about MMF?"

"Mumbai Music Factory."

"Exactly. They are celebrating 25 years."

"So what?"

"Jai, you have to be patient," she said, displeased; took a sip; and resumed, "MMF are celebrating their 25th anniversary. They are organising a song-and-dance competition on Friday, the 31st of this month. The auditions are on this coming Sunday. Just for one day. They will pick only five for the main competition."

"Who goes? Oksana or me?"

"It is for pairs," she clarified. "Boy and girl. But only one applies. If the boy applies, then he has to find his girl partner and vice versa. But both will share the prize money. It suits you both."

"Umm . . ."

"Don't hesitate," she said. "There is no big prize money: Rs100,000 for the winner, Rs50,000 for the first runner-up and Rs25,000 for the second runner-up. If you win one of the three places, then you might be noticed. Seize this opportunity. It is godsend," she concluded and looked at me with narrowed eyes, waiting for my response.

"But there may be many people," I asked, concerned. "It is very tough to get through the auditioning."

She shook her head in disbelief.

"Jai, nobody will give anything on a plate. There will always be competition," she lectured once again like a grandmother. "But this one is bit easy."

"How?"

"This is only for the Mumbai residents, and only pairs can apply," she clarified.

"How do we prove we are from Mumbai?"

"Show your driving licence."

"I am not sure."

"Jai, it will bring you both close."

"What close? She is going away anyway."

"Jai, take one step at a time," Dolce argued.

"What if it didn't work?" I dismissed her argument.

"Jai, listen carefully to what I am going to tell you now," she said and, leaning forwards, preached, "You don't cross a bridge in one jump from one side to another because you fear that it might break. But you cross it by taking one step at a time, hoping it would never break. Am I clear?"

She left me stunned and speechless with her powerful argument. The power of her argument seemed to belie her age. There was no way out for me now. She had forced me to commit.

"I'll do. But who will talk to her?" I fired the last and the only arrow left in my quiver.

"You will talk to her," she replied forcefully.

"She won't listen to me."

"Without trying?"

"I don't know how."

"I can help you," she said confidently. "The competition is on 31 October 2014, and she is leaving on the 27 November 2014. Why should she have any problem?"

"I'll talk to her," I said, yielding to her powerful arguments and persistence. I asked curiously, "How did you come to know about the competition?"

"You want to know that?" she asked, smiling.

"Yes."

"You really want to know?" she teased.

"Yes," I almost begged.

"You know, there is this person—" she said, leaving the sentence deliberately incomplete.

"Which person?" I asked, frustrated.

"Dolce Bond 007," she replied, winking.

I lifted my right hand, pretending to hit her. Oksana showed up smiling and hugged Dolce. She sat on the chair close to Dolce and looked at me, still smiling. She seemed to have recovered from last night. Why wouldn't she? She would have put that in her diary and then erased everything from her memory. Dolce, looking at me, rolled her eyes, communicating that I should now talk to Oksana. I was happy to talk to her in Dolce's presence.

"Dolce, remember I told you this Sunday we are going for an audition?" I lied with a fake smile on my face.

"Which audition?" Oksana asked, surprised with a beautiful and broad smile on her face.

Those two words from Oksana felt like music to my ears.

"Your best friend will explain to you," I said, pointing to Dolce.

Dolce repeated everything to Oksana, carefully choosing her words. I noticed that Oksana was listening very attentively, showing a lot of interest, which raised my hopes of her participation in the competition.

"I can go anywhere for dance," Oksana said enthusiastically. "I breathe, eat, and drink dance."

"We have to start preparing for the audition. It is almost upon us," I said, matching her enthusiasm.

"Jai, take the address. You have to be there before 9," Dolce said, hurried. "I've to go now."

"Give it to Oksana. Also, SMS me," I said while getting up.

I opened the door for Dolce and watched her, in admiration, walking towards the lifts. Suddenly, she turned, gave me a thumbs up, and then went inside the lift. I noticed a lot of pride and satisfaction on her face. Hurray, Dolce had done it again for me.

CHAPTER 24

We left the apartment at 8 in the morning for the auditions. On the way, I sought Oksana's opinion about my dancing skills. She advised me to be myself, remember the basics, and not to repeat the mistake I had committed at the TV station. I couldn't recall what exactly had gone wrong on that day. I decided not to think too much and treat today's audition as my first.

We reached the venue at 8.35 and waited quietly, hoping to be called for audition soon. It was a big hall full of people who were busy in talking, rehearsing, and some were even praying. All looked nervous including me except for Oksana who didn't show any signs of nervousness.

Earlier in the morning, I had convinced Oksana to wear the same Indian dance costume, which she had used to take the pictures. She was looking very pretty and stood out in the waiting crowd. The exposed midriff made her the centre of attraction. Within minutes, she had become well known, and many female participants started to flock around her. She smiled, talked, replied, and thanked whenever a compliment was made in a pleasing manner.

The names of the participants started to be called out. We saw couples after couples walking to the end of the hall, turning left and then disappearing. We waited, waited, and waited. Three hours had passed, but our names were not called out. I saw rejected candidates leaving the hall in tears or disappointed or stone-faced. The hall started to appear less crowded.

Suddenly, we saw a middle-aged man, with medium physique, heading towards us. He stood by Oksana's left side and started to whisper something in her ear. She got up and asked me to follow the man. We all started to walk together with the man on her left, Oksana in the middle and me on her right side. We reached the end of the hall and then turned left into a long corridor some 30 metres long. The man pointed to the door that was on the other end of the corridor.

Suddenly, the man put his right arm over Oksana's shoulders, prodding her right arm with his fingers. Oksana looked at him, produced a fake smile, and looked straight, acting to be normal. However, I noticed that she had an uneasy look as if a python had coiled around her, choking her throat. But she kept her calm in a dignified manner. The man started to tell her how he had noticed her, fast-forwarded her audition, and ensured that she didn't miss out because he felt that she deserved a chance. To me, it looked like she knew these advancements as she would have experienced many times in the past.

She didn't look at me, possibly not thinking me worthy enough to come to her rescue or not expecting any help from me. I thought she must have felt alone. But I wanted to tell her that if there were bad Indians, there were good Indians also. Just wait and watch. Next, I put my left arm over that man's arm and pressed his hand with my armpit so hard, blocking any movement. She looked at me and smiled. Her smile was spontaneous, a smile that was not fake or forced and a smile of a person who felt safe, secure, and protected. I wanted to tell how many times I defended her and offended the people who badmouthed her or insulted her. But how would she know? I had never told her.

I told the man that Oksana couldn't take the weight of his arm, so I used my arm to put a counterweight. He looked at me embarrassed and pulled his arm back, causing my arm to fall over her shoulders. But I didn't remove my arm from her shoulders, and she didn't ask either. That was the first time I had touched her since that Friday. It was a good omen. We reached the door, which was on the right side. That man went through the opposite door, disappearing soon. We stood outside the door for a moment. I removed my hand from her shoulders. We looked at each other, and she lowered her lashes, assuring me that all was well.

We crossed the door into a small auditorium, which had a stage fully lit with bright lights. There were two average-looking male judges sitting some ten metres away from the stage. There were no cameras, no TV screens, and no audience. We walked to the centre, greeted the judges, and then introduced ourselves. The judges asked us about the song and dance we were going to use for our audition. I told them that the song was our own creation and had been played only once at a TV station, which impressed them. They spoke softly, clearly, and didn't not ask any unnecessary questions to Oksana.

We were told to start the performance. We took our starting position and waited for the judges' orders. The stage was still lit with bright lights. We heard one of the judges saying, "Lights, camera, and dance." The music was about to start, but I could not hold my laugh. I moved away from my starting position and then burst into a loud laugh. No one was sure why. Oksana looked at me, bemused. The judges found my laugh very amusing, and they also joined me without knowing the reason. I stopped laughing, apologised, and then moved back to the starting position.

"Why did you laugh?" Judge 1 asked with a smile on his face.

"I heard someone saying lights, camera, and dance," I replied politely.

"That was me. That is how it's done. Is this your first audition?" Judge 2 asked seriously.

"No, this is my second audition. But the lights are already on, and there are no cameras here."

"Right. Right. Right. Good one," Judge 2 said, embarrassed.

"It is a habit. Come on now. Start your performance," Judge 1 ordered.

We prepared to start, waited for the orders, and then the music started. It was the routine I had practised many times recently. I made it sure that the start was done properly. My head, shoulders, body, legs, and feet were moving in a perfect harmony. I didn't feel any nervousness or stiffness in my body. There was no stage fright or inhibition or lack of coordination with Oksana. I didn't have to worry about Oksana because I knew that she knew her trade very well. As the ending neared, I quickly moved to my position and stretched my right arm out. Oksana started moving to the centre, her back towards my stretched arm; and with an impressive gentle backward jerk, she fell back on my stretched arm. With the last beat of the drum, we curled up our hands in a lotus shape. That was the end of our performance. We bowed before the judges who told us to wait outside. We started to walk back to the waiting area and soon found a spot very close to the one we had occupied in the morning. I looked at Oksana who greeted me with a smile. We didn't say anything but kept looking at each other. There was some kind of communication going on between us. A positive one, that of love. At least, that is what I felt.

We had been waiting for about an hour when our eyes fell on the same man who was standing at the top end of the corridor. He yelled out Oksana's name, gestured her to come to him, but told me to wait. I started to get worried. I looked at her who was preparing to walk to the man. She tried to appear calm, told me not to worry, and soon disappeared with the man into the corridor.

Five minutes had passed since she had gone. All types of evil thoughts started to appear in my mind. What could he do in five minutes? Quick one was a possibility. No, she would never allow that to happen. But what if she was trapped with nowhere to go and being forced to reward for moving us to the final round? I started to get restless, stood up, and started to walk towards the corridor. Halfway through, I saw Oksana appearing. She had a paper in her hand, but her face looked listless. There was no brightness or sparkle on her face. I immediately knew that something was wrong. I asked her, but she ignored me and then showed me the invitation to the main competition. We had made to the finals, but Oksana wasn't looking the same. I thought of keeping quiet until we reached home. I was not going to rest until I found the truth.

Back at home, she wanted to take a rest in her room. I gave her five minutes to change and asked her to come back as I needed to talk to her urgently. She agreed and went away. Meanwhile, I went to the kitchen to make coffee for both of us. While making the coffee, I felt pity for her as everybody was after her. I came back to the dining area with two mugs in hands and found her waiting. I asked her not to leave until I told her. I then sat down close to her for the first time, otherwise always preferring the chair opposite her. She seemed to have recovered but bore a forced smile on her face.

"What happened there?" I asked sternly.

"Nothing happened," she murmured.

I started to breathe heavily and looked straight into her eyes, showing my anger.

"Where is the invitation?" I yelled. "I want it now."

She looked at me terrified because she had never seen me like that.

"What is wrong with you? You look so different."

"Where is the paper?" I repeated.

"Why do you want?" she asked.

"I want to tear it apart. We are not going there," I said loudly in anger.

"This the last chance for you. Don't do it."

"I don't need any chance."

"Why?"

"Because I am tired."

"Tired of what?"

"Tired of defending you, tired of people who speak rubbish about you, tired of people who call you a bad woman and a prostitute, tired of people who touch you, tired of people who look at you in a lustful way . . . tired of—" I left the sentence incomplete in despair.

"Tired of me," she completed the sentence with a sad smile on her face.

"Yes. Tired of you. I never understood you. You never tried to understand me," I said, dejected.

"Why do you want to understand me?" she asked in a heavy voice.

"Because I . . . I like you," I said, hesitated.

Only if she knew how I was feeling last night. Only if she knew how much Dolce liked her.

"You have to control yourself. Let us be good friends until I leave," she addressed like a mature person.

"You should know the meaning of a good friend. They don't hide things. They share things, happiness, and sorrows." I matched her maturity with my own maturity.

"What do you want me to share?"

"What happened in the morning? What did that man do to you?"

"There is no point in thinking about it."

"So something happened?" I asked as my heart started to sink.

The thing she didn't want had eventually happened, and I couldn't save her. I started to curse himself at the very idea that I had agreed to participate. I didn't know how many more insults she had to face until her departure. I felt very guilty.

"What happened?" I repeated, but she again kept quiet.

"Give me the paper."

"No, I won't." She moved her hand back, trying to hide it from him.

"Why do you want to go there?"

"Because if we win, it'll cover the cost of my ticket," she replied.

I was impressed with her honesty. Everybody wants to make money. She was trying to earn it through legitimate means.

"I'll give you money."

"I want to earn my money," she asserted.

I should have known that she would never accept my charity because she was a proud woman.

"Find a new partner," I said and issued an ultimatum. "I am not going until you tell me the truth."

She looked confused, not knowing what to do. She kept staring into the vacuum. How hard was it to tell the truth? Why was she so rigid and reticent? There was no response from her, so I pretended to get up.

"Wait. Where are you going?" she pleaded.

"Tell me the truth or find your partner," I said plainly.

"On one condition," she pleaded again.

"As long as you tell me the truth."

"You won't react or do anything mad."

"I never do anything mad," I assured.

Finally, she agreed. She told me that after she went to him, he congratulated her for making it to the main competition. He said that the invitation paper was in the office so she should come with him to collect that. His office was exactly opposite the audition room entrance. When they reached the office, he got the paper out of his table drawer, held it in his hand, and then asked her to come close to collect from him. She went close, collected the paper, and then started to read. While she was reading, he put his hands on her face and started to rub her cheeks. He told her that he was in charge for calling out the names. Hadn't he seen her, she would've never been able to make it because the names were being called randomly. He also told her that she was looking very pretty in the Indian dance costume that caught his attention. He regretted that he wouldn't be able to help her in the main competition because he had been hired for just the day. She didn't know what to do as he kept rubbing her cheeks. Suddenly, the phone in his office rang. He went to attend and started talking to someone. She seized the opportunity and ran out. But he ran after, overtook, and then blocked her way. At this point, Oksana stopped talking.

"What happened after that?" I demanded.

"He told me not to tell anything to anyone."

"What did you say?"

"I said nothing. He also told me to stay careful from you."

"You mean me? Why?" I asked, astonished.

"He told me not to trust young people because they are not reliable." She giggled.

"What did you say?"

"Nothing. I pushed him aside and started running."

"Did he come after you?"

"No. He kept looking at me. When I reached the end, I looked back. He was still standing there. He smiled and waved at me."

"So what will you do now?" I quipped.

"I don't understand." She looked puzzled.

"Who will save you from me now?"

"Jai Grover because I trust him."

"I promise that I'll pay you back," I told, choking in emotions. "And you wouldn't know."

"I don't need anything back," she replied, bringing that ever-familiar bright, sparkling smile on her face, which had been missing since that episode.

I became very emotional. I got up, stood behind her, locked her with my arms, and then tried to whisper something in her ear.

"Jai, unlock me. I've told you not to touch me without my permission," she said seriously.

Shocked, I unlocked her and went back to my chair. She didn't say anything when I had my arm over her shoulders earlier today. She was so moody. I felt humiliated.

"Why didn't you object when I put my hand over your shoulders earlier today?"

"I think that was a smart move by you. Otherwise, that man wouldn't have removed his hand," she praised and ended sensibly. "Moreover, it wasn't an appropriate place or time to argue with you."

But I still failed to understand her logic. I just wanted to touch her out of affection. Apart from her dancing skills and beauty, I greatly admired her and in many cases respected her. I was so confused that I couldn't distinguish liking, infatuation, and love. Despite her rejections, I still liked her and needed her more than ever. I wasn't sure whether I would remember her instructions in the future and wouldn't repeat the same mistake. I had to keep trying to win her heart even if I was under a delusion.

"Can I call you Oksi from today? Just for few last weeks?" I pleaded.

"I like when people call me Oksi," she replied, smiling.

"Will you miss me?" I asked hopelessly, knowing her reply.

She blushed, smiled, and then shook her head slowly, implying no. It was not the violent shake I had seen few days ago but a gentle one with a blush and a smile. However, it still wasn't the yes I wanted to hear.

"Do we need to prepare for the main event?" I moved on.

"We need to practise more," she replied.

"Today is 12 October," I said thoughtfully. "I will ask Dolce to rehire the auditorium for a week close to the main event."

"Can I go now?" she asked as if seeking my permission.

"Why are you asking me?" I asked, surprised.

"Didn't you say not to leave until you told me?" she replied naively, which was nothing but her usual drama.

"I don't want you to go, but if you want . . ." I flirted.

She smiled and then went away. I called Dolce to arrange to book the school auditorium for nine more days between 20 October and 30 October, costing me Rs4,500.

CHAPTER 25

Oksana had gone out for a couple of hours to meet her friends whereas I chose to stay back. I never wanted her to go out without me. I always wanted her to be around me. But I had never interfered with her personal life. While eagerly waiting for her return, I started to think about the changes I had noticed recently in her behaviour. She had changed. She was talking, giggling, smiling, flirting, passing an odd comment, and behaving like a teenager. I knew she was 32. Once you crossed 30, you lose many freedoms. You needed to behave in a certain way and always appear mature. At the same time, you wanted to relive your gone years especially those teenage years. With only me around her, she didn't have any inhibitions to relive her teenage years. When I was in the tenth standard, we used to have a monthly calendar hanging on the kitchen wall. On every monthly page, there used to be a quotable quote. One of the months, which I still remembered, showed a bird soaring into blue skies with a beautiful quote: "If you love something, set it free. If it comes back, it's yours. Otherwise, it never was.'

For me, Oksana was a woman who always wanted to be free. I let her fly the way she wanted. I liked her in all forms as long as she was around. I didn't like the place without her. It looked so empty. The walls looked strange. I felt short of breath. She brought a breath of fresh air. She filled the whole place with her fragrance. She lit up the place with her big and sparkling eyes. Her laugh, smile, and giggle sounded music to my ears. She illuminated the apartment with her sheer presence.

But in the back of my mind, I knew she was not going to be around for long. She would be gone in the next four weeks forever, never to return. Mumbai had given her nothing but a bad name, insult, pain, humiliation, embarrassment, discomfort, and unease. She had to survive leering eyes, lustful looks, advancements, obscenities, and indecent touches. At least in her country, she would be among her own people whom she knew how to deal with, with her friends and relatives—happy, smiling, and free. She should go back to her country. There was no point in thinking about her decision to go back. Instead, I wanted to enjoy every moment with her till she was around.

There was hope that things might change for the better. If we won the main competition, we may get noticed and be flooded with work. I liked what Dolce had advised me few days back: "Take one step at a time." Meanwhile, I should enjoy dance practice with her, try to win the competition for her, and keep her happy. We had been practising for days for the main event, which was taking place tomorrow. I had gained some confidence since passing the auditions, but the main competition was not going to be an easy one. All the contests were chosen on merit, so the margin of error was little. For me, it was not just winning, but my future with Oksana depended on it.

I heard the click of the lock being opened. She came in smiling, and the whole atmosphere lit up again. I told her I needed to talk to her about tomorrow's competition. She said she needed ten minutes, allowing me enough time to make a call to Delhi. I came back, but she was still in her room. She came back in five minutes, but the wait sounded like five hours to me.

"So how is our Oksana today?" I asked casually.

"Good. In fact, very good," she replied gleefully.

"It's always good to be in the company of girls," I flirted. "Why should one care for poor Jai?"

"I am always here for rich Jai," she flirted back.

"Do you think I am rich?"

"I think so."

"What way?"

"Moneywise."

"Money doesn't give you everything in life," I said philosophically.

"What do you want?"

"I want someone not to go," I said, breathing slowly. She looked away smiling but didn't say anything. I continued, "No answer. Change the topic."

"What did you want to talk about?"

"I think once you go, you will have to come back to pick something you would be leaving behind."

"I'll be leaving behind?" she said, her eyebrows arched in surprise.

"Yes."

"What?"

"Your dressing table."

"Oh, that one. You can keep it."

"For memory."

"I don't know. Give it to someone."

The discussion was not going anywhere, so it was better to concentrate on tomorrow's competition, which should have been the case anyway. But first, I needed a coffee break to re-energise myself. She didn't want, so I went to the kitchen to make coffee for myself. I came back and took the first sip, infusing fresh vigour into my body.

"Oksana, what do you think about tomorrow?" I asked, resuming our conversation.

"Well, we have the last practice session tonight," she replied. "Then we forget until tomorrow."

"I agree," I said. "We shouldn't stress ourselves too much."

"Correct, Jai," she encouraged. "That is how you should look at it."

"Do you know how the competition is going to work?"

She shook her head.

"We will leave at 8 in the morning to be at the venue at 9. The first performance will start at 10. After every performance, there is a 30-minute break so that they could rearrange the stage for the next performance. The lunch break is between 12.30 and 1.30, and the last performance starts at 3.30."

I stopped in the middle to take a sip. I looked at her beautiful face, infusing an extra dose of vigour into my body. I resumed, smiling, "By 3.45, all performances would have finished. The winners would be announced at 5. The award ceremony is scheduled to take place the next day on Saturday in a hotel between 6 and 9 in the evening. Was I clear?"

She nodded, smiling, and asked, "Should we leave for practice?"

We left the apartment for our last session of practice. I regretted that it was going to be our last walk to the auditorium. I remembered the first day of our practice: how she had become upset with me, her angry face, her sitting on the front chair, her gaze moving away, my tricks, and the last trick of me pretending to call Mum. It all looked like yesterday, but actually, that was 15 September, and today was 30 October. So much water had flown down the Ganges since then. I sighed. *Time flies when you are in the company of someone as beautiful as Oksana.*

I woke up next morning very nervous. It was my first big public performance of that kind. My only hope was Oksana. I didn't want to fail her. To overcome my nervousness, I decided to do some meditation and use yoga breathing technique. I sat on the floor in a lotus pose and used the alternative breathing technique, completing six cycles. Next, I started meditation. Staying in the lotus pose, I closed my eyes and listened to my breathing. Just breathing to keep the focus on one thing. I stayed in that position for five minutes. Finally, I opened my eyes and started the third-eye gaze for about five minutes.

I felt much better. Alternative breathing had filled up my lungs with fresh air, and meditation balanced my mind. The nerves were calmed. I could do alternative breathing anytime anywhere even just before the start of our performance. How good is yoga? Simple, free, and effective.

I put my dance costume and shoes in my backpack. I took a shower, got ready, and waited for Oksana anxiously. Soon the queen appeared. Well, not exactly in a queen's dress. She was looking fabulous as usual in blue jeans and red tank top. I got tempted to roll my hands over her arms, but I could imagine that only in my dreams. Instead, I greeted her with a smile, which was reciprocated by a broad smile.

"Are we ready?" I asked.

She nodded.

"I want to make one thing clear," I said forcefully. "When we go out together, I take control of everything."

"What control?"

"Don't go anywhere without me. Even if you wanted to go to the loo. I'll come with you and wait outside."

"Why?"

"Why? If someone tried to touch you, we leave the place."

"You don't want anyone to touch me?" she teased.

"Only if you allow someone."

"Really?"

"It is your body," I said logically.

"You won't feel jealous?" she flirted.

"You like to flirt, don't you?'

"You also like to flirt."

"No. I am serious. Always serious."

"Time to leave now," she said hastily.

It was a light morning chat needed for the stressful day ahead. We reached the venue in 40 minutes. It was a proper studio with concrete fencing and a big iron gate. We walked about 30 meters and entered the main building door through the portico. It looked like a reception hall, full of people. On the right side stood a makeshift registration office consisting of two desks. We walked towards the desks where two young girls were checking invitations. We stood in the queue for a while when one of the girls yelled, "Any contestants in the queue?" We raised our hands, so she asked us to come forward.

"Show me you papers," the girl said.

Oksana handed over the invitation. The girl started typing something on her computer and then raised her head.

"Oksana Bzv . . . vo . . . sky," she said, struggling to pronounce.

"Bzovsky," Oksana corrected politely, smiling gracefully.

"Who is your partner?" the girl asked casually.

Oksana pointed to me. The girl looked at me with disdain. I couldn't understand her behaviour. Was it because I was with Oksana who was better looking than her? Or the girl didn't like men at all? I shrugged my shoulders, ignoring her rudeness.

"You are number 3 starting at 11," she said and then pointed to a man some ten metres away. "See him."

We went to the man who was an office assistant. He took us around the practice hall, waiting room, and toilet area. In the waiting area, there were four temporary tables for food. He asked us to wait in the room and feel free to have anything available on those tables. The time was 9.30, so we decided to go around to have a look at the practice hall. It was a large room with a mirror wall, lockers, and two change rooms. We didn't need any practice, so we put our stuff in one of the lockers and then returned to the waiting room. At 9.45 a man appeared in the waiting room, advising that the first three pairs should remain ready. We were number three, the only pair not ready. We quickly rushed to the practice hall, changed, and came back barely two minutes before the start.

At 10 we were led to the main competition area. It was really a nice auditorium. A large stage with dimmed lights, a place for the contestants on the right hand, an area for the judges facing the stage some ten metres away, and an area for the audience in the centre. There was a total of three judges. Two of them were the same judges whom we had met on the audition day. The audience area was a full house. There were three rows of couches for the contestants stacked one after another in a terrace style. We took the last row. I made sure Oksana sat in the corner, and I sat beside her. I looked at her. She assured me with a little hand wave. I liked her hand wave.

Suddenly, a young lady appeared on the stage, and she started to talk through the mic. She was the host of the show. She started to read the rules of the competition, which had already been communicated to the contestants. She said the winning pair would be decided by the judges. She announced that the marketing director of the MMF would address before the start of the competition. An old man appeared on the stage and started speaking about the history and future plans of MMF. He said although the MMF was a music company, they had organised the song and dance competition for a reason. They were soon starting a large dance academy. He gave the information about the proposed academy, i.e. types of dances, types of courses, etc., and then he left the stage.

The host reappeared on the stage and announced the start of the first performance. The stage was cleared for the performances, and the first pair went to the stage. The lights were dimmed. They took their starting position and waited for judges to say, "Lights, camera, and dance." The lights were turned on, cameras started to roll, and their performance started. They danced to a popular Bollywood duet, which they finished in three to four minutes. It was really a good performance. They heard the judges' comments and then came back to their seats. A break of 30 minutes was announced. It was a nerve-racking wait because I wanted our turn to come quickly, finish our performance, and return to our seat relieved. It was no different feeling from the period leading up to my semester-end exams. The time for the second performance was announced, and the pair started heading towards the stage. The same routine was repeated like the first one. The second pair returned to their seats jumping, happy with their performance and with the judges' comments.

Our turn had arrived, for which I had been eagerly waiting for. Suddenly, the nervousness gripped my whole body, and my legs started to shake. My heart started to pound in fear. I nervously looked straight into her big, blue, bright, and sparkling eyes. She smiled back, trying to calm me down. There were few minutes left, so I decided to perform alternate breathing. I closed my eyes, started alternate breathing, and then heard our names being called out.

We sprang to our feet and started walking towards the stage. I walked nervously behind her. She wasn't deterred at all, walking in full confidence. She had performed many times in front of people, so it was a cakewalk for her.

We both moved to the centre of the stage and took our starting position. I stood behind, our legs bent in a bow style, arms curled up, and hands in a lotus shape, waiting for the judges' orders. Next we heard, "Lights, camera, and dance.'

As the song and music started, we broke into opposite directions. This was the most difficult and intricate part of our performance. We shook and moved parts of our body—head, shoulders, hands, waist, and legs—in different directions: forwards, semi-forwards, backwards, and sideways. We bent and moved our limbs up with a hand roll. We switched, crossed, spun around, and jumped. For the third part, we started with shaking our hands. Our feet moving sideways to come close to each other to the centre. The song stopped, but the music continued. We locked our left arms and looked into each other's eye, moving in a circular motion. With the start of the song, we repeated part two steps. Next, I came back to the centre to prepare for the end part. I bent my legs in a bow style, left hand on the hip, and stretched my right hand outwards. Oksana danced back to the centre and with a gentle backward jerk dropped her body on my stretched right hand. Finally, the music stopped after a large beat of the drum. I curled my left hand up, and she curled up both her hands in a lotus shape.

We ended our performance with a loud applause from the audience. We stood together, bowed, and waited for the judges' comments. The moment of truth had arrived.

"We haven't heard this song before. Which movie was this from?" Judge 1 asked.

"This is not from any movie. It is our own creation," I replied.

"Really. Who sang?" Judge 3 asked.

"I and one Mini," I replied proudly.

"It is a good song you have created," Judge 2 said.

I nodded and felt assured that the judges had liked our song. But it was a general comment that had nothing to do with our overall performance. We waited for the judges' comments, my heart in my mouth.

"I thought the performance was very good. You both moved around very well. Lip-syncing and body movements were also good. However, there was a bit of problem with the coordination. Jai, your body looked a bit stiff. You need to open up a bit. But all in all, a good performance," Judge 1 commented and then looked at Judge 2 for his comments.

My heart sank after hearing his comments. Stiff. What was new? I always felt stiff in her presence.

We both thanked Judge 1.

"I liked the performance. They had a good measure of the stage. Definitely, there was a problem in the coordination, but Oksana tried to make up for Jai. She danced with absolute confidence, pride, and grace. I would say she stood out," Judge 2 finished his comments.

Still no relief for me. *Oksana is going to be the saviour,* I thought. If we won, then the credit should go to her.

"A brilliant performance. Oksana stole the show. Jai complemented her very well. Jai, when you dance with a good performer, your own performance would automatically improve. It was a ten-on-ten performance," Judge 3 commented.

It felt like music to my ears. It was the best comment for my any performance ever. I was relieved at the thought that I had contributed a bit. Amid the thunderous applause, we strolled back to our seats.

I looked at her. She was calm, not giving away much, but she looked happy with my performance. I recalled how she had told me few weeks back, "Because it's me, Oksana, who is your teacher." She was right like she had always been. We had to sit through more performances. We broke for the lunch break, which we didn't enjoy because it was cold and tasteless. Finally, the last performance ended at 4, leaving one full hour on hand before the winners would be announced.

"What do you think of the comments?" I asked eagerly.

"Overall good," she replied calmly. "But there were good comments for others also."

"So we wait and watch."

"Exactly."

"But what is your gut feeling?" I asked deliberately to prepare for my next sentence depending upon her reply.

"My feeling is always positive."

"Always. For everyone," I quipped.

She kept quiet, preferring to ignore me. She knew how to conduct in public. In the last two weeks, I was drawn closer to her, feeling desperate, restless, and uneasy. I had not been able to find a solution. The key to the solution lay in her hands because I was always ready. She was a mystery to me I was unable to unlock. Nothing had moved beyond her trust in me and occasional flirts.

We heard the announcement being made to advise the contestants to assemble back in the auditorium. We all headed back to the auditorium in complete silence.

The host came back on the stage and started with the most overused statement heard all over the world, "It didn't matter who won or lost. All the contestants are winners." I noticed that the host had three envelopes in her hand. I thought mathematically speaking we had one-fifth of a chance. She broke the seal of the first envelope and announced the names of the second runners-up. There was a huge applause from the audience. But it wasn't us. We had lost out in the second runners-up race. The good thing was that we now had one-fourth of a chance. We were inching towards the victory. The names of the first runners-up were announced, and it wasn't our names this time also. The probability of winning had increased to one-third of a chance.

I became tense, and my heart started to pound. All I could hear was the sound of the pounding: *lub-dub, lub-dub, and lub-dub.* The atmosphere was becoming very tense. Suddenly, I felt the warmth of her soft velvety hand on my right shoulder. I fixed my eyes kindly on her. She was smiling, and there was no tension on her face. She lowered her lashes as if saying, "Don't worry. Everything will be all right."

Finally, the seal of the last envelope was broken. The names of the winning pair were about to be announced. Our fate was hanging in the balance. She squeezed my hand, which I took as an indication of her own nervousness or urgency or excitement. A thunderous applause broke the silence. She released her hand and threw her arms up in the air. We had won. She had won. I was numb because this was my first major victory. I held my breath, then started to breathe slowly, and looked into the vacuum without any purpose. My concentration was broken when she shook my shoulder and then looked at me in a way, saying, "See, I told you."

I nodded, feeling privileged to be under the tutelage of an experienced and skilled dancer. There was something about Oksana.

CHAPTER 26

It was the cool morning of Saturday, 1 November 2014. Last evening we talked for hours about the competition, the contestants, our performance, winning moment, and more. We received congratulatory calls from Dolce, Amardeep, and others. Dolce asked for a treat. I agreed because I myself wanted to meet her to discuss something important. We decided to meet tomorrow at 2 in the afternoon. I called Mum who was pleased to know about my first real world success. She said Papa had to go to Singapore in the morning at a short notice. She was feeling alone. I felt for her but couldn't do anything.

I returned to the hall with a heavy heart. The thought of attending the award ceremony in the evening cheered me up. The ceremony was to take place in the same hotel where I had met Oksana in July. That didn't deter her. She said that it was a proud moment for her because she was going there as a winner, not as a dancer.

I decided to wear formal. Oksana said she wanted to buy a new dress for the occasion. She could now afford because she was richer by Rs50,000. That was the first time I had earned money since moving to Mumbai—in fact, in my life. However, it wouldn't make any difference to my bank balance because I had decided to give away my prize money to Dolce, Amardeep, Sachin, Neel, and Ajay Rs10,000 apiece. As a result, my current bank balance stood unchanged at Rs460,010.45. The fact that I had made my first earning should have made be happy, but the thought that soon she would be gone dampened my mood. I went to my room and prepared a brief acceptance speech. I folded the paper into half. I didn't want to fold the paper further, so I gave it to Oksana because it fitted perfectly in her bag.

At 2.30 in the afternoon, we left for the shopping centre to buy Oksana's new dress. At a ladies' fashion store, she started looking around for her new dress. "Pick this one, check, keep that back and pick another" type of thing kept on happening. We already had spent an hour in the store in vain. Finally, she chose one she seemed to have liked. She went to the fitting room. In about ten minutes, she called me for my opinion. I felt privileged. I nearly fell over when I saw her. She was looking absolutely gorgeous in loose black trousers, white short-sleeved shirt with a knot in the front, and high-heeled black sandals. The shirt had a white background with tiny black polka dots.

"How do I look?" she asked, excited.

"You always look good with or without clothes," I flirted.

"What do you mean without clothes?" she asked while narrowing her eyes.

"I've seen you without clothes."

"You still remember that?" she asked seriously.

"Have you forgotten?"

"Cut the crap," she replied sternly. I looked at her hopelessly and sighed. She asked again seriously, "Do you want to help? How do I look?"

"Buy this one," I replied impassively and took a deep breath.

She came out, paid, and we reached home at 4, leaving an hour for us to get ready. She unpacked her new dress and then started closely, checking her selection once again. She held her shirt from the shoulder corners and then displayed on her body. She repeated the same exercise with her trousers this time on her legs. She looked very happy with her selection, so she went to her room to get ready.

We reached the hotel at 25 minutes to 6. The lobby, as usual, was full of people. We went to the reception area to be told to proceed to level one where the award ceremony was taking place. We crossed the lobby, went past the arcade, and then took a lift to level one.

The door opened to a fairly large well-lit ceremony hall and a bar straight ahead some ten metres away where people were enjoying drinks of their choices. On the left side, we saw a row of tables on which food was placed, and the right side led to the main ceremony area. We turned right to walk towards the ceremony area. There were around ten rows of chairs. Each row was divided into two equal number of chairs separated by a walking space from the middle. The stage was two steps high, with a mic on the left, three chairs right in the middle, and a table on the right side where large bouquets had been placed. The toilets were just behind the last row facing each other.

There were around 50 people of different colours, shades, sizes, and heights. Oksana was looking dazzling in her dress. She wore a beautiful crown-braid hairstyle, popularised by Ukrainian politician Yulia Tymoshenko, which exposed her long neck, and a structured bag hanging by her left shoulder. People started looking at us, talking in hushed voices probably about Oksana. My mood soured the way people were looking at her. I started getting bad vibes from some people and feared something untoward was about to happen.

Soon we were greeted by a young woman who led us to our seats. The front row, on the left side, was reserved for the winners. The other winners had already taken their seats. The two corner seats were reserved for the main winners. It was a very proud moment for me to see a seat reserved for me. I asked Oksana to take the corner seat and sat beside her on the other. She sat in the most exquisite manner. She put her right leg over her left leg, rested her elbows on the side arms, and then locked her hands. The empty seats soon started to fill in. Three men walked by us, headed towards the stage, and then took the middle chairs. They looked like people from the MMF. Out of the three men, one was short, fat, and bald. He wore a thick moustache and was constantly laughing in a very weird manner.

We waited for the main ceremony to start. It was not until 6.30 the ceremony finally started off. The same woman who had greeted us earlier took the mic. She introduced the three men who were MMF's top executives. The short, fat, and bald man was the owner. She explained the agenda for the night. It was simple. The owner would speak about the MMF, the names of the pairs would be called out in reverse order, i.e. the second runners-up, first runners-up, and the winners followed by the acceptance speech by the winners. The whole ceremony would be wrapped up in 45 minutes, and then people could enjoy food and drinks until 9.

The woman requested the fat man to deliver his opening remarks. He started off with the usual stuff about his company, the charitable work they do, and their future plans about the soon-to-be-launched dance academy. He finished his remarks in about ten minutes, and the woman called out the names of the second runners-up. They got up and walked up the stage. They stood near the mic, facing the people. One of the two men handed them bouquets and a cheque for Rs25,000. A photographer took their picture. They bowed and came back to their seats. The same process was repeated for the first runners-up.

Finally, our names were called out. We got up to walk up the stage. I was in the front and Oksana behind me. The fat man was supposed to give away cheques to us, so he stood near the mic. As we neared, he extended his hand, pushing me aside, and then started to shake hands with Oksana. I stood there watching him shaking hand with Oksana with a broad smile on his face. Next, he put his left hand on Oksana's hand to give the impression that it was the two-handed handshake. Actually, he was stroking her hand with his left hand. Oksana was smiling gracefully, unaware of what actually was happening.

All eyes were on Oksana. It looked like she was the showstopper. I meant nothing to the crowd, and they seemed to be not interested in me. I felt humiliated, ignored, and alone. To divert my attention, I looked around at the people. I saw a man clapping constantly for no reason. A woman sitting beside hit him with her left elbow. He looked at the woman in pain. With her index finger over her lips, she gestured towards him to stop laughing. She must have been his wife, a wise one.

My focus returned to Oksana when I saw the fat man still shaking hands with her. It looked too long for a handshake, so she started pulling her hand back. The fat man let her hand go reluctantly with that weird smile on his face. He then looked at me with a forced smile but didn't shake hands with me. My humiliation was complete. I looked at her. Her face was saying, "I know what he's doing but don't say anything now." I took a deep breath and pretended to be normal. We were then presented with individual bouquets and prize money of Rs50,000 each. The fat man moved to Oksana's side for the group picture. He put his arm around Oksana's waist and squeezed her towards himself, narrowing the gap between the two but increasing the gap between Oksana and me. I looked at her from the corners of my eyes, disgusted and inwardly seething. Finally, the group picture was taken. Not contented, he flashed his mobile out and then took a selfie with Oksana with both of them making faces and sticking their tongues out. He then went to the woman and whispered something in her ear. The woman announced that the fat man wanted Oksana to deliver the acceptance speech. My humiliation wasn't yet complete. I still had to survive few more lonely moments until her speech ended.

She went to the mic and unfolded the paper I had given her. I saw a man sitting on one of the front seats, readjusting his position. He put his right leg over his left, rested his left cheek on his palm, smiled, and focused his gaze on Oksana as if it were his own wife that was going to deliver the acceptance speech. Oksana started her speech in her deep husky voice, which sounded music to everyone's ears. I looked around. Nobody was looking at me, except for the woman who had elbowed her husband. Oksana ended her speech with a loud thank-you and then raised her right fist like the black-power salute of Tommie Smith and John Carlos in the 1968 Summer Olympics. I thought probably she was protesting against Shabnam Seth's indecent proposal. As Oksana ended her speech, I saw a man gesturing with upturned palm towards her, a gesture often used in India for a "Wow" or "What a speech" or "What an item". I thought of telling the man that item was a big-ticket item but for my next plan. In the end, Oksana bobbed a shy little bow to the audience, her left hand on her chest, and gave a big shiny smile, which attracted more thunderous applause.

Finally, my ordeal was over. We started walking down the stage towards the exit. I had made a decision to leave the place without having anything. They could have their food or drinks, but I was not going to stay any longer. As we were approaching the lift, Oksana felt her throat had dried, so she wanted to have soft drinks to quench the dryness. I told her to pick one and watched her until she had reached the bar. Meanwhile, I turned to walk towards the men's toilet when I saw a man approaching me. I stood there waiting for him. He was of medium height, pale skinned, and well built. He had a big oval-shaped face, Mexican-style moustache, and big jaws. He was wearing an expensive suit, implying that he was a wealthy man. He came close and stood slightly diagonally in front of me directly facing the bar.

"Naresh Galhot," he introduced himself.

He pulled his visiting card out of his coat, which he gave to me. I read the card and then looked up at him. He was not looking at me. I thought that there were people who felt below their dignity to look straight into one's eyes, so I didn't mind his rudeness.

"Jai Grover," I introduced myself.

"Join my company," he spoke at length. "I've a big events management company. We manage big events in India, Dubai, and Singapore. You can go to places anywhere in India or Dubai or Singapore. We are planning to organise events in London, Toronto, New Jersey, and Bay Area wherever large Indian population resides."

"I'll think about it," I told him politely.

"You know, you could brush shoulders with big Bollywood stars. It is all fun. Travel, parties, and more."

"I am not alone, so I need to check with my partner first," I lied.

"You have my card. Contact me when you are ready."

He went away, disappearing somewhere. I was still waiting for Oksana, so I started to think about Naresh Galhot. He looked very sharp, shrewd, clever, smooth, and greedy. A person who could smell money in any opportunity. A person whose eyes would sparkle at the slightest mention of money. Above all, a person who could exploit anyone. He didn't give me any positive vibes; in fact, I felt very insecure.

I forgot about the toilet, turned back, and started walking towards the bar. I saw Oksana leaning on a stool, slowly shaking her hips. I stopped and looked back to search for Naresh Galhot. I couldn't locate him anywhere. A strange smile appeared on my face, and the whole conversation started flashing in front of my eyes. I understood why he wasn't looking at me. Why? Because he was watching Oksana all the time. He was more interested in Oksana than me. I went to Oksana and looked straight at her beautiful, radiant face. I thought, *Everybody likes Oksana. Wrong—everybody likes her body. They want a slice of Oksana night after night.*

CHAPTER 27

I left home to meet Dolce in the same food court where I had met her the first time. While on the train, I started to think about last night. I laughed and thought no one was going to get hold of Oksana. I knew her very well. She was Oksana. Sharp, strong, proud, intelligent, and beautiful. I then started to think about Dolce. I had to discuss few important things with her. I trusted her more than my life. She was my Shakespeare's famous quote: "A friend in need is a friend indeed." The acronym of her name was *DD*—Dolce Desai—but she could aptly be called Dolce Dear, Dolce Darling, Dolce the Doll, Dolce the Delight, and, of course, Dolce the Drummer. I felt privileged to have her as my friend and thought Sachin was so lucky to have her as his girlfriend. She would always keep him happy because she was that type of person. Suddenly, an evil thought crossed my mind. What if I hadn't met Oksana? What if Sachin wasn't Dolce's boyfriend? What if I had met her and found her unattached? Would have I wanted her to be my girlfriend? She was beautiful and rich. I shook my head in disbelief. No, never. The image that I had created for her would have remained the same. The image that of a most trusted friend and a close confidante. I felt relieved because these were hypothetical questions anyway.

I reached the food court and soon located her busy on the mobile, checking probably social media or on some kind of chat.

"How is my Dolce?" I asked.

She stopped fiddling with her mobile, looked up, nodded, and asked, smiling, "How was last night?"

"Winners are grinners," I replied, grinning, choosing not to disclose much.

It was she who had got us to the competition, so it wasn't fair to tell her how I had felt last night.

"I told you," she said, still smiling, and complained, "Why didn't you bring Oksi?"

"I had to talk something private with you."

"What?"

"I want you to convince Oksana to cancel her plans to go back."

"Why? She's already booked," she asked, alarmed.

"Why? I am thinking of something big," I continued. "Can't do without her."

"What big?" she asked, confused.

"I am planning to hold an event. I've done my research. It is possible. It requires hard work, so I need help—your help," I explained. "Could you all come to my place tomorrow, please?"

"Are you sure?" she asked suspiciously.

I nodded while giving her two thumbs up.

"What time?"

"Eleven in the morning," I said. "First, convince Oksana."

"What do I say?" she asked, pretending to be tired.

"I don't have to tell you. You know how to deal with her," I replied, smiling.

I suddenly remembered about the money. I gestured Dolce to wait, stood up, and took the money out of my pocket.

"This is my share of winning amount," I said proudly. "But it is yours."

"No, Jai," Dolce protested.

"Remember, our first meeting, you promised so you have to take."

"You talk to others," she said cleverly.

"If Dolce says yes, everybody says yes," I said forcefully and then threatened, "Otherwise, we finish our friendship."

"But you keep some."

I shook my head violently. She nodded reluctantly.

I felt relieved having been able to pay something back to them after so many months. If they were not with me, I would have gone back failed. Their kindness, friendship, and constant support had kept me going. As I had never been away from my parents, they had become my family in Mumbai.

"So you are talking to Oksana?" I said, resuming the conversation after a brief lull.

"Is it only the event?" Dolce asked suspiciously.

"What only the event?" I asked, sighing, which she noticed.

"You want her to cancel?"

"Yes."

"I don't agree with you. Do you like her?"

"I can't hide anymore. I have to tell you everything."

"Tell me. Tell me," she said, excited, moving her chair close.

"On one condition," I said seriously.

"I won't tell anyone," she said, outsmarting me.

"It's a very private thing I am sharing with you," I cautioned and then complimented, "But I trust you."

"Sure. Sure," she said, overexcited. "Tell me now, please."

I started to tell her everything in detail. I told her how I met Oksana. In the beginning, I just saw a dancer in her. She needed help, and I needed a dancer. It was a win-win situation for both of us. Even after she had moved into my apartment, I saw her the same way. But after that eventful Friday night, things started to change. She started to drift away while I drew closer and closer. I also told her about the three *R*s technique, but that also failed. I concluded by saying that in the last few weeks, I had become desperate, but I was controlling my emotions somehow.

"Do you know why she is drifting away?" Dolce asked.

"No. It could be anything," I replied. "Age gap or cultural thing or pure disliking."

"I bet it is not disliking. Otherwise, she would have moved out a long time back."

"I never thought about that."

"Does she trust you?"

"I think so," I said. "Trust is the only thing that is holding me."

"What do you mean holding you?"

"I don't know," I replied, confused.

"What would've you done, otherwise?"

"Nothing. I don't know," I replied, irritated.

"I think you need to talk to her in a plain language."

"I am dropping hints, but she ignores them."

"Go straight."

"I don't have courage."

"Are you a man or a woman?" she ridiculed.

"Ask her," I replied, winking. "She knows."

We both burst into laughter. We took a small break and walked around to order food. Gujarati Dolce ordered Punjabi cuisine for both.

She said she liked Punjabi cuisine. While walking back, she stopped. With a little hand wave, she told me to come close. I hesitated. What was she doing? Was she going to say something unexpected? Was she going to ditch Sachin for me? Seeing me hesitating, she came close to my left ear and whispered, "Don't tell that Punjabi that I like Punjabi cuisine."

Relieved, I started to laugh loudly. That Punjabi was none other than Amardeep. Their rivalry continued even when not facing each other. I laughed, thinking about Amardeep. We came back to resume some serious conversation.

"Why are you doing the event?" Dolce asked.

"I want to beat them the way Ivan the Great beat Tatars in their own game."

"Beat who? Who are Tatars?" she asked, confused.

"Beat people like Shabnam, Sharif Ahmad, and Ranganathan," I replied, "Don't worry about Tatars. It is an old story."

"I don't get you," she said, still confused.

"For our dance group, Shabnam could influence people. But an event is a public thing. She can't stop people going to an event. So we skip the idea of performing for others. Instead, we perform for ourselves," I reinforced my argument.

"When do you want to do it?"

"On 24 December 2014 between 9 and midnight."

"Are you serious?" she asked. "Today is second of November. You don't have enough time, Jai."

"I've worked everything out. That is why I need everybody tomorrow including Oksana. She is the key."

"Why do you want her to cancel? Why can't she postpone?"

"There are many reasons. First, she could prove a big-ticket item for our company. Second, if our event succeeds, then she doesn't have to worry much."

"What if it fails?" she challenged.

"I can find a job for her. She still has a valid visa until June 2015."

"How will you find a job for her when you yourself struggled?"

"There is someone who offered us to join his company."

"Who is this someone?"

"I'll tell you about him later," I replied, not wanting to disclose about Naresh Galhot whom I myself didn't like much, but he was the only hope.

"Moreover—" I paused in hesitation.

"Why did you stop?"

"I don't want her to go," I replied, looking away from Dolce.

"That is the main thing, isn't it, Jai?" Dolce teased. "Now I'll talk to her. Leave that to me."

"I knew you will help me," I said gratefully.

We prepared to leave. Dolce promised to get in touch with Oksana and also with others for tomorrow's meeting. I started to get worried because there was a lot of work ahead. A lot of planning was required for the venue, online ticketing company, the programme for the night, advertisement, website, logistics etc. I had to finish most of my work by 14 November. It was my 22nd birthday, so my parents wanted me to visit them. I had to book tickets for Delhi also.

I reached the building tired. My legs were screaming out for rest. As I was about to open the door, Dolce called. She had spoken to Oksana who had agreed to cancel her plan because she wanted to help me, which I greatly appreciated. It was a welcome relief that one major issue was sorted out because without her the event wouldn't have been possible. I opened the door to find Oksana sitting on the couch, ready to go somewhere. She looked over her shoulder and got up hurriedly to say something. I didn't know what was coming now.

"Did you ask Dolce to call me?" she shouted.

"No," I lied.

"Couldn't you have spoken to me directly?"

"I am scared of you."

"You told her that you didn't want me to go. Why?"

"Because you are beautiful," I quipped.

"Don't talk rubbish. Otherwise, I won't cancel my plan," she threatened.

"Sorry," I said, quickly falling in line, and pleaded, "Please don't do that."

She still had an ace up her sleeve. There was no respite for me. I was tired, but I needed to prepare for tomorrow's meeting. I wanted some peace around me.

"That is okay," she said with great difficulty. "I am going out."

My face lit up. For the first time, I didn't mind her going away for few hours.

I started working on the process of events management: goal, team, date and venue, programme, budget, ticket pricing, advertisement, and tagline. The goal was to organise a Bollywood night event. The date we knew of, and the team was already in place.

I contacted an online ticketing company who explained their charges: 2.5 per cent for processing, Rs100 per ticket for print, and 3.5 per cent for payment processing. Their deal included free advertisement on their website. I decided to hire two stand-up comedians and two C-rated Bollywood female stars just for appearance. There were many C-rated Bollywood stars who struggle to find roles after a movie or two. They then make money through appearing in events, inaugurating little shops, or appearing in little-known fashion shows. Some indulge in less-dignified work.

I prepared a rough budget. I thought an auditorium with minimum 600 seating capacity would return us a small profit. I worked out the ticket pricing based on platinum, gold, and silver types, allocating 200 seats each. For online advertisement, I chose to use Google AdWords and Facebook from next week until the event date.

I also booked the ticket for Delhi for 14 November, which cost me Rs3,421 return fare. The scheduled take-off time was 15:40, landing in Delhi at 17:40. I ended the day pretty much satisfied with my efforts.

Next day the whole team landed at my place at 11 in the morning for our first meeting. Dolce and Oksana left for the shopping centre to cancel the ticket.

Meanwhile, I told the guys not to worry about the expenses or any loss. I told them I was happy to share the profit. I needed their support for the successful culmination of the event. The guys listened to me without any resistance or expressions on their faces. Had Dolce been around, she would have definitely resisted and insisted that everybody shared the expenses or any loss equally.

Eventually, after a 30-minute wait, Dolce and Oksana came back from the centre. Oksana was very upset because she had lost some money in cancellation. We all sat around the dining table to start our first meeting.

"Dolce, I've told these guys that they didn't have to worry about the expenses," I said.

"Who will bear?" Dolce asked.

"Myself and Oksana," I replied, winking, but Oksana reacted as if she had touched a live wire.

"I am not doing anything. I already lost Rs5,000 in cancellation because of you," she said, red-faced, and then gave me a glare.

"Because of me? How?"

"How? You don't know?" she yelled.

"He is joking," Dolce comforted. "He'll compensate you for the cancellation."

"I don't need that money," she replied calmly.

"Don't worry, Oksana," Amardeep consoled, not wanting to be left behind. "We will talk about it later."

"Should we start?" I said.

"That is why we are here," Oksana said something sensible for the first time, normally never taking any interest, always choosing to be a mere spectator like Ajay, Neel, and Sachin.

"I've worked out everything. The programme, the cost, date, venue, advertisement strategy, and the tagline."

"Jai, how is the tagline going to be like?" Dolce asked.

"You will like it. It's very apt."

"Really, what is it like?"

"Since the event is on 24 December between 9 and midnight, I called it like this: Bollywood Night—Enjoy the Christmas Eve," I said and then asked, flashing a bright smile, "How is that for a tagline?"

No one said anything. My genius tagline had fallen apart.

"Do you have a better idea?" I asked, extremely disappointed.

No one had thought about it. However, there was a strong message in their silence. It was a good test because if it didn't excite them, how could it then excite the public? We needed more punch to the line, so we started to think in complete silence. While I was thinking, I looked at Oksana. She still bore that upsetting face. When our eyes met, she turned her gaze away disdainfully. OMG, such a hatred for me. My thinking process almost immediately collapsed. I covered my face with my hands and laughed.

"I got it," Dolce broke the silence and said, brimming in confidence, "Bollywood Night—Enjoy the Christmas Eve and Go Home on Christmas Day."

I looked around the faces. Amardeep was still thinking, probably deliberately choosing to ignore Dolce's tagline. I personally liked the new tagline. I started to clap, and soon others joined me. The tagline was approved.

"Now the programme," I explained. "We will hire two stand-up comedians and two C-rated Bollywood female actors. Two dance performances by Oksana."

There was no response from Oksana. I looked up. She, as usual, was not in the discussion. She was looking somewhere else, chewing something again like a cow. I waved my hand in front of her face to draw her attention. She stopped chewing and then squeezed her lips, trying to hide her chew.

"You have two dance performances," I repeated.

"I heard you," she whined.

"We will fill the gaps with music," I said, ignoring her whine. "All agree?"

"Yep, that is our job," Amardeep said, looking at the other three, who nodded.

"Are you interested in budget and pricing?" I asked, knowing that it wasn't really their concern.

"How will we know how much are we making?" Oksana asked seriously.

"I'll give the high-level details," I said. "First the cost. It is coming around Rs620,000."

"Do you have that much money?" Dolce asked, concerned.

"I don't have to pay everything now," I replied. "Just the advance. About Rs137,000."

"How much will we make?" Sachin asked.

"We have 200 platinum seats at Rs2,000 each, 200 gold at Rs1,500 each, and 200 silver at Rs1,000 each. How much is—"

Before I could complete my sentence, Dolce started to calculate on her mobile; so I let her, which allowed me to stretch my arms.

"Rs900,000. So we can make a good profit," she said.

"No, only a small profit. The ticketing company will deduct 2.5 per cent for processing, Rs100 per ticket print, and 3.5 per cent for payment processing," I explained. Dolce again tried to calculate, but I stopped. "Don't bother. I've got the figure. It is Rs786,000, which means we make a profit of Rs166,000. Around Rs23,714 each. All happy?"

"Only Rs23,714?" Oksana asked despairingly.

"Tickets are cheap. It is not a bad profit for first-timers like us," I said, staring at her. She grinned sheepishly. I continued, "No additional 5 per cent to you in this case."

"Why?" she asked with raised eyebrows.

"Tickets would be sold by the ticketing company," I replied.

She didn't say anything but didn't look happy either.

"Dolce, if you could now tell your friend to start her practice?" I asked deliberately to stir Oksana up.

She took it very seriously.

"I don't need any practice. I can do without practice," she replied angrily.

"Remember, your slogan," I reminded. "Practise, practise, and practise."

"That was for you. Not for me," she replied sternly after giving me a quick glare.

God, I had done a cardinal sin of comparing myself with her.

"Are we done?" Sachin asked.

"Yes. But I got a problem," I replied.

"What?" Dolce asked.

"I can't find any C-rated actors," I said, concerned.

"How did you work out the cost?" Dolce said.

"Good pick," I remarked, impressed.

"Even I was going to ask you," Amardeep said.

"Really?" Dolce teased. "If you had brains, then you would have asked first."

"Sachin, I am warning you. I'll kill her," Amardeep said, annoyed in his usual style.

I laughed. Their rivalry was a daily event. Sometimes many times in a day.

"Jai, how did you work out the cost?" Sachin asked, ignoring both.

"I just budgeted Rs300,000 for the two."

"What will you do now?" Dolce asked, concerned.

I started to think. Suddenly, his thought brought a big smile on my face. Where is he? It had been long since I had seen him.

"There is one who can help," I replied, relieved.

"Who?"

"Someone who promised Oksana to take to Lonavla," I said with a big smile on my face.

"Do you have a boyfriend?" Amardeep asked Oksana, disappointed. He sighed. "I wasn't bad."

We all laughed. Feeling embarrassed, Oksana blushed and then burst into laughter.

"I don't have any boyfriend," she said, still laughing. She completed her sentence, pointing to me. "He is his friend."

"We go out for lunch," I said. "I have to do a lot of work."

Back from lunch, I booked an auditorium costing Rs120,000 for five hours. The auditorium was close to a railway station, so the parking was not going to be a major issue. They demanded 10 per cent advance, which I had to pay immediately. I spoke to two stand-up comedians who demanded Rs150,000 each and 20 per cent advance. I placed an advertisement on Google AdWords and Facebook, costing me Rs10,000 each. I kept aside Rs20,000 and Rs10,000 for refreshments and logistics respectively. The refreshment supplier demanded 25 per cent advance.

I now needed to sort out the female actors' issue. I dialled his number, but it kept ringing. I decided to call him a little later. As I was about to disconnect, someone picked my call.

"Aah . . ." someone answered in a feeble voice, appearing to be in deep pain.

"Hello, VS," I said.

"Kon VS [Who VS]?" he replied in Hindi.

I laughed and thought that this man was a crack. First time when I addressed him by his proper name, he insisted on being called VS.

"Vishal. I am Jai speaking," I said, laughing. "How are you?"

"Oh! Jai. Not good," Vishal replied.

What he told me next made me laugh, but I had to control myself because he was in a bad condition. He said he was currently admitted in a hospital in Meerut after a road accident. He had arrived in Meerut last week to resolve a long-standing dispute with his uncle over an ancestral land. During an argument, they had come to blows. His cousin ran to the cowshed, came back with an axe in his hand, and chased him down the street only to be rescued by a passing policeman, unharmed. His cousin was arrested, and the police advised him to take the matter to the court. He also told me sadly, though, that he and his cousin used to play together when they were kids.

"So how did you end up in the hospital?" I asked sympathetically.

"Everything is wrong in North India," he complained. His tirade continued, "People don't have traffic sense. They think they are smart but actually are idiots. There is no privacy because people peep into one another's homes. The weather is bad because it is very cold."

"So how did you end up in the hospital?" I asked again, irritated.

He told me that three days back, he was going to the court on a scooter. One of his relatives was driving while he was sitting behind him as a pillion passenger. It was a foggy morning, a common thing in winter months in Delhi and cities close to Delhi. As they were travelling, suddenly, the traffic signal turned red, so they had to stop abruptly. A car coming from behind couldn't see them, so it rammed into their scooter. Vishal was thrown off his seat and fell straight on the road, his face down. As a result, he had badly bruised his face and dislocated his shoulder.

"How long will you be in the hospital?" I asked seriously.

"Three or four more days."

"Will you be coming back to Mumbai after that?"

"Didn't I tell you about the court case?" he replied, annoyed.

"I need your help."

I told him everything in brief about my event and the reason why I had called him.

"Are you sure?" he ridiculed. "Can you organise an event?"

"Yes, why?"

"Didn't I tell you that you are not smart?" he hurled an insult once again.

Vishal had insulted me with that "you are not smart" remark many times in the past. I always thought of telling him that his self-created superlative image was actually a false one. He was surviving with the help of his father's influence; otherwise, he wasn't capable of selling even a brothel. But today was not the right time because I needed his help. Moreover, I didn't want to engage in an unnecessary discussion with him on trivial issues.

"I think I can organise," I responded calmly.

"Why didn't you call me?" he demanded.

Why should have I called him? He had to be stopped, so I shot back.

"Why didn't you call me?" I asked, putting a lot of weight on *you*.

"Are you mad? I am in the hospital, and you expect me to call you?" he rebuked.

How was I supposed to know that? There was a certain method in his madness.

"I am sorry," I said. He had already wasted my 15 minutes. I asked, hoping to extract useful information from him. "How can I get C-rated female actors?"

"You know Vinay?" he replied finally.

"That bar manager?" I asked, relieved.

"Yes. Call him. He knows an agent."

"Thank you. What is Vinay's number?"

"I don't know. Call the reception."

"Thank you. I've to go now. I hope—"

He didn't let me complete my sentence.

"Kysi hey woh [How is she]?" Vishal asked coolly as if his pain had suddenly vanished.

I knew who he was asking about, but I thought of having fun with Vishal.

"Who are you talking about?"

"That Russian."

"Which Russian? I don't know any Russian."

"The one who lives with you," he said, irritated.

"Oh! Oksana," I said while trying to control my laugh. I needled, "By the way, she was asking about you."

"Really? What for?"

"You had promised to take her to Lonavla."

"Yes. I remember that." He sighed in grief.

It was the time to end our long and largely useless conversation.

"Bye, Vishal."

"Call me VS. Aah . . ." he reminded, ending with an aah.

I couldn't make out whether Vishal's aah was due to his injuries or Oksana. She was quite capable of inflicting pain on others. I had myself been a victim of her pain many times. I started to think about Vishal. No matter how irritating, irrational, or illogical he was, he was still a useful person. It was hard to deal with him, but with a bit of patience, one could get enough out of him. I also remembered when he had told that I should know people like Vinay. How correct was he?

I called the hotel, obtained the number from Vinay, and then phoned the agent. Initially, he demanded Rs400,000, which was way above my budget. After a hard-fought negotiation, he agreed. However, I had to pay 20 per cent as advance payment. All in all, I had paid Rs122,000 towards advance payments, leaving my bank balance at Rs328,090.15. To my dismay, I realised that I had spent more than 50 per cent in under four months.

I went to bed somewhat worried. I couldn't sleep. I needed to divert my attention. Suddenly, I recalled my conversation with Vishal about Oksana. A funny thought crossed my mind. What if Oksana and Vishal loved each other? How would they manage? He wouldn't stop dishing out his nonsense. She wouldn't stop pulling his leg. One thing was sure that they would drive each other crazy. I laughed my head off. I felt a bit relieved, but I now needed to prepare myself for the Delhi trip.

CHAPTER 28

It was my 22nd birthday today. Nobody in Mumbai knew about it because I hadn't told anyone. I was to fly up to Delhi in the evening to spend a night with my parents. Meanwhile, I started to look back at my previous 21 birthdays. My parents told me that my first birthday was celebrated at home with a great pomp and show. All our close relatives, family friends, and neighbours were invited to join my first birthday bash. I didn't remember much about my second and third birthdays. But my most memorable one was my fourth birthday because I celebrated at the McDonald's with my little friends. I was lucky because McDonald's had opened its first Indian branch on 13 October 1996, nearly a month before my fourth birthday, at Basant Lok, South Delhi. We continued to celebrate my birthdays at McDonald's until I turned 10. Thereafter, it became a private affair, always celebrating with my parents at home.

My flight to Delhi was due to take off in two hours. I was leaving for Delhi quite satisfied with the progress so far. The ticket sale had started. The public response had been good so far. The ticketing company had informed me that they were expecting to sell out by the second week of December. However, I was concerned about Oksana. That was the first time I was leaving her alone. It was just a night away, but I felt like going away for months. I didn't want to go, but I had to. I was torn between Oksana and my parents. I needed to talk to her. I yelled out her name. She came out beaming.

"Call Dolce if you need any help," I said, concerned.

"I don't need any help," she replied calmly.

"Will you be fine alone?"

"Much safer," she teased.

"Who were you scared of?"

"Someone."

"Is that someone me?"

"Yes," she replied, giggling.

"Do you want anything from Delhi?"

"What can you get for me?"

"You tell me."

"I don't want anything."

"If you didn't want anything, then why did you ask?"

"Because you asked me," she replied like a kid.

"I have to go now," I said. "I will be back tomorrow at 5 in the evening."

She shrugged her shoulders.

I picked my backpack, looked at her radiant face for the last time, and left without looking back again. It took me about an hour to reach the airport. I checked in and waited to board the plane. I called Dolce to make sure she remained in touch with Oksana until my return. An announcement was made, and I boarded the plane. It started filling in very quickly, and after some wait, it started to move. The final take-off was announced, and within minutes, we were airborne. I started getting a sinking feeling. It wasn't due to the take-off but the feeling of leaving someone behind, not seeing for 24 hours, and missing badly. I started to think about Oksana. What would she be doing now? Talking to Dolce or her friends, cooking, practising dance, or sitting alone in her most favourite pose.

The plane shook violently, breaking my concentration. It was the turbulence that caused the plan to shake because we were approaching the wintery north. I checked the time. We had been flying for 90 minutes. I couldn't think much thereafter because the turbulence wouldn't stop until we made the touchdown.

I got out of the airport and hired a taxi. I was back in Delhi after a gap of little under four months. I had left Delhi in the blistering summer on 20 July, and I was back in Delhi on a wintery evening of 14 November. I looked around. Nothing had changed in four months. Same buildings, same shops, same roads, and same people. Everything looked tasteless and listless to me. I didn't feel any vibrancy or energy in the city. It was here I was born, lived most of my life, gone to the school and the institute. I had turned 22 today, but there was no joy. But the people looked happy, laughing, shopping, walking, and talking like the people did in Mumbai.

Finally, I reached home. The security guard manning the gate opened the gate in such a manner as if I were a victorious prince returning from a war. He had never done it before, but then I had never been out for so long. I patted his back and enquired about his family. I saw my parents standing at the front door. They were the same parents I had seen four months back. They hadn't grown old. I ran towards my mother and hugged her tight. It was a long tight hug before she released me. I then hugged my father who looked very pleased to see me. I saw my mother wiping her tears from the corner of her sari. Once inside, I started looking around and went to one room after another and then the backyard. Nothing had changed, but everything looked strange. I came back and saw my parents whispering something.

"What are you talking about?" I asked, concerned.

"Nothing. Don't worry," Papa replied.

"No. There is something. I've never seen you like this," I insisted.

"That time you used to live with us," Mum said, complaining.

"Jai, she is complaining that you just came for one night," Papa clarified.

"That's too late on your birthday," Mum said sadly.

"Go and freshen up," Papa ordered.

"Come back quick, Jai," Mum ordered.

I came back in ten minutes to the dining area. Mum had already arranged the food on the table. Papa was sitting on one of the chairs. Mum was busy in the kitchen with something. I sat with Papa, waiting for Mum to join us. It was the same Indian drama. She came with a plate containing an incense stick, flowers, uncooked rice, *roli* for *tilak,* and Indian sweets. She gestured me to stand up and took my *aarti* by moving the plate in front of my face in a circular motion. She then asked to seek the blessing from Baba Nanak, the founder of Sikhism and the first of the Sikh gurus.

"My son is 22 today," Mum said proudly.

"Big boy," Papa said proudly.

Big boy. Yes, I had become a big boy in the last four months by meeting and dealing with people from different strokes.

"Where is the cake?" Papa asked.

"Should we cut it now, Jai?" Mum asked.

"I am 22. I don't like these things now," I replied, irritated.

"Yes, he is 22. We will have after dinner," Papa said softly.

We started having dinner quietly. I started to think about Oksana again. I was having dinner without her for the first time in the last four months. For a moment, I thought she was sitting across me, smiling and teasing me. I shook my head to bring my attention back and then drew a deep sigh.

I looked at Mum who was trying to communicate through her eyes: "Have this" or "You want this". Papa made sure that I had a bit of everything that was on the table. I laughed because they were treating me like a kid. Occasionally, I noticed that Mum was looking at me as if I were a stranger, searching for old Jai. We finished and headed to the TV room for the postdinner chat.

"How is your business going?" Papa asked seriously.

"Didn't Mum tell you anything?" I replied.

"Yes, but I want to hear from you."

"Well, for the event, things are looking bright."

I briefly explained to him everything: how I failed to get any business, about team Dolce, different people I met, and Oksana.

"Business is like that. There are always challenges you should learn to face. Success and failures are part and parcel of a business. Learn from your mistakes and don't repeat them," Papa lectured.

Papa had been in the business for so long. Small failures were daily things for him. Meanwhile, Mum came in with the cake.

"Jai, how are your friends?" Mum asked.

"Good," I replied. "Dolce is very intelligent, Amardeep is funny, and rest of the three are very quiet."

"How is she?" Mum asked, smiling mischievously.

"Who is she?" I asked, smiling mischievously.

"What's her name?" Papa asked curiously.

"Oksana," I replied to Papa then turned to Mum. "She is good."

"You like her?" Mum teased.

"No," I lied.

"Jooth [That is a lie]," Mum said. "I was watching you. Your mind was somewhere else."

"What is the matter, Jai?" Papa asked, worried.

"Nothing," I replied.

"Jai, you have never lied to your parents," Mum said seriously. "Something is wrong."

"I like her," I confessed.

"Does she like you?"

"I don't know," I replied impatiently. "I am dropping hints, but she is ignoring."

"Is that bothering you?" Papa asked.

"No. As long as she is around, I am happy."

"How old is she?" Mum asked.

"She'll turn 33 on the 27th of this month."

"Really 33? See the coincidence."

"What coincidence?"

"You are 22, she is 33, so the gap is 11 years," Mum said out of the blue. "It makes a good series—11, 22, 33."

"Don't use your engineering brain," Papa said, laughing. "She is not 33 yet."

"I had to sacrifice my engineering career for you two," Mum complained.

"Jai, she is too old for you," Papa said seriously.

"I know, but I really like her."

"It is your life, so live the way you want to live," Papa preached.

"Jai, your papa is right. Take it easy and hope for the best," Mum added.

"What do I do?" I asked, confused.

"The way you handled the business challenges", Papa said, "same way you handle your personal life."

"Don't know how," I asked, dejected.

"Buy her a gift," Mum suggested.

"She doesn't want."

"Jai, wait for the right opportunity," Mum advised. "You said her birthday is due this month."

It was the eureka moment for me. I got up, stood behind her, and locked my arms around her neck, almost choking her. She giggled and then slapped my wrist.

"Treat her well," she said seriously. "Remember, I told you something the night before you were leaving for Mumbai."

"I remember very well," I replied admiringly.

"What are you going to buy?"

"A wristwatch."

"Buy a good one."

"I'll."

"I want to talk to her," Mum said unexpectedly. She demanded, "Give me her number."

"No," I insisted. "You don't know her."

"Now I've to know her," Mum persisted.

I gave her Oksana's number reluctantly. I feared for the worst, not sure what would come out of Oksana's mouth. After all, she was a complex person. Anyway, Mum dialled her number and started talking to her. I heard Mum praising her for what she had done to me. Mum said I had matured—I always was. I was more disciplined—I always was. I was a better person—I always was. I was more orderly. How did Mum know? After some time, their conversation ended. Mum was very impressed with her. Mum said she had a beautiful voice. Only and only if Mum knew how she had screamed at me. I didn't know what was in store for me once I would be back in Mumbai tomorrow.

We had been happily talking without realising it had gone past midnight. We got up. Suddenly, Mum stopped, looked straight into my eyes, and said, "Jai, you have changed so much in the last four months."

Next, she whizzed past the kitchen and vanished into her room. I went to my room and started to think what Mum had just said. Yes, I had changed. Good people like Dolce, Amardeep, Ajay, Sachin, Neel, and Monik de Mellow had changed me. Bad people who had used foul language, indecently touched, and fantasised at Oksana had changed me. Above all, it was Oksana herself who had changed me. Not only had I changed, but I had become more mature, developed a good sense of humour, and learnt how to flirt. What hadn't changed? My parents. Supportive, considerate, friendly, and charming. There were no parents like Simrin Grover and Vijay Grover in this world. The evening had passed off happily, so I decided to sleep, eager to let the night pass off quickly and partly due to tiredness.

The plane made a touchdown on the tarmac, and I was back in Mumbai. The time was exactly 4 in the afternoon. I quickly hired a taxi to be at home by 5 as promised to Oksana.

Earlier in the morning in Delhi, I went to a Titan showroom in Connaught Place to buy a watch for Oksana. I chose a rectangle shaped, black dialled with a black leather strap costing me Rs51,900. I hated the watch Oksana wore. She wore on the right hand, which I hated even more.

This time, my parents didn't drop me at the airport at my insistence. Instead, I hired a taxi and asked the taxi driver to move quickly. I wanted to reach Mumbai as soon as possible. It wasn't the same feeling when I had left earlier in July. That time, I was going to an unknown city where I knew no one. This time, I knew the city very well, made friends, and met Oksana.

I reached home to find Oksana sitting on the couch, staring into the vacuum. Her hair pulled up into a knot at the back, exposing her long and beautiful neck. She looked over her shoulders, rolled her eyes all over me, gave me a mysterious Mona Lisa–type smile, and then went back into her vacuum staring. No hi. No hello. Frustrated at her behaviour, I went straight to my room, threw the backpack on the bed, and then lay down to take a breather. I thought she would never change. I was sure even if God descended upon the earth and told her that he would take her to heaven, she would tell him to go to hell. She was that type of woman.

Restless, wanting to talk to her, I went back to the dining area. I sat down, hoping that she would initiate a conversation. Her back was facing me. She didn't move from her position for a while. Suddenly, she got up, walked towards the table, and pulled a chair in Bond style. I thought next she would now say, "My name is Bond. James Bond 007." Nothing of that sort happened.

"Are you trying to trap me?" she asked sternly.

"What trap?" I asked, confused and surprised.

"Why did you tell your mother to phone me?" she asked angrily.

"How do you know?" I asked, shocked.

"How would she then know about a Ukrainian dancer?"

"You know she knows you", I replied, "but as Oksana, not as a Ukrainian dancer."

"Oksana," she said, making a face.

I failed to convince her that it was Mum who wanted to talk to her. Mum spoke so highly about her. I thought if Mum ever met her, she would surely die of a heart attack. I kept looking at her totally shocked at her behaviour. She started to walk back to her room. Halfway through, she turned, smiled, and then started to sing a famous Bollywood Hindi-English mix tune, "What is my name? What is my name? My name is Sheila. No. No. No. No. No . . . Main tere hath na aani . . ." It wasn't the song but that one particular line in Hindi she wanted to convey whose rough translation in English meant "I won't fall in your trap". She would have danced many times on that tune when she used to work for Shabnam.

I kept looking at her in amazement until she disappeared into her room. How come she was able to come up with such witty ideas? Why wouldn't someone fall in love with her? I got up and then spun around on my right foot elated for no particular reason but only having succeeded in talking to her.

CHAPTER 29

I was overly excited today because it was 27 November, Oksana's birthday. To make her birthday a memorable one, I had decided to surprise her. Last night I lied to her that we were going to meet someone in Mumbai for our event. My plan was to take her to Lonavla, a small hill station 96 kilometres from Mumbai, for a night trip. It was on the Mumbai-Pune Expressway, hardly a 90-minute drive from the place we lived. There were so many lovely spots in Lonavla that needed more than a day to cover them all.

Her birthday alone was not the reason of my excitement. Since my return from Delhi, things had been progressing very well. Almost 400 tickets had been sold. The ticketing company was confident that the remaining 200 tickets would be sold soon. Meanwhile, Dolce, Amardeep, Oksana, and I had made a visit to the auditorium. It was good enough for the beginners like us: close to a train station, on a busy road, and secured by a concrete wall.

The temperature today in Lonavla was going to hover around pleasant 29 degrees. It was time to leave. I picked my backpack and waited for her. She appeared in a crop top and skin-tight trousers. She looked happy and very pleasant, probably knowing that it was her birthday today. We left the apartment and within 30 minutes hit the expressway. I looked at her. She was sleeping, probably making up for her lost sleep. I concentrated on driving in peace. She didn't fully wake up until we reached Lonavla, only occasionally waking up, blinking her eyes, looking around, and then going back to sleep.

We reached the Ryewood Park. The sky looked dull and the weather sticky.

"Where are we?" she wheezed, fluttering her eyelids and feeling confused, trying to figure out the place.

"Lonavla," I replied calmly.

"Why are we here?" she asked, surprised.

"Vishal asked me to take you to Lonavla," I quipped.

"Vishal?" she said. "I know you are lying."

"Why should I lie?"

"Because you are that type of person."

"I've never lied to you."

"Didn't you tell your mother to phone me?"

She still hadn't forgotten. There was no way I could convince her. Without wasting more time, we went inside the park. It was a Thursday, so there weren't many people there. I felt very nice strolling around the pack with Oksana. There were an old Shiva temple and plenty of places for children to play. She looked at Shiva's statue mesmerised, trying to make out who he actually was. We sat under a large tree and started to talk.

"Who is Shiva?" she asked, yearning to know more.

This was typical of Europeans who have always been interested in mythical India—its spirituality, philosophy, and mystique.

"He is one of the three main gods in Hinduism," I replied, impressed with her keenness to know about Indian culture.

"Who are the other two?"

"Brahma and Vishnu."

"How many gods do you have in India?" she asked innocently.

"Thirty-three million."

"Why so many?"

"We have a large population. One god can't handle so many people," I replied seriously.

She seemed to have believed me. Next, I burst into a loud laughter because I myself didn't know why there were so many gods in Hinduism.

"Why are you laughing?" She grinned sheepishly, probably thinking that she had asked a wrong question.

"I don't know why there are so many gods in India."

"Why then three main gods?"

"Because there are three letters in *God*."

"What do you mean?"

"See, Brahma is believed to be the generator or the creator of this universe; Vishnu, the operator or preserver; and Shiva, the destroyer. Take the first letters from the generator, the operator, and the destroyer. What do you get? *God*."

"Really?" she asked surprised with wide eyes.

She was very impressed with my made-up story. I didn't know if it really was true. I was not a very religious person but had heard such thing on a religious channel whose need I found today to use on an unsuspecting and innocent European. Self-correction was imminent.

"I am sorry. Don't believe in what I told you. There is no connection between the word *God* and the three Hindu gods," I said, feeling relieved.

She looked at me suspiciously and said, "See, I told you. You lie."

I looked at her amazed, impressed with her presence of mind, and asked, "How many gods do you have in Ukraine?"

"I don't know. I am not a very religious person," she replied casually.

At least, there was one thing that was common between us.

"How is the place?" I asked while changing the topic.

"It is very nice. It's so green. A bit sticky, but the air is so clean here."

I nodded, and we left the park after spending an hour there. We had our lunch at a south Indian *dhaba*. She liked *masala dosa,* and I had my favourite: *idli sambar*. Idli-sambar reminded me of Mum. She would make once a month for me as a special treat. She had learnt South Indian cooking while pursuing her engineering degree there. Funnily enough, idli sambar is a Tamil breakfast dish. In the South, people have it daily, not once a month.

After filling our tummies, we covered three more spots. Valvan Dam supplied water to a local power station. It had a beautiful garden. The Lonavla Lake was surrounded by an absolutely majestic natural scenery. The lake was full because of the recent monsoon rains, which otherwise dried in summer, and finally the Duke's Nose, about 12 kilometres from the town, popular with hikers. We didn't find any hikers, though.

There was enough light left in the day, even though it had turned 6.30 in the evening. We decided to go around on a scenic drive with green hills on the right and equally green gorge on the left. The road was very narrow, so I was driving very slowly and carefully. After reaching the top, we decided to head back to the town. I reversed the car to start the steep descent to the town when, suddenly, I noticed a dirt road on the left side. I had missed that while going up the hill. Out of curiosity, I turned left into the dirt road. Approximately after 100 metres, the road led to a curved left turn; and farther 30 or 40 metres down, it ended. I reversed the car, parked, and then we both got off.

There was no one around. On one side were green hills and the other side the gorge—deep, green, and beautiful. At the foot of the hills, there was an old worn-out bench, around 20 metres diagonally across where our car was parked. It looked like an abandoned lookout point. The view across the gorge was majestic. Oksana, leaning against the railing, started to look around and down the gorge. She was looking pretty in her feathered hairstyle. I asked her to sit on the bench for a while, so we both cut across and then settled ourselves on the bench.

"It was a very beautiful day," I said, excited.

"Yes, but dull and sticky," she replied casually.

"It is not the weather I was talking about," I said. She stared at me in a meaningful way as if looking for more disclosure. I disclosed, "It is a beautiful day for someone who was born today."

"You knew," she muttered while her lips quivered.

We looked at each other. She became very emotional, lowered her lashes, and then looked away.

"You want a return gift?" she asked abruptly.

Another mood swing, I thought.

"When did I give you any gift?" I asked casually.

"This trip."

"Don't worry about this trip."

The look on her face changed. It was the same look I had seen in the past on that Friday night. Was there a soft chord somewhere in her I needed to touch? I looked around the scenery. The atmosphere was so serene and romantic. Moreover, there was no one around. Suddenly, my heart started to race up and down; and I felt my body stiffened, titillating my desire. The atmosphere and her sheer presence in a lonely place were becoming unbearable for me.

I got up and gently pushed her shoulders with my hands. She quickly moved her hands behind to support her body from falling backwards.

"What do you want?" she asked in a very feeble voice.

She looked straight into my eyes and then blushed as if getting some idea what I was looking for.

"Here?" she asked nervously.

"Yes, here," I replied forcefully. She started to think, somewhat confused. Encouraged, I assured, "Don't worry. There is no one around."

She sat across the bench, removed her sandals, put them on one side, got up, and then removed her trousers. She was now in her crop top and black shorts—barefooted and looking like a stunner. I also sat down on the bench to prepare myself for our second encounter. As she was preparing to remove her shorts, suddenly, we heard faint human voices coming from somewhere far away. We both stopped and started to look around, panicked. There was no one around us, but the human voices could still be heard from far away.

That was the climax of our failed second encounter. She picked her sandals in one hand, trousers on the other hand, and then ran in careful and small steps towards the car. I was still sitting on the bench, watching her beautiful body slowly running away from me. Her semi-exposed body looked celestial. As she reached the back door of the car, she stopped; turned her face, which was partially covered with her hair; and then yelled, "Open the door."

Her face bore a nervous and anxious look. She was looking even more beautiful. I unlocked the car. She quickly jumped into the backseat. I got up dejected and walked slowly towards the car. I sat on the driver's seat, looking straight down the dirt road ahead without any purpose. I didn't want to go, so I kept looking at the road. The human voices could still be heard. I turned back and laughed because she was still in her shorts. She had forgotten to put her trousers on because of nervousness. I looked straight into her beautiful eyes and smiled.

"Put your trousers on," I said.

Realising her mistake, she brought a shy smile on her face, pretended to hit me with her trousers, and then started to put it on. She was now back in her full attire, got out, and sat on the front passenger's seat, waiting for me to turn the ignition on. I was in no mood to miss the golden chance but couldn't do anything because the voices could still be heard. I thought I should go and check where the noise was coming from. But it was too risky to leave her alone, so I dropped the idea. It had started to get dark. In the next 15 to 20 minutes, it would be completely dark. I didn't look at her, just remained motionless.

"Move the car," she said.

I looked at her and shook my head, refusing to move the car.

"Why?"

"Why? Because my body is still stiff," I said, smiling.

"Find a hotel and do it there," she said, smiling mischievously.

"Do what?"

"The thing that will calm your stiffness," she said, giggling.

My eyes lit up. I turned the ignition on, not giving her a chance to change her mind, and pressed the pedal so hard that I nearly missed a roadside boulder. I regained control and then started negotiating the dirt road. Upon reaching the end of the dirt road, I turned left on the narrow road and saw a broken-down bus ten metres down. There were people talking while waiting for the bus to be fixed. As we went past the bus, Oksana looked out, smiled, and waved at the waiting people. I sighed in despair.

We reached the town in the dark. It was a quiet town compared to the Mumbai madness. The population of Lonavla at that time was around 55,000, which was very small by Indian standards. We found a good three-star hotel near the post office off the expressway. We went to the reception and booked two rooms costing me Rs10,000 for a night. Our rooms were located on level one, so we decided to take the stairs. The rooms were very neat and clean. I asked Oksana to freshen up before we ordered our dinner. I went to my room to drop my backpack, ordered food and cake, and then quickly ran down to buy flowers for her.

As I neared the door, I froze. I saw him going out. I could recognise him in millions from any angle. I stopped breathing, hoping him to disappear quickly before he saw me. Suddenly, he stopped, looked back, and spotted me. He waited, expecting me to come near to him. Having no option left, I started moving towards him.

"How are you, Grover?" Naresh Galhot asked.

He had not forgotten my last name.

"I am fine, sir," I replied politely.

This time, he talked, looking into my eyes. Suddenly, he rolled his eyes around the lobby, looking for someone. I knew who his eyes were searching for. But he was too shrewd to ask me about Oksana.

"I don't know where my friend is," he said calmly. "Don't worry. I'll find him."

"Why were you going out without him?" I asked.

"Oh! I was going to wait for him in the car," he replied calmly that only a shrewd person could quickly answer an unexpected question. "He might have gone to the toilet."

"Oh!" I said.

"Grover, I heard you're doing an event."

"How do you know?" I asked, surprised.

"What do I do?" he asked sharply.

"Manage an events company."

"I've to keep an eye on my competitors."

"Do you think I am your competitor?"

"Merge your company with my company," he said in a low but stern voice, bringing his face close to me.

I felt a chill in my body.

"Why? I am smaller than the smallest fish in the pond," I replied, trying to impress him with an unusual sentence.

His face turned serious. He looked at me for a while, came close, and then whispered in my left ear menacingly, "You should kill a cobra before it raises its head."

He waited for a while for my reaction. Deep down, I was very scared. But I stayed calm, holding my breath. He smiled mysteriously and said, "My offer is always open. Good luck."

And he left. He had openly threatened me. I was too small for these big operators—cultured and educated and no match for them. Nothing mattered in the real world. First, it was Shabnam who had screwed me up, and now I had to deal with Naresh. I felt a shiver down my spinal cord and started to sweat in fear. I somehow controlled my fear and then headed to buy flowers. I bought flowers. Fearing for her safety, I quickly ran upstairs. Suddenly, I stopped outside her room. I thought, why did I have to book two rooms? I shrugged my shoulders because I couldn't find any reasonable answer. I knocked at her door; and there she was—fresh, smiling, and looking beautiful. My whole tension evaporated into the air.

"This is for you," I said while giving her the roses.

"Thank you. So many?" she said while smelling the roses.

The roses were no match for her own fragrance.

"Thirty-three," I said.

"Why 33?"

"Because you are 33 today."

"How do you know about my birthday?"

"Guess."

"Oh! You took my passport the other day."

"Yes. I noted your birthday because I wanted to surprise you."

"When is your birthday, Jai?"

"It's gone, recently."

"Oh! That is why you went to Delhi recently?'

"Yes."

"How old are you?"

"I was born on 14 November 1992, which makes me 22," I replied, surprised because she still didn't remember my age.

"Really? Only 22?" she said, surprised. She spoke at length, "You are a Scorpio, who are known for their ability to heal others. They are analytical thinkers, practical, logical, stubborn, and determined."

"You know about these things?" I asked, impressed. "What are you?"

"Oh! I am a Sagittarian. We are kind of tactless people. We throw arrows in the air aimlessly. If we are lucky, sometimes an arrow might hit the bull's-eye. Otherwise, we are just honest. But we like our freedom, though."

Tactless, throwing arrows aimlessly, honest, freedom, and bull's-eye—that was the summation of her personality.

What was tactlessness in her? Probably her abruptness, anger, and mood swings. She had been throwing arrows aimlessly with her decision to move to an unknown place called India, quit Shabnam's job in a haste, move into my apartment, and that Friday night. She had given me ample examples of her honesty. She never lied, insisted on 5 per cent extra for agreeing to be the USP and her reason to participate in the dance competition. She was a free woman because she always liked her personal freedom.

Bull's-eye. I could have been her bull's-eye. Why hadn't she been able to see that so far? She might realise after throwing few more arrows. There was still a chance for me. Impressed with my analytical thinking, I drew a deep breath.

Somebody knocked at the door. It was the hotel staff with food and cake. I had ordered Chinese food. Oksana cut the cake, and then we started having food. She was very good at using chopsticks, which I had never mastered. She liked the food, and so did I. It was time to give her the gift.

"I bought a gift for you in Delhi," I said enthusiastically.

"What is it?" she asked, excited.

"Open and see for yourself."

"You got the watch for me. But I already have one."

"It is time to replace."

"Why?"

"Because I don't like that. It is round shaped with bracelet wrist. Bracelet wrists are normally loose, so they need to be pulled up many times."

"What will this one do?"

"It is rectangle shaped with a black leather strap, so it will fit very well around your wrist. You don't have to pull it up so many times. Also, the black colour will suit your skin well."

"Thanks, Jai."

"And put it on your left hand. Women shouldn't wear watches on the right hand."

"Really? How do you know that?"

"Because I don't like it on your right hand," I replied. "Try it now."

"Not today. I'll wear it on a special day."

"What is today?"

"No. Not now," she said, refusing flatly.

"As you wish," I said. I looked straight into her eyes in a meaningful way and reminded, "What about my return gift?"

"No. Not now," she replied, flatly backing out.

Another of her mood swings. I raised my eyebrows and exhaled my breath in a whistle.

"Remember, you promised me to calm my stiffness," I asked, annoyed.

"That was there," she said casually and quickly changed the topic. "But I'll cheer you up with a joke. Remember, I told you once that I'll tell you a joke."

"If a joke can calm my stiffness, then go ahead," I said sarcastically.

"One Indian man wanted to buy a suit, so he went to a shop. He enquired about the price. The shopkeeper told him that it would cost him Rs10,000. He requested for 10 per cent discount. The shopkeeper agreed to give him 10 per cent off. Encouraged with the shopkeeper's response, he asked for more discount. The shopkeeper went up to 50 per cent discount. The Indian man wouldn't stop asking for more discount. The shopkeeper got so much frustrated that he threw the suit at his face and told him to take it for free. The Indian said, 'Thank you. Can you give me two?'"

She finished her joke, giggling. I didn't say anything but kept looking at her, still feeling stiff. She asked, burning me more, "Did you like the joke?"

She then asked me to go to my room. I started to leave, dejected and reluctant. Then I stopped outside her room and turned.

"You were ready at that abandoned lookout point. What happened now?" I asked, still hopeful.

"Because I was alone there. If I had refused, you could have used force, so I had to agree."

"Why would have I used force?" I riposted after feeling insulted with her "you could have used force" remark.

"All men are like that," she replied, winking and blinking, and then she slammed the door.

I stood there for a while, shocked at her logic. My stiffness converted into a rage. I was expecting something different tonight, but she had slapped me with a joke on Indians and nearly branded me a rapist. Wow! Not one but she had given me two return gifts. I went to my room and fell asleep, laughing at her joke. It was really a good joke.

Next day we returned to Mumbai at 6 in the evening after covering the remaining spots at Lonavla. Oksana was quite normal throughout the day. I also had recovered from the last night's shock. Suddenly, some unknown fear started to grip me. Naresh Galhot had started worrying me. We still had little under four weeks to go for the event. It was my last hope. What if it didn't go through as per plan? I couldn't afford any further failure. I would have to go back to Delhi, losing Oksana forever. After all, it was a big leap I was taking.

CHAPTER 30

We just had three days left for the event. Everything was going well as per plan. The tickets had been sold out, so we were sure of making a small profit. My bank balance had shrunk to Rs221,123.90 because I spent a lot of money on the watch, Lonavla trip, and routine home expenses. But it was a matter of few more days before my balance reached to a healthy level once again.

Last few weeks had been rather dull. Nothing exciting because there was nothing much to do other than waiting for the big day. We were very happy with our efforts considering the fact that we were predominantly a bunch of teenagers. Oksana, anyway, never bothered to involve herself much, only ensuring her token attendance, nothing beyond that. We hadn't had any meeting for a long time because there was no need for one. In fact, our last meeting had taken place before Oksana and I went to Lonavla. We decided to have one last meeting before the event at Gaylord's.

It was Dolce's plan. She came up with a unique agenda. She said that for the first ten minutes we would review the progress, and then each of us will have to talk about an interesting event or a person or even a joke. Because she had made agenda very difficult for Sachin, Ajay, and Neel, they decided that it was in their own interest to not join us. So it was just four of us: Dolce, Amardeep, Oksana, and me. I didn't know what to expect from Oksana, but Dolce insisted that she had to join, so she was in.

Suddenly, her room door opened; and out she came looking fresh, happy, calm, and, of course, stunning. We left for the Gaylord's and reached there in under an hour to find Dolce and Amardeep already waiting us. For the first time, they had beaten us.

"Hi, Oksi," Dolce called loudly in joy.

"Hi, Dolce," Oksana replied, equally matching her enthusiasm.

We settled ourselves on a table. Amardeep was going to pay because he complained that he had never been able to do so. We all agreed happily.

"We haven't met for a long time. Only on the phones," Dolce commented.

"Sometimes we should keep a distance for a while," I lectured.

"That is true," Amardeep said.

"Jai, first the review. What is happening?" Dolce spoke, initiating her first agenda item.

"Nothing much," I explained. "Everything is under control. Now, we have to wait for the big day."

"We will go two hours early," Amardeep added, tapping the table with his hands to create some kind of music. "We need to set up our instruments on the stage and make sure they work."

"I think Amar is right," I said. "What do you both think?"

"Who is going to be the MC?" Dolce dropped the penny.

"God, we never thought about it," I said, rueing the omission while holding my head.

"It is not a worry. I'll do," Dolce said confidently.

I looked at Dolce, amazed. How quickly had she resolved the case she herself had reported? I shook my head in disbelief.

"Have you ever done it before?" I asked, still uncertain about her MC skills.

"Amar, tell him," Dolce said confidently.

"She used to be the MC in the school," Amar replied painfully.

"What else can you do, Dolce?" I asked, smiling.

"Not many things," she replied modestly.

"You need to know about the programme sequence and—"

"Be the drummer. I'll do both," she completed the sentence, delighted.

I looked at her in admiration because she never failed to amaze me.

"Is there anything left, Oksana?" I asked, deliberately needling her.

"I don't know. It is your company, not mine," she replied flatly.

"But you are also a director," I teased.

"Director," she said, laughing.

"We are done," I said. "But first we have to clap for Dolce."

"Why?" Amardeep objected.

"Because she reminded us about the MC. Otherwise—"

"We should give her a Nobel Prize for that," Amardeep commented bitterly.

We all laughed at his pain. My laugh faded away quickly because it was he who was going to pay today. We decided to order. Amardeep gave deliberately, still overcoming his emotions, the privilege to order to Oksana only. He said a flat no to Dolce. We all laughed at Amardeep's unique sense of humour. In the end, both ordered together.

"Dolce, now you drive," I said. "Show us your MC skills."

"Amar, you have to start. What have you prepared?" Dolce ordered.

"Nothing," he replied, laughing loudly.

"Don't fool around," she said seriously.

"I'll tell you something funny. I don't know whether it's from a movie or if I have read somewhere. I can't recall."

"What is it?" Dolce said, frustrated.

"There is an American young man and a young woman, like friends. They go to a country somewhere in the Middle East, which is ruled by a military dictator. So they are going around, and suddenly, three or four pickup vans surround them. They are forced into the vans by the goons of the dictator, saying, 'No broblem. No broblem.'"

We all laughed when he said "No problem, No problem" in the Middle Eastern accent.

"And then they take them away. Next, there is coliseum full of people who are yelling and shouting like how great their leader is. He is the wisest in the world and a bright star. He would soon conquer the whole world etc. The American man is suspended from a wooden structure upside down right in the middle. The American woman is sitting with the dictator in the VIP stand. The dictator tells her, 'You can save him.' She asks him how. He puts his hand on her thigh and says while stroking her thigh, 'You know I am a lonely man.' The woman looks at him, smiles, and replies confidently in the typical American way, 'You know what, in that case, you should f—— your own mother.'"

Everybody burst into laughter.

"Are you done?" Dolce asked impatiently, not expecting such a good joke from Amardeep.

"No, wait. Next, what happens is that Americans come searching for the couple. So there are three to four choppers. They land, and first, they free the man. Then they head towards the VIP stand. The dictator gets up and, pointing to the American woman, says, 'Take her. She is like my sister.'"

We all again burst into laughter. It was a good joke Amardeep had managed to pull out from somewhere. Meanwhile, the food arrived, so we had a mini break. I started to think that Americans are very good at rescuing their citizens from anywhere. They've the capacity, resources, and will. Many nations could do that, but it is a policy thing.

"Jai, how was your Lonavla trip?" Dolce asked.

"It wasn't bad," I replied. "The weather was a bit dull and sticky."

"Did you enjoy?"

"Very much. Ask your best friend."

"How was it, Oksi?" Dolce asked, turning to Oksana.

"I barely survived," she replied, looking at me with a mischievous smile.

"What happened?" Dolce asked, showing a genuine concern.

"Someone liked her so much that he went after her," I replied cynically.

"What happened then?"

"He saved me from that man," Oksana replied crisply with her index finger pointed at me.

I had no answer for her sharp brain. I squeezed my lips to suppress my smile and looked away.

"Is there something between you two?" Amardeep asked suspiciously.

I looked at Dolce.

"Amar, you are such an idiot," Dolce admonished him while looking at me in a meaningful way. "Wouldn't we know? After all, we are best friends."

"Did I ask you?" Amardeep shouted.

"Amar, she is right," Oksana said seriously, calming him down.

"Jai, it's your turn now," Dolce said, resuming her agenda.

"I don't know any jokes," I replied seriously.

"You don't know any joke?" Oksana said, needling me once again.

I gave her a strong glare because I knew she was referring to the Indian joke, which she had told me at Lonavla.

"No," I said flatly.

"What do you have then?" Dolce asked me.

"Something serious."

"Seriously. It's not about work."

"No. I want to talk about the growing population in India. We won't progress until we control our population. India is projected to reach to a $10 trillion economy by 2050, but the population would also grow to 1.66 billion people, which means per capita income of around $6,000," I paused to search for more arguments to substantiate my point. I soon resumed, "That too after 35 years from now. The wealth of a nation shouldn't be measured in GDP but in per capita income. In a nutshell, nothing will change."

"We should go the China way," Amardeep interrupted.

"No. That won't work here. We have elections in India, so no political party would dare to have this on their manifesto."

"How can we resolve then?" Dolce asked seriously.

"You know the family planning programme of the 70s failed. We should start incentivising all those couples who are about to start their nuclear families or still planning to expand."

"What do you propose?" Dolce asked seriously like an interviewer would ask a candidate.

"It is easy but requires government funding. Let us assume the government promises Rs500,000 to the couple who agrees to produce one child, Rs300,000 for two children, and nothing to the couple who produce more than two."

"They will take the money and start producing more," Dolce commented, which made a lot of sense.

"No. You deposit the money in a bank. Pay them only after 20 years."

"How will it work?"

"If they introduce now, they don't have to worry for the next 20 years. They just have to deposit, which they could use somewhere else until maturity."

"How if I promised one kid but actually produced two kids?" Dolce asked keenly.

"Will you produce only two kids?" Amardeep asked, seizing the opportunity to pull her leg. He added, laughing, "You are capable of producing a dozen, but Sachin would be dead by then."

He then went "ho-ho-ho" with everybody, laughing, except for Dolce who was busy processing the right reply in her brain.

"Amar, we are talking about the population control, not population increase," she said confidently. "I'll answer you when we are discussing the population increase."

She took the smile off everybody's face and then looked around us with wide eyes.

"Sorry," Amardeep apologised.

"What were you asking?" I asked.

"How if I promised one kid but actually produced two kids?" Dolce repeated.

"If you had signed up for one kid but produced two, then you get only Rs300,000. Similarly, if you had signed up for two kids but produced three, then you get nothing."

"What if I had signed up for two kids but actually produced one kid?" Dolce asked.

"What is so difficult in this? They will get Rs500,000," Amardeep replied overconfidently.

"Really, where will you get the additional Rs200,000 you had not planned for?" Dolce reacted intelligently.

"In this case, you get what you had signed up for," I said, supporting her argument.

"Why don't they do?"

"I don't know what is happening now. In 2010, the Congress refused to introduce legislation to reduce the population. It is really not an expenditure but kind of an investment. When people get their money, they would start spending, which will circulate into the economy," I concluded, feeling proud.

"Good topic you chose, Jai," Dolce praised.

"We youth need to really start worrying about it."

"Now, my dear Oksi, what do you have?" Dolce asked, caressing her hand.

"I don't know, but I've one question for Indian people."

"What?" Dolce asked, smiling probably at the mention of *Indian people* instead of *Indians*.

"What is those people you don't touch?" she asked innocently.

There was a pin-drop silence. We all knew what she was talking about. It was so embarrassing for Indians to talk about the subject to a foreigner where no such things existed. She was taking Shabnam's revenge on every Indian. Not only Shabnam but others who had cast an evil eye on her. But she was right. It existed and still exists.

"I think Dolce should answer," I proposed, knowing that she handled her well.

"Yeah, I'll. Why should we hide?" Dolce said boldly. She explained, "It did exist quite a lot in the past when less than 10 per cent of so-called high-caste people used to dominate the remaining 90 per cent people. The caste system is nothing but racism and slavery combined, which has significantly reduced now."

"How was it reduced?" Oksana asked curiously.

"Empowering the so-called low-caste people. There is more than 50 per cent reservation for them in the government schools, colleges, competitive exams, and jobs. They are now politically very much aware of their rights and have managed to occupy highest positions," Dolce concluded.

"But the undercurrent of caste system still exists like racism in America or elsewhere," I added.

During Dolce's explanation, I kept looking at Oksana. She was listening to the whole thing with rapt attention as if she had to write a thesis for her PhD.

"What happens when you touch them?" Oksana asked innocently again.

"Nothing happens," I replied, laughing. "Remember in the olden days people used to avoid touching lepers?"

"Yes."

"They used to isolate them from the communities. It is just the same mindset."

"In the last general elections, Modi smashed all the caste-based parties," Dolce said, beaming.

Modi was her hero. While driving back, I realised that Dolce was right about Modi smashing the caste-based parties in the 2014 general elections. He ripped through their stronghold and vanquished them all. One such party in North India couldn't win a single seat, losing all its 21 seats won in the previous general elections. Up until then, his party was seen as urban and so-called upper-caste Hindu party. He smashed this myth and said that he represented 1.2 billion people, not any religion, caste, or region.

At least, India had started to move in the right direction—not completely, though.

CHAPTER 31

I had been restlessly busy today making calls to the suppliers, Dolce, and Amardeep. Tomorrow was the moment of reckoning for all seven of us. A test of our hard work, teamwork, bonding, and exceptional camaraderie. At around 6.45 in the evening, I sat on the couch and started to think. What would we be doing tomorrow this time around? Probably busy in setting up the stage, inspecting various things, waiting for the external performers, making sure that the instruments worked, and making last-minute calls. There would be confusion, urgency, little clashes, consolations, occasional silence, and nervousness.

We had been advised by the auditorium management to open the main gates at 8.30. The waiting crowd would then rush in talking, smiling, laughing, and perhaps screaming. All types of noises would be heard—those of excitement, anxiety, impatience, screams, runs, and more. Finally, Dolce would take over the stage at 9, welcome people, introduce us, read the programme details, announce the first item, and then the event would formally start.

Once the event started, it would definitely end. We had deliberately kept one popular item for Oksana to perform in the end. It was scheduled to start five minutes to midnight. She was to make sure it finished after midnight. Dolce would then take over the stage again, call us on the stage, and we would bow before the audience. She would thank the audience and wish them all a Merry Christmas. We would watch people leaving, and soon the auditorium would be empty. There would be complete silence for a while. Next, we would look at one another and then burst into a big cheer, high-fiving one another, happy that we had pulled it off. Next day we would collect our payment from the ticketing company, pay off outstanding monies, relax for a few days, and then plan for an even bigger event.

I had been thinking about tomorrow so intensely that I forgot that it was time to make a call to Mum. I got up from the couch to head to my room. On the way, I saw Oksana standing in the kitchen, preparing dinner, her back towards me. Her hair was falling to the sides. She was occasionally stroking her cheeks. I stopped and looked at her, mesmerised. I became emotional and wanted to hug her from behind. Knowing that was not possible, I sighed and then went to my room. I spoke to Mum and repeated everything that I had been thinking about. I told her that I was feeling very nervous, to which she told me to be strong and wished me good luck. Mum fussed over whether I was eating enough, maintaining my chiselled body, and asking me, "How is she?"

I had never felt so nervous in my life, not even before my exams. But people like Shabnam, Naresh, and other evil souls I had met had dented my confidence. Not realising I was facing the real world, not an exam. We finished our dinner quietly. There was no tension or nervousness on her face. Why was she so strong? I was a qualified engineer from a premier institute, and she was a self-taught but a skilled dancer. Probably dancing and constant practice helped her release tension and stress. After all, tension and stress are a mental thing.

I decided to watch TV to divert my attention and to calm my nervousness. I turned the TV on after so many days. There was usual crap. Movies, dance, songs, soap, comedy, and cricket. Nothing piqued my interest. I kept on changing channels, and then I stopped. It was a news channel. I turned to another news channel and another. It was the same news everywhere.

I slumped on the couch, looked at the wall aimlessly, and then started to think about my future. Dolce called and said she was coming to my place with Amardeep soon. Oksana asked, "What are we going to do next?" I told her to wait until Dolce and Amardeep arrived. She said she would clear, wash, and clean because she wanted me to relax and stay calm. I looked at her in admiration. She was the only person I always felt so close since moving to Mumbai. Her presence was the only source of my strength. I went into a deep thought. The 2008 Mumbai terrorist attack flashed before my eyes.

Ten Pakistani terrorists had carried out a series of twelve shooting and bombing attacks lasting four days across Mumbai, killing at least 166 people and wounding around 293. They killed Indians, Americans, Australians, Hindus, Christians, Jews, and more but told a Turkish couple staying in the Taj Place Hotel that they would spare them because they were Muslims. Muslims of India prayed for India, fearing the backlash from Hindus. Ultimately, commandos were flown in from Delhi who bravely entered the besieged areas and started eliminating the terrorists one by one. It had been now more than six years since the attack, but for some, lives had changed forever. There was no backlash against Muslims. Hindus had become saner. Indian Muslims refused to bury the dead terrorists in their graveyards. The saner world, especially the democratic countries, sympathised and openly supported India. After all, terrorism was a global problem.

My concentration was broken by a knock at the door. I got up to open the door and saw Dolce and Amardeep with a pall of gloom all over their faces. I let them in and gestured to take seats. Oksana also joined us. We all sat around the dining table like we had been sitting in the past. However, there was no usual "Hi, Oksi", "Hi, Dolce", hugging, or handshakes. Instead, we greeted one another with fake smiles on our faces.

"Do you know what exactly happened?" Dolce asked impatiently.

"As much as I could hear in the news," I replied sadly.

I told them a bomb had gone off outside the auditorium, ripping through the wall and badly damaging the gate. It was an explosive-type radio-controlled IED incorporating a cell phone that was modified and connected to an electrical firing circuit. Luckily, there was no casualty. The whole area had been cordoned off, rendering it out of bounds for few days. The NIA sleuths were expected to fly down from Delhi to examine the site. The politicians were calling for calm, and the police commissioner had assured that the people responsible would be caught soon. That was all good, but we had been robbed of our event. It stood *cancelled*.

"I know who could have done it," Dolce said angrily.

"Who?" I asked, alarmed.

"You know who I am talking about," she replied, stealing her gaze away.

"Are you talking about Muslims?"

She kept quiet. Her eyes were wide open, nostrils blown up, and she was seething. I didn't expect this from Dolce. She was such a beautiful, intelligent, helpful, and caring 18-year-old girl. I needed to talk to her to make her more beautiful, intelligent, helpful, and caring 18-year-old girl. I had promised her in the past that I would make her a better person when the right time arrived. That time had arrived.

"Who are you talking about?" I asked sternly.

"You said that," she shot back.

"I need to talk you about this in detail. Promise you will listen to me."

"Uh-huh."

"You are talking anecdotal," I said. "How do you know it was them? Police have yet to identify the people responsible for the blast. Are you listening?"

"Yes."

"Don't draw your own conclusions."

"What if police find someone and I turned out to be right?"

"Still wrong. You should not generalise things or form an opinion. One or two or even ten people do not represent the whole community," I said forcefully.

"They've been doing it everywhere," she protested.

"It is not *they* but *some.* Those types of people exist in all communities," I contested.

"They did Mumbai, 9/11, London, Madrid, and Beslan."

I was shocked when I heard about Beslan. How did she know about it? It had happened in 2004 when she would have been only around 8 or 9.

"How do you know about Beslan?" I asked curiously.

"How do I know? It was on TV, and I was a kid then. I can't forget those kids and women who were trapped inside," she replied painfully in a choking voice.

She had a valid reason to develop such an adverse view about a community. As a kid, when you saw something that horrible, it sticks in your mind forever. Mumbai, 9/11, London, Madrid, and Beslan were bad examples for Muslims. They were all sheer acts of terrorism. Holding innocent hostage, especially children and women, as well as killing, injuring, and maiming people wouldn't help their cause whatever that might be. They couldn't bring down nations by holding few hundred hostages or through acts of terrorism.

At the same time, it was also true that more Muslims had been killed in the last 30 to 40 years in Afghanistan, Iran, Iraq, Bosnia, Syria, Egypt, and Libya—in millions—but nobody bats an eyelash because they themselves don't care. How many innocent women were raped in Bosnia? They were raped until they fell pregnant and held hostage until they couldn't abort.

"I don't support any act of terrorism whether by Hindus, Sikhs, Christians, or Muslims," I said.

"They only do that?" Dolce complained like a kid.

"Really? You know there are invisible competing forces who have conflicting interests," I argued.

"Who are they?" Oksana asked eagerly.

"You want to know?"

"Yes."

"Really?" I teased, smiling, looking straight into her big blue eyes.

"Yes," she shouted, irritated.

"I said invisible forces, so how do I know?"

"Invisible forces," she ridiculed while making a face.

She then stuck her tongue out and licked her lips like a lizard does after swallowing an insect. I laughed despite being in a mess because of the cancellation. Oksana couldn't care less because she didn't look upset at all. I shook my head in disbelief and then turned to Dolce for more lecture.

"How did you feel when Shah Rukh was detained at one of the airports in the US few years back?"

"Bad," Dolce replied.

"Why?"

"Because he is an Indian."

"But he is a Muslim too," I replied swiftly.

Dolce's face dropped, but she didn't look like convinced. When I mentioned Shah Rukh, Amardeep got up and then tried to imitate his signature move by stretching both his hands sideways and bending backwards. While trying to bend backwards, he struggled to balance his body and fell down. We all laughed. He got up laughing, brought a sheepish grin on his face, suddenly turned serious, and then complained, "You know how many Sikhs have been killed in the US since 9/11?"

"Do you think Americans are from Mars?" I asked, knowing that over a dozen Sikhs had been murdered in the United States due to mistaken identity since 9/11. "Because of their beard and turban, people in the US think Sikhs are Muslims."

"How to resolve the issue?" Dolce asked seriously.

"There has to be a truce between Saudi and Iran because they create proxy wars in many Muslin countries."

"Why?"

"To control different Muslim sects," I said. "But there are good Muslim countries."

The world, in general, might not know that such countries existed in the Muslim world. The problem with Muslim countries is that they've a very bad PR machinery. What we see in media is bad, bad—nothing but bad. Few jokers, with their strange world view, appear on TV in funny dresses and dish out nonsense, bringing the entire community down. They blame other countries for all their problems, totally ignoring the internal issues and the fault lines that exist in their own countries. I knew for certain that at least there was one country in the Muslim world that needed praise and wider exposure.

"Which country are you talking about?" Dolce woke me up.

"Have you heard of Azerbaijan?" I replied.

"I know Azerbaijan," Oksana said calmly. "I've been there when I was a kid."

"Of course you should know because it was a part of Soviet Union."

"I know that," she replied, irritated.

"Did you have to get the permission from Moscow?" I teased.

"What do you mean?"

"I thought if you wanted to pee, you needed permission from Moscow," I said, laughing.

"You look very happy," she said, shaking her head the way Indians normally do.

She was actually making fun of Indians.

"What is the point of mourning? I am not responsible for what has happened," I shot back.

We decided to take a coffee break, so Dolce and Oksana went to the kitchen to make coffee for all. Amardeep followed them in the kitchen, leaving me alone. I watched them make coffee where Amardeep was flirting with Oksana and pulling Dolce's leg. I heard him telling Oksana that he would only have coffee if she made it. Dolce, Oksana, and Amardeep came from the kitchen with coffee.

"The coffee is here. Thank you, Dolce," I said, deliberately omitting Oksana's name.

"I made it," she protested.

"Oh! That is why it tastes so terrible," I teased.

"Then don't have," she said, annoyed, and then sat down furious.

"Even if you ask me to drink poison, I would drink without any hesitation," I flirted.

It didn't make any difference. She turned her gaze away.

"There is something between you both," Amardeep said suspiciously.

"Yes, there is," I said.

"What?" he reacted, alarmed.

"We all love Oksana because she is sharp, strong, proud, intelligent, beautiful, and a skilled dancer. What do you say, Dolce?"

"Of course we all love our Oksi," Dolce said while hugging her.

She was the only person who could handle her.

"What do you think, Amar?" I asked.

"I love her the most, more than you all," he replied, making his feelings obvious for Oksana.

We all laughed including Oksana who couldn't control her laugh, bringing herself back to normal.

"Dolce, I thought you had an eight o'clock curfew," I asked, remembering that she had once told us that she was supposed to get back to her home by that time.

"Not for tonight. By the way, I am staying here tonight," Dolce chirruped.

"Where is your stuff for the night?"

"My bag is in his Scorpio. Amar, Please get it for me."

"*Pagal* [Mad]. I've to do everything for her," Amardeep said, smiling.

He went downstairs to get her bag.

"Dolce, you can stay here on one condition," I said seriously.

"What condition?" she asked, surprised.

"You have to change your opinion about Muslims. You are intelligent, so you shouldn't think that way."

"Oh! You were talking about that country. What was it?"

"Azerbaijan."

"What is so special about this country?"

"People and their constitution."

"What do you mean?"

"See, like India they also have a secular democratic constitution. People are tolerant, secular, educated, and resilient. They have ballet theatres, which you will not find anywhere in the Muslim world. Moreover, they call their country republic, not the Islamic republic," I concluded, detailing all the positive things about Azerbaijan.

"What is wrong in calling Islamic republic?" Oksana asked seriously.

"You have to ask them", I replied, winking, "not me."

That brought a little smile on her face.

"So why don't we hear about them?" Dolce asked.

"Because the whole world thinks that the Muslim world is only made up of Saudi Arabia and Iran," I replied. Dolce started to think about something. I wasn't sure whether I had been able to change her opinion. I woke her up. "What do you think now?"

"I'll try."

"Not try. You have to change," I asked sternly.

"Should we go to Starbucks now?" she replied, smiling.

"I am not sure Roshan Ali would be there," I replied, feeling over the moon.

Dolce had changed. With examples like Azerbaijan, Dolce's polluted mind had been cleaned of prejudice, ill will, or malice towards Muslims. It was a happy ending. For me, Dolce was a perfect and a complete person now. A good human being.

Amardeep came back and tossed Dolce's bag carelessly on the couch.

"Ask her to sleep here?" he said, thumping the table with his right hand, laughing loudly.

We all laughed except for Dolce. She ducked his jab by ignoring him.

"Where will I sleep?" Dolce asked, concerned.

"You sleep in my room. I'll sleep outside on the couch," I replied.

"Dolce will sleep in my room," Oksana said, showing magnanimity.

"Dolce is lucky," Amar quipped.

"What about Oksana, Amar?" I asked, smiling.

"She is unlucky," he replied, laughing loudly like "ho-ho-ho".

It was so funny that everybody started laughing. Even Dolce couldn't control this time. Amardeep said he had to leave, so I saw him off. Before leaving, he wanted to know what I was going to do. I said I would think about it tomorrow. I was feeling very tired, so I went to sleep, but the girls kept talking.

Next day I woke late at 9 in the morning fresh but quickly remembered about the cancellation, which stressed me. The good thing was with Dolce around, it was a different atmosphere like when a relative comes to your home for a sleepover. Oksana had no choice but to get up early, but surprisingly enough, she was in a very pleasant mood. It was a test for me to see whether it would be like two Indians versus two girls.

"How is India? How is Ukraine?" I asked deliberately.

"Jai, you should say, 'How are you, ladies?'" Dolce chided, pretending to be upset.

So it was clear that I was alone versus the two ladies. It didn't matter which countries girls come from. They are always united. I apologised and excused myself for ten minutes to make a call. I called the ticketing company who told me that they would start refunding money soon. But I owed them Rs168,000 for twice their processing fee, one-time ticket print, and twice-payment processing. I had lost all my advance payments. The only consolation for me was that I had saved Rs10,000 on logistics. I paid the ticketing company their dues and then checked my bank balance. It had dipped to meagre Rs53,123.90. Basically, I was gone. I came back in despair to join Dolce and Oksana.

"Who were you talking to?" Dolce asked.

"The ticketing company," I said, dejected.

"What happened? You don't look good," she asked, showing a genuine concern.

"They are refunding people."

"So?"

"I lost all the advance payments, and I owed the company Rs168,000."

"Do you have any money left?"

"Enough for the next 6–8 weeks."

"Dolce, let us book the tickets," Oksana said hurriedly.

"Wait until I work something out," I snapped at her.

"What will you work out now?" She frowned.

"You have to give me some time," I pleaded.

"Jai, she'll wait." Dolce calmed us down.

"Why didn't you do insurance?" Oksana asked.

"I didn't think about it. It is too late now," I replied, irritated.

"I want to ask you both a question," Dolce said, turning to me. She asked, "Do you like her?"

"You know that," I replied.

"He doesn't like me," Oksana said, fuming. "He likes only one thing."

"What is that one thing?" I frowned.

"You know that," she replied sharply.

"Time out," Dolce said.

We both kept quiet. I couldn't look into Dolce's eyes. I was feeling very embarrassed that an 18-year-old teenager was acting like an umpire to resolve my personal problem. I felt very ashamed of myself. I looked at Oksana who was looking straight at me, angry.

"Oksi, I want to ask you a straight question," Dolce said. Oksana nodded while bringing a fake smile on her face. She asked, "Do you like Jai?"

"I don't know."

"Different question. Do you dislike him?"

"No."

"Do you trust him?"

"Yes."

"What is the problem then?"

"I don't want to get involved," Oksana said. "I like my freedom."

"Then what happened on that Friday night?"

"Who told you about that?" Oksana asked, surprised, slowly moving her head away from Dolce.

"I told her," I replied calmly.

"Why did you tell her?" she screamed, red-faced.

"Because she is our best friend," I yelled.

"Who else did you tell?" she screamed her heart out.

"Nobody."

"I don't trust you now."

"Jai, Oksana, stop talking about it," Dolce said maturely.

Dolce was hurt. I could feel that. I didn't like Oksana's attitude; in fact, for the first time, I slightly hated her. I wanted her to be beautiful from the outside, which she was, as well as from the inside. I decided to keep quiet.

"Jai, we are going to the shopping centre," Dolce said.

The matter remained unresolved between Oksana and me. I had to do some serious thinking. I could still convince her as long as she was around. How could I stop her from going back? I slipped into deep thinking. Suddenly, my eyes lit up, and I started to see a glimmer of hope. There was one person who could help me. I made a call and secured an appointment for 30 December 2014 at 2 in the afternoon.

CHAPTER 32

I reached his Bandra Kurla complex office exactly at 2 in the afternoon. It was a large planned commercial complex, housing a number of buildings including banks, multinationals, Dolce's ex-school, National Stock Exchange, and US consulate, providing employment to around 600,000 people. His office was located in a modern building on level 4. I went to the receptionist and told her about my appointment. She made a call to someone and then asked me to take a seat. She told that I would be called in ten minutes. I took a seat and picked a magazine to kill my time. No finding anything interesting, I kept it back. I looked at the receptionist and admired her efficiency. She was very efficiently multitasking many things such as answering calls, checking emails, photocopying, and receiving visitors. After ten minutes, she told me to go inside the office, turn right, and his room was last on the opposite side. It was a small office of around 20 staff who were all busy taking calls, chasing payments, planning new events, and just talking to one another.

I reached his glassed cabin and saw him in his chair, talking to someone on the phone. He saw me and with a hand gesture asked me to sit on one of the two front chairs. I sat down nervously and waited for him to finish his call. It was a nice cabin with a street view, which I noticed when I had entered. He was talking to someone about an event, probably a TV award ceremony early next year. He kept me waiting for another ten minutes before he ended his conversation. He made another call to the receptionist and told her not to disturb him for the next half an hour. He asked me to close the door of his cabin, which I did. He didn't apologise for keeping me waiting. There was no need because I needed him more than he needed me.

"What happened to your event, Grover?" Naresh Galhot asked without preamble.

"It went up in smoke with the blast," I replied casually.

"Didn't you have any insurance?"

"No."

"How much did you lose?" He smiled probably at my inexperience.

"Rs305,000."

"That is too much to lose for a starter."

"I know."

"You know?" he ridiculed.

He was trying to humiliate me as much as he could to shake my little confidence that was still left in me. I didn't respond to his humiliation and kept looking at him. He picked a paper and then started to read something, totally ignoring me. I decided to stay calm, knowing that he was deliberately doing that.

"You learn from mistakes. Try again," he lectured, his eyes still fixed on the paper.

"I don't have money for that," I replied while trying to control my emotions.

I was already destroyed by the cancellation, and this man was making my life even more difficult. If he had continued like that, I would have certainly broken down. I kept looking at him without getting provoked or disturbed because he was my only hope.

"You want money?" he asked casually.

"How?" I asked, surprised.

"I'll buy your company for Rs1 and compensate you for your loss."

"You mean you will pay Rs305,000 plus Rs1."

"Uh-huh."

"What do I've to do?" I asked suspiciously, sensing some danger ahead.

He bent down, opened the drawer, and said while giving me a form, "These are the transfer papers. Sign them now and take your money. Simple."

"I can't sign now. I need Oksana's signature," I lied.

He looked at me as if he had caught me red-handed. He then brought a shrewd smile on his face.

"Who is Oksana? That Russian who was with you other night?"

"She is not Russian. She is from Ukraine," I protested.

"Don't worry. It is the same thing in India," he contested.

"Ukraine is not Russia, though," I protested again.

"You think I am a fool? I know she is not your partner." He frowned.

"How do you know?" I asked, surprised.

"A foreigner like her can't become a partner of a company in India."

"I still need time to sign the papers," I insisted.

He thought for a moment while scratching his head and said, "You get one day. Otherwise, the deal is over."

"You will get the signed papers tomorrow."

"Just the papers?" he asked, surprised.

"What else?"

"That Russian."

"What about her?"

"Convince her to join my company."

"What about me?"

"I don't need idiots like you," he replied disdainfully.

"Why do you want her?"

"I need a dancer. I know she is a good dancer."

"But you can get many dancers. Why her?"

"Why did you choose her?"

I was absolutely sure he knew the reason.

"I needed a dancer," I replied casually.

"No. You needed someone different to attract business."

"How do you know?"

"She is everywhere. On your website, your social media."

He looked down, shaking his head as if saying, "I know everything, you fool." I should have known that shrewd people like him always carried out background checks before any negotiations.

"What if I refuse to talk to her?"

He looked at me, narrowed his eyes, moved his head close to me, and said menacingly, "Grover, I've other means to get things done."

The message was clear to me. If I had refused, he would have had my bones broken. Or cut off my head to send to Delhi as a New Year's gift to my parents. Even given a *supari* in my name. I knew supari was a term used in the Mumbai underworld for contract killing. I had heard that term been used in many movies. Mumbai underworld is as dangerous as any other underworld in the world like in Italy or New York. They all work in the same fashion. Never leave a clue so they are never caught. Everybody knows them, but the law can't touch them. In Mumbai, they are called *bhai*. *Bhai* means *brother*. They often wear white trousers, white shirt, and gold chains around their necks. Not one chain but many. They control areas, brothels, and bars and even run a network of beggars. No one dares to mess with them.

I started to sweat. I requested for a glass of water, which he happily ordered, enjoying my plight. I drank water and regained some composure.

"Why do you want me to talk to her?" I asked nervously.

"She is a foreigner," he replied.

I started to get some idea. Because she was a foreigner, they couldn't touch her. There would be a diplomatic uproar if they harmed her. At least, she was safe from these ruthless people. I thought he had committed a big mistake by disclosing this to me.

"I know that," I said.

"Because it is only you who could convince her."

I thought that I had an edge. He wanted her desperately but couldn't approach her directly. I started to think about my next move. There was a chance to get a better deal for her.

"Why do you think I could convince her?"

"Isn't she living with you?"

"We are sharing the apartment. That is all," I tried to outsmart him.

"Why would you take her to Lonavla?"

So he knew she was with me. But how? I couldn't make out.

"Why can't I?" I asked.

He bent down and picked something from under his table. It was a small black briefcase. He opened it and then showed me. It had bundles of currency notes.

"This is Rs50,000 more for convincing her."

He then closed it and flicked the combination locks. Why was he giving me Rs50,000 more? That proved his desperation for Oksana, so a better deal was still possible for her.

"I'll try, but you have to make a promise," I said. He stared at me without saying anything. I added, "Treat her properly. She is not the kind of woman you think."

"Why do you worry about her?" he asked without showing any concern for Oksana.

For him, Oksana was a kind of toy he had to have, someone he could play daily. The very thought of how she would deal with people like Naresh saddened me. I knew she was sharp, intelligent, strong, and proud but only for me. She was no match for shrewd people like Naresh who could easily exploit her without giving a slight hint.

"Because I am selling her. You know that," I replied, dismayed.

"Keep her," he said bluntly.

"I don't have anything to offer her."

"She can go back to her country."

He had touched my emotional chord. The only reason I had decided to meet Naresh was to prevent her from going back. I was in a catch-22 situation.

"Please treat her well," I begged, losing all advantage I had gained over him.

I thought shrewd people never give you an advantage but only give a glimmer of hope to further entrap you.

"Of course. I've got good contacts in the industry," he said softly. There was certain deception in his softness. I started to get worried, but I kept listening. "I can get roles for her."

"What roles?" I asked anxiously.

"Item songs."

So he already had plans for her. He was going to throw her to the wolves.

"No," I said disapprovingly. "They will exploit her."

"What do you mean?"

"Casting couch."

"There is no casting couch," he replied dismissively.

"It happens everywhere. Hollywood, Hong Kong, and China. Bollywood is not immune to it."

"What do you want?"

"When will she get the first role?"

"It doesn't happen overnight. It takes time."

"How long?"

"I don't know. I've to sell her profile first."

"Sell her profile first and then sell her," I said sarcastically.

He chose to ignore my jab. I prayed Oksana never got picked up for any role.

"What do we do next?" I asked.

"You both meet me here tomorrow at 11 in the night."

"Here. In your office. Why?" I reacted in pain.

Naresh got up, looked outside through the window glass, and then asked me to join him. He had a very good street view. It was a busy lane full of shops, cafes, and restaurants.

"Can you see that?" he asked, pointing towards a shop that had a red board.

"What is that?"

"It is a restaurant," he replied. I looked at him, confused. He added, excited, "Tomorrow, we are having New Year's party there. The party starts at 8 in the evening. I'll leave the party for some time. Come here and then go back."

"Go back alone."

"I am getting frustrated with you. I've given you more than one hour now."

"I didn't force you," I shot back.

"Who is coming with you?"

"So you will go back with Oksana. Why here? Why not there?"

"There is some problem."

"I understand your problem. You are not taking her back there but somewhere else," I said sternly.

He looked at me, smiled, and then asked me to get back to my seat.

"What do you want to do?"

He knew once he had her he could do whatever he wanted.

"I'll come here alone, give you the papers, and then we go together to pick Oksana," I proposed.

"Pick? Where?" he asked, surprised.

"I am not telling you now," I replied, smiling.

"Okay. Okay," he said, slightly frustrated.

"Why do you want me to come at 11? Why not earlier?"

"I am busy whole day tomorrow. I want to end the last day celebrating with a happy note."

"Strange. I've to go now. Give me my money," I said while preparing to get up.

"Take this case. It has Rs50,000."

"Rest."

"Not until tomorrow. Sign the transfer papers and then take your money," he said firmly.

I picked the case and started to leave his cabin when he called my name.

"Grover, get the case back. I do most of my dealing with this. It is a lucky one for me."

"Sure," I assured.

"How will you open the case?" he asked, smiling.

I looked at the lock. It was a four-combination lock. I tried to open the case, but it wouldn't open.

"Give me the combination then."

"2233."

"Did you say 2233?" I asked in total disbelief.

"Yes. Why?" he asked, surprised.

"No. Nothing. I'll see you tomorrow."

I left his cabin, and before leaving the office, I looked back. He was again busy on the phone, probably talking to someone for my supari. I left the building, thinking about tomorrow's meeting. I positioned myself against a wall and looked around, searching for an appropriate place to park my car tomorrow. After a while, I began to walk slowly at a corner, looked up and down, crossed a couple of streets, and soon found a busy and safe road two streets away from the building. I surveyed the road thoroughly. Satisfied, I decided to park the car there tomorrow.

CHAPTER 33

31 December 2014, 6 in the evening. There were only six hours left for India to usher in the New Year. I thought many countries in the South Pole would already have celebrated or about to celebrate the New Year. There would a lot of people on the Mumbai roads tonight, making noises, partying, drinking, or honking cars. Everybody was in a celebratory mood, except for me. I had just five hours before handing over Oksana to Naresh.

What would I do when I come back alone? The thought saddened me. There was a tiny glimmer of hope. I had been thinking of various options since meeting Naresh. I had to weigh my options based on risks versus rewards, choosing the one with fewer risks and more rewards.

Option number one. I would permanently end my relationship with Oksana if at all there existed any. I would ask her to leave my apartment and be on her own. I didn't owe her anything. On the contrary, I had given free shelter, always defended and protected her. Once she was gone, I would pack up and go back to Delhi either to pursue my MBA in the United States or join my father's business. That would put my life back on track. I shook my head violently and thought, *No, that is wrong.* I owed her many things. She had won the first cheque for my business, helped me win the dance competition, put some order and discipline in my life, cooked for me, and cancelled her plan to return to Ukraine. If I let her go, she would be on the road, struggling to survive the mean streets of Mumbai. Not good so I dropped.

Option number two. Let her go back to Ukraine. That would make her safe from the mean streets of Mumbai. But there was a war going in Ukraine. What if she got killed? Even if she survived, what if she decided to marry an old American? There was no problem in marrying an American. They are good people much better than us, but she didn't deserve to marry an old American twice her age. She didn't deserve to marry me either because she was older than me. But that was my problem, not hers. In any case, I would lose her forever. I never wanted her to go in the first place. This option was not acceptable to me either.

Option number three. Tell her the truth. About Naresh and my meeting with him. That probably was the best thing to do. Be honest, transparent, and leave everything for her to decide. But I had never fully understood her nature. She was still unhappy with me for disclosing our little secret to Dolce. She remained unhappy whole day yesterday. It was after a lot of convincing and continuously apologising that she agreed to go out with me tonight. What if she didn't like my plan? What if she decided to go back? What if she decided not to go out tonight, upsetting the last night of the year? No way, this option was too risky.

There was only one option left, i.e. to introduce her to Naresh and then leave her to his mercy. I was happy with my meeting with Naresh yesterday. I had called a spade a spade. I had managed to strike a good deal for Oksana. There was one silver lining in this option. I could convince her to stay with me, giving me time and opportunity to win her heart. I could still defend and protect her. The most rewarding thing was, with Naresh's money, I could rebuild everything. Then get her back into my fold. This option was too good to be ignored, so I chose option number four.

I went to my room and closed the door. I got the suitcase out. There were ten bundles of Rs50, each bundle containing a hundred notes. I broke the seal of each bundle and separated each into individual notes. I spread them on the bed and started looking at them aimlessly. I left the notes on the bed and got hold of the transfer papers. It was a simple legal document, which I understood, if not fully, though. On the last page, Naresh had already signed the document on the bottom left. There were three dotted lines on the bottom-right blank yet to be signed by me.

Suddenly, I felt a chill all over my body. A fear gripped me, and I started to shake. My hands were shaking, and I started to breathe heavy. I put my right hand on top of my left hand in order to control the shake. I went to the kitchen and drank one full glass of water. I stayed there for a while and then came back to my room. I recalled Naresh saying, "I don't need idiots like you." He was right. I was an idiot. How could I do that? It was I who had suggested going there alone. It was a trap I had lain for myself. I was going straight into a lion's den alone. Naresh was a shrewd and dangerous businessman. What if he had a gun and forced me to call Oksana to his office? Everybody has mobile these days. At gunpoint, I couldn't lie. What if there were more people with Naresh? They would kill me first, dumping my body in a gutter, lying there for days. They then had everything: Oksana, Rs50,000, and transfer papers, which he didn't need because my company was worthless anyway.

I started to get worried about Oksana's safety more than my own. If they succeeded in bringing her up, she would find me dead, and then they would start ripping her apart one by one. The thought of sharp, intelligent, strong, proud, beautiful, skilled dancer and now helpless Oksana among those beasts distressed me a lot. I did know how they would do. From the front, behind, one at a time or together. She would either die in the process of their heinous act or they would kill her, thinking that her use-by date had expired, dumping us together. Even if she survived, they would keep her for their future pleasure; or if they took pity on her, they would let her go, throwing few notes on her face to add further insult to her injury. This option had far greater risks than those of the other options. I couldn't run away from Naresh because I had committed myself by accepting fifty grand from him. I had to save her even at the cost of my own life. What do I do now?

I started to think of some way out. After a while, a forced smile appeared on my face. My fear subsided. I wasn't that idiot Naresh had thought. I got hold of a blank sheet and wrote Naresh's name, his office address, and a message, "If I don't come back in the next 20 minutes, then call police control room number 100." I folded the paper, put it in an envelope, and then sealed it. I felt a bit relieved. The plan would definitely save her. However, there was one more thing that was still bothering me. The combination that Naresh had chosen to unlock his briefcase. Why did he choose 2233? Was it a coincidence, or did he know too much about us? How did he know I was 22 and Oksana was 33? Had he deliberately set that combination by combining our ages? I couldn't resolve the mystery, so I stopped thinking about it. I packed the notes in the briefcase, fiddled with its lock combination, and tossed it on the bed. I placed the transfer papers and the envelope on top of the case to ensure to pick everything up when I left to meet Naresh.

I checked the time. I had been thinking for hours. It was 9.30, just one hour left to get ready and leave. I came out and found beautiful Oksana sitting on the couch, reading a magazine. She was looking dazzling because she had spruced herself up for the night. She was wearing a full-sleeved black tee, smoke-coloured ripped jeans, grey snood, lace-up boots, and a brown cross body bag. Her smooth hair was heightened and given extra fullness over teasing or padding, which she told me was called bouffant. Her lips, as ever luscious, painted in glossy red. Where did she get that fashion sense? She could easily beat any Bollywood, even a Hollywood, star.

"You are looking very beautiful," I said honestly.

She gave me a look as if finding it hard to digest my compliment. I continued, "You don't trust me."

"No," she replied, agitated. "After what you told Dolce."

"I've already apologised."

"Apology is not enough."

"What else can I do?" I said, irritated.

"Tell her nothing happened between us." She winked.

I laughed at her logic. Her wink said it all that she herself was not serious.

"Why are you hard on me?" I complained.

"Be . . . ca . . . use. I am not telling you," she said, stretching *because* and then changing the idea like her mood.

"But you are a good Indian."

"I know what you are saying," I said, honestly pleased at her comment. "We may suffer from an image problem. But there is one thing we believe in which nobody in this world believes in."

"What is that?" she asked curiously.

"Vasudhaiva Kutumbakam," I replied. She looked confused. I explained, "It is in Sanskrit, which means 'The world is one family'. It's from our ancient scriptures dating back to 3000 BC."

I looked at her for her reaction. There was none because she couldn't understand what I was trying to say, so I continued, choking in emotions, "How could have I treated you differently from any other Indian?"

"What is Sanskrit?" she asked, carefree.

"Ancient Indian language now almost dead like Latin," I said, laughing.

"Why are there so many bad people in Mumbai?"

"Not everyone is bad," I protested. "Yes, there are some. It is all because of the modern rat race, greed, lust, money, and, of course, poverty. Even if there are only 30 per cent Indians who are good, that is around 360 million people. That is more than the entire population of the USA or eight times your country's population."

"Everybody in India should be good," she commented innocently.

It was an impossible expectation, but she meant well.

"Is everybody good in Ukraine?"

"Of course."

"Then we can produce a good Indian with the help of a Ukrainian," I said, winking.

She just smiled without saying anything. I got up to get ready. I came back in 15 minutes. She surveyed me from top to bottom for the first time in my memory.

"This is what you are going to wear?" she said, disappointed.

I was wearing blue jeans, matching shirt, and sneakers.

"Why? What is wrong with this?" I replied, confused.

"That is not a party dress," she said while pretending to make a sad face.

"I don't know who you are going to impress tonight," I said sarcastically. "But the person I want to impress is not interested in me, so I don't care."

"Who do you want to impress?" she asked, pretending ignorance.

I gave her a nasty glare. I went back to my room and came back with the briefcase.

"What is in the briefcase?" she asked.

"Don't bother," I replied coldly.

We raced down the parking lot. I tossed the case in the trunk, and we started to move.

CHAPTER 34

We reached the complex in about 30 minutes. I parked the car on the street I had surveyed yesterday. Luckily, I got a vacant spot. The street was busy and well lit, safe for her to remain in the car alone for some time. I looked at her and flashed a smile at her.

"Check the time. It is 11," I said, showing the time from my wristwatch. I gave her the envelope. "Keep this with you."

She took it, confused, and started turning up and down, trying to locate something written on it. There was nothing written on the either side of the envelope.

"What is this?" she asked suspiciously.

"Keep the car keys," I explained. "If I don't come back in the next 20 minute, tear the envelope up and do exactly what is written inside. And don't stay here. Just run."

"Where are you going?" she asked, worried.

She had an anxious look on her face, which I liked. At least, she was worrying about me.

"Don't worry. Just promise you open the envelope only after 20 minutes."

"Promise. But . . ." she asked, confused.

The fear had started to grip her face. I couldn't face her more. I got off the car, opened the trunk, and picked the case. I started walking towards Naresh's office, worried. I hated myself. It was like feeding a lamb before sending it to a slaughterhouse. Around ten metres down, I stopped. I felt someone was watching me. I turned and saw Oksana standing outside the car, looking at me. I looked at her. Her face was pale, and the sparkle in her eyes vanished. It wasn't the same Oksana I had spoken to at the apartment about an hour ago but a very worried Oksana. I took a deep sigh; waved at her, assuring that everything was fine; and gestured her to sit inside the car. She brought a fake smile and then went inside the car.

I started to make a hasty walk towards Naresh's office. I reached the building in five minutes but couldn't enter because the sliding door was locked. I made a call to Naresh who remotely opened the door for me. He was in his office, so I thought. I waited for the sliding door to close and soon located the black knob on one side of the wall near the door. I pressed it, and the door started to slide open. I felt relieved that I didn't have to reply on Naresh to get out of the building. I went to the lifts and found all the four lifts waiting for me at the ground floor. I got in and pressed number four. The doors closed, and then it raced up to level 4. There was complete silence inside. The reception area was empty. I started to think about the receptionist I had met yesterday. I went inside the main office area. There were few lights on, but Naresh's cabin was fully lit. I reached his cabin and saw him talking to someone on his mobile. He looked very excited. He saw me and pointed to sit on one of the front seats. I sat down and waited for him to finish his conversation. I deliberately ignored his conversation and adjusted myself in a comfortable position. He was alone, so there was no immediate threat. He finished soon this time and looked at me like a winner looks at a loser. He started to rub his palms in excitement.

"I am very happy that you made a good decision," Naresh said, extremely excited. I felt his words like rubbing salt to my wounds. "I've promised you that I will treat her nicely. Let us finish here and then we leave."

"Leave where?" I asked calmly.

"To get the Russian," he replied, surprised.

"She refused," I lied.

He almost jumped from his seat. His face started to turn red.

"Didn't you convince her?" he asked, annoyed.

"For me, no means no," I replied calmly. "Even if she had agreed, I would have never handed her over to you."

His face had turned red. He raised his eyebrows, blew up his nostrils, and started to breathe in anger.

"Suno beche [Listen, kid], do you know what you are saying?"

"For me, no means no," I repeated firmly. "Even if she had agreed, I would have never handed her over to you."

"You are gone now," he said angrily.

"What will you do?"

"What will I do? You want to know?" he said, enraged.

He reached to his mobile and started to dial a number. Before he could dial the full number, I quickly got up, snatched the mobile, and put it in my front pocket. I knew I was younger and much stronger. That was the first such violent act of my life. I came back and waited for his reaction. He was seething but didn't say anything.

"Listen carefully," I spoke firmly. "I've told her if I didn't come back in the next ten minutes, then call the police."

I still had fifteen minutes left, but I lied. He looked at me in absolute amazement and then slumped back on his chair. He looked very weak. No matter how shrewd he was, he knew that he had lost the plot. He quickly recovered and brought a forced smile on his face, which I thought was another sign of his weakness.

"Ab ka Kare [What do we do now]?" he said, grinning sheepishly.

"I'll tell you," I replied stylishly like a movie star.

I got up, opened the case, threw the notes up in the air, closed the case, took the transfer papers out of my pocket, tore them into small pieces, and threw them on his face. The notes started to fall everywhere: on the table, on his head, and on the floor. He had a shocking look on his face.

"Why did you throw them up in the air?" he asked, thinking I was mad.

"Naresh, there are 45 more minutes left in 2014," I replied in style, often seen in Bollywood thrillers, a la Amitabh Bacchan. "It will take you some time to collect them all. Then you will start counting them. After the count, you would be happy that you got your 50,000 in full and intact."

"So?" he screamed.

"What did you say yesterday?" I said, calmly ignoring his scream. I continued stylishly, "That you wanted to end the last day celebrating on a happy note. You can now celebrate with 1,000 notes of Rs50, not just on a happy note."

He wasn't very impressed with my dialogue. After all, I had ruined his night. And his future plans. I checked the time. There were only five minutes left before Oksana took any action.

"I am going now," I said seriously.

I left his cabin. When I was about to leave his office, I turned back. I had forgotten to give him the last jolt. I went to his cabin again and found him collecting the notes from the floor. He looked at me, embarrassed. He got up and sat back on his chair.

"How will you open the case, Naresh?" I asked, smiling.

He reached to the case and started flickering his fingers over the combination locks. It wouldn't open because I had changed the combination.

"Harami [Bastard], why did you change the combination?" he shouted.

I didn't like his abuse. I was the only legitimate son of my parents. But I chose to ignore it.

"I changed it," I replied, shrugging my shoulders. "I will tell you the new combination. Is it hard to restore?"

"I told you this was my lucky case," he said, frustrated, and started to pant. "That combination was given to me by an astrologer. He had advised me not to change it—ever."

I started to laugh, thinking that in this 21st century, India was full of superstitious people. It was an irony that people like Naresh sought divine intervention but actually lived double and sleazy lives. I drew a lot of pleasure at the thought that it was the beginning of the start of his bad luck.

"Do you want the new combination?" I teased, enjoying every moment. "You will like it, I promise."

"Ullu ka patthe, jaldi batao [You son of an owl, tell me quickly]," he said aggressively.

"You really want to know?" I asked, equally matching his aggression with restraint.

"Madar [You mother]—" he swore, leaving the abuse incomplete.

Actually, he wanted to say, "You motherf——." That was it. I was not going to tolerate someone as sleazy as

Naresh—and now nobody—to abuse my mother. I had to leave the place quickly.

"Suna nahi [Didn't you hear me]?" he yelled.

I somehow controlled my emotions. I looked at the watch. There were 30 minutes left to midnight. I should have been with Oksana now.

"It is something that will arrive in the next 30 minutes."

I started to leave. He didn't understand and came out of his cabin.

"Please, tell me," he pleaded.

I liked the way he was pleading.

"Two, zero, one, five," I shouted from the office entrance.

"What?"

"I said 2015. Coming soon," I replied, hastily leaving his office without waiting for his reaction.

I raced down, came out, and started to run towards the car. I reached the street where my car was parked. I was relieved to see my car around 20 metres away from me. But I couldn't see Oksana, so I started to get worried. I ran even faster, reached to the driver's side, and found her inside the car. I looked at the watch. I was exactly eight minutes late. There were 22 more minutes left in 2014.

I looked at her from the outside and then smiled. She had pulled back, lowered the seat, and slept, the envelope firmly in her hands. I looked up the sky. It was a full-moon night. Her face was glowing like a full moon. The window on her side was half open. Occasionally, the cool breeze was causing her hair to stroke her face. The paleness and worry from her face had disappeared. She looked very relaxed and calm. How did she know that everything was all right now? Not wanting to disturb her sleep, I chose to spend few moments outside. I leant against the car and started to look back at my last six months in Mumbai.

I realised that I had achieved nothing. I had wasted my six months and almost all money gifted by my parents. I had been unable to get the dancing group going and failed to hold my first event successfully. I had not failed because of my incompetence but because of jealous people like Shabnam and the miscreants responsible for the blast. This was just to console myself because, in reality, I had failed.

However, I had learnt many things I would have never learnt had I not moved to Mumbai. I had learnt about the real world that operated out there in Mumbai or elsewhere. About the people, good or bad, that the world was made of. I had learnt how to deal with bad people in the most sophisticated way without losing my dignity. I had learnt how to set up a new business, how to acquire and manage a team, and how to negotiate things. I had made good friends like Amardeep, Sachin, Ajay, Neel, and, above all, Dolce. I had met, helped, defended, and protected someone called Oksana Bzovsky, a sharp, strong, proud, intelligent, beautiful, and skilled dancer from Ukraine. I thought, *Success is not happiness, but happiness is a success.*

I was happy the way I had taught Naresh Galhot a lesson and the way I had saved Oksana from his clutches. I was surprised how easily Naresh had caved in. Or was I lucky? Naresh was too shrewd, cunning, and dangerous. It could have been the New Year's Eve that saved me because his goons might have been busy enjoying. But in my heart of hearts, I knew he wouldn't give up so easily. He would definitely come after us. Mumbai was no longer safe for me. I needed to get out of Mumbai real fast. Meanwhile, for my own safety, I decided to visit a police station the next day to record my statement.

I took a deep sigh and decided to get inside the car. I opened the door slowly, sat inside, and closed the door back very slowly. I hadn't disturbed her because she was still sleeping. I looked at her face, admiring her beauty for a while; and then again, I went into a deep thought.

I became very emotional. I wanted to tell her many things.

How much I had defended her from the people who had spoken badly about her. How much I had protected her from the mean streets of Mumbai. How much I had admired her for enforcing discipline and order in my life, her fashion sense, her honesty, her sharpness, and her witty replies. How much I had enjoyed her cooking, her fragrance, her flawless skin, and her beautiful body. How much I had liked her smile, her flirts, her anger, her screams, her laugh, her mood, and her facial expressions.

How much I had disliked her enigmatic and reticent nature, her sleeping habit, her choice of wearing a watch on her right hand, and her deliberate attempts to ignore my hints.

I wanted to tell her how much pain she had given me over the last few months. I wanted to tell her that the only right she had given me was to allow me to call her Oksi, which I had never exercised. I wanted to impress her with the quote: "Even after thousand years from now, when the people of Ukraine would look up the sky on a clear starry night, they would find a new star called OKSANA." I wanted to tell her how much I liked her, wanted her, and wished to remain with her forever.

All of a sudden, I became very emotional, and tears started to roll down my cheeks. I thought, why did I alone have to be good? This was after a long time I had wept in my memory. Last time I had wept was when I was four riding my tricycle when it tipped over and I hit a brick. I received a gash on my forehead and then started to weep. Mum came out running, took me in her arms, and hugged me. Weeping, I asked her to hit the brick, and she laughed at my childish suggestion. I sighed and quickly wiped my tears to not give a wrong impression to Oksana that I was a weak person.

By now, I was fully convinced that I wasn't a smart person. Vishal had always thought that way about me. Naresh Galhot had called me an idiot. Ranganathan had outsmarted me, and Sharif Ahmad had fooled me in thinking that he was a good man.

At the same time, I was proud of my decision that I had made tonight. I had kept my promise given to Mum and Oksana. I remembered what Mum had told me the night before I was fly to Mumbai in July: "I don't mind you find a girlfriend but be always good to her. Don't deceive or take undue advantage of or ditch her." I remembered what I had promised Oksana when she had reposed her trust in me: "I promise that I'll pay you back. And you wouldn't know." She didn't know and would never know.

I hated India because of people like Naresh Galhot who was the filth on the face of the country, and I loved Ukraine because of people like Oksana who represented purity and innocence.

I checked the time once again. There were ten more minutes left in 2014. I decided to head back to the apartment. I reached to her hands, took the envelope, and tore it into small pieces. I looked at her again and felt an extreme urge to touch her lips. Next, I rolled my index finger over her big luscious lips two to three times. Her lips quivered, and she opened her big blue eyes. She blinked many times, rubbed her eyes, and then started to look left and right, trying to come out of sleep. She narrowed her eyes and looked straight into my eyes.

"Did you touch me?" she asked suspiciously.

I nodded. She didn't say anything but kept staring at me and then smiled. This was the first time she hadn't felt upset at my touching her. We both kept staring down the road without talking for a while when she broke the silence.

"What are you going to do now?" she asked seriously.

"You messed with Shabnam, and I messed with someone else," I replied, smiling.

"Who did you mess with?"

"You don't need to know him," I replied. She was asking me about the person who would have fancied her. I muttered, "Mumbai is no longer safe for us."

"Why? Is everything all right?" she asked anxiously.

"As long as you are with me, you don't have to worry," I replied calmly. Her anxiety faded into calmness. I disclosed, "I am going back to Delhi forever."

She stared down the road for a while, turned to me, lips squeezed and a mischievous smile on the face.

"I won't leave you easily," she said, winking, and completed her sentence, which felt like heavenly music to my ears. "I am also coming with you."

She didn't wait for my reaction. Instead, she yawned carelessly and went back to sleep. I sat motionless. I started to breathe slowly. I thought I was dreaming. I pinched myself. I wasn't dreaming. The thing I had been waiting to hear for the past six months had finally happened. I wasn't under any delusion, but it had come a long way, which was not unexpected from a complex person like Oksana. I had not failed, but my success was postponed for some time.

I took a deep breath, turned the ignition on, and moved the car. As I was about to leave the complex gate, my mobile started to beep. I slowed down and looked through the rear-view mirror. There was no one behind, so I stopped the car right in the middle of the road. I checked the time. There were four more minutes left to midnight. I took the mobile out of my pocket. It was a text message from that abnormal Vishal. What surprised me the most was that the message was for Oksana. Why did he use my mobile to send her a message? It wasn't rocket science to figure out because anything was expected from that abnormal Vishal. I shook my head in disbelief, smiling. I started to read the message:

> Hi Oksana
> Happy 2015.
> I am back. ☺
> Let us meet 2moro. 😉
> Bye. 😘
> Vishal

I closely looked at the emoji pictographs. It was a happy face, a winking face, and a face throwing a kiss. I laughed and thought that abnormal Vishal had a good sense of humour. He had left no stone unturned to pour his love for Oksana.

Next, I started to get worried. My affairs had barely started, and my competitors had already started to spring up. Anyway, I thought of showing the message to Oksana. I looked at her to find her sleeping comfortably. I decided not to wake her up for that abnormal Vishal. He had to be stopped, so I decided to text him back:

> Hi Vishal
> Happy 2015 to you too.
> Glad you are back.
> Can't meet because you are late.
> Bye.
> Oksana Bzovsky

I switched the mobile off after sending the message. I pressed the pedal, the car surged forwards, and we left the complex.

As I hit the main road, she pulled the sleeves of her tee up, and what I saw brought a broad smile on my face. Her right hand was bare, and the watch I had gifted her was on her left hand, sitting firmly around her wrist. She had promised to wear the watch on a special day. She had kept her promise because it, indeed, was a special night for both of us. I started to concentrate on my driving and then saw a building, a kilometre or two ahead, had started showing the countdown to the New Year. Ten, nine, eight, seven, six, five, four, three, two, one—it kept flashing for a while and then HAPPY NEW YEAR.

The End

ABOUT THE AUTHOR

Born in Kashmir, India, Anil Dhar is an information technology professional whose main interest has always been in history, culture, world events and conflicts, current affairs and travelling.

Oksana is his first novel, and writing it was quite an experience.

He is a naturalised citizen of Australia and lives in Sydney. More information is available by email at anil.dhar@live.com or Twitter @ZippyAD.

Printed in the United States
By Bookmasters